PRAISE FOR LAURIE R. KING

WITH CHILD

"King's prose is immensely readable and her characters [are] complex and interesting. King is a damned fine prose-smith . . . too good a writer not to read."
—*Mystery News*

"A contemporary, somber psychological thriller, more character study than caper . . . A compelling cast of characters."
—*San Francisco Chronicle Book Review*

"Laurie King knows how to keep a plot boiling, and her crusty, sharp-tongued Kate is appealingly vulnerable."
—*Philadelphia Inquirer*

"Laurie R. King manages to create from Page 1 of every book the feeling that the reader will be in good hands. Martinelli is the kind of person you'd like to know and talk with over many lunches, a smart and tough woman."
—*Chicago Tribune*

"Laurie R. King makes every sentence and every nuance of every character count in WITH CHILD . . . the author has developed a fine cast of complex characters to accent an intelligent, tightly woven police procedural . . . King makes us empathize with her realistic characters while unfolding an intricate mystery that never falters."
—*Sun-Sentinel*

MORE RAVES FOR LAURIE R. KING

TO PLAY THE FOOL

"Beautifully written, with clearly defined and engaging characters."
—*The Boston Globe*

"Confirms King's status as one of the most original talents to emerge in the '90s."
—*Kirkus Reviews*

"King has once again demonstrated that the praise she earned with her Edgar award-winning first book was well deserved."
—*Mostly Murder*

"An awe-inspiring work . . . In Erasmus, King has created one of the most unforgettable characters in mystery literature."
—*The Drood Review of Mystery*

"Its characters, and its language, linger in the mind long after more conventional entries in the genre are gone."
—*San Jose Mercury News*

"King practices her own magic here, conjuring up . . . an indelibly affecting narrative from unexpected material."
—*Publishers Weekly* (starred review)

"Combines a thoughtful complexity of crime and character with graceful writing."
—*The Orlando Sentinel*

"King is a talent to be reckoned with."
—*Feminist Bookstore News*

A GRAVE TALENT

WINNER OF THE EDGAR AND JOHN CREASEY AWARDS FOR BEST NOVEL

"Well-crafted, prickling with excitement, full of intriguing characters . . . A story told well enough to hook and hold Rendell and P. D. James fans."
—*Booklist* (starred review)

"Amazing first novel with intelligence, intrigue, and intricacy . . . [Laurie R. King is] a writer to watch."
—*Library Journal*

"Unusually sensitive and densely imagined."
—*Kirkus Reviews*

THE BEEKEEPER'S APPRENTICE

"[A] delightful and well-wrought addition to the master detective's casework."
—*Publishers Weekly*

"A fascinating and often moving account of a friendship so unusual and so compelling that one almost accepts it as being historically real."
—*The Denver Post*

"Uncommonly rich."
—*Kirkus Reviews*

"May have the guardians of the Sherlock Holmes canon howling while the rest of us eagerly rush into its heady pages."
—*The Washington Post Book World*

WITH CHILD

LAURIE R. KING

BANTAM BOOKS
New York   Toronto   London   Sydney
Auckland

This edition contains the complete text of the original hardcover edition.
NOT ONE WORD HAD BEEN OMITTED.

WITH CHILD
A Bantam Book / Published by arrangement with St. Martin's Press

PUBLISHING HISTORY
St. Martin's Press hardcover edition published February 1996
Bantam paperback edition / May 1997

ISBN 978-0-553-57458-6
Published simultaneously in the United States and Canada

Bantam Books are published by Bantam Books, a division of Random House, Inc. Its trademark, consisting of the words "Bantam Books" and the portrayal of a rooster, is Registered in U.S. Patent and Trademark Office and in other countries. Marca Registrada. Bantam Books, New York, New York.

PRINTED IN THE UNITED STATES OF AMERICA

OPM   20   19   18   17   16   15   14

FOR MY SISTER, LYNN DIFLEY
AND ALL HER FAMILY

When a writer of fiction makes shameless use of actual institutions, such as the Green Tortoise bus company or the police departments of various jurisdictions, it may be necessary to point out that the actual people affiliated with them and the fictional characters presented in the story are two separate things.

The real people are much more helpful and infinitely more efficient.

A book, like any other child, is a communal project. I would like to thank the members of my community for their help with this one, particularly Barbara Kempster and Leila Lawrence.

WITH
CHILD

A CONVERSATION

*So it was settled: Jules would come and stay with Kate
from the wedding until New Year's.*

With one adjustment to the plan.

*On the phone, the afternoon before the wedding, Kate
talked to her partner at his house on the other side of
town.*

"Al, I was thinking. If it's all right with you and Jani, I
thought Jules and I might go north for a few days over
Christmas. Maybe as far as Washington."

"To see Lee?"

"Possibly. If we feel like it. I had a letter from her last
week, asking me to come to her aunt's island for Christmas if I could get it off."

"Does she know you're on leave?"

"She doesn't know anything. I didn't tell her about the
shooting, or that I got hurt. I didn't want to worry her,
and once I got out of the hospital, it didn't really seem like
something I could put in a letter, somehow. She did say
she was sorry not to make it to your wedding, that she's
writing you and sending you a present."

"Are you two about to break up?" he asked bluntly.

"Jesus, Al, you do ask some good ones, don't you? I

1

don't know. I just don't know anymore. I don't even know if I care. I haven't even talked to her in four months, just these damn stupid cards of hers. But there won't be any scenes, if that's what you're worried about. I wouldn't take Jules into that. If we do go—and I really haven't made up my mind one way or the other—then we'd just go for the day, maybe overnight, depending on the ferry schedule, but then we'd leave and go do something else. Does Jules ski?"

"Better than I do. Which isn't saying much, I admit."

"Maybe we could go to Rainier or Hood, then. If Jani approves."

"I'll talk to her, but I doubt she'll have any problems with it. Do you want the car?"

"I'm going to take the Saab off its blocks. And if driving turns out to be a problem, we'll come home. I'm not going to risk passing out or anything while I'm driving Jules. You know that, Al. I'd never put Jules into danger. Never."

◆

AUGUST,
SEPTEMBER

◆

ONE

KATE CAME awake to a question. She lay inert for a few seconds until it was answered, by the familiar groan of the Alcatraz foghorn, seemingly a stone's throw from the foot of her bed. Home. Thank God.

Fingers of sweet sleep tugged at her, but for a moment she held herself back, mildly, dutifully curious. Funny, she thought muzzily, I wouldn't have thought that noise would wake me up. I hear it all summer, like living inside a pair of asthmatic lungs, but the only time I noticed it was when they tried replacing it with that irritating electronic whine. The telephone? Don't think it rang. If so, it's stopped now. Let them call back at a human hour. The neighbor's dog? Probably the dream, she decided, which had been stupefyingly tedious even to a sleeping mind, a cop's variation on the "moving luggage from one place to another—Oh God, I've lost one" theme, involving the transfer of prisoners, one at a time, from cell to hallway to van to hallway to cell, each step accompanied by forms and signatures and telephone calls. Better than the hell of the last few days, she thought, but thank God I woke up before I died of boredom. Poor old gray cells too tired to come up with a decent dream. Back to sleep.

She reached up and circled her right arm around the pillow, pulled it under her with a wriggle of voluptuary delight, reached back over her shoulders for the covers and pulled them over her head, and let go, deliciously, slippery as a fish into the deep, dark, still pond of sleep.

Only to be snagged on the viciously sharp point of the doorbell and jerked rudely up into the cruel air. Her eyes flew open. Seconds later, the message reached the rest of her body. Sheets and blankets erupted, feet hit the carpeting, hand reached for dressing gown and found only the smooth wood of the closet door, reached for suitcase and found it still locked tight, reached for keys and found— she waved the search away in a gesture of futility. From behind a pair of swollen, grit-encrusted lids, her eyes steered two distant feet through the obstacles of strewn suitcases, clothing, boots, jacket, toward the stairs, and all the while she was mumbling under her breath.

"It's Al, bound to be, I'll kill him, where's my gun? Hawkin, I'm going to blow you away, you bastard, I'm not on duty 'til tonight, and here you are with your jokes and your doughnuts at dawn"—she picked up the bedside clock, put it down again—"near enough dawn. Christ, where'd I put those keys? Why'd I lock the goddamn suitcase anyway, it was only in the trunk of the car, here's my gun, I could shoot off the lock, cutesy little padlock, break it off with my teeth. Oh, the hell with it, most of me's covered, it's only Al. No, it can't be Al; he's off with Jani somewhere, that conference with the name. Not Al, must be the milkman, ha, funny girl, just as likely to be a dinosaur or a dodo or—Christ Almighty!" This last was delivered in a shout as the sleeve of a denim jacket, discarded a very few hours before in the process of unburdening herself to fall into bed, caught at her bare ankle and tried to throw her down the stairs. She deflected herself off the newel and landed on all the knobs of the chair of the electric lift, which, as her last act before leaving the house, Lee had sent back up to the top, out of the way—an action Kate had thought at the time was merely thoughtful, but which, at some point during the last few days, she had decided was symbolic. Disentangling herself from the contraption and rubbing her left thigh, Kate limped down the stairs, muttering and unkempt as a street person, a young, muscular, well-fed street person wearing nothing but a navy blue silk tank top, a pair of Campbell plaid flannel boxer shorts, and a thin gold band on the ring finger of her left hand.

She flipped on the door viewer and was surprised to see only the small porch and the street beyond. No, wait—there was a head, the top of a head of dark hair bisected by a perfect sharp part. A child. Kate reached out both hands to turn bolt and knob.

"Look, kid, if you're out here at this ungodly hour selling Girl Scout cookies, I'm going to report you to . . . Jules? Is that you?"

The child on her doorstep nodded, a subdued movement so unlike the daughter of Jani Cameron that Kate had to lean forward to examine her. She wore a white T-shirt with some kind of foreign writing on it, cutoff shorts, sandals, and a backpack hanging from one thin shoulder; her glossy black hair was in its usual long, tight braids, and she had a Band-Aid on her left knee and a tattoo on the right—no, not an actual tattoo, just a drawing done in blue ink, smudged and fading. Her skin was browner than when Kate had seen her last, in the winter, but it had an odd tinge to it, Kate noted, and a strange, withered sort of texture.

"What's wrong with you?" she asked sharply.

"I just needed to see you, Casey. Kate. Do you think I could come in? It's kind of cold out here."

Kate realized simultaneously that she was huddled behind the door more from self-protection than from modesty, and that the reason the child looked so gray and pinched was that she was half-frozen, shivering and damp in the dripping fog on this lovely late August morning in sunny California. Perceptive of you, Martinelli, Kate told herself as she stood back to let Jules in. Just call me Shirley Holmes.

"It was warm when I left this morning," said Jules

apologetically. "I forgot about the fog you get here. It comes over the hills like a giant wave, doesn't it? A tsunami, it's called, a tidal wave. It looked like it was about to crash down and wipe out everything from Palo Alto on up. It's the heat inland that brings the fog, you know. I read an article on it; it's a cycle, a cyclical thing, heating up, the fog coming in, cooling off, and then there's a few clear days while—"

During this informative monologue, Kate led her visitor into the kitchen, switched on the electrical baseboard radiator and waved her hand at the chair nearest it, walked over to the coffee machine, abandoned that, and went out of the kitchen (Jules raised her voice but did not slow down a fraction), coming back with the tan alpaca throw rug that lived on the back of the sofa, dropped it on Jules's lap, then returned to the coffeepot, where she went like an automaton through the familiar motions of beans and grinder, filter and water before switching it on and standing, one hip against the counter and arms akimbo, completely oblivious of Jules's voice, watching with unfocused eyes as the brown liquid began to trickle out into the carafe, the gears of her mind unmeshed, idling, blessedly near to stillness, to sleep. . . .

"Are you angry, Kate?"

Startled into awakeness, Kate turned and nearly knocked a coffee mug from the edge of the counter.

"Jules! Hi. Yes. No, I mean, I'm not angry. Why should I be angry?"

"You looked annoyed when you opened the door. I must've gotten you out of bed."

"All kinds of people get me out of bed. No, I'm not angry. Are you warmer now? Want something hot to drink? You probably don't like coffee."

"I like coffee, if you have milk and sugar."

"Sure. Ah. This milk doesn't look very nice," she noted as the watery blue blobs slid from the carton into the cup. She squinted at the due date. "Looks more like yogurt. I don't suppose you want yogurt in your coffee? Doesn't smell very nice, either."

"No, thank you," said Jules politely. "Black with sugar will be fine, but just half a cup, please."

"Fine, fine," said Kate, and nodded half a dozen times before she caught herself and took the milk carton and the mug to the sink to empty them. She rinsed the mug, dumped the milk down the drain, pushed the carton into the overflowing garbage can under the sink (hurriedly closing the door), then took out sugar, spoon, and another mug, and resumed her position in front of the gurgling, steaming coffeemaker, watching the coffee dribble slowly, hypnotically out.

"Are you all right?" interrupted the voice behind her. Kate's head snapped upright again.

"Yes, of course. Just not awake yet."

"It is nearly nine o'clock," said Jules in mild accusation.

"Yes, and I went to bed at five. I haven't been sleeping well lately. Look, Jules, are you just here for a friendly visit? Because if so, I'm not very good company."

"No. I need to talk to you. Professionally."

Oh hell. Kate scrubbed her face with both hands. A lost dog or a playground bully. The neighbor exposing himself. Do I need this?

"I wouldn't bother you if it wasn't important. Weren't. And I have tried the local police."

"Okay, Jules, I'm not going to throw you out. Just give me ten minutes to jump-start the brain and then I'll put on my cop hat for you."

"I didn't think homicide detectives wore uniforms."

"A feeble attempt at humor." She poured the coffee into two mugs and carried both of them out of the room. "There's food if you want, Jules," she called from the stairs.

A minute later, Jules heard the shower start. At twelve, she was, both by nature and through her mother's distracted style of nurturing, quite able to look after herself. She stood up and folded the alpaca throw neatly over the back of the chair, and began a systematic search of the kitchen cabinets and drawers. She found half a loaf of

9

rock-hard French bread and some eggs in the refrigerator, a few strips of bacon in the freezer compartment, a bowl and a frying pan behind the low doors, then began with deliberate movements to assemble them into breakfast. She had to lean her entire weight against the Chinese cleaver to chop the bread into something resembling slices, and substitute frozen orange juice concentrate for the milk, but she had just decided that necessity may have given birth to an interesting invention when a ghastly noise from upstairs, half shriek and half growl, froze her arm in the motion of shaking nutmeg into the bowl. Before the noise had faded, though, she resumed, realizing that Kate was only reacting to a stream of suddenly cold water. Al made the same sorts of noises in the shower sometimes, though not quite so loud. When she had asked about it, he told her that it helped him wake up. She'd never had the nerve to try it herself, and reflected that it must be something they taught you at the Police Academy. She found a sugar bowl and added a large pinch to the beaten eggs.

Kate bounded down the stairs a few minutes later and burst into the kitchen.

"God, it smells like a Denny's in here. What have you been making?"

"There's a plate of French toast for you, if you want it, and some bacon. I couldn't find any syrup, but there's warm honey and jam and powdered sugar."

Kate swallowed five thick slices and more than her share of the bacon, stopping only because Jules ran out of bread. She ran the last corner of the eggy, buttery fried bread through the pool of liquified honey, put it into her mouth, and sighed.

"I take back the insult. It smells like heaven and tasted like paradise, and what do I have to do to pay you back for it?"

"It's your food; you don't have to pay for it."

"Wrong. Rule one of being an adult: Nothing in life is free. So, what do you want, how did you get here, and do people know where you are?"

10

"I took the bus and walked from the station. I actually thought I'd have more trouble, because I've only been here once, but your house is easy to find from downtown. You just walk uphill."

"Well, that answers the least of the questions, anyway. Do we need to make a phone call so somebody doesn't report you missing?"

"Not really. I left at my normal time this morning—I'm going to a summer school course at the university on writing software. It's really interesting, and I'm sorry to miss today because we work in teams, so I'm wasting my partner's time, but he's always got something of his own he can do. He's a genius—a true genius, I mean, his IQ's even higher than mine. He sold a game to Atari when he was ten, and he's working on another version of it now, so he won't worry or anything if I don't show up. In fact, he might not notice; he has a strange sense of time when he's working. Anyway, nobody expects me home until three or four. Mom arranged for me to have dinner with the family next door while she's gone, and their daughter Trini, who's only two years older than I am and a real airhead—but because she's older, they think she's somehow magically more responsible—she stays the night with me. May I use your bathroom?"

"Huh? Oh, sure, it's under the stairs there."

"I remember."

Kate, detective that she was, had caught the one relevant fact as it shot past her, that she had six hours to return this short person back to her proper place. She began to shovel the breakfast things in the musty-smelling dishwasher, pausing first to pour the last of the coffee into her cup. Not that caffeine would enable her to keep up with Jules Cameron. Cocaine, maybe. Although, come to think of it, Jules had changed in the last year. Physically, of course: She was nearly as tall as Kate now, and she wore a bra between her T-shirt and the nubs on her chest. More than that, though, was her attitude: At eleven, she had brazened out her turmoil—braces, brains, no father, and a long-distance move could not have been

11

easy—with an almost comic maturity, even pomposity, to her speech. That seemed to have been toned down, either by design or because she'd grown out of the need. Kate hoped the latter—it would be a pity to have this little gem shove her light under a basket because of the lesser minds around her. Particularly, Kate reflected, those inhabiting male bodies. Jules must be getting to the age where these things mattered.

She finished loading the dishwasher, turned it on, and went out into the living room, where she found Jules looking out into the fog, where the neighbor's garden was beginning to materialize.

"Was it this window?" Jules asked.

It took an instant to click.

"The one above you." She watched Jules step back to peer up, then retreat farther until she could see the branches that had held the SWAT marksman on a night eighteen months earlier.

"From that tree?"

"Yes."

"It wasn't Al, was it? Who shot . . . that man."

"Of course not."

"I didn't think so. I mean, I was young then, and I sort of imagined it was Al up in the tree, even though I knew it wasn't."

"Al doesn't climb trees. It's in his contract. So," she said sharply before Jules could inquire about contract clauses or ask to see the bloodstains that lay, all but invisible to any eyes but Kate's, three inches to the right of her foot, hidden beneath the new Tibetan carpet, "what is it you want me to do for you? 'Professionally.' "

It was a long and convoluted tale, filled with extraneous detail and looping into unnecessary excursions, speculations, and a pre-teenager's philosophical reflections, mature and mawkish by turns, but Kate was an experienced interrogator, and if she lacked Al Hawkin's natural ability to read and lead the person being questioned, she had at least learned how to keep things on track.

Jules went to a private school. To the parent of a public

12

school child, the idea of private school evokes high academic standards and close discipline, a broad education for already bright children balanced with encouraging each student to develop his or her own interests and abilities to the fullest. This paradisaical image loses some of its solidity once inside the walls of the ivory tower ("I mean," commented Jules, "two of the high school girls got pregnant last year, how's that for brains?"), but it can be said that the teaching is no worse than that of a public school, and classes are certainly smaller. Too, a privately funded school is safe from the state's fiscal blackmailers, who had turned most of the schools in the area where Jules lived into year-round schools, with students popping in and out of one another's desks for twelve months of the year. Where parents pay the bills, parents choose the calendar, and it was no accident that many of the parents whose children went to school with Jules taught on nine-month schedules at colleges and universities. The date for the school's winter music program was always chosen with an eye to the university's exam schedule. With this groundwork out of the way, and reduced to an adult perspective, Jules's narrative amounted to the following.

Immediately after university grades had been posted the previous June, Jani Cameron had picked up her bags and her daughter and flown to Germany to examine certain manuscripts in Köln, Berlin, and Düsseldorf. Jani spent the two weeks in quiet ecstasy and filled two notebooks with references and addenda to the manuscript she was hoping to finish before October.

Her daughter was less than ecstatic. Jani had never gotten around to teaching Jules German, for one thing, and then she arbitrarily ruled that Jules could not go beyond hotel, park, or library without her mother—that is, she could not go. Kate had the strong impression that some dark unpleasantness had taken place, and her detective instincts stirred, but she was not sure how much of that impression was from Jules's dramatization of a mere argument, so she decided not to allow herself to be distracted. At the end of the two weeks, as mother and daughter packed to leave for San Francisco, Jani was brought out of her academic dream to the harsh realization that her remarkable but normally reasonable little girl was deeply entrenched in a case of the adolescent sulks.

No, Jules had not had a good time. She did not like to play in parks with children; she did not care for libraries filled with books she could not read; she did not think it unreasonable that she hadn't learned German in fourteen days. Furthermore, she did not like having been taken from her friends and from a summer school offering in computer programming that interested her, just to tag along behind her mother.

The two Cameron women fought with polite implacability all the way across the Atlantic, interrupted only by meals and the movie, which Jules watched while her mother pretended to sleep, trying desperately to absorb this radical change in her daughter. By the time the plane touched down in San Francisco, they had come to an agreement. The next morning, Jani sat down at her desk while Jules went off to talk her way into a late registration at the computer course. As they nodded off over their respective keyboards, both felt a sense of uneasy victory beneath the heavy fog of their jet lag, and a vague awareness of business unfinished.

All of which was to say that, while Jani wrote her book and edged further into her relationship with Inspector Alonzo Hawkin of the San Francisco Police Department, Jules had a great deal of time on her own. She went to school four mornings a week to fill the crevices of her voracious mind with the intricacies of RAMs and ROMs, artificial intelligence and virtual reality, but the afternoons and weekends, which normally she might have spent at home reading or floating in their apartment house's minuscule pool, she spent on her own, pointedly away from her mother's presence. Friends were thin on the ground in July and August, sprinkled across the globe from Yosemite to Tashkent, but there were enough left to keep Jules from boredom, and there was her computer partner, and there were the library and the bilingual books her mother had ordered so that she could start on German, and there was the larger swimming pool in the park, and the park itself to read in.

Which was where she had met Dio.

"It must be a nickname," said Jules. "I mean, who would name their kid God, except maybe a rock star or something? He said it was his real name, but another time he said his mother was secretly in love with some piano player named Claudio and named Dio after him. He never told me his last name."

Dio lived in the park. It was both an indication of Jules's naïveté and the unlikely surroundings that she had not believed him. She'd seen him before, a few times in early July and then more often. Finally, in the last week of July, he came and sat next to her and asked what she was reading. He seemed baffled that she would want to learn German; he was more interested in one of her other books, a novel by Anne McCaffrey, and settled down at a distance from her for the rest of the afternoon, reading. He read slowly, and asked her what a couple of words meant, but he was possessed by the book. When it was time for Jules to go home, Dio asked hesitantly if she would mind if he borrowed it. It was a paperback and belonged to her, so she let him take it, said she'd be in the park again the following afternoon. She then went home to dinner.

He was there the next day, and the next. He returned the book as if it were a precious stone, she gave him another one, and they read in odd companionship for the rest of that week.

And he was odd, she had to admit that. Or, no, not odd himself, but there was something strange about him. It was not merely that his hair was long, though clean, or that he seemed to have only two T-shirts—neither of these made him stand out even in a wealthy neighborhood. However, he seemed to have no family or friends, he never bought an ice cream or brought a snack, and he seemed uneasy at accepting anything from Jules. Then she discovered that he did not have a library card—an inconceivable impoverishment to Jules. He was vague about where he lived, what school he went to. And he wouldn't come to dinner when Jules invited him. That was the final straw.

"What is it with you?" she had asked irritably. "You're this big mystery man all the time. Every time I ask anything about you, you look off into space and mutter. I don't care if your father's a garbageman or something, or if you don't have one. I don't have a father, but that doesn't mean I won't go to a friend's house for dinner. I thought we were friends, anyway. Aren't we?"

Well, um, er, yes, but.

"You don't have to invite me to your house if it's dirty or something. Mom's making hamburgers, is all, and she said I could invite you."

"You told your mother about me? What did you tell her? What'd she say?"

"I told her there was a new kid I'd met in the park who liked to read, and she said, 'That's nice, honey,' and went back to work. She's writing a book." That distracted him.

"What kind of book?"

"Like I told you, her field is medieval German literature. This one is on marriage as a symbolic something or other. Pretty boring, really. I looked at a few pages, and even I couldn't make any sense of them. So, will you come to dinner?"

"Your mother will ask questions, and her cop boyfriend"—"Sorry, Kate, that's what he said," Jules explained—"will come looking for me."

"Why, are you some kind of criminal?"

"No! I mean, in a way. He might think I was. Thing is, Jules, I live here, in the park."

There followed a lengthy discussion with an incredulous Jules slowly being convinced that yes, a person could actually sleep here, could live in the gaps of her own staid community. Actually, Kate had to admit, the boy

16

sounded smart, and he had found an ideal place for a residence—for the summer, at any rate. He bathed in the backyard swimming pools of dark houses; he ate from the garbage cans of the rich and the fruit trees and tomato vines of the weekend gardeners. He even earned a bit of money, posing as a neighborhood kid willing to mow lawns and do chores (of whom Kate could imagine there were few enough in that particular town). He probably did his share of trying for unlocked back doors and helping himself to small items from cars, but without a criminal brotherhood to back him up, he would have found it a problem to fence goods or sell drugs on any scale. No, he sounded like a springtime runaway who had discovered a superior resting place, an urban Huck Finn's island, until the winter drove him in, into the arms of the city's predators. Kate wished him luck, but she had seen too many of them to hold out much hope, or to feel a great urgency to action.

Jules, however, was worried. Not just because he was without a home—she, too, had read enough Mark Twain to take the edge off the reality the newspapers told her about—and not for fear of what the harder life of October would push him toward. She was worried because he had disappeared.

Kate let her talk on, half-hearing the anxious recital of her visit to the police and sheriff's office, the patrolman who had laughed at her, the park maintenance man who had told her to go home, the downstairs neighbor, Señora Hidalgo, who had thrown a fit when she heard Jules admit to speaking to a stranger and then had listened no more. Kate had known what was coming from the moment Jules had mentioned a boy in the park with an unlikely name. The only surprises were the resourcefulness of the runaway and the persistence of the girl who had befriended him. Kate also noticed, when she more or less automatically got a physical description of the boy from Jules, the complete lack of romance in the girl's words. Dio was clearly a friend, not an adolescent fantasy.

"I know that Al would help," Jules was saying, "but

17

he and Mom won't be back until the day after tomorrow, and I would have called him and asked him to make the police listen to me, but then I remembered you, and I thought you might help me look for Dio, at least until Al gets back."

Kate felt her professional cynicism gently nudged by this declaration of faith—until she called forcefully to mind just whom she was dealing with here, stared hard into the large, innocent, barely-out-of-childhood hazel eyes before her, and saw reflected in them the dim, cool glow of a computer display. Kate, Kate, she chided herself, lack of sleep is no excuse for being taken in by the patter of a twelve-year-old con woman. The kid knew damn well that Kate would jump through flaming hoops for her. Al Hawkin was Kate's partner, but he was also her superior; Al was fighting hard to make points with Jani Cameron; the way to Jani Cameron was through her daughter; therefore, performing this small service would ultimately boost her, Kate's, position. Kate might even work harder to find Dio than Al would—but that was getting too cold-blooded, and surely the timing of Al's absence was coincidental.

"Right," she said dryly, letting Jules know that she hadn't fallen for it. Nonetheless, she would look. Sure, the boy was likely to be in Los Angeles, or working the streets closer to home, but she was not about to tell that to Jules. Not her job, thank God, to educate a privileged and protected girl about the monsters lurking in the shadows, about the parents with the moral awareness of three-year-olds who, when faced with the problems of a child, be it a crying infant or a prickly teenager, took the simple response of hitting it or getting rid of it. Disposable children, Dio and thousands like him, thrown away by his family, picked up by a pimp for a few years, and thrown away again to die of drugs and disease and the depredations of life in the streets. He had started by bathing in the swimming pools of affluent families, but that wasn't what he was doing now.

None of this to Miss Jules Cameron, however. Something prettier.

"Jules, the policeman you talked to was probably right. I know street people, and the chances are very good he just left—for a few days or weeks, or permanently. Yes, I know he wouldn't have left without telling you, but what if he had to? What if, say, his parents showed up and he didn't want to go home? Wouldn't he then just take off without a word until the coast was clear?" Kate hurried over the thin patches in this argument. "Does he know how to get in touch with you?"

"Yes. I gave him a notebook for a present, a little one, to fit in his pocket. It had a rainbow on the front. He told me he didn't know when his birthday was, which is ridiculous, of course. I still can't think why he wouldn't tell me that—you can't trace someone by his date of birth, can you? Anyway, I gave him an unbirthday party, made him some microwave brownies with candles and some ice cream, though by the time we ate it, the ice cream was melted and we had to use it like a sauce, and for his present I bought him the notebook. I wrote his name on the front page, just Dio, but in Gothic script, using a calligraphy pen, and on the second page I put my name and address and phone number. You think he's in trouble, don't you?" she said abruptly. "Kidnapped by a serial killer and tortured to death, like that one up in Seattle, or the man you and Al caught, Andrew Lewis. You just don't want to tell me."

So much for pretty deceptions. Kate ran her fingers through her still-damp hair, thinking idly that she would really have to get it cut. "That was a completely different thing, Jules, you know that."

"But there is someone killing people up in Seattle. He just goes on and on. What if he moved down here?"

"Jules," Kate said firmly, "stop trying to frighten yourself. He's killing young women, not homeless boys." Five of them so far, and granted, all were young and small and most of them had cropped hair, but still.

"You're right," Jules said, and let out a long sigh. "I

always let my imagination run away with me. In fact, sometimes I—" She stopped, and looked away.

"Sometimes you what?"

"Oh, nothing. It's stupid. It's just that when I was little, I used to believe that if I could imagine something bad, it wouldn't happen to me. Childish, huh?"

"Oh, I don't know," Kate said slowly. "It's always the unexpected things that knock you for a loop."

Jules glanced at her quickly, then away again. "Yeah, well. It was probably some psychological interpretation of a statistical probability, like saying lightning won't strike the same place twice. I used to lie in bed at night trying to think of all the terrible things that might happen, and it was always a relief to come up with something really awful, because if I could imagine it clearly enough, it was as if it had actually happened, and then I would know that at least I was safe from *that*."

The adult vocabulary combined with the earnestness of youth made it difficult to get a grip on Jules Cameron, but for the moment Kate put aside the question of what Jules was telling her and went for the most immediate consideration.

"Jules, I truly do not think you need to worry about serial killers and torture murders. The newspapers make you think that kind of thing happens all the time, and sure, there are a lot of things someone like Dio can get into, things that are not very nice. The world isn't a good place for a kid on his own. But I think it's much more likely that, for reasons known only to himself, Dio decided suddenly to move on. And I do honestly think he may just show up again. Without more information, I can't do much for you, and of course you realize that I personally have very little authority outside of San Francisco. However, I will go and ask a few questions, see what I can find out about him, see if I can set the ball rolling. Okay?"

"Thank you." She practically whispered it, overcome by the relief of a burden handed over. For a moment, she looked very young.

"I want you to remember two things, Jules. First of all, Dio seems to be pretty resourceful at taking care of himself. Most kids end up living in boxes under an overpass and falling in with some real shit—with some really rotten characters. Your Dio sounds fairly clever, and I'd say that if he manages to avoid drugs, he has a good chance of staying on his feet."

"He hates drugs. He told me once they make him sick, and they killed his mother. It's the only time he said anything about her, when he was telling me where his name came from, and I think he meant it. Both parts of it."

Jules did not seem to have faced the implication that if the boy knew that drugs made him ill, he at least had to have tried something, but Kate was not about to point this out, either.

"I hope so. The other thing to remember is, even if he has taken off, even if, God forbid, he's dead, he had a friend—you. A lot of runaways never do make friends, not normal friends. It's something to be proud of, Jules." To Kate's horror, the child's lips began to twitch and her eyes fill. Jesus, after the last few days, all she needed was another scene. She moved to cut it off. "However, I also agree with Señora Hidalgo. Befriending some stranger in a park is a damn fool thing to do, and if I were your mother, I'd turn you over my knee."

As the words left her mouth, Kate wondered why on earth conversing with a child invariably turned her into a cliché-mouthing maiden aunt, alternately hearty and judgmental. Don't interrupt, child. It's not polite to point. Wash your mouth out with soap. However, in this case it did the trick: Jules's eyes went instantly dry, her chin rose.

"My mother never hits me. She says it's a shameful abuse of superior strength."

"So it is. But I'd still do it. However," she said, rising, "I'm not your mother, and I don't want you riding the bus home. Let me put on some shoes and I'll drive you back."

"But you have to be at work today. They told me."

"Only on call, and then not until tonight. There's loads of time."

"You should go back to sleep, then."

"I'll sleep later. Nobody dies on a Tuesday night."

"But—"

"Look, Jules, do you have some reason you don't want me to drive you home? Hiding something, maybe?"

"Of course not."

"Fine. I'll go and put on my shoes. Be back in a minute."

"Okay. And Kate? Thank you."

◆

In the basement garage, Jules paused between the two cars. She looked at the gleaming white Saab convertible up on its blocks, and then she took in Kate's dented, scruffy Japanese model, covered with road dirt and smeared with engine grease from the recent repairs, strewn inside with debris and rubbish. She said nothing, just took an empty pretzel box from the floor and with fastidious fingernails gathered up the apple cores and grape stems and dropped them into the box along with the Styrofoam cups, empty wrappers, grease-stained paper bags, and generic garbage. She ran out of room in the pretzel box and used a McDonald's sack for the remainder, then neatly placed both box and bag on the cement floor of the garage just under the driver's door of Lee's car. She carefully gathered up all the cassette tapes from the seat before getting in, then set about matching nineteen scattered tapes to their boxes while Kate backed out of the garage and headed toward the nearest freeway entrance. By the time they had negotiated the most recent route complications, inserted themselves into the flow of determined truckers, and dodged the inevitable panic-stricken station wagons with midwestern plates that decided at the last moment that they needed to get off *right now*, Jules had the tapes securely boxed and arranged in their zippered pouch, the titles up and facing the same way. She placed the zip bag on the floor under her knees, put her hands in her lap, narrowed her eyes at the truck in front of them, and spoke.

"Where's Lee?"

Kate took a deep breath and flexed her hands on the wheel.

"Lee is visiting an aunt, up in Washington."

"The state?"

"Yes."

"We used to live in Seattle, when I was really small. I don't remember it. She must be feeling better, then."

"She must be." Kate felt the child's eyes on her.

"How long has she been away?"

"I just got back this morning from taking her."

"You drove her? That's a long way, isn't it? Is she phobic about flying?"

"She just finds it difficult, with her legs," said Kate evenly, giving absolutely no indication in her voice of the previous two weeks, of the nasty surprises and the queasy blend of loneliness, abandonment, sheer rage, and the dregs of the worst hangover she'd had for many years.

"I suppose she would," said Jules thoughtfully. "Planes are so crowded anyway; with crutches, they'd be awful. Or does she still use the wheelchair?"

"Sometimes, but mostly she uses arm braces."

"And didn't you have a man living in the house, too? Lee's caretaker. I met him. Jon, without the *h*."

"He's away for a while, too."

"So you're all alone. Do you like being alone in the house?" When Kate did not answer immediately, she continued. "I do. I like coming home to a house—or to an apartment, in my case—when you know nobody's there and nobody will be there for a while. I can't wait until Mom thinks I'm old enough to stay by myself. It's a real pain, having Trini the airhead there all the time. She's all right, but she takes up so much space, somehow, and she always has music going. I like being alone, for a while anyway. I don't know how I'd like it all the time. I guess

I'd get lonely, at night especially. How long will Lee be gone?"

"I don't know." Now Kate's control was slipping, and she heard the edge in her voice. Jules looked at her again.

"How are her legs, anyway? Al said she could get around pretty well, compared with what they were expecting—"

"Let's not talk about Lee anymore," Kate said, her voice friendly but the warning signs clear. "I'm totally pissed off at her right now. Okay? Tell me, what's that say on your shirt?"

Jules dropped her chin to look at the foreign writing. "It says, *'Panta hellenike estin emoi.'* That means, 'It's all Greek to me.' This guy in my programming class puts himself through college by selling T-shirts. I thought this one was kinda neat."

Kinda neat, Kate thought with a smile, and the psychological interpretations of statistical probabilities. "Tell me about your class," she suggested. The topic lasted Jules until Palo Alto, when Kate left the freeway and asked for directions to the park.

TWO

KATE SATISFIED herself with a slow drive-by and a pause in the parking lot, although Jules was anxious to show her around.

"No, I just wanted to see," she said firmly. "And you used to meet him under that tree? What direction did he usually come from? No, just to get an idea. Now, show me where you live. No, Jules, I'm not just going to drop you off."

Ignoring the girl's protests, Kate parked in a visitor's slot behind the large brick building and walked up the stairs behind her, feeling like a truant officer. The apartment turned out to be larger than the one Kate had seen in San Jose, where Jani and her daughter had lived two floors above a particularly vicious psychopath, but it retained the old one's personality as the lair of a distracted academic and her serious and equally intellectual daughter. The high ceilings seemed to be held up by bookshelves—no neatly arranged storage spaces, either, but depositories laden with volumes in the disarray of constant use. Some improvements had been made over the last place: the ghastly motel furniture had been left behind, the plastic and chrome dinette set traded for a wooden dining table with six matching wooden chairs, the flowered sofa replaced by a suite of comfortable-looking overstuffed chairs and sofa in corduroy the shade of cappuccino. Even the heaps of books seemed less precarious here; a few surfaces were actually free of them.

Jules picked up two mugs, one with a spoon in it, and carried them into the kitchen. Kate followed her.

"Nice place."

"I like it better than the other one. Nobody lived in that building but Yuppies, and then after . . . I kept thinking I saw him in the hallways." She turned away, furiously embarrassed by this admission, to thrust the mugs and a couple of other things into the dishwasher.

"Spooky," Kate agreed. "Where does Mrs. Hidalgo live?"

"Oh, she won't be expecting me for hours yet. I don't get home 'til two sometimes." It had been "three or four" earlier; Jules, among her many accomplishments, was not a practiced liar.

"I suppose you could forge a note for school," Kate said easily, looking out the window at a desk-sized balcony and a postage stamp–sized swimming pool below, "but Mrs. Hidalgo would probably find out, and your mother would blow up. Best defuse the bomb before it starts spluttering."

Jules was silent; then Kate heard her sigh. "You're as bad as Al," she complained. "Okay, let me just dump these books. You want to see my room?"

"Sure," said Kate. Jules caught up her backpack and led Kate to the other end of the very ordinary apartment. The room, as Kate had suspected, was not ordinary. It was, in fact, like no other teenage bedroom she'd ever seen, and in the course of her professional life she had seen quite a few.

To begin with, it was tidy. Not compulsively so, but beneath a minor accumulation of papers, books, and Coke cans, things were obviously in their assigned and logical places. The shelves were free of dust, and the bed had even been made.

The room was very Jules. The top end of the bed was buried under an arrangement of stuffed animals; on the foot of the bed were two books, each of them weighing at least five pounds. The one on the top was a biography of Mary Wollstonecraft. A high shelf, running around three sides of the room, was solid with more toys, teddy bears in the full gamut of pastels, a grouping of stuffed cows and another of elephants, and so on through the bestiary. The shelves below that held books—paperback novels on the higher shelves, solid books lower down; tomes such as few adults had even held were down at waist level. This was a logical-enough arrangement in earthquake country—some of those books would kill a person if they fell from a height of eight feet—but she was amused to see a collection of old and obviously much loved picture books shoulder-to-shoulder with a collection of glossy coffee table art books. The cross between childhood naïveté and adult sophistication extended to the walls as well: Three framed prints from the pages of *Goodnight Moon* were arranged on one wall, facing a poster of a Renaissance woman's face on the other, an ethereal blond portrait with the name of a German museum underneath.

Jules had dropped her backpack on the desk and gone across to open the door of a wire cage. A black-and-white rat came blinking out onto his mistress's hand, but Kate was distracted by a piece of paper that had been pinned up to the corkboard over the desk, on which was printed the word *sesquipedalian*.

"What's that?" she asked, pointing.

"That's my word for the day," Jules told her matter-of-factly. She had been cuddling the rat to her chin, and she now kissed his pointy nose and allowed him to scramble onto her shoulder. "It means long words. Literally, it refers to something a foot and a half long." She took a peanut from a jar and held it up to her shoulder. Kate watched the rat manipulate the nut between his delicate paws and nibble it down to nothing, and she wondered briefly how to respond to the word of the day before deciding that she didn't actually have to.

"What's his name?" she asked instead.

"Ratty."

"I loved *The Wind in the Willows* when I was a kid," Kate agreed.

"Actually, his full name is Ratiocinate," said Jules, putting him back in the cage with another nut. "But I call him Ratty."

Kate laughed aloud and followed Jules back to the kitchen. The girl looked into the refrigerator. "Would you like a Coke?" she offered. "Or I could make you some coffee. Mrs. Hidalgo never has anything but juices to drink; she believes in healthy living." It sounded like a quote, as did many of Jules's remarks. Kate was not actually thirsty, and she didn't much like Coke either, but without knowing why, she found herself accepting the offer. She and Jules stood in the kitchen for a while, talking about the apartment and drinking from the cans, until eventually Kate suggested they should be going downstairs.

Then, on their way out of the apartment, an odd thing happened, one that would have made little impression on Kate had it not been for Jules's reaction. The telephone rang as they walked toward it, and without hesitating, almost without breaking stride, Jules simply picked up the receiver and let it drop immediately back onto the base. No, not drop: Jules slammed it down in a small burst of fury and continued on out of the apartment. Kate followed, waited while Jules dug the key from her shorts pocket and locked the door, and then spoke to the back that she was following down the hallway.

"Get a lot of wrong numbers, do you?" She was totally unprepared for the girl's reaction: Jules whipped around, long braids flying and her face frozen, as if daring Kate to push an inquiry, and then she started down the stairs at a pace so fast, it was almost running. Kate caught up with her at the downstairs neighbor's door, putting out a hand to touch the girl's arm.

"Jules, are you getting a lot of crank phone calls?"

The girl stared at the doorbell, and then the rigidity in her shoulders gave way and she exhaled.

"No, not a lot. I just had one a while back that was really weird, and I guess I'm still jumpy when the phone rings if I'm alone. Stupid to just hang up like that, isn't it? I mean, what if it was Mom?"

"Or Dio?"

She turned to stare at Kate. "God, I didn't think about that. He's never phoned me," she said doubtfully. "But he could."

"If you're having a problem, Jules, you can always have your phone number changed. Or you can arrange with the phone company—"

"No!" she said fiercely. "I don't want to change the number, and I don't want to bring the phone company into it."

"Use the answering machine, then, to screen your calls."

"I do, sometimes."

"Have you told your mom, or Al?"

"It only happened once!" Jules nearly shouted. "It's not a problem."

"It sounds to me like it is."

"Really, Kate, it's not. It's just all the stuff about Dio—it's getting to me. But if whoever it is starts up again, I promise I'll ask Mom to change the number." Jules reached for the doorbell again, and this time Kate let her ring it.

The matriarch of the Hidalgo clan did not quite match the short, squat, big-bosomed surrogate-grandmother-to-the-neighborhood image Kate had formed. True, her skin was the color of an old penny, and true, the smell of something magnificent on the stove filled the stairwell; there was even the clear indication that half the children on the block had moved in. However, the good señora had a waist slimmer than Kate's, and the jeans and scoop-necked pink T-shirt she wore covered a body taut with aerobic muscles. She also wore a small microphone clipped to the front of her shirt, like a newscaster's mike,

29

only pointing down. She looked at her two visitors with concern.

"Julia, you are home early. Was there a problem at the school?" She gave the name a Spanish pronunciation, but her accent was mild.

"*Buenos dias, Señora,*" said Jules carefully. "*No hay problema. Este es mi amiga Kate Martinelli. Yo tengo . . . tiene . . . yo tenía una problema, y ella va a ayudarme con, er . . .*"

"That was very good, Julia; you're coming along rapidly. I'm pleased to meet you, Ms. Martinelli. Rosa Hidalgo." She put out her hand, which was as firm as the rest of her. "Come in. I was just finishing here. Fieldwork for my thesis in child psychology," she added, looking over her shoulder.

The room was awash with children, along with a number of maternal types planted around the edges like boulders. Rosa Hidalgo moved surely through the small multicolored heads, avoiding the clutter of blocks and toys that covered the floor like debris from a shrapnel bomb.

"That's great for today. Thank you all. How about lunch now? Eh, amigos," she said in higher tones, "you hungry? Burritos, peanut butter, tuna fish, and tell Angélica what you want to drink." She began folding away tape recorder and mike while various boulders moved forward to scoop the abandoned toys into containers and the children, all of them small, marginally verbal, but astonishingly noisy, washed off to the next room, where her daughter, a tall girl of perhaps seventeen, presided with an immense dignity over sandwiches and pitchers of drink.

"Have you eaten, Kate? Jules? There're vegetarian burritos; I hope that is all right. I use adzuki beans. Jennifer, this is Kate. Show her where things are, would you? Tami, I know you need to leave, but I must clarify something. When Tom junior was talking about the dog, was he saying—"

Although Kate was no more hungry than she had been

thirsty when offered the Coke upstairs, she ate two of the superb fat burritos, which were everything their fragrance had advertised, and refused a third only at the thought of the already-straining waistband of her trousers.

"Do you have a child here, Kate?" asked the woman whom Rosa had addressed as Jennifer.

"Sorry? Oh, no. No, I don't have any children. I'm a friend of Jules, the girl over there. She lives upstairs. Do you know how much longer—"

She was interrupted by a rapid escalation of shrieks from the next room, at which point Jennifer was suddenly just not there, only her plate teetering on the edge of the sink. Kate rescued it, and was relieved when she saw that the furious quarrel at the children's table was the signal for a mass departure. Twenty minutes of potty visiting and prying toys from clenched fists later, Kate was finally alone with Rosa Hidalgo.

"Whew! *Madre*, I need a cup of coffee. How about you?"

Kate thought a slug of bourbon more like it, but she accepted the lesser drug with thanks. It was real coffee, from a press-filter machine, thick and gritty and exactly right.

"I thought at first you were running a nursery in here."

"Twenty three-and-a-half-year-olds, it sounds more like the monkey house in the zoo. Every six months, they come here in the mornings for a week." She paused, reviewing the syntax of the sentence. "Twice a year, I have them here, every morning for a week."

"Must seem quiet when the week is over," Kate commented.

"*Madre*, my ears, they sing. Next February will be the last time. I wonder if I will miss them."

"You said it was for a thesis?"

"Yes, I am tracing the development of gender characteristics, which boys play with toy cars and which girls prefer dolls, comparing them with the results of a number

31

of other researchers doing similar studies. I have been following this group since they had one year."

"Since they were one year old, Mama," corrected her daughter, clearing dishes in the background.

"Since they were one year old. Thank you, Angél. My English suffers after one of these sessions," she remarked to Kate, her pronunciation more precise than ever. "It is a symptom of stress. Angél, go and get your suit on; we will go for a swim. You, too, Julia. Leave those dishes; we'll do them later. Now"—she turned to Kate when the door had closed behind the girls—"you will please tell me what problem you are helping Julia with, what is troubling her, and why she did not go to her computer class today."

"I think you're aware that Jules made a friend in the park this summer, a homeless boy." Rosa Hidalgo nodded. "Well, he's disappeared, and she's concerned. She came to ask me to look into it. I'm with the police department," she added. "In San Francisco. I work with her mother's . . . boyfriend."

"Alonzo Hawkin, yes. And you live in San Francisco?" Kate nodded. "I see. And she went during school hours that I might not know."

"She thought you'd worry."

"She was correct. Why do the bright ones always do such awesomely stupid things?" The shake of her head was the gesture of an experienced mother rather than that of a trained psychologist. "What will you do, about the boy?"

"There isn't much I can do, to tell you the truth. Talk to the local sheriff's department, put his description out over the wire if he doesn't show up in a few days, see if he's shown up in L.A. or Tucson."

"That does not sound very hopeful."

"Juvenile runaways are nearly impossible to trace. I haven't said anything to Jules, but I think she is aware of the difficulties. She also seems aware of the dangers, though if anything, I'd say she has an overly dramatic view of the threats to the boy. AIDS and hepatitis are more likely than the murdering maniac she visualizes."

Rosa Hidalgo's gaze narrowed to attention at Kate's last words, and she spoke sharply.

"What precisely did she tell you?"

"I think she was worried about a serial killer torturing him to death. Something like that."

"*Madre de Díos,*" she muttered, shaken.

"I told her that was completely unlikely," Kate hastened to say. "And really, it's a credit to her that she's concerned about him. It doesn't even seem to be anything romantic, just that she feels responsible for a friend she's just realized she badly misunderstood. She's a good kid. Don't come down too hard on her for lying to you."

"If 'coming down hard' means expressing anger, then no, I will not. I will, however, strongly urge her mother and Alonzo to educate her as to the dangers the world holds for young girls. Talking to a boy in a well-populated public park is one thing; taking a bus to San Francisco without telling anyone is quite another. Her mother has a strong tendency to be overly protective, and to avoid unpleasant topics with her daughter. She must be shown that it only makes the darkness beneath Julia's brilliance all the greater. I shall speak to Alonzo about it, I think. It was very perceptive of you to see beneath the armor of Julia's mind, Ms. Martinelli."

For a cop, Kate supposed she meant.

"The name is Kate. Here, let me give you my phone number, in case anything else comes up. That's my number at work, and—do you have a pen? This," she continued, writing on the back of the card, "is my home number. I have to run, but would you tell Jules I'll call her tomorrow night? Maybe you'd better give me your number, too," she said, taking back the pen and writing down the number. As Rosa escorted her to the door the two girls reappeared, clutching scraps of bright nylon and brighter towels. Kate sidled past them into the hallway and, reassuring Jules that she was going to look into

Dio's absence, that she would be in touch, and that she would be discreet, she made her escape.

◆

Kate parked on the far side of the park from the swimming pool, in case Jules ended up there. Kate had no intention of allowing Jules to tag along while she followed her nose to what might turn up as a two-day-old decomposing corpse bent over a spray-paint canister. Jani—and Al—would not thank her for that.

However, a circuit of the park, which took less than half an hour, brought no whiff of the utterly unmistakable, primally unnerving smell of a rotting human being. The park was partly grass and playground, partly scrub woodland around an arroyo—masses of tick bush, madrone, live oak, and great billows of poison oak beginning to take on the spectacular red of its autumnal coloring. She went back to the car and drew out a mechanic's coverall that she kept there, more as emergency-clothing-cum-rag than because she worked on the car in it. It was made of tightly woven gabardine, and as she zipped it up, she felt as if she had stepped into a sauna. She also put on socks and running shoes and a pair of driving gloves. She thought of tying her hair in a towel, but decided that would be just too awful. She locked the car and walked along the road that wrapped the wilderness portion of the park until she found a vague deer trail, then pushed her way into the stifling, hot, dusty, fragrant brush. When that trail petered out, she reversed her steps and tried another.

Forty minutes later, she found the boy's lair. He must have been immune to poison oak, because Kate had to swim in the stuff, and twice she had gone past the low entrance before registering that one of the branches seemed even more dead than the others.

There was a tent, brown and dusty and pushed in among the bushes on all sides, carefully zipped up, but with the flaps only casually draped across the door and left down at the windows. She cleared her throat and said

34

the boy's name loudly, but the only movement was a blue jay over her head. With a beat of apprehension she pulled up the door flap and looked through the screen into the tent, claustrophobic in its branch-crowded windows. There was no body, sprawled and swelling. There was a pair of cloth high-top tennis shoes, mostly holes, in one corner next to a neat pile of folded clothes which, she soon found, consisted of a pair of shorts and one of jeans, a T-shirt, two graying pairs of undershorts, a pair of mismatched, once-white athletic socks, and a sweatshirt. There were also half a dozen two-liter plastic soft-drink bottles filled with water that appeared dirty with the beginnings of algae; a worn beach towel; a sleeping bag with several holes and a broken zipper; and half a dozen shoe boxes in a neat pile. Some of these last were empty, others held a variety of undoubtedly scrounged treasures: two or three half-empty notepads—stained with what, coffee grounds?—three pencils, two pens. Another shoe box held string, twine, elastic bands, broken shoelaces, a snarl of twist ties, and some neatly folded plastic grocery bags. Another—surprise: jewelry. Most of it was of the costume variety, but there was also a man's gold signet ring with a small diamond, the metal scratched and slightly misshapen as if it had been buried in sand, and three odd earrings for pierced ears, all of which had lost the post's anchor. One of the earrings had three gold chains, each ending in a small ruby and dangling from a center stud with a larger ruby, to Kate's eyes genuine and worth a few dollars at a pawnshop or jeweler's. She closed the shoe boxes and put them back as she had found them, then continued her search. Inside a cracked plastic file box about a foot square and with a rock on top of it, she found Dio's library, including a hardback science fiction novel from the local public library, due the following week. Checked out to Jules? After an inner battle, she removed it from the others, most of them worn paperback classics like *The Adventures of Huckleberry Finn*, *The Three Musketeers*, *David Copperfield*, and *Peter Pan*. Deliberately collected, she wondered as she thumbed through them, or just what someone in the neighborhood happened to throw out? There was no rainbow notebook, no identifying papers aside from the much handled photograph of a woman with large teeth laughing into the camera on a beach. It was the only thing in the tent that she thought Dio might regret, were it to be damaged by rain, so for safekeeping she stuck it inside the library book and put that to one side.

No sign of a struggle; on the other hand, it was doubtful that he'd pack up and leave without the bits of jewelry that could buy a hungry boy several meals. But there was nothing more she could do here, except . . . She took one of the pads and a pencil stub out of the appropriate box and wrote her home phone number on it. Below it, she added: *I'm a friend of Jules. Please call collect.*

She left the pad on the sleeping bag, picked up Jules's book, and let herself out of the tent, where the close day seemed cool compared with the stifling tent. She fastened the zip and pulled the door flap across the tent, then pushed her way back out of the brush.

By the time she had gained the road, she could barely keep from ripping off the drenched and sticking coverall. She did unzip it completely, stuffing the gloves into a pocket. Oh God, she thought, I'm itching already, and scratched her head.

She had company. A sheriff's car had pulled authoritatively, if ineffectually, across the front of her car, and the two deputies were standing side by side, watching her puff up the road.

Kate knew immediately that these two would drawl, though they had probably been born in California, that they'd make some remark about her clothes, and that they would attempt to bracket her at close quarters to strut their power. Well, they'd just chosen the wrong woman on the wrong day for that little game. She walked past them without a glance, went to the trunk of her car, unlocked it, tossed in the library book, and took out two bottles of mineral water. One she drank, letting it spill down her throat. She bent over and let the other one glug across her face and into her hair. Still ignoring the two deputies, who were now standing on either side of her, she capped the bottles, tossed them into the trunk, ran her fingers through her shaggy hair to comb it roughly into place, and brought her right foot up to the bumper to untie her shoe. Only now did one of the young men speak, the one on her left.

"Afternoon there, Miss."

"Martinelli. And it's Ms."

"Why, we got us a card-carrying feminist, Randy," said the second.

"Randy," she snorted, kicking her shoe into the trunk and bending to untie the other one. "And I suppose your partner's name is Dick." Before he could figure it out, she distracted him by shrugging out of the coverall and tossing the filthy garment in after the shoes and socks, then reaching in for a pair of rubber thongs, dropping them to the ground, and slipping her feet into them. "You drive that car?" she asked.

Totally disconcerted, he actually answered.

"Yeah, I drive it."

"Well, don't worry, parking gets easier as you gain experience. Now if you'll pardon me, boys, I've got things to do." She thrust a hand into the pocket of her running shorts and when she looked up, she found herself staring into the ends of a matched pair of 9-mm automatics.

Afterward, she thought it amazing that she hadn't been frozen with terror, in the sights of two small cannons manned by lunatics, but at the time all she felt was incredulity. She slowly stretched out her arm and let the key chain dangle from her fingers, and the two sheriff's deputies straightened up, beginning to look sickly.

"You stupid shits," she said conversationally. "How long have you two bozos been out of the Academy? A week? You don't go waving your gun around unless you're prepared to use it, and you don't use it unless you're prepared to spend six months filling out the goddamn forms. For Christ's sake, can you possibly think that a person dressed like this could conceal anything bigger than a Swiss army knife?"

She gestured at herself, and the two louts looked again at the nylon running shorts and the damp and clinging tank top, then finished holstering their guns.

"We had a report, ma'am . . ." began the shorter one, the driver, with no trace now of a drawl.

"Some old lady in one of those houses over there no doubt, who saw me poking around and took me for a mad bomber. And now she's watching you making asses of yourselves."

"Yes, ma'am. But do you mind telling us what you were doing?"

"This is a public park."

"Now, look you—"

"Shut up, Randy," hissed the driver.

"But Nelson—"

"Nelson?" snorted Kate. No wonder he had a chip on his shoulder. She stood and waited for further grumbles of authority, but there was more apprehension than aggression in their faces.

"No, I'm not going to file a complaint. But you two better think three times before you pull that kind of damn fool stunt again. I don't expect to have to ID myself every time I go for my keys, and it's too damn hot to wear a uniform."

Kate waited an instant before this penny dropped, and she was suddenly aware that she felt better than she had in a long time. Happy, even. She stepped forward and held out her hand to Nelson.

"Inspector Kate Martinelli, SFPD. Homicide."

She was still feeling marvelously cheerful as she pulled her car in beside Nelson and Randy's black-and-white in the parking lot of a nearby hamburger joint, and she could feel the bounce in her steps as she accompanied the two looming uniforms inside. She ordered a large iced tea, excused herself to scrub her face and hands in the rest room, and then joined the men at the table, where she flipped her ID onto the table and sat down.

"Okay," she said without preamble. "What I was doing there in that weird outfit was looking for a boy. Friend of mine met him in the park a few times; he disappeared five days ago. He told her that he lived there, in the park, so I thought I'd have a look. He was telling the truth, but he's not there now, hasn't been for a few days, by the look of it, left behind some things of value—a ring, a couple of odd earrings, pair of shoes. He's a light-skinned Hispanic male, age maybe fourteen or fifteen, five seven, slim, no distinguishing marks except for a chip on the top right incisor, calls himself Dio and his name may be Claudio, hung around the park a lot. Any bells?"

"Sounds like half the kids in the park, come summer," Nelson said, all business now and damned glad if nobody referred to that little episode earlier.

"This one was a loner, would've avoided group activities, didn't use the pool or take classes, just drifted. Talked to a young girl a lot; she's twelve, five four, black braids, hazel eyes, slightly Oriental-looking. Pretty, acts older than her age."

"She sounds familiar. Reads a lot?"

"That's her."

"I remember a boy," said Nelson. "Never talked to him, though."

"I'd appreciate it if you'd keep an eye out for him. He hasn't done anything, not that I know of, and he sounds the kind of kid who, if he's been pulled into the game or onto the needle, might cut all ties."

"Some self-respect, you mean?" asked Nelson. He wasn't a total loss, then, in the brains department.

"Might be salvaged," she agreed. "Well, gentlemen, it's been real. When you find out who made the call about that dangerous madwoman in the bushes, you might ask her if she's seen our young man. Here's my card, and my home number." (Handing out a lot of these lately, she reflected.) "Give me a ring if you get anything. Thanks for the drink."

♦

Kate drove the thirty miles home without thinking of much of anything, parked on the street in front of the house, and let herself in the front door. When she closed the door behind her, she was hit by the miasma of a house that was not merely empty but abandoned. She stood in the hallway of the house and heard its silence, smelled the staleness beneath the remnants of the breakfast Jules had cooked, and thought how happy she had once been to come home to this place; remembered how she and Lee had loved and labored to free it of its decades of neglect; remembered how she and Lee had loved. It had been their joy and their delight, and now its walls rang with emptiness: no Lee upstairs or in the consulting rooms on Kate's right, no Jon making magic in the kitchen or down in the basement apartment listening to his peculiar modern music, none of Lee's clients, none of Jon's impossible friends, no nothing, just the ache of its emptiness and Kate, standing in the hall.

She poured herself a glass of wine, ignoring the clock, and trudged up the stairs. At the top, not meaning to, she found herself in Lee's study, standing at Lee's desk, opening its right-hand drawer, and taking out the letter from Lee's mad aunt that had begun all this:

> *My dear niece,*
> *We have only met twice during your life, and as during our brief second meeting you were clad only in a pair of wet diapers, you probably do not remember me. I trust that you are at least aware that your father had a sister. If not, then I imagine this will come as a considerable surprise. Nonetheless, he had, and I am she. Hard to think of my brother—young enough to have been my own baby, come to think of it—as a man of fifty, but as I turn sixty-eight this year, that would have been the case. Except that he died in uniform, you never saw him, and I was kept from you by your mother, because I reminded her of her great loss, or so she said.*

I returned to this country a year ago, taking up residence on an island in the Strait of Juan de Fuca that has no electricity and virtually no neighbors. I find it a delightful contrast to Calcutta, and is not contrast the spice of life? Upon my return, I instructed my lawyer to find what he could about my family members, which may explain why I am writing to you now. He seems to have employed a private investigator—a curious thought—who charged what seemed to me an excessive amount of money for a folder full of newspaper clippings. I apologize for inadvertently trespassing upon your privacy; had I known that I was doing so, I would have instructed the man to desist.

Thus I have learned of your injury, and although I was certainly distressed to hear of it, I understand that you are progressing rapidly, and as, after all, you could hardly stagger about when last I saw you, I suppose one could say that from my viewpoint there has been little change.

Which brings me to my purpose in writing, other than to arrange for an annual exchange of Christmas cards and other nonsense. If you are ever wishing a period in an extremely rustic retreat with an ill-tempered old woman who has no time for sympathy and no craving for service, my island is at your disposal. It is not set up for a disabled person, but then neither is it set up for a sixty-eight-year-old woman with malaria, so we would be evenly matched, and no doubt would cope.

I realize you may be feeling perfectly horrified at the idea, in which case toss these pages into the bin and don't give me another thought. I write only as a gesture to my brother, of whom I was very fond and whom I still miss daily. If something of him has surfaced in you, and particularly if that element makes the proposal of

an island sojourn appealing, please write to tell
me when you wish to arrive.

Agatha Cooper

And to think, Kate reflected, that my first reaction was to laugh in delight at its absurdity. The memory made her feel ill, because in reality Lee's aunt had spoken, and Lee had answered, and now Kate was alone in the big house. She put the letter away and went into the hallway, where she gathered the shed clothes from the night before and took them not into their bedroom, but down to the small guest room at the end of the upstairs hall. She hung the denim jacket in the closet, stripped off her tank top and shorts and threw them along with the other dirty clothes into the guest hamper, and walked nude up the carpeted hall to get her work clothes out of the big bedroom. At the mirrored closet, she paused and eyed her reflection sourly. She wouldn't be surprised to find two more pounds on the scale: Long drives and comfort eating were killers. She looked pale, restless; her hair was nearly in her eyes. Even her fingernails were dirty and overlong.

"Christ, you're a mess," she said to her reflected self, and went to take a long shower with a great deal of soap.

She did not consult the scales; she did cut her fingernails.

Going back downstairs, she checked a second time, but the answering machine was still obstinately free of messages, not a red light to be seen. She even pushed the playback button, rationalizing that the light could be broken, but it merely clunked and beeped at her and was silent. She decided to go in to work after all, although she was only on call.

After the brooding quiet of the house, the gritty chaos of the Department of Justice was almost a balm to Kate's spirit. She had been away for little more than a week, but it might have been a few minutes. Kitagawa nodded as he passed her, deep in conversation with a man in the garish uniform of a doorman. Tom Boyle raised a finger in greeting but did not take the phone from his ear. She went to her desk, stowed her gun and a thermos of coffee in the bottom drawer, and sat in her chair: home again.

Dellamonica had a new tie. April Robinette had spilled something on her skirt. Gomes came through cursing furiously and carrying a massive electronic typewriter under his arm. There was another new plant on Al Hawkin's desk, already looking resigned to a lingering death. The top of Kate's desk was covered with scribbled messages that would take most of the day to decipher and deal with. Among them she found a flyer with the grainy photograph of a young girl with short hair, and she did not need to read the description of the missing girl to know that the police in Washington—no, she corrected herself, this one was from Oregon—were afraid that the so-called Snoqualmie Strangler had claimed a sixth victim. It had been several days since Kate had heard or read any news, but Jules was no doubt more up to date: This was the maniac who worried Jules, although there was no boy among his victims. Kate thought briefly of the girl's apprehension—no, her fear—that the telephone call had caused, and then her own phone rang.

Despite what she had told Jules, people did die in San Francisco on a Tuesday afternoon. In this case it was a drive-by shooting, in broad daylight, in the Castro district, with three dozen eager and contradictory witnesses to sort out; she would not have much opportunity to doze off over her files that night.

Dropping the flyer into her wastebasket, Kate retrieved her gun and her thermos, and went out to do her job.

THREE

WITH SEPTEMBER began the phone calls from Jules. In the first week, the girl called twice, to check on the search for Dio. They were brief calls, depressing for both of them. Kate was, in fact, looking for him, even after Al Hawkin had returned, because although Al had told Kate to concentrate on her own work, not sweat over some kid Jules shouldn't have been talking to in the first place, Kate could hear the pride and the loneliness in Jules's voice, and she remembered what it was like to feel abandoned by the adults you loved. Jules was going through a bad patch, and Kate could justify only just so many hours at work, so anything that filled the hours at home was all right with her—even talking to an angry twelve-year-old.

The tone of these telephone conversations evolved rapidly under the pressures from both sides. After the brief, uncomfortable calls of the first week, Kate half-expected that Jules would not try again; instead, the calls began hesitantly to take on a life of their own. Under the impetus of her summer experience, Jules's inevitable back-to-school essay of "What I Did During Vacation" evolved into a major project on homelessness, with Kate as her primary resource.

Even after the paper had been turned in to the astonished but pleased teacher, the phone calls continued, always beginning with the ritual "Anything about Dio?" before wandering off into twenty, even thirty minutes of discussion about homelessness; the ethics of capitalism; the lack of good teachers in the universe; her word for the day (*meniscus, braggadocio,* and *haruspex* were among the sesquipedalian ones, but the shorter *mensch, spirit,* and *vagrant* interested her, as well); the difficulties of getting a good education when surrounded by fools who were obsessed with clothing, hair, and boys; the psychological need for a peer group; the homeless again, and what they did for companionship; the friends Jules had made in her new home; the difference between a boyfriend and a boy friend; clothing, hair, and boys; the politics of clothing, hair, and boys; the pros and cons of short versus long hair; a boy friend called Josh; Kate's work; life in general; life in particular. To her surprise, Kate found herself patient with these adolescent maunderings, and, more than that, positively missing them when three or four days passed without a phone call.

The truth was, the house on Russian Hill was too damn big and too damn quiet. One night, she came home and found a message on the answering machine: Jon was thinking of hopping over to London, since Lee was not there to need his assistance; he would ring when he got back to Boston. "Cheerio, ducks." He did not explain how he knew that Lee was still away. Pride kept Kate from calling him back on the number he had left, but the inevitable conclusion that Lee and Jon had been in communication made the house ring with silence. She tried leaving the radio on, to defuse that first awful minute of coming home to rooms that had not breathed since she left, but the ruse did not work.

One day in mid-September, unpacking the bags after a desultory trip through the aisles of the supermarket, Kate discovered a box of cat kibbles in a bag between the packages of dried pasta and a jug of red wine. She held it up, a totally unfamiliar box she could have sworn she'd never touched before. The orange cat on the front of it grinned at her.

"My subconscious wants me to get a cat," she said aloud in disgust. She took the kibbles to the back door, poured half of them onto the brick patio for the birds, and left the box next to the door. No damn cat.

The next night, late, she was getting into bed when she heard a strange slapping noise down on the patio. Cautiously, she looked over the upstairs balcony and into the face of an obese and disgusted raccoon, who all but shook the empty box at her and tapped its foot. On her way home from work the following day, she stopped at the local corner store and bought five boxes of bone-shaped dog biscuits. The Vietnamese man who ran the cash register looked at her in surprise.

"You have dog now, Miss?"

"No, it's a payoff to the neighborhood protection racket, so they won't turn over my garbage cans."

The man smiled his polite incomprehension and gingerly held out her change.

In one of her long letters north, she told Lee about the raccoon, whom she called Gideon ("Rocky's friend," she wrote in explanation). She also told Lee about work, the neighbors' building project that filled the street with pickup trucks, Dumpsters, and lumber deliveries, the new owners of the exercise club, a rumor that the restaurant at the base of the hill was about to reopen, a phone call from a client of Lee's who had wanted to tell her that his HIV test was blessedly negative, about Al and Jani and Jules and a few mutual friends. She received a handful of brief notes in return.

She did not tell Lee everything—not how she hated opening the door when she came home, nor how she'd taken to sleeping in the guest room or on the sofa. She did not write Lee about her fruitless search for Dio through the shelters and the streets, the hot lines and church soup kitchens and crack houses, the continual rounds of her informants. She did not write Lee about the brief, bloody spasm of gang killings in late September, set off by a theft from a high school locker, that left three kids dead and four bleeding in the space of a few days. She did not write to Lee about these shootings because they proved to be the shock needed to begin the process of coming out of the drifting malaise she had been subject to since driving Lee north in August.

The youngest of the three students to be killed was a slight thirteen-year-old girl with a plait of long black hair that curved down her thin backbone and across the rucked-up remains of what had been a white blouse. When Kate arrived on the scene and pulled back the blood-soaked flowered bedsheet that someone had covered her with, her heart thudded painfully for two fast beats: Her eyes had seen the body as that of Jules Cameron, lying in a pool of crimson agony on the weed-choked sidewalk.

She went on with her job; she took her statements and began her paperwork for the case, forgetting that moment of shock in the familiar routine. She went home and had her dinner and put out the dog biscuits for the raccoon; she ran a hasty vacuum cleaner over the floor and bathed and went to bed half-drunk, and toward morning she dreamed. It was not a particularly nasty dream, just wistful, and in it she was talking to the kid sister who had been killed by an automobile when Kate was in college many years before. They talked about a book and a baseball game, and when the conversation ended and Kate was beginning to wake, she saw that the person she had been talking to was actually Jules.

She came fully awake with a wry smile on her face. For some people, messages from the unconscious mind needed to be pretty blatant. Kate got the point.

When the sun was a bit farther up, she phoned Jules. Jani answered, a lovely, low voice with a lilt of accent.

"Good morning, Kate. Are you looking for Al?"

"Er, well, no, actually. I was hoping to catch Jules before she left for school."

"She is still here. Just one moment." Kate heard the muffling distortions of receiver against hand as Jani

47

called, "Jules!" and then, again to Kate, "She will be here in a moment. How are you, Kate?"

"Fine. Just fine."

"And Lee, how is she progressing?"

"Lee's fine."

"Will you come to dinner soon? Both of you?"

"Well, that might be difficult."

"I understand," she sympathized, not understanding in the least. "But as soon as it is possible. Here is Jules."

"Kate?"

"Hey, J. How're you doing?"

"Did you find him?"

"Find . . . Oh, Dio. No, I'm sorry, nothing's come in. I was calling to see if you'd like to go and do something this weekend. I'm supposed to be off, unless something comes up, and I thought you might like to spend Saturday in riotous living. If it's okay with your mother," she added, belatedly aware that she sounded like an acned teenage boy with sweating palms, asking for a date.

"What would we do?"

"Whatever you like. Movie, the beach. Shopping," she suggested desperately. What do girls like Jules do in their spare time, anyway? Go to the library? Maybe this wasn't such a great idea.

"I'd like that. Let me ask Mom." Again the muffled sounds, the occasional mutter and word of a brief conversation. "Kate? She says fine, what time, and do you want to come back here for dinner?"

"Ten too early for you? And if you want, we could stay out, have a hamburger or some Chinese. Cruise the bars, look for some action?"

That raised a giggle, unexpected from that particular set of vocal cords.

"Ten is fine. Thank you."

Twenty minutes later, the telephone pulled Kate out of the shower, where she'd been berating herself for such a dumb commitment, picturing herself locked up in the car with Jules, driving up and down mumbling, So, what do you wanna do? and Jules answering, I dunno, what do you wanna do?

"Hello?"

"Kate? It's Jules," the girl said, sounding oddly furtive. "There's something I would like to do on Saturday, if it's okay with you."

"Is it legal?" Kate asked warily.

"I think so. If it isn't, don't worry—it was just an idea."

"What is it?" Kate wiped a dribble of shampoo away from her eye with the edge of the towel.

"I'd like to try shooting a gun somewhere."

Probably the very last thing Kate had expected.

"Sure. What kind of gun?"

"What do you mean?"

"Pistol? Rifle? Machine gun? Grenade launcher?"

"Just the pistol, I guess."

"Fine, if your mom doesn't object." Silence. "You think she would?"

"Probably," she said darkly.

"I really couldn't take you if she didn't approve. Ask Al to convince her."

"She doesn't like guns."

"I'm not crazy about them myself. They make a lot of work for me," she said darkly, Lee and the murdered Jules-like girl very much on her mind. "Ask Al."

"Okay."

Kate returned to her shower in a better frame of mind.

◆

Nothing came up to keep Kate from her appointment with Jules, and on a gorgeous crisp autumnal morning, she drove down the peninsula and parked outside the apartment building. She was buzzed in, took the elevator up, and Al opened the door, unshaven and in a dressing gown and slippers. He nodded Kate in. She looked everywhere but at the partner who was in fact her superior officer. He did not seem to notice.

"Coffee?" he asked, holding out his own cup.

"Not if you made it, thanks."

"I think Jules did." She followed him to the kitchen and they examined the glass carafe. The coffee was still more brown than green. "Not too old."

"Yes, then I will have a cup."

"Taking her to the range, then?"

"If it's all right with Jani."

"Jani connects guns with some unpleasant things in her past, but she agrees that Jules has the right to an education."

"I don't want to create a problem here."

"You're not creating it. Ah, here's the Juice now."

"The name is Jules, Alhambra," she growled in the mock disgust of a long-standing joke, and in an aside added, "Good morning, Kate."

Today's T-shirt read, in delicate gold writing: WHEN GOD CREATED MAN, SHE WAS ONLY JOKING. Kate grinned.

"Hey, J, like the shirt. Ready to go? Oh, hi, Jani."

Jani came into the room, dressed more casually than Kate had ever seen her (though rumor had it that when Al Hawkin had first met her, she'd been wearing nothing but a towel, no doubt an exaggeration)—in yellow-orange cotton shorts and a loose white blouse, both crisply ironed. There were also sandals on her feet, two pencils through the heavy bun she wore her gorgeous black hair in, and a pair of reading glasses in one hand. When she entered the room, her daughter immediately stiffened and looked out of the window.

"Hello, Kate. Have you been offered anything to drink?"

"I've got coffee, thanks."

"And you, Jules, did you eat breakfast?"

"I'm not hungry, Mother."

Ah, said Kate to herself, so that's how it is.

What a world lay in those four words, a minor salvo in the bitter civil war between mother and daughter, a family of two turned in on itself in dependency, infuriated at itself. The four words brought with them a flood of memories, of battles and uneasy peace treaties made all

50

the more terrible by the love that lay beneath. Kate drained her coffee cup, still standing, and held it out to her partner with a smile that felt pasted on.

"Thanks, Al, that was great." He handed it to Jules.

"Put it in the sink, would you, Jujube?"

"Anything you say, Altercation."

When the child had left the room, Jani spoke quietly, with surface nonchalance. "Before I forget, Kate, Rosa Hidalgo would appreciate it if you could stop by before you leave today. Nothing terribly urgent, merely a question that arose concerning one of her young clients."

"But what—" Kate stopped, surprised at the stillness in Jani's posture, the urgency in her eyes. "Sure, be glad to," she said easily, and Jani relaxed and held Kate's eyes for a split instant longer, in warning, before nodding her head in an informal leave-taking and disappearing back into her study. Jules stood in the doorway and watched her mother's retreating back, glowering with suspicion.

"Shall we go?" Kate suggested.

"Have a good time, Emerald," Al said. Jules roused herself.

"I'll try, Allegheny."

"Be home by midnight, Pearl." He stifled a yawn.

"Or you'll turn into a pumpkin, right, Alcatraz? And by the way," she said as a parting shot, "I don't think pearls qualify as jewels."

He laughed and closed the apartment door behind them. On the stairs, Jules dropped the joking attitude as if it had never been and turned to Kate.

"What did she want?"

"Who, your mother? Oh, at the end there. She didn't want anything," Kate said easily. "Had a message from Rosa downstairs, probably about a case she asked me about a while back. Why?"

"She's always talking about me to people."

"That's hardly surprising; you're an important part of her life. It would be a bit strange never to mention you, don't you think?" Kate knew that her face gave away nothing—there were too many hours of interrogation behind her to let her thoughts be read by a twelve-year-old. Even this twelve-year-old.

"That's not what I mean."

"No? Well, in this case, I don't think your suspicions are justified. Your mom probably just thought it was a private message, that's all."

In silence, Kate and Jules walked down the two flights of stairs, Kate feeling absurdly on trial, as aware of the child's inner turmoil as if she could see it on a screen: Which side was Kate on? Kate wondered if it mattered, knew that it did, knew furthermore that she wanted Jules to trust her loyalty, and realized that she'd be a damned fool to get herself between child and mother, with Al Hawkin standing over it all. Have to watch your step, Kate.

Still in silence, she started the car and drove the half mile or so to the park with the swimming pool. Jules walked away onto the grass, and Kate trailed after, to the shade of a tree on a low rise. Jules settled down as if sitting in a familiar chair. Kate sat down beside her.

"This is where you used to meet him, you said?" she asked after a couple of minutes.

"His father used to beat him. Did I tell you that?"

"No, you didn't, but it doesn't surprise me. A lot of runaways come from abusive families."

"He's dead, isn't he?"

"He may be. But in all honesty, Jules, I think the odds that he's alive somewhere are considerably higher."

"Did you ever read *Peter Pan*?" Jules asked abruptly.

"*Peter Pan*?" Kate wondered where this was going. "Not in a very long time."

"I hate that book. It's detestable. I read it again last week, because I was thinking about something Dio said, and when you take away all that cute, cheerful stuff they put in the movies, you see it's about a bunch of boys whose parents throw them away, or anyway don't care enough to bother looking for them when they get lost, who get together to try and take care of each other, only to have another group of grown-ups try to kill them all.

What's the difference between a pirate and a serial killer, or a drug pusher, or a . . . a pimp, I ask you?"

Kate was shocked, though whether by the words or the ferociously dry eyes, she could not have said.

"Um, what makes you think—"

"Oh, get real, Kate. I'm not stupid, you know. I do read." She jumped up and stalked off to the chain-link fence around the swimming pool and stood with her fingers hooked into the wire, staring at the lesson going on in the water. Kate followed her slowly, then leaned with her back against the fence, facing the opposite direction.

"You having problems with your mom?"

"I suppose."

"Most people do, at one time or another. She loves you."

"I know. And she has problems. God, who doesn't?" she said with a bitterness beyond her years.

"We don't," said Kate lightly. "Not today. Today is not for problems. Come on."

♦

They spent the next few hours at the shooting range, and Kate considered that she had done the job well, acquainting Jules with the intricacies of the handgun (a borrowed .22 and Kate's own heavier .38) to the point that Jules could hit the target a respectable number of times, and further, she kept the girl at it until she began to show signs of boredom with this, her mother's bugbear. Ravenous, they ate hamburgers, went to an early movie, ended up, of all places, at a bowling alley, and arrived back at the apartment at 10:30 that night, disheveled, exhausted, and reeking of gunpowder, sweat, hamburger grease, popcorn, and the cigarette smoke of the alley. Jules jabbered maniacally for twenty minutes before she began to flag, and then was dispatched to bed. Jani went to make coffee.

"You gave her a good time," said Al, approving and amused.

"She's a nice kid. And tell Jani I think the fascination

with guns will fade, now she knows they're just noise and stink."

"How's Lee? Do you need to call to tell her you'll be late?" Hawkin knew the routine as well as Kate did: Call in whenever you're away.

"No, I don't. She's . . . she isn't there."

Hawkin looked up quickly. "Not in the hospital again?"

"Oh, no, she's doing fine. Or I guess she is. She's up at her aunt's."

"Still? It's been weeks."

"Five weeks, not that long. She writes. She's okay, getting her head straight." That she could admit this much to Al Hawkin was an indication of how very far she'd come since they first began to work together. However she added, "Don't say anything, around the department."

"No," he said, but he watched her closely for a long minute before he stood up to get himself a drink. Kate thought vaguely of leaving.

"I've asked Jani to marry me," he said abruptly. "She said yes."

"I did wonder." She grinned. "I'm very happy for you, Al. For both of you."

Al Hawkin and Jani Cameron had met a year and a half ago, only days before Lee had been shot in the culmination of the same case that brought him to the Cameron door. Since then, Al had paid court to this woman with all his might and every wile at his command. "Laid siege" would describe it more accurately, Kate had occasionally thought over the months. A very polite and solicitous siege, true, but for all the chivalry, there was an underlying single-minded determination that made the final result inescapable.

Jani, coming in with a tray of coffee, was also happy. At any rate, there was a softness in her that had not been there before, and conversely, her spine was straighter. Al had won her, and she was freed from solitude, and Kate heard the heavy footsteps of returning melancholia as she sat on the comfortable ugly sofa and drank coffee with these two friends who had obviously spent this gift of an unexpected free day mostly in bed. She drained her mug, took her leave of them, and drove home to her empty house on Russian Hill. She looked at the keyhole with loathing, opened the door. No lights, no warmth, no smells, the only noise the sharp echo of the door closing. The only life here was an importunate raccoon.

"You miserable house," she said loudly, and went to feed Gideon his dinner.

FOUR

KATE WOKE early after a night of fitful sleep, and she decided the time had come to find her running shoes again. It took her a while, but she uncovered them at last in a box on a shelf in what she had begun thinking of as Lee's closet, where Jon must have put them some months before in one of his fits of tidying. They were old friends on her feet, and she did a careful round of stretches before letting herself out into the gray half rain of an early, foggy morning.

By the base of the hill, her calf muscles were quivering, and the intended easy run of two miles was whittled down still further. At the end of the short circuit, she returned up Russian Hill, walking, and slowly at that, with a red face and heaving lungs. Inside the house, the red dot on the answering machine was glowing, an excuse to sit down on the carpeted stairway to listen to the message—three messages, it turned out; the telephone must have rung the whole time she was out. The first one was from Jon, his voice sounding distant, exaggerated: defensive.

"Katarina, dearest, *why* do I always get the machine? Are you never at home? I *do* hope you're getting these messages; I'll feel terrible if you haven't been. Anyway, I'm back in Boston, but only for a few days. A friend wants me to go to his place in Cancún, and you know how I adore Mexico. Just for a week or two, maybe a bit more, I don't know. I may be back in the City first, but if not, I'll drop you a line and let you know just where I am, exactly. If you really have to get ahold of me, that same number in Boston will do; they'll know where I am. Did you get my postcard from London? Don't you think those helmets the bobbies wear are just so adorable? Why don't our boys wear them? Couldn't you suggest it to the police commissioner or whoever is in charge of the uniforms? Ah well, enough of this, I'll use up the whole tape. Toodle-oo now, Kate, as they say in jolly old. I hope you're well. I'll be in touch soon."

The next message was a brief one from Rosa Hidalgo, who said, "Kate, I just wanted to tell you that if there's anything I can do to help you with Jules, just call me. She's a real sweetheart, but she can be a handful, and I'm happy to offer advice." Kate stared at the machine, wondering what on earth the woman was talking about. She shook her head at the neighborhood busybody and dismissed her from her mind.

Fortunately, the third message was from Jules.

"Hi, Kate. I, um, I suppose you're asleep, and don't bother calling me back. I just wanted to say thanks for yesterday; I really enjoyed it. Especially when that guy in the next lane who was giving you a hard time turned around and dropped the ball on his foot. God, that was funny. Anyway, thanks, I really had a great time, and, if you ever want to do it again, I'd love to. I mean, not just the same things, but anything. Oh, this is Jules—I forgot to say. As if you wouldn't have guessed by now, duh. Gotta run—the French club's going to the beach. Bye, Kate. And thanks again. Bye."

Kate was grinning when the tape clucked to itself, and she pushed herself off the stairs to go shower.

The message from Jules was to prove the high point of a very long and very trying week, a week designed by malevolent fate to push the most phlegmatic of detectives over the edge. Kate was not exactly riding the most even of keels to begin with.

Monday her car would not start.

Cable car and bus got her to work late, irritable, and with leg muscles still quivering from Sunday's run, to find that Al Hawkin was out with the flu and she had been paired with Sammy Calvo, easily the most abrasive and inefficient detective in the city. And of course they caught a call first thing, so she had the pleasure of listening to his offensive jokes—told in all innocence; he truly could not comprehend why a woman might not think a rape joke funny—and going back over his interviews to see what he had left out.

Tuesday, the tow truck was delayed, so she was late a second time. She was further irritated by the truck driver's friendly offer to take Lee's Saab down from its blocks so Kate could drive it—because the thought had already occurred to her and been squelched by the need to reinstate its insurance at a moment's notice, by the knowledge of the comments a Saab convertible would stir up when she climbed out of it at a crime scene in one of the more unsavory parts of town, but mostly by pride. The car was Lee's; Kate would have nothing to do with it.

Wednesday, she sat in the department's unmarked car and had a shouting match with Sammy Calvo over his treatment of a witness, the fifteen-year-old mother of the child whose death they were investigating. His final querulous remark made her blood pressure soar: "I don't understand why you're so hot about this, Katy. I just asked her if she'd ever heard of the Pill." Although sorely tempted to whack him over the head with the clipboard he invariably carried, she satisfied herself with snarling, "It's because you're an insensitive jerk, Sammy. And for Christ's sake, don't call me Katy." She slammed the door of the car behind her and went back into the house to calm the teary young mother and her angry family, finally retrieving some of the answers she needed.

It was a long time until night, and longer still before

she came through the door of the house, her very skin aching with the stress and frustrations of a fourteen-hour day, aching for a friendly voice, aching for Lee, aching, most of all, for a drink, many drinks; craving alcohol like a drowning person craves air, she yearned for the world's oldest painkiller to knock the edges off the intolerable day. She heaved her things onto the kitchen table, plucked a bottle of wine from the rack without looking to see what kind it was, took it over to the drawer to get the corkscrew, and then stood with the corkscrew in one hand as a strong and distressing thought intruded itself into her actions.

How long has it been since you did not finish off the better part of a bottle of wine at night? Since the middle of August, maybe?

Oh God—she shook her head—not tonight, no guilt tonight. It's been a hell of a day.

What day isn't? If not tonight, when?

Fuck off; it's only wine.

Only . . . ?

I want a drink.

Or six.

She stood there for a very long time, aching and frightened and knowing at last, on this gray and dreary night, that she was walking on the edge of a precipice, the one that began with just a bit of letting go and ended up with a few shortcuts and reassuring herself that nobody would notice, until finally she would be just another cop who gave up the fight, a woman who couldn't cut it with the big boys, a lesbian who wasn't as good as she thought. And no, she was not exaggerating the importance of this night's bottle of wine that she held in her hands, because she had at last admitted that if she opened it, the wine would be drinking her, not she it, and if knowing that, she went ahead, then she was also being consumed by tomorrow's bottle, and Friday's. . . .

And oh God, who would care? She put the point of the corkscrew to the foil over the cork, and no further.

It was, oddly enough, Jules who pulled her back from

the edge, that annoying young reminder of yet another responsibility unmet. The thought of Jules was bracing. Maddening, but bracing, like a slap in the face. She put the bottle away and made herself a cup of hot milk in the microwave, then sat with it at the kitchen table while she sorted through the mail.

Junk mail, bills, catalogs, *Psychology Today* and the *Disability Rag* for Lee (at least she hasn't changed the addresses on her subscriptions, Kate thought with black humor), and two letters—one for Lee, one from Lee.

She put everything but this last in a precise stack, largest on the bottom and smallest on top, the lower left corners aligned. She leaned the cheap envelope addressed to her in Lee's heavy black pen against the saltcellar, then took a swig from her mug, grimaced, got up and found an apple and a piece of leathery pizza in the refrigerator, and ate them standing at the sink. Then she took a can of split pea soup from the cupboard and two slices of bread from the refrigerator, opened the can, put half of the soup into a bowl and put that in the microwave oven, dropped the bread into the toaster, ate the soup, ate one slice of toast plain and the other with a sprinkling from the clotted shaker of cinnamon sugar, reached into the cupboard for the bag of coffee beans and then put them down on the sink and turned and took three steps to the table and ran a finger under the flap of the envelope and pulled the slip of paper out and smoothed it open on top of the table with one rapid hand before it could burn her. Then, because it lay open before her, Kate read Lee's brief letter.

"Dearest Kate," it began. That was something, anyway. Doing well, getting stronger. Learning to use a hatchet, could Kate believe that? Wearing one of Agatha's flannel shirts and a down vest, cold mornings. Beautiful trees. Strong hills on wise islands. Pods of orcas in the Sound. All of burgeoning nature helping her to find herself, transferring the energy of the hills into her body. Still confused, though, and sorry, so very, abjectly sorry, to be putting Kate through this, but . . .

But she couldn't say when she would be home. But

Kate couldn't come to visit. But she couldn't tell Kate what to say to her clients, her friends. But as soon as she had her head together, Kate would be the first to know; be patient. "Love, Lee."

Kate looked down at her hand on the table. She had clawed the page together into her fist and it lay there now in a tight wad. She opened her hand, picked at the edges of the letter, smoothed it onto the tabletop with long movements of her hand as if trying to bond it to the wood of the table. She leaned forward, stood, pushing the chair away with the backs of her knees, and turned away.

Beaten, flayed, and too weary to weep, Kate went upstairs to bed.

♦

Thursday's brightest spot came early, when Kate succeeded in running two miles and still managed a (very slow) near jog coming back up the hill. The rest of the day went downhill fast.

On Friday, Hawkin was back, and she and Calvo went out to the Sunset and arrested the dead child's father, a pleasant, rather stupid, frightened, unemployed eighth-grade dropout who had been abused himself as a child and who sobbed uncontrollably when Kate read him his rights, then—sure sign they had arrested the right man—fell asleep in the squad car from sheer relief.

His interview and confession brought no satisfaction. He was only a cog in a deadly mechanism, grinding on to produce yet more poverty and brutality. He was no killer, yet he killed, unforgivably, his own child.

Al Hawkin was near the interview room when Kate came out. Waiting for her? He dropped in beside her as she marched away.

"Al, good to see you. You should be home; you look like hell."

"How'd it go?"

"We got a confession."

"And?"

61

"And what? He'll go to prison and get himself a fine set of muscles in the weight room, and when he gets out, he'll find his girlfriend has two more kids by two other men, and everyone will go on beating everyone else, happily ever after."

"One of those days, I see."

"Do you ever think, Al, that maybe someone should just sterilize the whole goddamn human race, admit that it was a mistake, leave the planet to the dolphins and the cockroaches?"

"Often. Let's go get some dinner."

"I can't, Al. I have to see a man about a car."

"What kind of car?"

"A piece of junk, by the sound of it, but cheap."

"Oh, right. Tony said you'd been having car problems."

"I don't have a problem now. I just don't have a car. Three thousand dollars to fix it so it won't quit on me—I don't have the money."

"What's wrong with Lee's?"

"Nothing. Everything. It's too complicated to go into, Al. And Jon lent his to a friend while he's away."

"So where's the car you're looking at?"

"It's just up Van Ness."

"I'll take you; then we can have dinner."

"If I'm buying, it's a deal."

The car proved impossible, too big to park, too shaky to corner, and probably had had its odometer turned back at some point. They went to a Greek pizza house to eat a feta and pesto pizza, and at 9:30 Hawkin pulled up in front of her empty house and turned off the engine.

"Lee's not back yet," he said after a glance at the windows.

"Nope."

"You heard from her?"

"Short letters. They're in her handwriting, but they're not Lee."

"What's going on?"

"Ah, shit, Al, I wish I knew." When he continued to study the side of her face, she sighed and squinted at the house. "She's been getting flaky over the last few months. She said she wants—" She stopped, realizing that she really didn't want to go into Lee's fantasies and desires, not even with Al. "She wants all kinds of things she can't have, in the shape she's in. And she's become secretive. She's never been one to hide anything, but suddenly there were all these things she wouldn't talk to me about—Lee the therapist's therapist, who's always talked over every little nuance, suddenly there were these areas she'd go silent about."

"Any pattern to them?" asked Hawkin the detective.

"Any discussion about the future was off-limits. Her future, our future."

"You think she wants out?" he asked bluntly.

"I did finally ask her that; she seemed, I don't know, shocked. Desperately unhappy that I'd think it. She's just going through a lot of stuff, I think," Kate said weakly. "Part of it has to do with her job—you know she's dropped most of the AIDS therapy? She hated to give it up, but it was too much for her, after the shooting. She doesn't have any stamina. She's seeing a lot more women now, and kids. I thought it might be money that was bugging her, because we still have heavy bills and she's not earning much, but when I suggested we move, she got really upset. I mean, look at this place. The taxes are unbelievable. She could retire on what it would bring, but she wouldn't hear of selling it—'Not yet,' she said."

"It is a beautiful house."

"I'm beginning to hate it. It's like living in a mausoleum. And that car of hers in the garage—she'll never drive it; she could sell it and buy something with manual controls and still have money left over, but she won't hear of it. Won't even say why, just refuses to talk about it."

They sat in the cooling car, neither of them making a move to go. Hawkin finally spoke.

"She may be finding it difficult to choose a future, having so very nearly had none, and then for a long time able to see only an intolerable future. Choices must be . . . painful. I just hope for your sake this phase doesn't go on too long."

"I think that's part of it," Kate surprised herself by saying. "I think she's testing me. Seeing just how long my patience will last. Seeing if I still love her."

"Or maybe—"

"Maybe what?"

"Hell, Kate, I'm no marriage counselor. I screwed up my own marriage thoroughly, too, so I'm no one to talk."

"Just tell me. I'm a big girl."

"Well, maybe what Lee needs to know is not how long you'll continue to be patient, but how long it will be before you get your own feet back under you, the way she's done."

"What do you mean?"

"The Lee Cooper I knew before she took a bullet in the spine, which I admit was not long, would have hated the thought of being in an unequal, dependent relationship."

"But I've been so careful to maintain her independence. Jon and I have sweated to let her be strong."

"I don't mean Lee has been dependent. I mean you."

"What *are* you talking about?" Kate asked testily.

"Caring for an invalid can be addictive," Hawkin said simply, and Kate felt as if the air had been thumped from her lungs. "I'm not saying it's the case, but I'm wondering if Lee might have thought you were becoming dependent—on her dependence, if that makes sense."

Kate sat there, struck dumb by the bolt of his perception. She remembered Lee saying it wasn't her legs not working that made her a cripple. "I'm a cripple because I can't stand alone," Lee had said. "I can't stand alone when I'm surrounded by people who want to protect me."

"Kate," Al was saying, "listen, don't take my amateur psychologizing to heart. I think you should go talk to one of the department's shrinks. You got along well with Mosley last year, didn't you? Go see him again. I mean that, Kate."

"Yes, I hear you. I think you're right, Al—not just about that, though I suppose I should go and have a talk with him, but about the other, as well. I must have been smothering her. No wonder she went off with Aunt Agatha."

"Is that the name?"

"You haven't met her. A rare treat," she said bitterly.

"Kate," he said, in a voice almost soft with affection, "just forget it all for the weekend, get some rest."

"I'll try to forget it, but I won't get much rest, not if I'm hunting down a car."

"And you told Jules you'd do something with her Sunday, didn't you? I'll warn her you may have to back out."

"Don't do that. I'll make it somehow."

"You don't have to."

"I want to."

"You're good for her, Kate," he said unexpectedly. "It does her good to be around someone like you. Her mother . . ." He paused, drumming his fingers on the bottom of the steering wheel. "Jani is a remarkable woman who has come through more than her fair share of hell. She's a strong woman, but only in some areas, and I'm afraid she's most unsure about herself in just those places that Jules needs her to be strong. I don't suppose I'm making much sense, but it's a long and ugly story and not for tonight. I just wanted to say that we both appreciate the efforts you've gone to for Jules."

"It's not an effort, Al. I like Jules."

"I like her, too. I love the girl. But I sometimes wonder just what the hell I was thinking, volunteering to go through the whole teenage thing all over again with a kid who makes my first two look like saints."

"Oh, come on, Al, you must be getting old. I know

65

she and Jani are having a rough time, but I got the strong impression that she feels comfortable with you."

"Thank God for that," he said under his breath.

"You're not telling me that there's some real problem with Jules, are you?" Belatedly, she remembered Rosa Hidalgo's peculiar message on the answering machine.

"Jules was very nearly expelled from her school last month—the very first week of classes."

"Jules?" Kate said incredulously. "What on earth for?"

"She had her English teacher in tears and then said some inexcusable things to the principal. We had to promise to get her into therapy before they would let her back in."

"I can't believe it."

"Believe it."

"But why? She seems so . . . together. Balanced."

"She did to me, too, until suddenly in the last few months . . . I have an idea of what set her off, but she won't talk about it. It's basically an accumulation of things: her brains, her history, her mother, her mother's history, puberty—like I said, I can't get into it now, even if I had Jani's permission. Let's just say there's a big head of pressure inside Jules, and some of it finds its way out in anger. Being with you seems to help her a lot, though. She becomes almost herself again for a while."

Kate stared out the window, then shook her head slowly. "I wish you hadn't told me."

"You'd have to know sooner or later. In fact, the psychologist Jules is going to wants to see you."

"No."

"Why not?"

It had been an instinctive response, and Kate searched for the reasons behind it. After a minute, she said hesitantly, "I think it might be a mistake to identify me with all the other adults in her life. If I am important to Jules, as you seem to think, it's because I'm an outsider. Kids her age think in terms of 'them' and 'us.' You wouldn't gain anything by making me one of her 'thems.' " And,

she added to herself, I could lose the friendship of someone I've grown surprisingly fond of.

"You could be right."

"I'm always right, Al. High time you recognized
that." She put on a smile and turned it toward him.

"I'll keep it in mind," he said, matching her light tone.

"I've got to go, Al," she said. "There's a raccoon who
comes by to pick up his hush money about now, and if I
don't give it to him, he starts pulling shingles off the
house. See you Sunday."

Even in the dim light, Kate could see her partner
waver, then decide not to ask what she was talking about.
Instead, he just said, "Good. And don't worry if you
haven't got a car sorted out by then; you're welcome to
use Jani's or mine."

"Thanks. Good night."

" 'Night, Kate. Thanks for the pizza."

She stood and watched him drive cautiously down
Green Street; then his left signal went on and he turned
south toward his own, increasingly seldom-used house in
the Sunset district. She lifted her head to the sky, where
no stars were visible, and then turned and dug around for
her key. Damn and blast, she thought; the one thing in
my life just now that I thought was uncomplicated turns
out to be on the edge of an explosion. Jules, what the hell
is up?

Gideon was prowling about the edge of the patio and
heard her come in. When she crossed the living room to
the glass doors, he was staring in at her, nose against the
glass, his small eyes glittering malevolently from the bur-
glar's mask of his markings. She cracked open the door,
tossed out a handful of the multicolored dog biscuits, and
watched him waddle over and choose one. He sat with
his back to her and crunched his way through one after
another, then hoisted himself up and stalked away into
the shrubbery. The small dog next door barked hysteri-
cally until the neighbor cursed and a door slammed. Silence descended. Kate locked the door and went sober to

bed, and it was not until her head was on the pillow that she remembered Al Hawkin's earlier little torpedo, before the revelation about Jules and her problems.

Jesus, she thought, staring up at the pattern of lights on the ceiling, Lee left because I was smothering her, and now Al says I'm still smothering her from a thousand miles away. It's not enough that I nearly killed her; I have to suffocate her, as well.

Nineteen months before, Kate had nearly been the death of Lee. It was Kate's job that gave Lee a bullet in the spine, and the fact that she was against Lee's involvement in the case from the beginning had nothing to do with it. She should have insisted.

But she had not, and Lee had nearly died. The doctors had told Kate that Lee probably would die, but she had not. They had told Lee she was almost certainly a paraplegic, but she regained the use of her feet. Then they warned her that she was about at the limits of what could reasonably be expected in the way of recovery, but Lee no longer listened to doctors. She no longer listened to anyone, for that matter; certainly not to Kate.

The months since the shooting had been a constant round of adjusting to Lee's varying needs. When Lee was feeling strong, Kate would back off; when Lee was immersed in despair, Kate was a bastion of encouragement. A year and a half of guilt and struggle and financial problems, week after week of Lee's agonizingly slow progress, losing ground and clawing back, all of Kate's existence, even at work, geared to her lover's ever-changing needs, her physical suffering and her blind determination and those odd pockets of cold air that appeared without warning, unexpected areas of extreme sensitivity such as Lee's Saab: symbolic, emotionally charged, tabu.

After all these months, Kate no longer paused to think, just reacted automatically in her role as counterpoise, shifting as required, making all the minute adjustments that kept the marriage balanced, because the one thing that could not be allowed, that must not happen no matter the cost, was that the balance collapse. The end of the marriage was the end of everything.

But now, there was no weight to balance. Caring for an invalid might not be addictive, but it was clearly habit-forming. She had to admit that she'd been sent sprawling when her burden was removed; it was time now to adjust, she told herself. Get used to an empty house. There might even be a degree of satisfaction to be found in having only her own wants and needs to take into account.

She lay there, considering Al's brutally honest judgment, running her mind over the texture of her relationship with Lee, becoming more and more convinced that he was right. She was smothering Lee. She would stop it. She contemplated how she would go about freeing Lee and herself, and as she lay there, she grew more awake every minute, until she was twitching as if she'd had two or three double espressos rather than a cup of weak decaffeinated coffee. Finally, she threw off the covers, went into Lee's study, and began to write a letter.

It was a long letter, full of love and understanding, of apology and the commitment to change for the better. The phrases flowed, two pages filled, three: "Lee," she wrote, "I am so grateful to Al for pointing out what I was doing; it must have been intolerable to you, even though you knew I was on'y trying to help. But I'm aware of it now, and I promise to keep hands off your life. I'll let you walk through the SoMa district at midnight if you want; I'll—"

She stood up so rapidly, the chair fell over backward, and she hurled the pen across the room and took the letter and tore it down the middle, then again, and a third time. She walked out of the study, turning off the lights behind her, then, picking up a warm blanket from her bed, went out onto the balcony. There she sat, bundled up, looking out across the northern edges of the city at the waters of the Golden Gate, reflected in lights from shore and ship and the island opposite.

Yes, Al, I'm terrified. I'm so angry at her, I never want

69

to see her again, but if she doesn't come back, I don't know what I'll do. I can't imagine life without her; it would be like imagining life without air. I love her and I hate her and I'm lost, completely lost without her, and all I can do is wait for her to tell me what she is going to do with me.

She slept, finally, and woke in the deck chair, with a mockingbird singing and Saturday's sun coming up. She watched the dawn, and as the sky lightened, her inner decision dawned as well, until, with a peculiar mixture of bitter satisfaction and gleeful mischief, she knew what she was going to do.

♦

Sunday morning, Al Hawkin pulled open the door of his fiancée's apartment and stood blinking at the apparition in the hallway. He had reassured himself through the peephole that the unidentifiable figure had no visible weapon, and now he pulled the belt of his robe a bit tighter and ran a hand across his grizzled hair.

"Can I help you with something, er, ma'am?" he asked uncertainly. "What apartment number were you—" The figure before him reached a gloved hand up to the helmet strap, bent over to remove it, and straightened up, shaking her hair out of her face. Even then, for a split second he failed to recognize her; she had more life in her face than he'd ever seen there.

"Kate!" She grinned at him, glowing with enthusiasm and exuding waves of fresh air. He ran an eye over her, new boots, new gloves, old leather bomber jacket a bit snug around the waist, the massive new helmet under one arm. "Let me guess," he said, stepping back to let her in. "You bought your new car. What kind?"

Jules came out of the kitchen behind him and stopped dead. "Why are you wearing that outfit, Kate?" she asked, but Kate answered her partner.

"A Kawasaki."

"Kawasaki doesn't make an automobile," he said, studying her leather jacket.

"By God, the man's a detective."

"You're not thinking of taking Jules out on it?"

A cry of protest rose from the kitchen door, but Kate ignored it. "Of course not," she said, and her grin became even wider. "Can I borrow the car keys, Dad?"

OCTOBER,
NOVEMBER

FIVE

OCTOBER CAME. Jon arrived back from Boston and London, flitted around the edge of Kate's vision for a few days, and, before she could catch hold of him, was off to Mexico with his friend. Short letters from Lee: She was well, getting stronger. Yesterday she'd dug clams for dinner; had cut a cord of stove wood already, could Kate believe that? And the trees were so beautiful, so calming. Finding herself, yet still filled with confusion, and sorry, so very sorry, to be putting Kate through all this, but . . .

But she still couldn't say when she'd be home.

In October, Kate's baffled anguish began to turn, to harden. Her letters north became shorter, sharper. She bruised her thigh once too often on Lee's chair lift at the top of the stairs, and in a fury at two o'clock one morning she took a wrench to it, dismantled it, and heaved the seat, followed by the wrench, into Lee's room, the room that had once been theirs. The next things to go were Lee's books in the dining room, again into Lee's room. She began deliberately to leave the dishes in the sink overnight, for two nights, a thing neither Lee nor Jon could have tolerated. She even began to leave the bed unmade and the cap off the toothpaste.

October settled into a pattern of work and home. Her new form of transport set off another flurry of raucous comments and irritating harassments from her coworkers, and she lost count of the number of Xeroxed articles about Dykes on Bikes she had found on her desk or tucked into the cycle, but she had, after all, expected something of the sort, and if her teeth ached from being gritted, at least she did not show that any of it bothered her.

She told herself that it would pass, and concentrated on the pleasures of a motorcycle in California. The fall weather held, a whole month of Indian summer, and she took long rides north into the wine country and the mountainous land behind it, glorying in the nearly forgotten freedom and sweet spark of risk that two wheels brought. When she needed four wheels, she hired the neighbor with his immaculately restored 1948 Chevy pickup, or she used Al's car. Even the house on Russian Hill did not seem quite so aggressively empty as it had; merely quiescent.

By the end of the month, the pleasure of her minor rebellions against the absent householders began to wane, when she found an unmade pile of sheets and blankets an unbearably slovenly greeting at the end of a long day, and found, too, that leaving the cap off the toothpaste tube made the contents go hard and stale. Still, she allowed the dishes to accumulate until she had no clean ones, vacuumed and swept only when her feet began to notice the grit, and ate when and what she felt like, rediscovering the illicit joys of pizza for breakfast and cereal with ice cream on top for dinner. She ran every morning, got the weights out of storage and set them up in Lee's consultation rooms, and began to sleep more soundly.

Other pleasures slowly began to reemerge into her life, as well. Before the shooting, she and Lee had had a few friends—not many, but good people, mostly women.

Then for the long months of Lee's recovery, Lee had possessed friendly helpers, and Kate had had her work.

Now, in her solitary life, the arid landscape showed signs of softening. Rosalyn Hall, a minister in the gay community, invited her to help at the church's annual Halloween bash for the neighborhood kids. Kate dutifully went, a cop doing a community service, but long after the neighborhood had retrieved its well-sugared offspring, and even after the minister's adopted daughter had been put to bed for the fourth and final time, Kate was still there, sitting and talking and drinking beer with Rosalyn and her partner, Maj.

"Do you know the word for that shape of a liquid when it sticks up over the top of a glass?" she asked, examining her freshly filled glass with a somewhat owlish seriousness. The two women shook their heads in equally inebriated interest. "It's called meniscus." Kate had finally found a use for a "word of the day." The word, and the evening, were successes, and when the two women asked her for Thanksgiving dinner, she went, not as a cop, but a family member.

She even had a single, sort of, almost date, when a woman she knew in the DA's office called and asked if Kate wanted to use a theater ticket intended for a friend, who was sick with the flu. Before leaving the house, Kate contemplated the thin gold band on her left hand. She even pulled it off, briefly, but in the end it stayed on her hand for the world to see, and the evening remained merely friendly. Which, she decided later, was much the better. The last thing she needed was another complication in her life.

As Kate's muscles toughened along with her attitude, other physical pleasures took the place of the one. She found she enjoyed the sensation of wearing her leathers and her cycle boots. She rediscovered the joys of growing physical strength and ability, and she thought about rejoining a martial art group.

But the true high point in the month was Jules's thirteenth birthday. Following a lengthy consultation with

Al and Jani, Kate arrived at the Cameron apartment on the Saturday following the actual day, in her full cycle regalia and carrying a box under one arm. That afternoon, Jules rode behind her on the cycle, wearing the new (secondhand) leather jacket and the helmet that Kate had bought for the back of the Kawasaki.

They went to San Francisco, at Jules's request. They cruised the streets, circling the tourist sites and through Chinatown, up the steep hills and down the drop-offs. Toward the end of the day, Jules decided that she wanted to parade through the Hall of Justice to show off her finery. Kate told her that few of Hawkin's colleagues would be in, but Jules wanted to go, so to the Hall of Justice they went, with Jules swaggering through the corridors in Kate's wake.

It wasn't until they reached the Homicide Department that Kate began to realize that this wasn't such a hot idea, but by then it was too late. When they stepped out of the elevator, two men she knew slightly were getting on, and as Kate paused to exchange a word with one of them, the other looked at Jules's retreating back, glanced at Kate, and then in a loud and jovial voice said, "Isn't she kind of young for you, Martinelli?"

Kate whipped around to find Jules, but the girl had already cleared the corner. When she looked back at the man, the elevator door was closing, but she heard the other man saying, "Jesus, Mark, put your foot in it, why don't you? That was the daughter of Al Hawkin's—" The door closed on the rest of it.

It had probably not been meant cruelly, or even crudely; the man Mark was simply one of those who thought that the way to demonstrate tolerance for gay women was to treat them as one of the boys. Still, when Kate caught up with Jules, she looked closely for red ears or other signs of discomfort, and was relieved when she found it obvious that the girl had not heard him. Kate got her out of there as soon as she could, infinitely grateful that the bad taste was only in her own mouth.

And still, all that fall, she looked for Dio. Once a week, she made the rounds of the homeless, asking about him. Always she asked among her network of informants, the dealers and hookers and petty thieves, whenever she saw one of them, and invariably received a shake of the head. Twice she heard rumors of him, once at a house for runaway teenagers, where one of the current residents had a friend who had met a boy of his description, over on Telegraph Avenue in Berkeley, or it might have been College Avenue, though it might have been Dion instead of Dio; and a second time, when one of her informants told her there was a boy-toy of that name in a house used by pederasts over near the marina. She phoned a couple of old friends in the Berkeley and Oakland departments to ask them to keep an ear out, and she arranged to be in on the raid of the marina house, but neither came up with anything more substantial than the ghost she already had. She doubted he was in the Bay Area, and told Jules that, but she also kept looking.

That autumn, in one of those flukes that even the statistician will admit happens occasionally, it seemed for a while that every case the Homicide Department handled involved kids, either as victim or perpetrator, or both. A two-year-old with old scars on his back and broken bones in various states of mending died in an emergency room from having been shaken violently by his eighteen-year-old mother. Three boys aged sixteen to twenty died from gunshot wounds in less than a month. Four bright seventeen-year-old students in a private school did a research project on explosives, using the public library, and sent a very effective pipe bomb to a hated teacher. It failed, but only because the man was as paranoid as he was infuriating, and had called the police before he touched the parcel; the four were charged with conspiracy and attempted murder, and might well be tried as adults. A seven-year-old in a pirate costume was separated from his friends on Halloween; he was found the next morning, raped and bludgeoned to death; the investigation was pointing toward a trio of boys only four years older. Kate saw two of her colleagues in tears within ten days, one of them a tough, experienced beat cop who had seen everything but still couldn't bring himself to look again at the baby in the cot. The detectives on the fourth floor of the Department of Justice made morbid jokes about it being the Year of the Child, and they either answered the phone gingerly or with a snarl, according to their personalities.

♦

NOVEMBER,
DECEMBER

♦

SIX

THE END of November drew near.

Christmas lights went up in celebration of the feast of Thanksgiving, and the following morning, still bloated from her dinner at the house of Rosalyn and Maj, Kate rode around Union Square on her way to the Hall of Justice, just to look at the windows of the big stores, filled with lace and gilt, velvet and silks, sprinkled with white flakes to evoke the wintery stuff seen in San Francisco perhaps twice in a century, set up to attract throngs of shoppers anxious to recapture the fantasies of a Victorian childhood, no matter the cost. The pickpockets and car thieves had a merry season, a coke dealer in the Tenderloin took to wrapping his packets in shiny red and green foil, Al and Jani set their date for the eighteenth of December, and people went on killing one another.

It was wet and miserable outside three days later, on the last Monday of November—a fact Kate could well attest to, as she'd been out in it a fair part of the day, following up witnesses to a domestic shooting in Chinatown. She had used departmental vehicles for the trips out, but she was now faced with either climbing into her damp moon-walk outfit, which would keep her mostly dry on the motorcycle, or getting a ride up the hill and having to cope with public transport in the morning.

The phone on her desk rang. She eyed it sourly, making no move to answer it. At the fourth ring, the man at the next desk looked up.

"Hey, Martinelli," he called. "That thing's called a tel-uh-phone. You pick it up and talk into one end; voices come from the other. Really fun, you should try it."

"Gee, thanks, Tommy boy. Thing is, my psychic reader told me never to answer any call that comes two minutes before I want to leave—it's sure to be a bad omen."

They both sat and watched it ring.

"Who's on call?" he asked.

"Calvo." There was no need to say more: They both knew he would be late. He was always late.

"Could be the lottery," he suggested.

"I never buy lottery tickets."

It rang on.

"You answer it, Tommy."

"It's my wife's birthday tonight; she'd kill me if I was late."

Ring. Ring.

"If you wait long enough, the shift will be over and you can leave."

Ring.

"Sounds pretty determined," he commented.

Kate stretched out a hand and picked up the instrument. "Inspector Martinelli."

"Kate? I thought I had missed you. This is Grace Kokumah, over at the Haight/Love Shelter. We talked, three, four weeks ago?" Her voice added a slight question mark at the end of the sentence, but Kate knew her instantly: a big, dignified black-black African woman with the flavor of her native Uganda rich in her voice and her hair in a zillion tiny glossy braids that ended in orange beads. Kate had met her three years before, when Lee had worked with her on the case of a fourteen-year-old boy with AIDS.

"Yes, Grace, how are you? Enjoying the rain?" Too many years of drought made rain the central topic of most winter conversations.

"We have many holes in our roof, Kate Martinelli, so I do not enjoy the rain, no. We have run out of buckets. The entire neighborhood has run out of buckets. We are making soup in roasting pans because our pots are busy catching drips. Kate, are you still interested in a boy called Dio?"

Thoughts of time clocks and home vanished.

"Do you have him there?"

"I do not have him, no. But one of my girls, who heard from a friend of a friend . . . You know?"

"Is she there? Will she talk to me?"

"To the famous Inspector Casey Martinelli? Yes."

Kate made a face at the receiver.

"I think it is better for you to come here," Grace suggested. "Tonight?"

"I can be there in half an hour, less if the traffic's clear."

"We will be very busy for the next hour, Kate. We are just serving dinner. Best you come a little later, when we have finished with the dishes. Then Kitty will be free to talk with you."

"If I come now, can you use a hand, with serving or washing?"

Grace's laugh was rich and deep. "Now I think you know that to be one stupid question, Inspector Martinelli."

"Fine, see you soon." She dropped the phone onto its hook and started to gather up her papers.

"Sounds like a hot date there, Martinelli."

"Sure you don't want to bring your wife? Dinner at the soup kitchen, give her a slice of life for her birthday present?"

"It's not my wife's birthday. What gave you that crazy idea?"

"I can't think. G'night, Tommy."

"Stay dry. So much for your psychic reader."

Kate's steps faltered briefly as his words triggered a vivid memory: Jules, speaking with such seriousness about her long-past childhood, when she lay in bed inventing horrors as a talisman to keep the real ones at bay. Anything that can be imagined won't happen.

Now why should I think of that? Kate asked herself as she waited for the elevator. Dio, I guess, and Jules, and meeting Dio at last and what I will see in his eyes and his nose and his skin, how far gone he'll be.

♦

The serving was over and the nonresident recipients were reluctantly scattering for their beds in doorways and Dumpsters and the bushes of Golden Gate Park when Kate blew into the Haight/Love Shelter. Grace Kokumah stood with her hands in the pockets of her sagging purple cardigan and watched without expression as Kate came to a halt next to the thin and already-yellowing Christmas tree and dropped her burden with a clatter before beginning to strip off the astronaut helmet, the dripping and voluminous orange neck-to-ankle waterproof jumpsuit, and the padded gloves. When Kate had popped open the snaps on her leather jacket and run a hand through her brief hair, the woman shook her beads.

"The city's finest, a vision to behold."

"Do you want the buckets or don't you?" Kate growled.

"Where did you find them?" She studied the waist-high stack, no doubt wondering instead *how* Kate had managed to transport them without being lifted up, cycle and all, by their wind resistance and dropped into the San Francisco Bay.

"Stole them from the morgue; they use them for the scraps. Joke! That was a joke!" she said to the horrified young people at Grace's back. "Macabre cop humor, you've heard of that. The cleaners buy soap in them, nothing worse than that. Do you have anything to eat? I'm starving."

"This is a soup kitchen, despite the temporary absence of stockpots. We have bean soup tonight, which has had a dry ham bone waved through it, we have white bread with margarine, and we have weak orange drink."

"The season of plenty, I see. Do I have to wash dishes first?"

"A person who brings us eight five-gallon buckets is permitted to eat before she labors. Kitty, would you please show Kate where to wash her hands, and then give her a bowl of soup?"

Once in the cramped corridor that wrapped around the kitchen, Kate touched the girl's arm.

"Grace tells me you might help me find a boy named Dio."

The girl cringed and fluttered her hands to shush Kate. "Not here. Later. I'll come to Grace's room." She scurried off.

So, Kate thought, I wash dishes after all.

◆

After bean soup, and after a largely symbolic contribution to the piles of dirty dishes, Grace rescued her and sent her off to the room she used as counseling center, doctor's examining room, office, and, occasionally, extra bedroom. Within five minutes Kitty skulked in, shutting the door noiselessly behind her. She wasted no time with small talk.

"You're lookin' for a guy named Dio?"

"That's what he called himself last summer, yes."

"What do you want him for?"

"I don't, particularly. Why don't you sit down, Kitty?"

"God, I don't know if I should do this. I mean, I don't know you."

Kate reached into the pocket she'd taken to using instead of the awkward handbag and held out her identification folder between two fingers, mostly as a means of keeping the girl from bolting. Kitty took it, looked at it curiously, handed it back. She sat down and studied

87

Kate's tired face, recently cropped hair, and biker's leathers.

"You look different."

Kate snapped shut the picture of the good Italian girl with the soft hair and the wary smile without glacing at it.

"Don't we all."

"You *are* that dyke cop whose girlfriend got shot?" she asked uncertainly. Kate did not wince, did not even pause in the motion of putting the ID back into her pocket.

"Yep. Now, tell me, how did you hear I was looking for Dio?"

"Grace put it on the notice board. Course, I don't know if it's the same guy, but it's not like a common name, is it?"

"She posted a notice that I was looking for Dio?"

"Not you. Just that there's word for him. You haven't seen the board? It's in the dining hall, just a bunch of those really ugly black cork squares Grace glued up and sticks notices on, like if someone calls her from Arkansas or something saying, 'Have you seen my little girl? Tell her to call Mummy.' There's just his name and a note to see Grace. Lots of them have that. She talks to kids and tries to convince them to call home, once they know someone's interested." From the way she spoke, nobody at home had expressed any interest in Kitty for some time.

"So you met Dio."

"Not me. A friend. No, really," she said, seeing Kate's skeptical look. "This guy I met walking down the Panhandle, you know? He gave me a cigarette—and honest, it was just a cigarette. Grace throws you out if she smells weed on you. Anyway, we got to talking about, well, things, you know? And he came back here for dinner and to look at the board and see if maybe . . . Well, there wasn't nothing for him on it, but then he sees the name Dio and acts kind of surprised, and he goes, 'I thought Dio was an orphan,' and I go, 'You should tell Dio his

88

name is up'—I mean, not like anyone wants to go home, you know, but still, it doesn't hurt to make a phone call, does it, and they might send some money or something. Well, anyway, he said he'd tell Dio if he saw him."

"When was this?"

"Last week. Friday maybe. Thursday? No, I remember, it was Friday because we had a tuna casserole and we talked about Catholics and that fish thing they used to have."

"Have you seen him since then?"

"Well, yeah, I mean, that's why I talked to Grace, isn't it, 'cause Bo—because my friend asked me to. He came here this afternoon. Well, really this morning, but I wasn't here, so he came back. He said he found Dio, and he's really sick—Dio is, I mean—and a couple of Dio's friends are really worried about him."

"Sick how? OD?" If so, he'd be long dead.

"I don't think so. Bo—my friend said he was coughing real bad, for the last week or so."

"Why didn't his friends take him to the emergency room? Or the free clinic?"

"Well, that part I didn't really understand. There's something about this guy Dio lives with, him and a bunch of other kids, all of them guys, I think. Anyway, there's this old guy who kind of heads up the place they're living in. It's a squat in a warehouse the other side of Market, down where the docks are? Anyway he—the old guy—doesn't like outsiders, like doctors."

I'll bet he doesn't, Kate thought bleakly. "I'd like to talk to your friend about this."

"He said no, he doesn't want nothing to do with it. He's just worried about Dio and thinks somebody should take him out of there before he dies or something. He'd probably freak if he knew I was talking to a cop about it. He said he doesn't want the old guy to know, 'cause he makes my friend nervous. Oh, there's nothing wrong with him. I mean, he takes care of the kids and doesn't feel them up or anything, but he's just . . . weird. That's what Bo says, anyway. Bo's my friend."

Secondhand and from a limited vocabulary like Kitty's, "weird" could mean anything from a drooling madman to an Oxbridgian with a plummy accent and boutonniere.

"Okay, I'll go see him. And I won't tell how I knew he was there. What's the address?"

Kitty had to stand up to get her hand into the pockets of her skintight jeans. She pulled out a grubby scrap of paper folded multiple times into a wad. Kate unfolded it, saw that the address was clear enough, and put it into her own pocket.

"Thanks, Kitty. I'll do what I can. It was good of you to take the chance, talking to me."

"Yeah, well. If us kids on the street don't look after each other, who will?"

◆

The rain was taking a break when Kate left the center, and the wind had dropped below gale force, so she decided to go by the address on the scrap of paper Kitty had given her. She was almost surprised to find, when she got there, that it actually existed. It proved to be a deserted three-story warehouse with plywood sheets nailed up across all the ground-floor windows, in an area slated for redevelopment. Kate went past it slowly, continued on a couple of blocks, and then doubled back, blessing the Kawasaki's efficient muffler system. Pushing the big machine into a recessed entranceway that stank of urine but was at the moment unoccupied, she climbed out of the bright orange jumpsuit, opened the storage box, took out a long flashlight and shoved in the wet jumpsuit, closed and locked the top, and clamped her helmet onto the bike with the rigid lock. She thrust the flashlight into the deep front pocket of her leather jacket and cautiously approached the building.

The front was, predictably, padlocked. She found the entrance currently in use down an alleyway on the side of the building, covered by a sheet of corrugated metal that screeched loudly when she pulled it aside. Over the noise of the wind and the occasional heavy drops, she could not tell if there was any movement inside the building. Trying to reassure herself that this really wasn't so stupid, that even though she felt like an empty-headed female on a late-night movie investigating attic noises with a candle in her hand, she actually was an armed cop (admittedly, with no official reason for being here, far less a search warrant), she stepped through the gap.

She had fully intended to make her presence known in a straightforward manner. After all, she hardly looked like a police officer, and she only wanted a chance to talk with the boy Dio. She even had her mouth open to call a placatory greeting when it began, the cold ripple of the skin up along the back of her hand, over her wrists, and up her forearms to her shoulders and the nape of her neck, the creepy-crawlies that told her something really bad was about to go down. She hadn't expected this, had only planned on talking with some unwashed boys in a squat, had arranged no backup, but the moment it started, she didn't stop to think, only reacted.

Gun up in both hands and ready, back against the wall, every hair alert, and . . . nothing. Nothing.

There were people in the building, though, she would swear to it, could feel them over her head, silently waiting for—what?

She, too, waited in the darkness, long minutes straining to hear, see, anything, tried to make herself open her mouth and call a friendly "Hello, anyone there?" but the ghostly touch along the tops of her arms did not go away. Finally, moving as stealthily as her heavy boots would allow, she sidled back through the gap, trotted down the alley (keeping a wary eye overhead) for a quick glance at the rear of the building, and then made her way back up the alleyway and through the shadows to the cycle, where she unlocked the storage compartment again and took out her mobile radio. She turned the volume right down and spoke in a mutter.

The marked unit arrived within three minutes, drifting to a stop with its headlights out. The dome light did not go on when the two men opened their doors with gentle clicks, and neither of them slammed his door. Kate was relieved; they knew their business. She cleared her throat quietly and walked over to them.

"Kate Martinelli, Homicide," she identified herself. "What do you know about that three-story building just this side of the garage?"

"It's been a squat for a couple of months now. No problems," said the older one. "We reported it, but the attitude this time of year is, if it stays quiet, let it go. There aren't enough beds for them in the shelters, anyway," he added defensively.

"I know. But it's been quiet? No sign of johns, not a crack house, shooting gallery, anything like that?"

"No customers of any kind. Why?"

"I don't have a warrant. I'm just looking for a boy, was told he was in there sick. I went in, but I . . . I don't like the way it feels inside. Wanted some backup." The younger man looked at her sideways, but the older one just nodded.

"I know what you mean. I'll go in with you," he offered. His voice sounded familiar. Kate looked more closely.

"Tom Rawlins, isn't it? Rawlings?" He seemed pleased to be recognized. "Thanks, but I think I'd better go in alone, I don't want to scare them off. Just watch my back? And maybe your partner here—"

"Ash Jordan," he said, introducing himself.

"Maybe Ash can watch around in back? There's a fire escape."

"Fine."

"What's he done?"

"As far as I know, he's only a status offender—assuming that I have his age right. I'm trying to track him down as a favor to a friend."

The men both accepted this, understanding the language of favors and friends and the problems of runaways.

"He calls himself Dio, light-skinned Hispanic, five seven, skinny, looks about fourteen."

"If he comes out, we'll just sit on him for a while," Rawlings assured her.

"That's great, thanks. This shouldn't take more than a few minutes."

She went back through the hole behind the metal sheet with the reassuring feeling of a brother cop at her back, and it made all the difference. She made her way cautiously, although not afraid, and found herself in a warren of what had once been offices and a showroom, empty now of stock but in an appalling state of dilapidation, Sheetrock drooping off the walls, ceiling joists exposed, filthy beyond belief. If there was a group of boys in the building, she decided after a quick search, they did not live down here.

Her flashlight found the stairs, stripped of the rotted carpeting, which had been left in a heap in one of the offices. They were firm, although they squeaked here and there as she started upward. She held the gun in one hand, the light in the other, and though her flesh still crawled, there was no turning back now.

At the top of the stairs, she stood just outside the door and stuck the flashlight and one eye around the corner, and here she found the boys' living quarters. It was a big room, one single space with a heavy freight elevator on one end, frozen with its floor two feet beneath the ceiling. Ropes of dust-clogged cobwebs dangled from the steel beams fifteen feet overhead, but on closer observation, she noticed there had been some effort to clean the floor, which lacked the jumble of bottles, needles, glue tubes, paint cans, used condoms, and general squalor that these places usually held. In the middle were a rough circle of chairs and milk crates on top of a frayed circular rug, pillows on some of the crates, one of them upended with a camping lantern set on top. Around the edges, against two of the walls, there seemed actually to have been an attempt at marking out eight or ten separate quarters with a hodgepodge of crates, cardboard boxes, and bits of wood draped with pieces of incongruous fabric, from flowered bedspreads to ancient paint-splattered tarps. Keeping well out in the center of the room, her ears straining for the least sound, Kate began to circle the floor. She probed each of the quarters with the beam of her flashlight, finding the same semblance of order that the circle of chairs showed. Some of the mattresses even had their rough covers pulled neatly up, though others . . .

She paused, went back to one Spartan and tidy cell, and ran the flashlight beam over the heap of—well, for lack of a better word, bedding. Yes, that was indeed a foot that she had seen protruding from the pile, enclosed in at least two layers of frayed sock. And now that she was closer, she could hear the sound of labored breathing above the slap of heavy raindrops against the black plastic someone had nailed up against the broken windows. She slid her gun back under her arm, transferred the light to her right hand, squatted down, and reached out gingerly for the covering layers at the opposite end of the mattress from the exposed sock. Black hair, long and greasy and soaked with sweat, straggled across a flushed face that had the high, broad cheekbones of a Mayan statue. His breathing sounded like a pair of wet sponges struggling to absorb a bit of air—it hurt Kate's chest just to listen to it. The boy's forehead was burning, and she pulled the covers back up around his neck. Somehow she was not surprised to see a neat stack of shoe boxes, two wide and three high, next to his mattress. On top of them lay a small, grubby notebook: There was a rainbow on its cover.

"Hello, Dio," she said quietly. She stood up, took the radio from the pocket of her leather jacket, spoke into it, and had gotten as far as "We've got a sick boy here at—" when all hell broke loose.

With a distant thunk, the overhead lights went on, and Kate's body was already automatically moving down and back when the gun started roaring at her from the freight elevator. She dove into the base of the makeshift walls, sending boxes and wood scraps flying and keeping just ahead of the terrifying slaps at her heels, until finally she had her own beautiful piece of metal in her hand. From the spurious protection of a packing crate, she aimed her gun at the source of the murderous fire. Her fifth bullet hit something.

A noise came, half yelp, half cough, followed immediately by a sharp clatter of metal dropping into metal.

"Police!" bellowed Kate at the top of her adrenaline-charged lungs. "Anyone reaching for that gun, I'll shoot!" She heard voices, then panicking shouts, and a number of feet on the floor overhead broke into a run, heading for the back of the warehouse. At the same time, one pair of feet came pounding up the stairs toward her, stopping just outside the door.

"Police!" he shouted, then said, "Inspector Martinelli, you okay?"

"Yeah, I'm fine. There was a single gun from the freight elevator; doesn't seem to be another. I hit him and he dropped it. See it? Hanging just under that strut?" She narrowed the beam on her flashlight to illuminate the spot.

"No, I—yes, got it."

"Keep an eye on it; I'm going up."

"Wait—"

"No. Is your partner around back?"

"Yes."

"Hope he stayed there—I don't want these kids to get away. I'll clear the elevator and then call you up. Oh, and the one I was looking for is down at the other end. I was just in the middle of calling for an ambulance—it sounds like pneumonia."

Kate had lost her radio in her rapid trip through the walls but had miraculously retained her flashlight, which even more miraculously still functioned. As Rawlings spoke into his own radio, giving rapid requests for backup and ambulance, she took off across the dusty wooden floor at a fast, low crouch, hit the now-well-lit stairs at a run, and, at the top landing, seeing no switch, put her leather-clad arm up across her face and then reached up in passing to swipe at the hanging bulb with the butt end of the heavy flashlight. Safe now in the concealing darkness, she pushed the flashlight into her pocket, took up a position to one side of the door to the third floor, turned the handle, and pushed it open. Nothing. Silence came through the doorway at her, but for the wind and the raindrops, and the only light was the dim illumination creeping in through the windows and up the elevator shaft. Gun at the ready, she slipped inside; there were raised voices outside and three floors down—Rawlings's partner, Jordan, had indeed stayed in his place. And then the most beautiful sound in the world: sirens, from several directions at once, getting louder every second. Beneath them, half-heard, came a low groaning sound from the direction of the freight elevator. Out came the flashlight again, and, holding it well to the side of her body, she flicked it on. The room was open and empty of anything large enough to hide a person. Just a matter of making sure the shooter couldn't retrieve his gun. Kate took two steps away from the wall, and no more.

There was no pain, no burst of light, no time for fear, much less anger, just the beginning awareness of movement above and behind her, a faint swishing noise registering in her ears, and then Kate was gone.

SEVEN

SOMEWHERE, DEEP down, she was aware. Some part of her concussed and swelling brain smelled the dust on the floor beneath her, heard the boots running toward her and the sirens cutting off, one by one, somewhere below, felt the hands and cushions and neck brace, dimly knew that she was being lifted and carried, that there was rain in her face and blue strobing lights and then the harsh flat surfaces of the hospital. A buzzing as her hair was shaved, a cold wash against the scalp, and eventually a mask on her face.

She knew all these things as textures and tastes: velvet soft black night studded by hard, sharp blue beads; the hospital as slick and cold as tile but overlaid with the warm, soft touch of a nurse whose words wrapped around her, incomprehensible but as comforting as a fur blanket. Cops like pillars, doctors like whips, these sensations washed over her while she lay stunned and unmoving, imprinting their textures on her battered brain, to appear in later life—never while she was conscious, but as dream images: fellow cops who smelled of dust, a nurse covered with luscious warm fur, words that tasted like broken glass.

And there were memories, drifting in and out as she lay in her hospital bed in the intensive care unit: moments of fear, times of great pleasure. Memories of Lee. Mostly, during the following days, she was back in August.

A letter.

It had begun with a letter, and now Kate lay in her hospital bed and remembered—

—*a day in early August. San Francisco had sweltered for ten days, longer, everyone complained, the weatherman explained, with his highs and lows—until finally that afternoon at three o'clock the people on the sidewalks at Fishermen's Wharf had felt the first damp fingers of fog on their sunburned faces, and by five o'clock the city was cool and cocooned.*

The house on Russian Hill retained the day's heat, but the food on the stove smelled good, appetizing after a week of cold salads and refrigerated soups. "That smells great, Jon," she said, greeting him from the hallway. She poked her head into the kitchen. "Hi."

"Hello, Kate, isn't it lovely to be cool again? I've been waiting for weeks to try this Ethiopian meat thing."

"Smells incredible." She turned to the closet and peeled off her windbreaker and shoulder holster, kicked off her shoes, stowed her briefcase on the floor, then put her head around the door to the living room, saw it was empty, and went back to the kitchen. "I know what you mean. I haven't felt like eating in days."

He looked up from the cutting board, his thinning hair in damp disarray. "Then the mice are getting pretty pushy, taking plates of food from the fridge."

"Squeak," she admitted. "Want a glass?" At his nod, she poured him some, and then filled a third glass. Pushing one toward him and picking up the other two, she asked, "Is Lee upstairs?"

"She is. The new physiotherapist was by this morning, seemed impressed," he reported. "And she had a couple of letters. One of them seemed to upset her."

"Upset her? How?"

"Maybe upset isn't the right word." He paused, one

hand on his hip, the other flung back with a sauce-coated spoon in it. He'd dropped most of his limp-wrist caricatures in the last year, thank God, but tended to strike poses when distracted and mince his words when uncomfortable. "Excited, maybe? Like a child with a secret, or a present. She said it was from her aunt." He shrugged and went back to his fragrant alchemy. Kate did not tell him that, as far as she knew, Lee had only one aunt, and she had died years ago.

"Everything else okay?"

"Fine. Dinner in twenty minutes," he said, dismissing her. She paused in the hallway to leaf through the mail on the table, seeing only bills and circulars, then carried the wine upstairs, where she found Lee in her study, reading something at the desk.

"Howdy, stranger," Kate said. Lee started violently, dropping the letter, and swung her chair around sharply. "Sorry, hon," Kate apologized, "I thought you heard me coming." She placed a glass on Lee's desk, kissed her, and dropped into the armchair with her own glass.

Lee looked flushed, but not with exertion, and it was cool up here. Excitement? Embarrassment? Kate's eyes flicked to the letter and away. She would not ask—Lee had little enough privacy, though Kate tried hard to give her as much as she could.

"Glad you could stop by," Lee said, regaining her calm. "Are you here or just passing through?"

"Here. And tomorrow off."

"You caught your baddie?"

"We did that, and a right little shit he is, too." Most murderers were someone close to the victim, family or friend, who lost control for a brief, fatal minute—not villainous, not particularly bright, and soon apprehended. Bread and butter for a homicide detective, but there was no denying the hard satisfaction of putting cuffs on someone to whom murder was more than an accident of chance.

They talked for a few minutes of this and that and

nothing in particular, then Kate said, "Jon said you had some letters."

Was Lee's evasive glance so obvious, or was the professional habit of interrogation so strong that she read guilt where there was none? "A postcard from Vaun Adams," Lee said. "From Spain. Where did I put it? Here." A photograph of Antoni Gaudí's Sagrada Familia church, and in Vaun's neat handwriting:

> Architecture like this makes a person feel that human beings ought to be a different shape— Ray Bradbury hiring Frank Lloyd Wright to build a house on Mars. Head nearly full, be home soon. Gerry and his wife send greetings.
>
> Love, V.

"The last one was from Kenya, wasn't it?"

"Egypt, and before that, Kenya. She's getting around."

"Nothing else exciting?"

"Couple of things, nothing thrilling."

"Fine," Kate said easily. "Do you feel like going down to dinner, or shall we eat up here? Jon's cooking up a storm."

"I've been smelling it all afternoon, drooling on the rug. I'll go down."

"Need a hand?"

"Carry the wine, please."

Lee rolled her chair over to the stair lift, maneuvered herself from one seat onto the other while Kate stood by making trivial talk and being unobtrusively ready to catch her. At the bottom, she checked that the walker was where Lee could reach it, then walked away, leaving her to it. She washed the grime of the day from her face and hands, then got to the table in time to hold the chair for Lee to lower herself into. Food, talk, paperwork, bed: just a day like any other.

Later that night, cuddling close for the first time since the heat wave had begun, Kate spoke into Lee's ear.

"You don't have to tell me whom you got a letter from."

"Don't I?"

"Of course not. It's your perfect right to have secrets, nasty, horrid secrets, secret lovers probably—I don't mind." Here she began to nibble down the back of Lee's neck while her fingertips sought out the sensitive areas along Lee's ribs. "I'll just tickle you until you tell, but I don't mind if you don't tell me. I can lie here all night tickling you, until you fall out of bed and have to sleep on the floor and—" Lee began to giggle and writhe away from Kate's hands and teeth, and the two of them wrestled until Lee, whose upper-body strength after months in the wheelchair was greater than Kate's, succeeded in pinning down Kate, who was not really trying very hard. Panting, Lee looked down into Kate's dark and astonished eyes.

"You sure you feel like just lying there all night?" she demanded in a husky voice, and put her mouth to Kate's.

It was the closest they had come to a normal night in a long, long time.

Much later, Kate muttered into Lee's shoulder, "Don't you think that will get you out of telling me about the letter."

"Tomorrow, my sweet Kate. Tomorrow."

♦

"It was from my aunt," Lee said, when tomorrow had come and they were still in bed, drinking coffee.

"But your aunt died." Lee's mother's sister had been a real terror, the sort of ramrod-spined old lady who regarded fitted bedsheets as a sure sign of the country's moral decay, who had left a clause in her will making it quite clear that Lee was to get not one cent to support her abominable lifestyle. "Don't tell me her will included posthumous letters."

"No, this is my father's older sister."

"I didn't know your father had a sister."

"Neither did I. Well, I knew he had one, but she disap-

peared so long ago, everyone assumed she was dead. You can read the letter if you want to. It's in the top right-hand drawer of my desk."

Kate padded down the hallway and brought it back, three pages of cotton bond covered with strong, thick writing. *What would a handwriting analyst make of that hand?* she thought idly, and sat down on the edge of the bed to read it.

"My dear niece," it began. By the middle of the second page, Kate's face was crinkled up in amusement, and when she came to the end, she laughed aloud. She took a moment to look back over the peculiar document. "A twenty-four-karat loony, isn't she?" she said with a chuckle. "As if you'd jump at the chance to join an old lady you've never met out in the sticks. You could borrow one of Jon's flannel shirts to chop firewood in. That is a truly great letter—I especially like the idea of hiring a PI to gather information about a niece. The throwaway line about malaria is good, too." She retrieved her cold coffee and took a swallow.

"I'm going, Kate."

Kate looked at her for a long minute. "That isn't very funny, Lee."

"No joke. I decided last night."

"You decided last night. When last night?"

"Kate—"

"When? Was it before you decided to give me a taste of what it used to be like? Or after you found you could do it?"

"Don't, Kate."

"Don't what? Don't point out to you that insanity seems to run in your family? How can you even think about it?"

"It's what I need, Kate. I knew it as soon as I read the letter."

"Right, fine, next summer we'll go and visit your loony aunt Agatha, up on her island without any electricity. Next summer, when you can walk and climb stairs and drive the car."

"I need it now, Kate, not a year from now. Sweetheart, I know you don't understand, but I'm asking you to trust me. I need this. I'm suffocating, Kate." She was pleading now, this strong woman who hated to ask for anything. She even put out a hand to Kate's arm. "Kate, please try to understand. I just need to be on my own for a while."

Kate made a huge effort. "Lee, look. I realize progress is slow, and God knows how frustrating you must find it, but throwing up your hands and doing something crazy isn't the answer. If you think you're ready to be on your own, then okay, go on a retreat, hire a cabin in Carmel, or what about that place in Point Reyes where you had that workshop? You've had to learn to walk all over again, one small step at a time. Regaining your independence is the same thing: one step at a time, not jumping off a cliff. Write your aunt, tell her to bring her malaria down for a visit, and then when you've had a few tries at roughing it, go and visit her."

"That makes a lot of sense."

"Good."

"But I'm going now."

"Jesus Christ!" Kate shouted, and slammed her mug down on the bedside table so hard, it dented the wood and sent a spray of coffee to the ceiling. "What the hell kind of game are you playing here? It isn't like you to be so completely pigheaded. You're acting like a child."

"Okay, I'm a child, I'm crazy. While you're name-calling, don't forget 'cripple.' I'm a cripple, right? And I am, but not because my legs don't work and I sometimes pee my pants. I'm a cripple because I can't stand alone. Kate, your life has gone on, but you forget that I had plans for my life, too, plans that all depend on my being able to take care of myself. If I can't take care of myself, how could I—" She broke off, but Kate was too upset to pursue Lee's train of thought.

"Take care of yourself, then. Start cooking again. See more clients. Get back on track. But this . . ."

"I cannot stand by myself when I'm surrounded by people who want to protect me," Lee cried. "I have to be around someone hard, like Aunt Agatha seems to be. Someone who doesn't love me. I know it's crazy, Kate, but it's something I have to do. I have to try at least. I may only be able to stand it for two days and then scream for help, but I am going to try.

"Kate, don't you see? I want to have a life again. I want to have my independence. I want to have . . ." She threw back her head and looked defiantly at Kate. "I want to have a baby."

Kate sat stunned. They had talked about it, of course, before the shooting, it was a natural concern of any permanent couple. But Kate had never had any wish to bear a child, and Lee in a wheelchair—well, she hadn't thought . . .

"Is that what all this is about?"

"All what?"

Kate shrank back from Lee's dry-eyed glare. "I'm sorry, love, I didn't know you were still . . . interested."

"Because I'm in a wheelchair all my instincts have atrophied, all my desires and drives just vanished, is that it?"

"I didn't mean that, Lee."

"And you don't even get mad at me. Do you know how long it's been since you shouted at me? Eighteen months, that's how long. You pussyfoot around like I'm about to break, you and Jon. I can't breathe!" Her voice climbed until it tore at her throat and at Kate's heart. "I have to get out of here. I have to have some air, or I'm going to suffocate."

◆

And so Kate traded leave days and indebted herself to her colleagues, and drove Lee north to Agatha's. She really had no choice, since she knew that if she refused, Lee would ask Jon. Or hitchhike.

She anticipated a long, tense journey, but to her surprise, as soon as the decision had been reached, Lee seemed to relax.

In the hospital bed, Kate's body, which had begun to

worry the ICU nurse with its raised pulse, also relaxed as Kate relived the good part of the trip.

They drove north on the coastal highway, slow but beautiful, reaching the redwoods by the afternoon. They dutifully made the rounds of the memorial groves, oohing at the height of the trees, admiring the immense cross sections with their little flags to mark the birth of Julius Caesar and the crossing of the Mayflower, and wondering at the enormous bearlike figures carved out of redwood with chain saws, which loomed up at the side of the road with a myriad of other beasts and cowboys and figures of St. Francis around their knees. SASQUATCH COUNTRY proclaimed one of them, and BIGFOOT LIVES HERE read another.

They stayed the night in a run-down cabin surrounded by the ageless hush of Sequoia sempervirens, a quiet broken only by the fluting voices of children coming home from the nearby state park's campfire program and later by the huge juddering roars of the logging trucks gearing down two hundred feet from their pillows. At one in the morning, when Lee announced that she had counted forty-three of them since they turned off their lights, and expressed some concern that there might be no trees left if they didn't get an early start the next morning, Kate reassured her that the noise wasn't logging trucks, it was a Sasquatch with digestive problems, and Lee got the giggles and began to sputter childish jokes about Bigfart, and on that high note they fell asleep.

In her damaged sleep, Kate's mouth curved into a smile.

The next afternoon, Kate's car, veteran of many wars, broke down in Reedsport, a town on the Oregon coast not exactly bursting with rental agencies, but even then, Kate managed to salvage the trip and divert the underlying tension by bullying the mechanic into lending them (for a price) his wife's two-year-old Ford. When it was loaded with their things, they shifted to the bigger, and faster, interstate highway and continued their way north.

Lee, reading the map, discovered a town with the unlikely name of Drain. She then began to search for further oddities, coming up with Hoquaim, Enumclaw, Pe Ell, and finally let out a cry of triumph.

"My God, Kate, there's a town in Washington called— are you ready?—Sappho."

Kate took her eyes off the road. "No, I won't believe that. You're making it up."

"I swear it! Look," she said, thrusting the map under Kate's nose.

"It has to be a misprint."

"I must go to Sappho," Lee declared.

Kate grinned, picked up Lee's left hand and kissed the ring she wore there, and managed to convince herself that everything was all right.

And on one level, it was. They drove through Oregon's lush Willamette Valley, two women in a foreign and well-watered land, where massive sprinklers hurled sparkling jets of water hundreds of feet through the air. They found two lakes to swim in, one noisy and crowded, the other newly opened and pristine. They stopped at two Pioneer Days museums to look over the rusty plows and make the requisite comment that women must have been tiny in those days, or else the leather of those shoes must have shrunk considerably in a century.

Kate, desperate to believe that all was well, saw only the sunshine, heard only Lee's laughter in the water and her shriek when the tiny fish nibbled her leg. She did not see that Lee's smiles were occasionally just a bit forced; she closed her ears to the long silences, put a succession of tapes in the Ford's player, talked a lot to herself.

She did not take conscious notice of the fact that Lee had not touched the wheelchair since they had left San Francisco. When Lee had Kate stop at a drug store so she could go in and buy some aspirin, the fact that Lee was chewing the things like peanuts was miraculously hidden behind the surface irritation that Lee had not asked Kate to go in for her. Bit by bit, as the miles passed, Lee became less and less willing to acknowledge her disabilities. They spent more than an hour every day at rest stops, Kate walking up and down the cement paths between the summer-worn lawns and the crowded parking strips while Lee hobbled, sweating and determined, to the toilets, refusing the wheelchair, ignoring the wide-doored handicapped stalls, feeling the eyes on her like so many burning coals, ready to snarl at Kate should she dare offer help or to stab a stranger's hand with icy politeness: *Thank you, I can manage.*

Outside the yellow rest rooms, cars came and went, truckers parked and used the toilets and rolled away, picnics were packed away and others spread out, and finally Lee emerged, one aluminum prop after the other, and made her way, three inches at a step, to the car. She would not allow Kate to park in the handicapped slots, would coldly rage and spit and wound if Kate tried to save her some steps, made it easier, acknowledged Lee's limitations. It was painful to stand by helplessly as Lee drove her legs to take one step, then another, excruciating to witness the effort Lee went through that Kate could so easily save her, agony to stand and watch as Lee battled furiously to compel her body to obey her will.

A six-month-old golden retriever flew past Lee, trailing its leash and its indignant, laughing owner. Lee teetered, leaned into the arm braces, stayed upright, and Kate began to breathe again. A fall, every fall, meant either long minutes of wracking effort or an assistance from Kate, followed by hours of bitter silence and (until recently, when Lee had renounced them) a surreptitious pain pill at night. No fall this time, not even descending the Everest of the four-inch curb. She had not even noticed that Kate had moved the car one space closer, six precious feet, or at any rate, she said nothing. *Perhaps this will be a good day after all,* Kate thought, starting the engine and putting the car into reverse.

◆

The next day, they reached Puget Sound, and the following morning set out for the ferry to Aunt Agatha's island. Through the foggy, low-lying pastureland, around the northern end of Fidalgo Island to Anacortes, Kate followed the signs, finally steering down into a huge parking lot next to the water, where they were directed into a loading lane. She cut the engine and opened her door to go and buy their tickets, but she stopped at the touch of Lee's hand on her arm and Lee's first word since they had left the motel.

"No."

"I was just going to buy the tickets. I'll be back in a minute."

"No, don't."

"I think we have to buy them before they let us on."

"Not now," Lee ordered sharply, and Kate stared at her profile, feeling uneasy now. Lee was getting terribly worked up about something. Kate knew that Lee had a lot of unresolved and probably unresolvable feelings toward the father she had never known, but Kate had had no indication before this that she was transferring those feelings to the man's sister. This is not good, she thought unhappily, but she pulled her door shut, and felt Lee relax a shade beside her.

Long minutes passed. A ferry appeared through the thinning fog. It docked, then began to spew forth a stream of speeding cars and trucks, like a shark spawning, with a smaller but no less determined string of pedestrians appearing along the other side of the waiting area. She'll be one of those, thought Kate; there's no point in paying to drive a car across if the people you're meeting have one. An older woman came into sight—no, too young. There was another, looking more likely. Kate leaned over the seat and began to pull the bits and pieces over to one side, and suddenly Lee made a noise in the back of her throat, flinging open her door to heave her clumsy legs laboriously out onto the pavement and begin hauling herself upright against the car.

Kate stopped her clearing activities and opened her own door. She stood out on the asphalt, looking toward the off-loading pedestrians for a straggling senior citizen, and then she realized that Lee was looking in the other direction, the direction they had come from. Kate looked, but she saw only the latecomers being directed into their lines—cars, campers, and a flashy red motorcycle weaving between the others. Lee waved her hand wildly, and Kate looked more closely. Could it be—yes, it was the motorcycle that had attracted Lee's interest. A messenger from Aunt Agatha? But how could Lee know? Suspicion began to blossom in Kate's mind, and she looked at Lee over the top of the car until, reluctantly, Lee answered the pressure of Kate's gaze and looked back, and Kate, seeing the same wrenching mixture of excitement and guilt and fear and defiance that she had seen there the day Aunt Agatha's letter arrived, only ten times stronger, knew instantly what it meant, knew why Lee had been silent and why she'd stopped Kate from buying the tickets. The truth was so devastating, so utterly appalling, she could feel nothing else, not even the anger that Lee was obviously expecting from her. She just stared, at Lee and then at the motorcyclist, who was somehow now standing in front of Lee.

The small figure in the bright red leathers with a zigzag of purple down each arm bent over in a deep bow, pulled off the purple helmet, and straightened up, shaking out a head of pure white curls. She held out a hand to Lee.

"You're Lee," she stated. "You look like your father."

"Aunt Agatha," Lee answered, with an uneasy sidelong glance at Kate. The woman followed her glance, then stretched her hand over the roof of the car to Kate.

"And you must be Kate."

Kate looked at the small brown hand, the wrinkled little face, sallow beneath a deep tan, the sparkling blue eyes that looked like Lee's, but she did not see them, saw only, clear before her, the evidence that Lee had made a great number of plans that patently did not include her. There had been nothing at all vague about this arrangement, how she intended to meet Aunt Agatha. Kate looked away from the older woman, back to her beloved.

"What has happened to you, Lee?" she whispered hoarsely. "This is . . . it's foul. Deceitful. You never intended me to go to the island, did you?"

"Oh dear," said Aunt Agatha with a sigh, and stood back.

"Kate, I never meant—"

"Oh Christ, Lee, don't make it worse." Kate found herself shouting, and she did not care. "You manipulated me to get you up here and now you want me to leave you alone. It's a shitty thing to do, and I'd never have believed it of you. You may not love me, but I thought at least you had some self-respect. Obviously I don't know you, not at all, not anymore. Well, fine, you're here, your aunt's here, and you don't need me." She yanked the back door open and began to heave Lee's possessions out onto the blacktop, beginning with the wheelchair. Lee, babbling incoherently and with tears on her face, began to inch her way around the car, leaning her full weight on the dusty hood. Her aunt followed—making no move to interfere, just shadowing this unknown crippled niece of hers. Kate finished in the backseat and turned to the trunk. She dropped a carton to the ground, sending books spilling out under the front of the car behind them, which for some reason had its engine running. A number of cars had started up, she noticed. The ferry was boarding, and the car was now empty of Lee's things except—Kate slammed the trunk shut and continued around to the passenger side, where she leaned in, pulled out Lee's arm braces and the waist pack she used as a purse, plucked a pair of sunglasses from the dashboard and a paperback from the door pocket and threw them onto the ground, slammed the door (Lee had reached the trunk by this time), and walked forward again around the front of the car and back to the driver's door. Lee, too, was back where she had started from, looking across the Ford's roof at Kate, protesting, crying, reaching, and cars were driving past, the passengers staring with greedy curiosity at the scene. A horn sounded. Kate opened her door, pausing before getting in.

"Do you want me out of the house when you get back?"

"NO! Oh God, Kate, if you'd just listen, you don't understand—"

"No, I don't. I don't understand anything. Let me know when you're coming home," she said. She got into the car, turned the key, put it into gear, and drove away, leaving Lee staggering at the sudden loss of support. She would have fallen but for Agatha. Kate drove between the white lines that led down the loading area toward the ferry, then cut back in the opposite direction to the empty off-loading lane. As she passed the two figures with their piles of luggage and the gaudy motorcycle, she heard Agatha Cooper's penetrating voice asking, "Can you ride on the back of a motorcycle, Lee?" She could not help looking back in the rearview mirror. Her last view of Lee for many months was of Lee watching her, but also of Lee beginning to straighten up and formulate the answer, a determined "Yes."

Kate had not even stayed to watch the ferry depart, had not even hoped that Lee might change her mind at the last moment. Instead, she drove up the hill, away from the sea and around the corner from the ferry terminal, where she pulled over into a wide spot, put her arms on the top of the steering wheel, and began to weep.

When she was empty and exhausted from the effort of tears and her eyes and head ached and throbbed, she drove on, somehow missing the way back to Seattle and ending up instead on the next island, where a cluster of motels and bars had sprung up around a military base. She checked into a motel, walked to the next-door bar for a drink, and woke up two days later, sick and wretched and wishing she were as dead as she felt.

She did not die; instead, she drove her hungover body out to the shore and sat watching the waters ebb out of the Sound, toward the sea, and then turn and push their way back in. The next morning, she checked out of the cigarette-permeated motel room and drove to Reedsport, where her car was still not ready. She walked far up and down the hard wet sand of the Oregon beaches all the following day, until finally, barely twenty-four hours be-

fore she was due back at work, the car was running. She drove back to the City, fueled by coffee and kept awake by food, to arrive home at five in the morning. And four hours after that, she was awakened by Jules, leaning on her doorbell.

The memories faded; Kate's body quieted, and then she slept.

EIGHT

WAS IT still August? There was a man in the bar, she remembered, a small man in a shiny suit; that was why she'd bought herself a bottle to take back to the hotel room, to get away from him.

No, it was December now, although inexplicably August's hangover was still with her—a head so fragile that if her queasy stomach did what it wanted to, her skull was sure to split right down the middle. Someone groaned, she thought, and grinned like a skull.

"Kate?" said an unfamiliar voice. "Katarina Martinelli? Are you awake?"

She worked her throat a bit, swallowed, cleared it gingerly. Her head didn't split, although she thought it might be a good idea to keep her eyes shut.

"Somebody had a headache," she muttered.

"What did she say?" said the voice.

"She seems to be disassociating herself from her experience," said another woman. Something familiar about this second voice. "How interesting."

"Not," began Kate, and then thought, The hell with it. Let them be interested.

"Not what, Kate?" said the second voice, the one with

the mild accent, and when Kate didn't answer, she continued, "Do you know where you are?"

"Hospital," Kate answered immediately. She knew these smells and noises even with her eyes shut and a hangover thudding through her. She'd know them even if she lay here dead.

"Do you know how you got here?"

Kate had no immediate answer for that one.

"Who had a headache?" voice two persisted.

"Joke," said Kate to shut her up, but the word set off an echo and bits of memory began to flake off and fall down where Kate could gather them up. Joke (*joke/buckets from the morgue catching scraps—no, drops, drops of rain/macabre cop humor, sorry, Grace/is he with you?/ you're looking for a boy called—*)

"Dio," she croaked, and opened her eyes into those of Rosa Hidalgo. "Dio. Is he alive?"

"The boy? The doctors say he's responding well, he'll be fine. You know how you got here, then?"

"I was in the squat, with, um. Rawlins. Rawlings," she corrected herself. "Did I get shot?"

"You were hit, with a piece of pipe. You were lucky, it seems, that God has blessed you with a thick skull."

"Thank you, God. How long was I out?" Kate was aware that the other woman was fussing with vital signs, her hand on Kate's wrist, but she ignored her.

"You were hit the day before yesterday, so it is about forty-three hours. And if you are wondering why I am here, I am acting as Jules's representative. Hospital policy does not allow children in the I.C.U.," she added with amusement, "and Jani has a lecture this afternoon."

"I can imagine Jules had words about hospital policy," Kate said, and closed her eyes.

◆

When she next woke, Hawkin was there, and a different nurse. Before she could speak, the nurse shoved a thermometer into her mouth, and everything waited until pulse and blood pressure had been taken and the high-tech thermometer beeped.

"How's the boy?" Kate asked as soon as her mouth was clear.

"He'll do. He's still on a drip but his fever's down. I talked with him just before I came here."

"Has anyone come for him yet?"

"He won't give us his last name, where he's from, anything."

"You might ask Grace Kokumah to come and talk with him. You know her?"

"Of course. I'll do that, when he's better. How are you doing?"

"I feel like hell, but everything seems to be in the right place. I haven't seen a doctor yet, not to talk to."

"I'll try and find one for you. You owe Rawlings, by the way. He managed to be in the way when they were moving you into the ambulance, so the papers didn't have any pictures of you this time. They had to make do with Reynolds."

"Who's Reynolds?"

"Sorry. Weldon Reynolds, the guy you shot. He has a record, but only small things, creating a disturbance, selling grass and mushrooms, resisting arrest. Not a sexual offender, as far as we can find out, and none of the other boys in the squat accused him. Looks like he had a fantasy of creating a society of outcasts, petty thievery and selling joints, with the profits coming to him, of course."

"Dickens," Kate commented.

"Fagin," agreed Hawkin. "He'll be okay, by the way. Your bullet caught him at a funny angle, probably bounced off one of the struts in that elevator, traveled up through a couple of ribs and collapsed a lung, but it didn't reach the heart. You were lucky."

"Yes," Kate said with feeling. A shooting, even justified, was always a serious thing; killing a perpetrator could haunt, or end, a cop's career. To say nothing of the cop.

"Are you okay about it?"

"I don't know. I haven't thought about it. I guess so."

"You remember shooting him?"

"Oh yes. I remember shooting, anyway. I never saw him, just the gun flashes, and I aimed at them, and then the gun fell. I never saw him," she repeated. "Am I on suspension?"

"Administrative leave," Hawkin confirmed. "There'll be a hearing when you're on your feet again, but you won't have any problems. You were entirely justified. *He* was shooting at *you*, for Christ's sake."

"I didn't have a warrant."

"He had no right to be there, either. I talked to the owner of the building. It'll be all right, Kate. Don't worry about it; just get better. Do you want me to call Lee?"

"No!"

Hawkin stood beside her bed and looked down at her for a long time, but in the end he did not comment, merely nodded and said good-bye. Kate was tired, but her throbbing skull kept sleep at bay for a long time—the throbbing, but also the tangled memories of Dio's sweaty face, the gun kicking in her hand, and the strangled cough of the man when her bullet hit him.

◆

One of the things Kate hated most about being in the hospital was that people were forever coming in on her while she was asleep. Not so much the hospital personnel—she was resigned to them; after all, they were body technicians, and having them wandering around the room while she was out like a light was much the same as having a doctor doing a yearly exam, prodding and looking into areas of her body that even Lee hadn't seen much of.

It was the others who were given free rein to come in and stare at her who drove her mad. Over the next few days, especially when she was moved from the I.C.U., there was a constant stream: The man from Internal Affairs, the police psychologist, the social workers and investigators and everyone connected with the squat and its boys and the criminality of its leader—all had come in at one time or another, and most of them had caught her sleeping.

And now, yet again, five days into her stay, she was struggling up into alertness, knowing someone was standing beside her bed. Two someones, she saw, Al and a boy who was either extremely short or else sitting down, a boy with a Mayan face and long hair as black as Jules's, a boy who looked embarrassed and shy and determined.

"Kate, this is Dio," Al said.

She tried to lift herself upright, then remembered the switch and raised the head of the bed. The boy was sitting, in a wheelchair, though by the looks of him it was more due to hospital policy than need.

"Well, you're certainly looking better than when I last saw you," Kate told him, and put out her hand. He shook it with the awkwardness of someone who is more familiar with the theory of a handshake than with its practice. That seemed true of dealing with the adult world in general, as well; when he had his hand back, he didn't seem to know what to do with it, and his gaze flitted about the room, landing only briefly on Kate's face and veering away from the thick bandages around her head.

"I, um, I wanted to say thank you," he said. "They're discharging me, and I wanted to see you before I left. To say thanks."

"You're welcome," she replied, swallowing a smile. "I'm just glad I found you. You should thank Jules, and Grace Kokumah."

"Um, I—I did. I also wanted to thank you for getting the library book back to Jules."

"Library book?" She looked to Al for explanation, but he only shook his head in incomprehension.

"Yeah, the one I had in the tent. I was really worried about it," he said in a rush. "It's been bugging me ever since I left, 'cause I know how careful Jules is with books, especially library books, and I knew the tent would leak as soon as it rained."

"I see. Why didn't you give it back to her before you

left?" And, she thought, why didn't you take your bits of jewelery with you?

He looked down intently at his fingers, which were plucking at a worn spot on the arm of the wheelchair. Al moved casually away to examine a wilting flower arrangement.

"I was gonna go back. I only came up here for the day, you know? There was this other kid in the park—he wanted to come up and he had a ride, so I came with him. Then we met Weldon, and it got late, so we stayed with him, and then, well, we just got busy, you know?" He looked up, and read the expression on her face as disapproval. "He always had things for us to do. And I was afraid that if I went back down, I might have problems getting up again, like if the cops—the police'd found my stuff and thought I stole it, so I just kept putting it off. But I felt really bad about that library book."

The smile tugged itself out of the corners of Kate's mouth. "You're something else, you know that, Dio?"

His head came up, looking for ridicule but looking relieved, and when he realized she meant it as a compliment, his brown skin blushed copper.

"You just stayed on in the squat because it was better than living out in the open, with winter coming on?"

"Yeah. It was an okay place. It was dry, and we had lots of blankets, and some of the other kids were cool. Weldon was a little weird sometimes, but he was good at getting food and stuff, and he knew some great stories. He used to tell us things at night. Called it 'sitting around the campfire.' " A crooked smile softened the boy's face for a minute, and then it was gone.

"How was he weird, Dio?" she asked, and when he didn't answer, she said, "I think I deserve to know. He nearly killed me, for Christ's sake."

"That was Gene that hit you."

"I mean with the gun. Or didn't you know that Weldon tried to shoot me?"

"I heard, yeah." He shifted uncomfortably. "I don't know. Weldon was kind of paranoid. He used to tell us how he'd protect us against people—cops and CPS and people who'd want to break us up. He used to call us his family. He even tried to get us to call him Dad, but only a couple of the littler kids ever did." He sounded regretful, as if he had failed a friend.

"Why didn't you let Jules know you were okay? She was terribly worried."

"I know. I did write. Twice."

"What happened?"

"I gave them to Weldon to mail," he said flatly.

"And he never did."

Dio shrugged.

"What are you going to do now?" she asked.

"I'm gonna live with a family for a while. The Steiners."

"I know them. They're good people."

"I guess."

"Well, good luck to you, Dio. Stay in touch, and look, if things get rough, give me a call, okay? I might be able to help."

His eyes went to her wrapped head, and he winced, but his parting handshake was more assured than the first one had been.

Al took the chair's handles and began to push it toward the doorway, but Kate had remembered something else.

"Dio—who was the woman in the picture? The snapshot I found in your tent?"

Al turned the chair around, but the boy's face was closed up and he said nothing.

"Anyway, did Jules give it back to you?"

After a moment, he ducked his head. "Yeah."

"That's good. Well, take care, man. See you later, Al."

Their voices faded down the noisy hallway, and Kate lay back to await the next interruption.

◆

She was in the hospital for a week, refused release because of occasional spikes in her temperature and a cycle

119

of blinding headaches that entertained a series of doctors and worried the nurses. Finally, however, her fevers left, and with the possibility of an infection inside her brain out of the way, she was discharged. Even then she had to lie to the head nurse, saying that there would be someone to care for her at home, but eventually, her shaven scalp cold around the smaller bandage, she eased herself from wheelchair to Hawkin's car, and he drove her home.

She let him take the bag of accumulated possessions into the house—things he or Rosa Hidalgo or Rosalyn Hall had fetched for her—and walked cautiously through to the living room sofa. Hawkin brought her the alpaca throw blanket, turned up the heat, made her a cup of hot milk, and carried her bag upstairs. He came back with her gun in its holster.

"Where do you want this?" he asked.

"The top drawer in that table with the phone on it, thanks."

He stepped back into the hallway and she heard the squeak of the drawer.

"Can I get you anything to eat?"

"No thanks. They fed me lunch." The doctor whose approval was required before Kate could leave had been in surgery, delayed by an automobile accident and leaving Kate to sit in her room, waiting and picking at a tray of hospital food, until he swept in, still wearing his surgical booties, looked in her eyes, asked her two or three questions, and left. "What I'd really like is to be alone, if that's not too rude."

"I understand. I'll stop by on my way home, but call if you need anything. Where's the—I saw it in the kitchen." He went out again and returned with the portable telephone, checking that the batteries were charged before he put it on the table in reach of Kate's hand. "You remember my beeper number?"

"Al, I had a concussion, not a lobotomy. Go do some work. Solve a crime or something, and let me sit and be quiet."

And it was quiet, once the door had closed behind

him. A light, steady rain was falling, soaking the shrubs and pots and the bricks of the patio, where the moss in the cracks rose up to drink it in. Streaks ran down the windows and the French doors, a mild gurgle came from the downspouts, an occasional seagull floated across the gray sky, and Kate slept.

It was dark outside when she woke, although a light from the kitchen gave outlines to her surroundings. She woke bit by bit, dozing warmly inside the cocoon of the soft blanket, grateful for the familiar room and the sounds of home. Hospitals were cold, clanking death traps, and she was aware, for the first time since August, of the innate goodness of life.

Easing onto her back to look at the digital clock on the video machine, she felt a twinge along the right side of her skull, but that was all. Just after eleven—she'd slept for seven hours. Gingerly she tried sitting up, then got to her feet, and other than a couple of dull thuds at each change of position, the headache remained lurking in the background—not gone, but not actively attacking, either.

Enjoying the freedom of movement, exploring how far it would stretch, Kate folded the blanket and tossed it across the back of the sofa (a brief awareness of pressure at the throwing motion, not really a pain) and went to look out the window at the night. All the lights seemed very distant, but it was a comforting sensation, not an alienating one. The wind stirred the bushes, and she wondered how long Gideon the raccoon had continued to come before deciding that she was a lost cause. Maybe she would put a handful of dog biscuits out tomorrow night, on the off chance he cruised by.

She was thirsty, and, yes, actually hungry, although there was not likely to be much that was edible in the refrigerator. She pulled the curtains against the night and went to the kitchen.

There was a vase of flowers on the table, a fresh, fragrant mixture of florist's blooms, and beside it a note, the first part of which, strangely enough, was in Al's handwriting. Surely he would have mentioned any message that afternoon? She picked it up and read:

> *Martinelli—I turned the ringer on your phone off and the sound down on your answering machine. Call if you need anything, otherwise, I'll drop by in the morning. The flowers are from Jules.*
>
> *—Al*

Beneath it on the page, in the same ink but by someone with a much lighter hand, was another message:

> *Kate,*
> *We didn't want to wake you, but I thought you might like some food and wouldn't feel like cooking. You can eat the soups cold or micro them for a couple of minutes, ditto the beans in the glass casserole, but don't heat the noodles— it's a salad. I'm going to be at the civic center tomorrow morning, and may stop by around noon. Oh yes, that's Maj's tiramisu in the white bowl. Take care.*
>
> *Rosalyn*

Kindness, the simple kindness of friends, the last thing she had expected, and it reached in through her weakness and she felt tears start up in her eyes as she sat at the table and read the words over again. On the third time through, it occurred to her that she had been driven in here by hunger, and she seemed miraculously to have at hand something more appealing and substantial than the bowl of cold cereal she had resigned herself to.

Six containers of food awaited her: two white deli cartons, two glass jars, and two ovenproof containers reminiscent of potlucks. Noodle salad with the spicy, fragrant sesame dressing Kate loved—how had Rosalyn known? One jar with a strip of masking tape labeling it mushroom soup, the other chicken vegetable. Two kinds of beans. And a large bowl of creamy white pudding, drifted with black-brown powdered chocolate. Kate reached in and began greedily to pull out containers.

At midnight, replete and much steadied, Kate turned off the kitchen light, turned on the light over the stairs, and began the climb to bed. Halfway up, she paused, then reversed her steps back into the kitchen. She found a stemmed wineglass and a pair of scissors, turned to the bouquet on the table and teased a few of the flowers from it, trimmed their stems short, and dropped them into the wineglass. She put the scissors in the drawer, ran some water into the glass, put the denuded stems into the trash, turned off the light again, and took the miniature flower arrangement up the stairs with her. The flowers sat on the table beside her bed, keeping her company while she looked at the television, and later they watched over her while she slept.

NINE

KATE WAS in the garden chopping weeds with a hoe when she heard the doorbell. The garden was on the north side of the house, and usually cool and shaded, but despite being mid-December, it was one of those warm winter days that explains why California is overpopulated, and Kate was sweating with the effort. She straightened and, with resignation, felt the inevitable jab in her head travel on down her spine and seize her stomach, setting off the vague nausea she had come to dread.

She was by now a connoisseur of headaches, a seasoned expert in knowing just how far she could go, when to back off and fetch the dolly rather than lifting a heavy object, how a change in the weather would affect the nerve endings inside her skull. Two weeks after the injury now, and she was beginning to resign herself to a permanent degree of ache. It was bearable, however, if she took care not to push herself.

Except for the other headaches, those bolts of pain that came out of the blue like slow lightning, rippling across her brain and turning her stomach upside down. Those sent her straight for the powerful tablets the doctor had given her, left her groping up the stairs, blind and retching and seeking the dark sanctuary of the bedroom. They would pass, after four or five hours, as suddenly as they had come, although the combined dregs of pain and pain-killers in her body meant that she was worth nothing for the rest of the day. Kate had had three of these since leaving the hospital, and she would have given a great deal to avoid having another one, but the doctors said there was no knowing what triggered them or how long they would be with her. What they did tell her was that she could not go back to active duty until she was free of the threat.

This headache that was now settling in seemed to be somewhere in between the basic nagging kind and the bullet-in-the-brain sort, which all in all might be a hopeful sign, Kate thought as she pulled off her muck-encrusted shoes against a boot scraper and walked through the house to the front door.

Any change was for the better, and any visitor a welcome one. Kate was thoroughly fed up with sick leave. The first two days home she had spent in front of the television, falling asleep over the large collection of unwatched videos Lee and Jon had taped for her over the months. On the third day, boredom had set in, and she found herself wandering through the house cataloging the unfinished jobs she found there, until eventually she went downstairs for a screwdriver and replaced the switch plate that had cracked back in September.

In the five days since then, interrupted only by an afternoon when she had to put on her official clothes and go in for a hearing about the shooting, she had trimmed and rehung two sticking doors, replaced the broken sash cords in the upstairs window, fixed the drip in the bathtub, finished grouting a patch of tile in the under-the-stairs bathroom that she and Lee had put up two years before, climbed a ladder to replace a cracked pane of glass and touch up the paint around it, and shifted everything in the living room to wax first one half of the inlaid wood floor and then the other.

The floor had been the worst, because having her head

down made her skull pound so horribly that she could only bear an hour at a time, whereas with an upright job she could stretch it to two hours before she had to lay down her tools and take herself trembling to bed for an hour or two. On the whole, however, physical work, done with care, seemed actually to help, particularly in the fresh air. Today she had been digging and weeding for nearly three hours before the doorbell interrupted, she saw as she glanced at the clock on her way through the living room. It looked as though she was going to pay for the exertion.

Kate picked up the loose knit cap she had taken to keeping on the table in the hallway and pulled it on as she went to answer the door. At first she saw nothing through the peephole; then, with a growing and fatalistic sense of déjà vu, she looked down, and there she saw the top of a head of black hair, neatly parted. She slid the bolt and opened the door.

"Morning, Jules."

"Uh-oh, you're not feeling well."

"I'm okay."

"Are you mad at me, then?"

"Why would I be mad at you?"

"It's just that you usually say, 'Hey, J.' 'Good morning, Jules' sounds so formal."

"So I'm feeling formal. Don't I look formal?"

Jules examined her muddy, sweat-stained clothing and grubby bare legs. "No, you don't. We tried to call, but we kept getting your machine, so we thought we'd come by anyway. Can I come in?"

"Who's 'we'?"

"Al." Jules turned and waved at the road. Kate bent to look and saw Al's car pull out from the curb and drive away. She cursed under her breath as Jules continued. "He has to pick something up from the office. I wonder why you call it an office when it's just that big room you guys share. Anyway, I wanted to say hi, so he said he'd drop me and come back. He won't be long. Are you sure you're feeling okay? You don't look like it."

"I'm fine. Come on in, Jules."

"I like that hat," Jules said, looking over her shoulder as she headed for the kitchen. "Where did you get it?"

"A friend made it for me. It hides the stubble."

"Can I see?" Jules asked, turning to face her, going suddenly serious.

"Not much to see," Kate said, but she pulled the cap off anyway and dropped it on the table. Rosalyn's partner, Maj, a woman of many talents and with a recipe for killer tiramisu, had come by the house with it and a pair of electrical clippers the week before. The resulting haircut was not all that much shorter than Kate's last one, though slightly lopsided, but it necessarily revealed too much of the still-clear lines where the surgeons had cut a flap in the skin to give access to the bone below. Maj's hat was pretty, but there was angora in it, and the damn thing itched. She pretended not to feel the girl's eyes on her as she reached for two glasses and took a bottle of juice from the refrigerator.

"You like cherry cider?" she asked.

"Sure, I guess. They didn't have to put a metal plate in your head, did they?" Jules demanded.

"No. They thought they might, but it wasn't that bad."

"That's good. A friend of mine has an uncle with a big plate in his skull. He has to carry a letter from his doctor around with him, because he sets off metal detectors."

Kate came near to laughing at the thought of the number of detectors she went through in the course of a week, all of them going off madly in her wake.

Jules absently accepted the glass of cider that Kate handed her, but her mind was still on the topic of the consequences of metal plates. "That must be a real pain," she reflected.

"It must be," Kate agreed seriously, and sat down. "It's good to see you. How've you been? How's Josh? Have you seen Dio since he got out of the hospital? And why aren't you in school?"

"It's a half day, for finals week. Dio's fine. And I

haven't seen Josh in a while, except in school, of course. He has a girlfriend." She sounded disgusted.

"I thought you were a girlfriend."

"I was a friend. Am a friend still, but he's busy. He'll get over it," she said, as if talking about the flu, which Kate thought reasonable enough.

"What's your shirt say today?" Kate asked. Jules held the lapels of her windbreaker open so Kate could see the writing, and when she saw the words, she began to laugh.

"Good, huh?"

"It's great." Kate did not tell her she had seen it before, worn by women who intended a rather different take on the message, but it was still a fine shirt: A WOMAN WITHOUT A MAN IS LIKE A FISH WITHOUT A BICYCLE.

Kate was about to ask about the word for the day when the girl blurted out, "Can I come and stay with you when Mom and Al go on their honeymoon?"

Kate opened her mouth, then shut it again.

"They were going to take me with them to Baja, and at first I thought it sounded great, but then I realized it was impossible. Talk about spare wheels." Kate wondered if she was hearing the voice of a friend behind the girl's words, that devastating peer criticism that could reduce even a self-contained person like Jules to a quivering mass. "Taking the kid along on a honeymoon," Jules said dismissively, her demeanor cool but with a clear thread of discomfort through it, and Kate stood up to take a random plate of food from the refrigerator in order to hide her smile. Jules, she guessed, had belatedly connected the traditional activities of a honeymoon couple with her mother and the amiable cop she was marrying; the mortification when her friends pointed this out must have been extreme.

Still. "I don't know when I'll be going back to work, Jules. I couldn't have you here alone while I'm out. They can be long days."

"Do you know when you'll be going back?"

"I see the doctor tomorrow afternoon. What were you planning on doing if I wasn't available?"

"Staying with Rosa, I guess."

"Or have Trini the airhead stay with you?"

"Not her. She's in trouble. She got caught shoplifting the day after Thanksgiving, and Mom won't have her in the house."

"Don't you have any family?" Kate hoped she hadn't sounded too plaintive, but Jules seemed not to have noticed.

"Mom has some relatives in Hong Kong, but nobody here. My father's dead," she said in a tight voice. "I don't know if there's anyone on his side, but Mom says they all hated her. Anyway, there's nobody to stay with."

"Have you met Al's kids? Not to stay with. I just wondered if you'd met them."

Jules relaxed suddenly and grinned. "You mean my sister- and brother-to-be? I met her—she's really cool. Him—Sean—I'll meet this weekend."

"They're coming up for the wedding?"

"Sure."

"I'm glad to hear it."

"It's important to Al, I know. Kate, do you think I should keep calling him Al if he's my mother's husband? I don't know if I could call him Daddy."

"Give it time," Kate suggested mildly. "*Dad* may feel comfortable after a while."

"I guess. Maybe he'd rather be just Al."

"I think, if you're asking me, that Al Hawkin would burst with pride if you took to calling him Dad, but I'm also sure he wouldn't want to push it. He loves you very much."

Jules became very interested in the trace of cider in the bottom of her glass. "He must be nuts," she muttered.

"Nuts because he loves you? Jules, you're one of the greatest people I've ever met."

"You don't know me," the girl said darkly.

"I know you better than you think I do." At this, Jules shot her a hard look composed of equal parts suspicion and apprehension, with a dash of hope thrown in. However, Kate had done about all she could just then.

All the time she had sat talking, the ache in her head continued to build, until it could not be ignored. Hating the display of weakness, she went to the cupboard and took out the pill bottle, shook a tablet out onto her palm, and swallowed it with the last of the juice in her glass.

"You aren't okay," Jules said with concern.

"I have a perpetual headache. I'll live."

"I should go." Jules stood up.

"Not until Al comes back."

"I'm sorry, Kate, I shouldn't have bothered you with all this."

"I'm glad you came. Did I ever thank you for the flowers, by the way?"

"Yes. Twice."

"Good. Those tiny white ones—what are they called? Baby's breath, I think. They dry well—did you know that? I have a sprig of them upstairs." Jules began to look positively alarmed at this uncharacteristic show of sentimentality, and Kate, peering at her through the distance of the headache and the onset of the painkiller, would have laughed if she hadn't known how much it would hurt. "It's okay, Jules, I'll go to bed and sleep it off. It comes and goes. You stay here until Al comes. Promise?" And what was it Jules had come here for? Oh, yes. "And I'll talk to him tomorrow, when my head is straight, about having you here. Bye, girl. Take care."

She did not hear Hawkin come, but when she woke five hours later, refreshed and ready to start the next cycle, the house was empty. Whistling tunelessly, she went to put in another hour with the hoe before dark.

TEN

"So what do you think, Al?" Kate was on the phone to her partner, the following evening.

"You're on workman's comp now?"

"Sick leave is just as boring as suspension."

"Must've been a relief, though, to be cleared."

"God, yes."

"Pretty hairy?"

"Oh, not really. The worst part was anticipating it. Have you ever . . . ?"

"No. I fired my gun once, though I didn't hit him, but that was in the old days, not even forms to fill out. But about Jules; you'll be out for another couple of weeks, you said?"

"At least that. The doctor wants to see me then, before he approves me for even light duty."

"You sure you want her? It's a long time, when you're not used to having a teenager around."

"Two weeks is nothing. We'll go sit on Santa's lap, have turkey with all the trimmings while you and Jani are so sunburned that you can't touch each other and have the squits from drinking ice in your margaritas."

"God, you're such a romantic."

"It's a talent. Jules and I will have a good time. If anything comes up, I'll call Rosa, have her come and pick Jules up."

"If you're not up to it, dump her. Promise? It's her own damn fault she's not going. The reason we chose this date in the first place was that she's off school for the holidays, and then she says she'd rather stay home."

"She wants to give you two some privacy, Al."

The phone was silent for a long time.

"Did she tell you that?" he said at last.

"More or less."

"God, I can be a damned fool sometimes. Why didn't I think of that, instead of assuming she was just being— What a sweetheart. She's nuts, of course. This is a vacation, not a honeymoon. I'll talk to her, see if I can get the other room back at the hotel."

"Al? Don't. Just leave it."

"But—"

"Jani might prefer it this way, and I know Jules will. Baja will be there next year. You two go away and relax; Jules and I will stay here and wrap presents."

"If you're sure."

"I'm sure, Al. So, how are the wedding preparations coming along?"

"Why didn't we elope to Vegas?" He groaned. She laughed.

"Let me know if I can do anything. Otherwise, I'll see you at the church on Sunday, and I'll bring Jules home with me then. I won't be on the bike," she reassured him.

"You're okay for driving?"

"No problem. There's no danger of blackouts or blurred vision, just these migraines; they don't know what's causing them or when they'll stop. But I will say, I'm getting a hell of a lot done on the house."

◆

The next interruption caught her again working outside, two days after Jules's visit. She was in the bottom of the garden, a place nothing human had ventured into for

132

at least two years, and she seriously thought of ignoring the doorbell. However, she was thirsty, and the compulsive rooting out of brambles would be waiting for her anytime. She dropped her tools on the patio, pulled her rubber boots off against the scraper, and went to answer the door.

This time, it was Rosa Hidalgo, looking cool and neat in linen pants and blouse, every hair in its place. She looked startled at the apparition in front of her, and Kate looked down at herself: tank top and running shorts dark with sweat, ingrained dirt to the wrists and in a line above where the rubber boots had covered her calves, and red welts, some of them dotted with dried blood, where first the roses and then the blackberries had had at her.

"I was gardening," she said in explanation.

"I see."

"Come in." She gestured down the hallway toward the living room and followed her guest through the house. "I don't know if you can call it gardening, really. 'Gardening' always makes me think of Vita Sackville-West in her jodhpurs and floppy hat. What I was doing was committing assault on the weeds. What would you like to drink?"

"Whatever you're having."

They took their tall glasses of iced tea onto the brick patio, which was cool and would allow the earthy fragrance Kate knew she was exuding to dissipate in the open air.

"I never really thanked you for everything you did for me when I was in the hospital," she told Rosa.

"You did thank me, and it was nothing."

"How've you been? How are the herds of small children?"

"One at a time, they are very appealing," she answered brightly, swirling the ice around in her glass.

"And Angelica, how is she?"

"Angél is fine, thank you."

Shallow conversation was tiring, Kate reflected. "Was there anything I could do for you, or did you just stop by to say hello?" she asked, knowing full well it was not the latter. Saying hello did not cause women like Rosa Hidalgo to be nervous.

"Ah, yes, I did have a reason to talk to you. Actually, Jani and Al asked me to come."

"This is about Jules, isn't it?"

"It is. There are some things they thought you ought to know, before you have her under your care for a number of days." Her accent was back.

"I told Al I didn't want to know. More than that, I think it's a bad idea."

"I know that is what you think. I presumed that was why you did not return the call I made a few months ago."

"Jules thinks of me as a friend, not a therapist, not an authority figure."

"I am aware of her feelings for you."

"Then, pardon my rudeness, but why are you here?"

"I am here because you are nearly the age of Jules's mother, and because Jules has chosen you, her soon-to-be stepfather's partner, to confide in, and because I feel I can trust you to use your knowledge of the child's past with care."

"I don't want to know," Kate said forcibly.

"Of course you don't. But you must. Because you won't know Jules unless I tell you about her."

Kate put her face in her hands. The woman was not going to leave without telling her what she thought Kate had to know. Kate might forcibly eject her, or lock herself in the bedroom until the woman went away, or plug her fingers into her ears and hum loudly, but by this time she was undeniably curious. She was, after all, a policewoman, to whom curiosity—nosiness—was both nature and training.

"Okay. All right. If you have to, then let's get on with it." Kate sat back in the chair and crossed her grubby legs in the woman's face. The body language of noncooperation, she thought with an inner smile.

"It begins a number of years ago. In the years after the

revolution in Russia. To put it simply, Jules's mother and her grandmother were both born as the result of rape."

Kate's crossed leg came down.

"*Both* of them?"

"Jani's mother was born in Shanghai in 1935, of a Russian Jewish mother raped by a soldier, either Japanese or Indian. Twenty years later, the child of that event was caught up in a riot in Hong Kong, and she, too, was raped. Jani was born nine months later. When Jani was three months old, her mother took her to the local Christian missionaries, then went home and committed suicide."

"Good . . . heavens," said Kate weakly.

"Jani became the brightest student the missionary school had seen in a long time. She received a scholarship, then came to this country to go to university. She was a sheltered young woman who was nonetheless aware of her past, and it was an almost textbook example of the cyclical nature of abuse when she met and married a young man who loved her extravagantly, wanted desperately to protect her delicate person, and turned on her whenever she stepped outside the guidelines he set. He began to beat her. And although it was not at the time legally recognized that a husband forcing himself on his wife is rape, that is what it was.

"However, Jani was not living in a war-torn city, and she had a few friends and some very employable skills. She left him, and she saw a lawyer. A restraining order was granted, he violated it, and when they came to arrest him, he had a gun and he used it against one of the policemen, who fortunately was not killed. Jani was there when it happened, and Jules, who was about six months old, was sleeping in the next room. He was, somehow, granted bail, but when he came, inevitably, to look for her, she was already gone. She divorced him while he was in jail. He was killed a few months after the divorce was finalized, apparently in a prison brawl, but Jani had the satisfaction of knowing that she had broken free, that she, of her own will, had saved both herself and her daughter.

"You will understand now why it took her so long to accept Al."

"Does he know all this?"

"Of course."

"And Jules?"

"Jani told her the bones of it last summer, just after school was out. Not the details, not the extent of his violence nor that he had threatened Jani with a gun, just that he'd threatened her, she had divorced him, and he was later killed."

"Last summer, huh?"

"The incident in Germany becomes more explicable, does it not?"

"What incident in Germany?" Kate asked, then kicked herself. She didn't want to know.

"Of course. Why should I think you knew about that? Curious. When they were in Köln, Jules disappeared from the hotel one morning, after what was apparently a mild argument with her mother. When she didn't come back by noon, Jani called the police. They found her just before midnight, coming out of a movie theater. Jules said that she'd spent the first part of the day in the park, and the evening in the theater, which was playing an American movie dubbed into German. Jules said she'd sat through it three times. She was trying to teach herself the language, she claimed, and chose the movie because she had seen it already in English."

Kate had to laugh. "You know, that sounds like Jules."

"It's possible. Nonetheless, Jani was insane with worry."

"Who wouldn't be? I'm not saying it excuses Jules, but it does sound like something a kid would do. A kid like Jules, anyway."

"And would a kid like Jules have screaming nightmares regularly every four or five days? You need to be prepared for those, Kate. And would that kid attack a teacher the first week of school, following a writing assignment to describe one's family history?"

"Attack? Al told me there had been some trouble, but

he didn't say she'd attacked anyone. Physically, you mean?"

"Verbally. The woman was in tears, shamed before the class. Young and inexperienced, she could have used a greater degree of tact in the assignment—after all, many children come from broken homes, and at that age they are going to be sensitive about it. Still, the degree of hostility shown by Jules was extraordinary. And quite devastating."

Kate sat and listened to the silence for several minutes, then stirred.

"What else? Any attempts at suicide, or threats?"

"Strangely enough, no. I agree, it might have been expected."

"Drugs? No, I would have noticed that. Tattoos? Body piercing? Shoplifting, for Christ's sake?"

"Nothing. She seems instead to have befriended a cop."

Kate thought about this statement for a few seconds, then decided that although the woman had not actually meant to rank friendship with a cop alongside bodily mutilation, a degree of irritation, if not anger, might be allowed nonetheless.

"Mrs. Hidalgo, I haven't heard—"

"Rosa, please."

"I haven't heard anything that would even begin to justify your presence here." Kate was surprised to find that the spark of irritation was actually something that burned hotter, and she gave in to it: straight for the woman's professional pride. "Frankly, I don't think you had any right to tell me. I think that if Jules had wanted me to know, she'd have found a way of telling me herself. She's a tough young lady, and I don't know that you or her mother give her credit for that. Personally, I think she's coping very well with what must have been devastating news: some nightmares and a tantrum against a teacher who probably deserved it strike me as a damned healthy way to react. If anything, she seems in better shape now than she did a year ago." Kate was working herself into a fine old rage, and enjoying every second of it. "When I first met Jules, she talked like an eleven-year old college sophomore. I'll bet she didn't have a single friend her own age. She was a prig with a big vocabulary, and if that isn't a defense mechanism to rival a brick wall, I don't know what is."

"I didn't mean to—" Rosa Hidalgo tried to interject, but Kate plowed on.

"Now she's a human being, as close to being a normal kid as you can get with a brain like hers. She's got friends—kids her own age, not just one inappropriate friendship with a cop." She put an ironic bite on the word *cop*, and again ignored the other woman's protests. "I know you people live in a hothouse down there, and I can see that Jani has a load of problems of her own, but I really think you'd be doing Jules a great service if you'd just back off and let her find her own way. Stop coddling her on the one hand and watching her like a hawk on the other, waiting for signs of mental and emotional problems. Give her a chance, for God's sake. Try trusting her."

The final exhortation came out more as a whine than as a command: Kate's rage had deflated as quickly as it had grown, leaving her with a bad taste in her mouth and no choice but to sit while the woman across from her earnestly explained the need for therapy and guidance and supervision. By the time she got rid of Rosa Hidalgo, Kate was feeling like a sullen teenager herself, more firmly convinced than ever that Jules was on the rightest possible road.

But, oh my, she thought as she climbed back into the muddy rubber boots, it was fun to get mad.

◆

Kate half-expected that after Rosa reported back on their interview, permission for Jules's plans would be withdrawn. However, the rest of that day and all the next went by with nothing said, so it appeared to be settled:

Jules would come and stay with her from the wedding until New Year's.

With one adjustment to the plan.

On the phone, the afternoon before the wedding, Kate talked to Al, who was at his own place on the other side of town.

"Al, I was thinking. If it's all right with you and Jani, I thought Jules and I might go north for a few days over Christmas. Maybe as far as Washington."

"To see Lee?"

"Possibly. If we feel like it. I had a letter from her last week, asking me to come to her aunt's island for Christmas if I could get it off."

"Does she know you're on leave?"

"She doesn't know anything. I didn't tell her about the shooting, or that I got hurt. I didn't want to worry her, and once I got out of the hospital, it didn't really seem like something I could put in a letter, somehow. She did say she was sorry not to make it to your wedding, that she's writing you and sending you a present."

"Are you two about to break up?" he asked bluntly.

"Jesus, Al, you do ask some good ones, don't you? I don't know. I just don't know anymore. I don't even know if I care. I haven't even talked to her in four months, just these stupid cards of hers. But there won't be any scenes, if that's what you're worried about. I wouldn't take Jules into that. I really haven't made up my mind one way or another. I just wrote and told Lee that I'd leave a message at the post office by the twenty-third if I decided to come—but if we do, it'd just be for the day, or maybe overnight, depending on the ferry schedule, but then we'd leave and go do something else. Does Jules ski?"

"Better than I do. Which isn't saying much, I admit."

"Maybe we could go to Rainier or Hood, then. If Jani approves."

"I'll talk to her, but I doubt she'll have any problems with it. Do you want the car?"

"I'm going to take the Saab off its blocks. And if driving turns out to be a problem, we'll come home. I'm not going to risk passing out or anything while I'm driving Jules. You know that, Al. I'd never put Jules into danger."

Al talked to Jani, Jani talked to Kate, Kate talked to Al again, and after that, she called the car insurance company, and finally went downstairs to see if she could get the Saab down from its blocks and running.

◆

Half the department seemed to be in the church, from the brass to the foot patrols, contrasting oddly with the ethereal academics Jani had invited. It was an afternoon affair with an informal potluck-style meal afterward in the church hall, when the motley friends rubbed shoulders and piled their rented plates high with dishes ranging from tamale pie and Jell-O salad to spanakopita, vegetarian spring rolls, and hummus.

But the real surprise of the day was not the sweet, honest innocence of the ceremony, nor seeing a SFPD lieutenant talking football with a Chinese professor of mathematics and a black lecturer in women's studies, nor even the quartet of two cops, a graduate student in history, and a technical writer singing dirty rugby songs. The real shock was the newlywed couple's daughter: Jules had a new image. With a vengeance.

Her waist-length braids were gone overnight. In their place stood a cropped black bristle nearly as short as Kate's, with a longer mop on the top held in place with a thick application of gel. Her makeup, though admirably restrained, added five years to her age, and the short jacket, short skirt, and short heels she wore made it equally apparent that this was not a child, but a young woman. Jani could barely bring herself to look at her daughter, merely shooting agonized glances at her from time to time, but Al seemed for the most part amused, even proud, at the transformation. The younger males present were attentive; Jules was aware of them, as well.

When the wine had begun to flow and the conversations flourish, Kate found herself standing next to Al over a platter of barbecued chicken wings. He was looking over to the other side of the room, where Jules in all her self-conscious punk splendor was talking animatedly with her new stepbrother, Sean, a serious, handsome young man a head taller than his father. Kate leaned over to speak in her partner's ear. "Quite a family you've got there, Al."

"Isn't Jules something else? The fledgling takes on her adult plumage. God, I thought Jani was going to die when Jules came home looking like that on Friday. She'll settle down."

"Jules? Or Jani?"

"Both."

The noise in the hall rose higher, and Kate escaped for an hour, to sit in the Saab under the shade of a tree and drift in and out of sleep. When she felt restored, she went back into the hall, to find that an impromptu dance had started up in one corner with a portable tape player. She found a chair in a corner, talked to various colleagues, then Jani, and then Al's daughter, until eventually the tables of food had been reduced to a shambles of scraps and crumbs, the new couple fled out the door, suddenly realizing that they were going to be late for their plane, and the life began to seep out of the party. Jules, flushed with exuberance and reluctant to let go of her triumphal entry into maturity, eventually remembered the shaky state of her guardian and pulled herself away from the nineteen-year-old premed student she was dancing with. Kate drove first to the Cameron apartment so Jules could fetch the bags she had packed earlier and to empty the refrigerator, and then to the house on Russian Hill. They stayed the night in San Francisco, and on Monday morning, they emptied Kate's refrigerator, as well.

After that, the girls were on the road.

ELEVEN

♦

"Oh hell. I don't think I turned off the coffeemaker."

"You did."

"You're sure?"

"Positive. And you locked the back door and turned off the oven and checked that the upstairs toilet wasn't running."

"Thank God for your brain, girl. So, I thought we'd stop in Berkeley on the way. I need a raincoat and there's a good outdoor store there."

"I wonder if they have boots."

"I wasn't going to say anything, but those shoes you're wearing aren't going to do it. Athletic shoes are great for California, but the rest of the world is a little tougher."

"It'll be wet up there, won't it? And we may be in the snow."

"Count on it."

"God, Kate, this is going to be so great. I love snow."

"Let's look at boots, then. Or heavier shoes, anyway.

142

And we'll stop in Sacramento tonight, to get your school project out of the way."

"You sure you don't mind?"

"Not at all. The last time I went to the capitol building was when I was your age. I wonder if it's changed."

◆

"You don't think I should have gotten those heavier boots?"

"These will be much more useful. And they really are waterproof."

"I like your hat."

"At least this one doesn't itch."

◆

"What a boring thing it must be, to be a state legislator."

"One more career option to cross off your list, eh?"

"I'd rather teach kindergarten, or be a garbage collector. Or a cop."

"Thanks a lot."

"No offense."

◆

"Is anything wrong, Jules?"

"No. Not at all. Why?"

"I thought you were going to fall out the window looking at those soldiers, and they weren't even very cute."

"I wasn't looking at them. I mean, I was, but not at them in particular. I was just thinking the other day that I didn't really know any soldiers; I don't know anything about them. When you were growing up, you must have had a lot of friends who went to Vietnam."

"I was a little young. I had a friend whose older brother was killed over there, but that was before I knew her. Why do you ask?"

"I don't know, just curious. Wearing camouflage clothes in a city seems kind of . . . incongruous, I suppose. And having to keep their hair so short, and wear those heavy boots and . . . well, the dog tags."

"Dog tags."

"Yes, the identification tags they wear."

"I know what dog tags are. Why are you so interested in dog tags?"

"I'm not."

"You sound like you are."

"They're just kind of strange, that's all."

"How so?"

"Well, what do they do with them when a soldier dies? And could they be faked? How can you check up to see if the number is real? Do they keep records?"

"Um, yes, they certainly do. The Veterans Administration could tell you about that, although they have to preserve confidentiality. I suppose a set of dog tags could be faked—they're only pieces of metal—although the number would have to be backed up by actual identification—for example, if the vet were trying to apply for benefits. They're not like a driver's license. And as for what they do with them, I've always assumed they send them to the next of kin. Why are you interested?"

"I just am, all right? Can't a person be curious? God, you sound like a cop."

"I am a cop, for heaven's sake."

"Yeah, well, don't act like one all the time, okay?"

"Sorry," Kate said to the back of Jules's head.

◆

"Why did you become a cop, Kate?" This time, they were not in the car, but in a pizza parlor near their motel north of Sacramento.

"I thought I could do some good. And I guess . . . I don't know, I suppose the tight structure of it appealed to me. It does to a lot of the people who join the police. You know where you stand, and who stands with you. At first, anyway; it gets more complicated as time goes on."

"Sounds like a family."

"It is, a bit. Tight-knit and squabbling."

"It's my word for the day."

"What is, *family*?"

"You sound surprised."

"Most of your words for the day are more complicated than that."

"I'm beginning to think that some of the most basic words are the most difficult. You know what *family* comes from? The Latin *famulus*, which means 'servant.' It meant all the relations and servants who lived together under one roof. In my dictionary, it's only the fifth definition that gets around to describing a family as two adults and their kids."

"Really?"

"Yes. Which would make you and Lee and Jon a family. When you're all together, I mean."

"That's a terrifying thought, being related to Jon."

"Ashley Montague says that the mother and child constitute the basic family unit."

"Well, I'm safe, then. You want that last piece?"

"Can I have the pepperoni off the top?"

"Sure."

◆

"Dio's family sounds pretty awful, doesn't it?"

"Has he told you anything about them?"

"Just little things, here and there. It's what he doesn't say that makes me think it was pretty bad."

"You're probably right."

"You must see a lot of that kind of thing."

"Too much."

"Why do parents do that to their kids—ignore them and hurt them and push them out?"

"A lot of them never learned how to be parents. Their own parents abused them, so they never learned the skills, and never had the self-confidence to make their own way."

"Sounds like those experiments on animals, when they take baby monkeys away from their mothers. It's so sad."

"It is. But it doesn't excuse them."

"It explains them."

"To some degree."

"Yes."

◆

"What is your father like?" Jules asked.

"My dad? Oh, he's been dead for ten, eleven years now. He was a good man, honest, hardworking. He ran a store that sold fresh fish and seafood. My grandfather—his father—had a fishing boat out of San Diego, and Dad had all sorts of cousins and uncles who let him have the pick of their catch."

"He sounds . . . well, ordinary."

"He was, I suppose. What they call 'the salt of the earth.'"

"I wonder what that means? I'll have to look it up when I get home." She took out a slim book with a sunflower on the cover and made a note.

"Do you write everything in your diary?" Kate asked.

"I write a lot. My words for the day, things to remember, ideas."

"Not so much daily happenings?"

"Sometimes, if I think they're the kinds of things that will interest me in ten years."

"Ten years, huh?"

"Did you keep a diary?"

"For a while. Just daily things—who did what to whom, tests, teachers. Dull stuff."

"I like keeping a diary. It helps me think about things."

"What kind of things?"

"Just . . . things."

◆

"You want me to put on a tape?" Jules offered.

"Sure."

"You have some great music, but some of these people I've never heard of. Who's Bessie Smith?"

"Old-time blues, real old-time."

"Janis Joplin I know; Al has a couple of her tapes. She's incredible."

"The woman sings straight from her—she sings with feeling."

"What were you going to say?"

"A word your mother wouldn't want me to use. I'm afraid I'm not a good influence on you, Jules."

"I know all the words."

"I'm sure you do. And their derivation from the original Anglo-Saxon, no doubt."

"I'm sorry. I must've been showing off again."

"Showing off? Hell no, I get a kick out of the sorts of things you know."

There was a brief silence as Jules went through a shoe box full of cassettes.

"Do you want k.d. lang or Bessie Smith?"

"Bessie Smith is a little hard on the ears. Put on k.d."

"She's supposed to be gay, isn't she?" Jules slid the tape into the player and adjusted the volume.

"So I heard."

"Did you know you were gay, when you were a kid?"

"No."

"Sorry. Do you mind talking about it?"

"No, not really."

"Meaning you do."

"Meaning I don't. What did you want to know?"

"Just if someone always knows their orientation."

"Some part of you knows from the beginning. Lee knew from the time she was eight or ten. I was in denial for years."

"Until you met Lee?"

"Until long after I met her."

"Did your family think she had made you into a lesbian?"

"Good heavens. How did you guess that?"

"It was in a story I read one time. Actually, being gay or straight seems to be inborn, doesn't it?"

"About the same percentage of the population is born

gay as is born left-handed. Left-handedness used to be seen as a moral flaw, too."

"Are you serious?"

"The word *sinister* refers to the left hand."

"God, you're right."

"And you can force a leftie to write with the right hand, just as you can force a lesbian to act straight. With much the same damage to their psyche."

"Do you think I might be a lesbian?"

"Frankly, no. Do you?"

Jules sighed. "I'm afraid not."

Kate began to laugh. "Being straight is nothing to mourn over, Jules."

"I know, but I always wanted to be left-handed."

◆

"Are you sorry you didn't go to Mexico with your mom and Al?"

"No. Not at all."

"You just seem distracted."

"Tired, I guess. It's been a really busy fall term."

"You're sure that's all?"

"Yes."

◆

"Jules, why did you cut your hair off?"

"I just wanted a change."

"You sure it wasn't out of solidarity with my bald head?"

"No. I think I cut it because my mother didn't want me to." Silence followed this admission. Then she said, "Guess it's kind of a stupid reason."

"Hey, if you can't use that reason when you're thirteen, when can you?"

"Oh well. It'll always grow back."

TWELVE

ANOTHER REST stop on the same freeway, but this one was more of a park than a mere parking lot with toilets, and this time, without Lee, Kate did not have to take the closest possible spot to the block of rest rooms. Instead, she drove past the center of activity, past the RVs and dogs and cranky children, around the van giving free coffee and brochures about the dangers of drunk driving, to pull the Saab into the farthest parking spot. Silence descended. Kate reached back for her jacket, and handed Jules hers.

Outside, on the tarmac, it was cold, but a bleak afternoon sun struggled for an illusion of warmth. Jules walked off to the toilets, and Kate left the parking area to stroll up a small rise of scruffy lawn. There was a river on the other side of the grass, fast and full and gray and cold, although, when she had scrambled cautiously up onto the boulders that formed the banks, Kate could see a lone fisherman downstream near the freeway bridge. She chose a flat rock on the top of the ridge, pulled her hat down over her ears and her coat down as far as she could, and she sat, watching the water go past.

Jules came after a while, stood and looked; then she,

too, sat. Her hand came up to brush at the cropped hair on the back of her head.

"Still feels funny?" Kate asked.

"I'm getting more used to it. I don't feel so . . . naked anymore."

"You sorry you did it?"

"No, I like it. It feels . . . How does it feel? Unprotected. Risky. Daring."

"Freedom is always a risky business," Kate intoned.

"Philosopher cop," Jules jeered. "But I don't think I'd go as far as Sinéad O'Connor. I'd get frostbite of the scalp."

"She probably wears hats a lot, in Ireland."

"I want a hat like yours—a nice warm hat." Jules pulled her collar up around her unprotected ears and pushed her bare hands into her pockets. "I wonder where fishermen get their clothes," she said after a while. "That water must be freezing." They watched the still figure, totally swathed in hat, coat, gloves, and hip waders, standing in the water. The only bits of human being actually showing were the circles of wrinkled skin around his eyes and nose—which were surrounded by the balaclava hat—wisps of white hair straggling from underneath, and the very tips of his fingers. He noticed them watching him, and raised one hand slightly. They waved back at him. "Those are cool gloves," Jules said, the final word accompanied by a shiver. Kate stood up. Her head was clear now, but it was beginning to ache from the cold. She handed Jules the keys.

"You get in the car; I'll just be a minute." Kate walked across the vacant portion of parking lot toward the ugly green cement-block building, where she gingerly eased her bare skin onto the icy toilet seat, washed her hands in water from a glacier, and walked out of the open doorway into an arctic blast and what at first glance appeared to be a tribe of Afghan gypsies with Frisbees. At least twenty college-aged kids, swathed in layers of colorful ethnic garments, had emerged from a resigned-looking bus and were spilling out across the pavement in chattering confusion. Three neon green plastic disks sailed back and forth between gloved hands while sandwiches, plastic food containers, and thermoses were pulled from nylon backpacks. The odors of damp wool, cigarettes, curry, and stale dope hit Kate's frozen nose, and she paused to absorb the spectacle. She had been too young for the first onslaught of the true hippie movement, but each generation of university students seemed to discover it anew. Once, her second year at UC Berkeley, she had taken a trip like this, with half a dozen others to New Mexico during the winter break. . . .

A trio of nearly identical twenty-year-olds pushed unseeing past her, three lithe bodies in boots and jeans and Mexican sweaters, carrying on a high-speed conversation.

"—think they'd have a microwave or something. My uncle has one you can plug into the cigarette lighter—"

"Yeah I mean, cold lentils are pretty gross."

"That sauna we stopped at was pretty cool, though."

"I don't think that bus has a cigarette lighter—"

"Why couldn't they put them in these rest stops? I mean, they have those hand dryers, so why not a microwave?"

"Yeah, like you could put a dime in for thirty seconds—"

"Like for a Tampax or something."

"Why not? It'd be a public serv—Oh God!"

"Oh shit, that's cold!"

"Jesus Christ!"

"Why can't they heat these goddamn toilets?"

"I'd pay a dime for—"

"—Stand up on the seat like they do in—"

"God, I wish I was a man!"

Grinning hugely, Kate tucked her hands under her armpits and walked back to the Saab. Another group of refugees from middle-class America were on the ridge overlooking the river, one of the girls looking like a sheep with a camera. She waved her furry arms to arrange her victims, two boys and a girl wearing a glorious coat, into a pose of buffoonery, and when she was satisfied, she snapped two pictures, took one of the frozen fisherman, and turned to take two or three more of her companions below, arrayed around the sides of the bus. Jules was standing outside the car, shivering and watching the activity with the half-envious interest of a younger generation. Kate shook her head at lost youth, got in behind the wheel, and started the car. They drove off beneath a shower of Frisbees.

The car warmed up rapidly, as did they. Kate's cold-induced headache did not fade, however, and she was torn between the desire for fresh air and the soothing stuffiness of the heaters. Then, when half an hour later Jules suggested they stop for dinner early, her stomach gave a lurch at the thought of food, and her heart sank.

"Well," she said in resignation, aware now that she really was beginning to feel ill, "I had thought we'd make it to Portland tonight."

"That's okay then," Jules said. "I'm not starving."

"No, I mean I don't think we'll make it. I'm afraid we're going to have to stop, anyway."

Through the incipient nausea and the tightening throb of her peripheral vision, Kate saw Jules look at her quickly.

"Your head?"

"I'm afraid so. I haven't had one for nearly a week; I thought they were over. Sorry."

"Oh God, Kate, don't apologize. Just stop."

"I could go on for another hour, I think."

"Why?"

Why indeed?

"We can't just stop. It'll have to be a place for the night, so I can go to bed. I'll be fine in the morning," she lied. She would be shaky and distant tomorrow, but functional.

"There're a couple of motels and restaurants two exits from now—that's what made me mention dinner. The sign said five miles."

"Would that suit you?"

"Sure. I have a book."

"I'm really sorry about this."

"Oh hey, it's a real hardship, stopping at four o'clock instead of seven. Like, major downer, man, I just can't stand it; I'll have to walk to Portland without you."

"Is *downer* back in? I've heard *cool* and even *bummer*, which was out of it by the time I was growing up. *Bad trip* will be revived next." Kate was trying, but it was getting bad fast.

"*Cool* is cool, but *out of it* is out of it," Jules informed her.

"Wouldn't you know?" she said lightly, and in a few minutes, she asked, "Which do you want, Best Western, Motel Six, or TraveLodge?"

"Which one has cable? This one says it does, but that one is farther from the freeway, so it'd be quieter."

"Jules, choose. Now."

"Turn right."

Kate signed the register with unsteady hands, one small and fading part of her carrying on in the onslaught inside her tender skull, arranging cable for Jules's room, arranging meals on the bill, taking the keys, aware of Jules, solicitous and worried at her elbow, practically guiding Kate up the stairs and dumping Kate's bag on the chair.

"Can I do anything for you?"

"Pull the curtains shut, would you? That's better."

"Do you want a doctor or something?"

"Jules, please, I just need to be alone and quiet." She squinted across the room at the girl and saw the fear in her eyes. "Jules, I promise you, I'm okay. It's just a kind of spasm that happens. I've had them before, and I'll probably have them again. They're"—she had to hunt for the word—"temporary. In the morning, I will be fine. Now, you go have some dinner." The lurch of her stomach was almost uncontrollable this time, and she swallowed the rush of saliva in her mouth. "Watch MTV until midnight, and I'll see you tomorrow. Did I give you the car key?"

"Yes. I have it. And should I take your room key, just in case . . . ?"

"I really don't want you to come over, Jules, but if it makes you feel better, take it." And go! she wanted to shriek. Jules either saw the thought or sensed it, because she picked up Kate's room key and went to the door.

"Jules. I'm really sorry."

"Don't worry, Kate. I hope you sleep well."

"G'night." The door started to close, but one last stir of her carrying-on self urged Kate to say, "Jules?" and the girl stuck her head back in. "Don't go anywhere, will you? Other than the restaurant."

"Of course not," the girl said, and closed the door firmly behind her.

Kate took six rapid steps to the toilet, where she was comprehensively sick. Afterward, she washed her face with tender care, brought each shoe up to untie the laces before stepping on the heels to pull them off, and then slid gratefully between the stiff, sterile sheets. And slept and slept.

♦

In the morning when she woke, Jules was missing.

THIRTEEN

It DID not help, being a cop. There was no armor against this, no reserves of professional impersonality to draw from, no protection. If anything, being a cop only intensified the horror, because she knew the dangers all too intimately. Kate had a full portfolio of images to draw from, all the dead and mangled innocents she had seen in her job, feeding into the standard reactions of any adult whose beloved child has disappeared: the rising tide of panic when there was no response next door and no familiar butch haircut in the restaurant, the muttered fury of just what she would do to the child when it turned out to be a false alarm—how could she put Kate through this routine, she who had always seemed so responsible? Why didn't she leave a note, a message? And by God, if she was in the shower all this time, oblivious to the pounding and shouting—The only way to keep from losing it, Kate's only hope against the almost overpowering urge to just to bash her aching skull against the metal post that held up the overhang on the walkway, was to find the armor of Police Officer, buckle it on, and cope.

She tried very hard, but it would not stay in place. "Yes, of course I looked in the restaurant. I looked in all three restaurants," she told the man at the reception desk, a different man from the sharp-eyed Middle Easterner who had been there the night before, though like enough to be a brother or cousin. But stupid. "Nobody saw her since last night. I just want the key. Yes, I know it's on the hook—the man who was on duty yesterday gave it to us—but the girl in that room took it, and I can't find her. Just let me borrow your master key; I'll bring it right back. Oh, surely you can leave the desk for two minutes." The armor slipped, and the elemental and terrified Kate looked out. She leaned forward and snarled into the clerk's face, "I'm a police officer, and I'll have your balls in jail if you don't have that room open in thirty seconds."

It was not until Kate stood in the doorway of the empty room and saw the bed and the three keys on the table—one for the car and two for their rooms—that the cold precision of routine slid into place. The coverlet was wrinkled, the pillows piled against the headboard, a black remote-control device lying to one side: the bed had not been slept in. The television at the foot of the bed was on, showing the menu screen and giving out no sound.

Kate's hands went automatically into her pockets, her ingrained response to avoid contamination of a crime scene. The clerk was peering over her shoulder, but Kate did not move from the doorway. "Go and call the police," she told him, her voice impossibly level. "Tell them there may have been a kidnapping." How can I be saying those words? her brain yammered. I'm the one who answers the call, not the one who makes it.

"There is a telephone just there," the clerk said.

"Call from the office." When he did not move, she snapped, "Sir, now. Please."

He left. She stepped into the room, her eyes darting across every bit of floor and surface. At the door to the bathroom, she took her right hand from her pocket and, using the backs of her fingernails, pushed the door open. The toilet had been used but not flushed (a true child of

California's perpetual drought, Kate thought absently), one glass had been unwrapped, and there was a crumpled hand towel on the fake marble of the sink. Beside the towel lay the new zip bag Jules had bought on the shopping trip in Berkeley, filled with the new cosmetics she had bought in the drugstore in Sacramento, but Kate could see no sign of a toothbrush or hairbrush, and she did not want to disturb the bag to look. Back out in the room, Kate checked the closet: empty, though one hanger had been pulled out from the cluster that was pushed against the end. She felt in her pocket, pulled out a pen, and used it to open the drawers: empty, all of them, but for one that held stationery and a Gideon Bible. She closed the drawers and went out of the room just as the excited clerk came back up the stairs. She put the key that he had given her into her pocket and asked him, "When does your cleaner come?" His face was avid, greedy as a panhandling drug addict, and she had to push down a surge of pure hatred.

"She's down at the other end, downstairs. She works her way up here by about ten or so—another hour at least."

"She mustn't go in. No one can go in there. Tell her."

"But what happened?"

"I don't know. Go back to your desk. And don't go off duty without permission."

"Whose permission? Look, I must be somewhere at noon—" But Kate turned her back on him, and he went off reluctantly to deal with the checking-out guests.

The vehicles of officialdom drifted in one at a time, the local police in a marked car, a curious sheriff's deputy and an equally bored highway patrol officer, on his breakfast break, followed by an unmarked police car. With each of them, she found herself answering familiar questions, could hear herself sounding like every adult she had ever questioned regarding a missing child, panicky and guilty and under thin control. The sense of unreality that always followed one of the bad headaches increased until she felt as if she were taking part in a dream.

At about this point, a middle-aged detective who reminded her of a rural Al Hawkin stopped the series of questions he was asking and looked at her closely.

"Are you all right, Inspector?"

Kate took a deep breath and pinched the bridge of her nose. "No, I'm not all right," she said aggressively. "These goddamn headaches leave me feeling like a zombie."

"Migraines?"

"Not exactly, but close enough. They're the tail end of an injury."

"Car accident?"

"What the hell does it matter?" she snapped, and then immediately said, "Sorry. No, I got hit in the head with a piece of galvanized pipe. Stupid. I was going in after a perp I'd wounded and one of his friends was waiting for me. I forgot to duck. My own damn fault."

As soon as she looked back at him, she knew that she had inadvertently said the right thing. The half-suspicious expression that had dogged his features miraculously cleared, and she could almost see the man recognize her, not as the butch-looking San Francisco cop, one of those affirmative-action females who would fret over a broken fingernail and be unreliable in a tight place, but, rather, as "one of us." A real cop. Oh well, she thought. Anything that helps.

"When did you eat last?" he said abruptly.

"I don't know. I'm not hungry."

He got up and went to the door of her motel room, which had been left open a crack despite the cold.

"Hank, go grab us some sandwiches. You want a beer, glass of wine, something?" he asked Kate, who became dimly aware that it must be closer to noon than morning.

"Alcohol's not a good idea just now. A Coke is fine, or coffee."

The food, she had to admit, had been a good idea.

Reality approached a few steps when the sandwiches had hit her system, and her mind started to work again.

"I'm sorry, what did you say your name was?"

"Hank Randel."

"Hank. What have we got so far?"

A deep, melodious, and sardonic voice cut across any answer Hank Randel might have made. "Sergeant, I'm sure you weren't going to answer that, so I'll save you the embarrassment of having to refuse."

Kate had been a police officer long enough to know the voice of authority when she heard it. She stifled an impulse to stand to attention and instead turned to look at the figure that now filled the doorway.

"Inspector Martinelli," said the man, coming into the room. "Lt. Florey D'Amico." He was a huge man with a quiet voice, and his hand as it shook hers was cautious with its strength. He was a foot taller than Kate and weighed two of her. She felt like a child, or a doll, in front of him as he took off his hat, shook the rain from it, and examined her thoughtfully. "I'm sorry this has happened, Inspector Martinelli. The child, she isn't yours I was told."

"No, she's . . . a sort of goddaughter. A friend. She's my partner's stepdaughter."

"I see. Well, what say we leave these gentlemen to get on with their work and you come back with me to the office."

Kate dug in her heels. She had no standing here to speak of, but she could be an obnoxiously well-informed private citizen, with rights.

"I want to know what you are doing about locating Jules."

He inclined his head to the door in invitation. She thought he was merely ignoring her demand, and she considered fighting him, then decided that she probably could do it better in front of witnesses. She picked up her coat and went to the door she had not been out of in nearly two hours, and when she stepped out onto the walkway, she felt her jaw drop. The motel parking lot was a writhing hive of police activity: a dozen marked cars and as many more distinctively dull sedans, uniformed officers and plainclothesmen in all directions, even a mobile command post in the process of being set up. Civilians were lined up outside half a mile of yellow tape, and she knew were she down there, she would hear the sound of news cameras and shouted questions. Voices from the room Jules had occupied drew her, and she looked in, seeing the final stages of the Crime Scene technicians' activities.

Kate was completely bewildered at the intensity of response to a missing girl. Portland was quieter than San Francisco, granted, but this? There were even television news vans, for God's sake. She looked up into D'Amico's face.

"I don't understand," she said.

"Ah. I wondered. Well, Inspector Martinelli, you obviously did not think of it, but your young friend Jules Cameron is young, slim, and has short dark hair, and as such *(Oh God, Kate thought)* we have to recognize that she fits the profile of victims for *(oh God, no)* the man the press has taken to calling the *(No. Oh, no, no, no)* Snoqualmie Strangler."

When he saw her reaction, D'Amico grabbed her arm and all but lifted her back inside the room, allowing her to drop onto the bed and shoving her head down onto her knees. She had not fainted, did not even cry out, but she sat with her head down and bit the side of her hand so hard, there was blood in her mouth.

It seemed a very long time, but in fact it was less than five minutes before Kate sat upright on the bed. This time she had no questions, merely followed the lieutenant meekly out the door and to his car.

◆

D'Amico's office was warm, light, and surprisingly tidy. The telephones and voices were muted by a glass-topped door. He pointed Kate to a chair, went on down the hallway for a minute, and when he came back, he closed the door and went around the desk to his own chair.

"Tea?"

"I'd rather have coffee."

He scooped up the telephone receiver in one paw and spoke into it. "Two coffees, one cream and sugar."

When it came, Kate drank the sweet mixture obediently.

"Tell me what happened," he said.

She rubbed one hand tiredly across her ridiculously short hair, vaguely aware that she had forgotten to pull on the knit cap before leaving her room. Her head was throbbing again, though so far her stomach had not joined in the revolt. "I don't know what happened. Jules and I checked in to the motel yesterday at about four-thirty, and this morning when I woke up, she wasn't in her room. That's all I know."

"When did you leave San Francisco?"

"We left . . . What's today? Wednesday? We left Monday morning. Stayed Monday night near Sacramento. Jules wanted . . . Jules wanted to . . . Oh God."

"Inspector Martinelli," he said, and his voice, quiet as ever, nonetheless brought her spine straight. "I require your assistance. You will give me a report of your movements since you left San Francisco on Monday morning."

"Sir. Jules's mother and my partner were married on Sunday afternoon. We had made an arrangement that Jules would spend two weeks with me while they were on their honeymoon, and after the wedding she went back with me to my house in San Francisco. We left the house at nine o'clock Monday morning. We stopped in Berkeley to do some shopping, and then about noon we drove north and then east onto highway Eighty. We detoured to Sacramento because Miss . . . because Jules needed to see the capitol building for a school project. We stayed the night at a motel just north of town, got back the next morning onto the I-Five, and continued north. We'd planned on staying the night in Portland, but we

161

didn't quite get that far." She described the trip, the stops, and the meals. About ten minutes after she began, another man came in, a young man in a dark suit with FBI written all over him. She broke off, but he just nodded at D'Amico, pulled up a chair, and waited for her to resume. She made it to the end of the report, and Jules was still missing from her room. Then the questions began.

"Inspector, why did the two of you come here?"

"I wanted . . . My lover is visiting her aunt, in the San Juan Islands." Neither of them reacted to the word *her*. "I haven't seen her since August, and I thought—I'm on sick leave—I'd come up for Christmas."

"And Jules Cameron? Why was she with you?" asked the FBI man.

"Her mother and my partner just got married, on Sunday," Kate repeated patiently. "They're in Mexico on their honeymoon, but Jules didn't want to go with them; she asked to come stay with me instead. I was happy to have the company. She's a good kid. No, she's better than that. She's a lovely human being, very smart, frighteningly smart, and mixed up, and she wanted . . . she likes me." Suddenly the tears came, unexpected and unwelcome in front of these men, but unstoppable. D'Amico put a box of tissues on the desk in front of her, and they waited until she gained control.

"God," she said hoarsely. "How am I going to tell Al?"

"Al is her stepfather? Your partner."

"Al Hawkin."

D'Amico's head came up. "I know Al Hawkin. I thought he was with L.A."

"He was. He transferred to us a couple of years ago."

The FBI man spoke up. "The Eva Vaughn case."

"I remember," D'Amico said. "Were you involved with that one?" He was asking her, and she nodded. "And the Raven Morningstar case, during the summer following?" he added slowly, as recognition and memory came. She nodded again, blew her nose a last time, and sat up to look straight at him, bracing herself. However, he did not comment about her notoriety or the mess that had been made of that latter case, but went back to her partner. "I heard Al Hawkin speak at a conference a few years ago. He's an impressive man. His subject . . . the subject was child abduction," he said in a voice gone suddenly flat.

Kate's mouth twisted into a bitter laugh. "It was his specialty," she said. "Oh God."

FOURTEEN

KATE MET the newlyweds at the airport early the following morning. Beneath their incongruous fresh sunburns and bright holiday clothes, they both looked deathly ill, flabby with exhaustion and grinding terror. Jani seemed unaware of her new husband's arm across her shoulders, unconscious of the coffee stains down the front of her lightweight yellow linen jacket. Her eyes flicked across Kate to fix on the large man at Kate's side. Hawkin spared Kate a longer glance, taking in his partner's equally derelict state in the moments it took to walk from the gate to where she and Lieutenant D'Amico stood waiting. Kate said nothing. Before Al Hawkin could speak, Jani walked straight over to the tall man in authority and looked up into his face.

"Is there any news about my daughter?"

"Nothing yet, ma'am. The search team is assembling now; they'll set out with the dogs again as soon as it gets light. Let's take you to a hotel, get you something to eat, and we can talk. Do you have any luggage?"

"It'll catch up with us later," Hawkin said absently. "They held the plane for us in L.A.; the bags got left behind." Kate could see that he badly wanted to seize

D'Amico and demand every detail and was keeping himself in only because he knew that loss of control would mean loss of time.

"I'm Florey D'Amico," the lieutenant said belatedly, sticking out his hand.

Kate trailed behind the three of them through the quiet airport and to D'Amico's unmarked car outside the baggage-claim area. After a brief hesitation, he put Jani in the front seat, but Al was leaning over the seat, waiting for him as soon as he got behind the wheel.

"What have you got so far?" he asked.

"Your little girl disappeared from her motel room south of here sometime after nine o'clock Tuesday night. We have yet to find anyone who saw anything, though of course we're still tracing half a dozen hotel guests who left before we were called. I should make it clear," he added, peering at Jani to see if she was listening to him, "that we have no evidence of foul play. Nothing to indicate that she did not walk away from her hotel room all by herself."

Jani was looking at him, but she might as well not have heard, for all the impact his words had on her expression. Al Hawkin brushed away the reassurances, if that is what they were meant to be.

"You must have more than that," he said impatiently.

D'Amico looked again at Jani, then turned to look at the traffic behind him before pulling out into the roadway. When the terminal was behind him, he said to Hawkin, his voice heavy with warning, "I think we ought to get you settled first, before we go into the details."

"Jani should hear it, too."

The heavy shoulders in front of Kate shrugged. "If you say so. Okay. As I said, there's nothing real yet aside from the fact that she wasn't in her room when Inspector Martinelli here woke up. She hadn't seen her since they checked in at four-thirty, although the waitress in the coffee shop says that Jules had a hamburger at about six and charged it to the room. The register tag is timed at six-forty-eight, and the waitress says the girl was reading, by herself, and took a long time to eat.

"So far, two people remember seeing her walking back toward her room a little after quarter to seven. She had the book in her hand. One of them commented that she looked cold and was hurrying, because a wind had come up and it was starting to sprinkle. She wasn't wearing a coat.

"We don't have anyone yet who saw her enter her room, but the house log shows she began watching a pay-per-view movie at eight-thirty-five. The family that stayed in the room next to hers isn't sure about anything. They knew the room was occupied because they heard movement and television noises from time to time, but they have two kids, and it wasn't until they got the kids settled at nine that their own room went quiet. They then heard nothing but the TV from Jules's room until they turned off the lights and went to sleep at about ten-thirty. The wife did hear voices sometime later. She thought before midnight, but she didn't look at the clock, and she couldn't tell where they were coming from. Could have been the parking lot or the hallway or the room on the other side.

"You have anything to add yet, Kate?"

"Just that I was sleeping so soundly that I probably wouldn't have heard voices unless they were pretty loud. I had taken a pain pill," she added. Jani said nothing, but Al looked at her. "My head was bothering me," she said. "That's why we stopped so early in the first place. I didn't think it was safe to drive."

"So you abandoned her instead," Jani said from the front seat, her voice thick with loathing and her jaw clenched.

"I—" Kate started, but Al reached forward with his right hand and placed it on his wife's shoulder.

"Jani, no," he said. After a minute, he looked at Kate, and she resumed.

"I didn't hear anything from Jules's room. In the morning when I tried to wake her up, at about eight-thirty, I couldn't get an answer, so I got the key from the desk and we opened her door. She'd been there, had a glass of water, sat on the bed for a while watching the TV. Her room key was there, along with the keys I'd given her to the car and to my room, but some of her stuff was gone: her jacket, the book she was reading, her diary, her pen, and some of her bathroom things. Her toothbrush and hairbrush were missing from the zip bag. Her makeup was still there."

"Jules doesn't wear makeup," Jani interrupted, her voice dripping scorn. "She borrowed some of mine for the wedding."

Kate looked at Hawkin. "Er, she doesn't exactly wear it, no. But she does experiment with it sometimes," she told the mother in the front seat.

"She didn't before she got to know you."

Kate looked helplessly at her partner, who offered her an infinitesimal shrug.

"That's all. Except for the boots. Her new boots were missing."

"She doesn't own any boots, and certainly not new ones." Jani again. "Al, this is ridiculous." She spoke over her shoulder, still looking only at the windshield. She can't bear to look at me, thought Kate, who became aware of a tiny spark of wholly inappropriate and utterly inexpressible anger.

"She does own a pair of boots," Kate said quietly. "A pair of waterproof Timberland hiking boots she said she's been wanting for a long time."

"Jules wouldn't want a pair of boots."

"I was with her. We bought them on Monday, in Berkeley. In fact, I put them on my credit card," Kate said baldly. Silence fell in the car, and Kate knew that it was all Jani could do not to insist that Kate be put out of the car, right there on the freeway.

"Was she wearing them during the day?" D'Amico asked unexpectedly.

"Yes."

"Well, she took them off at eight-thirty."

His three passengers gaped at him, astonished at this obscure bit of knowledge.

"We're not sure about it, of course, but it looks as if she was lying on the bed, watching her movie, and she must have kicked them off, one after the other, over the side of the bed. We found some chunks of dried mud in the carpeting from a sole with a deep tread," he explained. "And the guy downstairs was turning on his television when he heard two thuds from overhead, about thirty seconds apart. He said they sounded like shoes dropping." He shot Hawkin a glance over his shoulder. "You can see that we were interested in the mud and in the noises, but I'd say it's pretty certain they're connected. Besides, he heard her moving around a while later. Unfortunately, he went to sleep early."

"So that's it?" Hawkin asked him. "That's all you have?"

"So far. They're still running prints, and as I said, the search parties will be out again in a little while."

"They found nothing yesterday?"

"Not a thing. But the dogs didn't get here until the afternoon, so they had only a couple of hours."

"You haven't received a note?"

The brief hesitation before D'Amico answered said a great deal about the chances that she was being held for ransom. "No." That Al had even asked, his expression said, was a surprise; but then the Al who had asked was not the investigator; it was the father.

◆

What followed in the ensuing days seemed to Kate like a cross between being inside a tumble dryer and being shot from a cannon. Because she had no standing here in Oregon, she could take on none of the usual roles of questioning or directing or even acting as liaison with the unofficial volunteers. Still less could she talk with the press, which had seized on her familiar name with the glee of a pack of hounds and came howling to life whenever her face crossed their cameras.

She ended up collating, filing, and answering the telephone, performing her tasks with a grim ferocity, aching to do more and constantly aware of things going on just outside her sight and hearing. She saw Al a few times, Jani twice, looking so pale that her brown skin seemed as translucent as a lamp shade.

On Friday night, Kate caught at D'Amico's arm as he went past her. He looked at her as if he had never seen her before.

"You've got to give me something to do," she said, in what she had intended to be a demand but that came out a plea. "I'm going crazy here."

After a minute, he asked, "You have waterproof clothes?"

"I can get some."

He took a pen from his pocket and leaned over the desk, wrote a few words, and handed her the paper.

"Tomorrow morning, they start at first light. Go past the motel about half a mile. Give that to the man in charge. And get a jacket with a hood. They might not spot you quite so quickly." He walked away before she could thank him. Kate abandoned her filing and went to buy herself clothes to scramble over hills in. She did not think for a moment that they would find Jules anywhere near the motel, but it was better than sitting inside under the headache-inducing fluorescent lights.

Kate had already been forced to rent an anonymous small car when word got out among the press that she was driving a Saab convertible—a car that stood out in rainy Portland. She had gritted her teeth over the cost, and she winced when she saw the price tag on the jacket, a parka combining the most modern materials with traditional goose down, but the monetary penance seemed appropriate, and at least she would not collapse because of cold and wet.

And cold and wet it was, beating the bush, working on an ever-widening circle out from the motel, covering her assigned segment before staggering back to swallow hot drink and food, not even able to indulge in the luxury of camaraderie with the other exhausted searchers lest she be recognized, then zipping her coat again and going back out into the miserable afternoon. The rain turned into a dispirited sleet before dark. One of the search dogs slid into a frigid stream and was taken away for a rest. A volunteer cracked his head open against a branch; another took his place. Half-frozen mud glued itself to the outside of Kate's new boots; inside, blisters formed on her feet despite doubled socks. Her knees ached, her hands were raw, one cheekbone was black and blue from an incautiously released branch, and the left sleeve of her expensive parka bore an already-fraying patch of duct tape to keep the feathers from drifting out of the rip it had suffered at some point.

The next day was Christmas. During their breaks, the searchers ate turkey and pie until they could burst, but they found no sign of Jules.

On Kate's third day, the search parties split in two and shifted their centers of operations east and west of either side of the freeway. Kate went with the easterly party, farther up into the foothills. They found articles of clothing by the bushel, skeletons of various animals, and a few fresh animal corpses. One of those last caused a great convulsion of fear and excitement among the searchers, until it was determined to be the flayed remains of a deer, stretched out by scavengers among the dead leaves. The search went on.

Dogs and helicopters and human eyes traversed the hills in the filthy weather. Searchers faltered and dropped out, some of their places going unfilled now, six days after Jules had disappeared. Gray hopelessness was in all their minds. Everyone knew they were not going to find her, and the knowledge made the physical strain nearly unbearable, until only the habit of determination kept them at it, step by step, one tree, one boulder, one stream at a time.

After nine days, beneath a low sky dribbling wet snow, the search was called off. Had it been likely that Jules had simply wandered away, the search would have continued, but the chances of this were minuscule. Some-one had taken her, and despite the total lack of evidence, people from one side of the country to the other knew who that someone was, if not his actual identity.

There were news cameras at the center of operations to record the closing down of the hunt, and Kate in her exhaustion failed to dodge them. One minute she was trudging through the mire of the field turned parking lot, exchanging a few clichéd but deeply felt phrases with two fellow searchers, a young brother and sister who had driven three hundred miles from eastern Washington to join the hunt. The next minute, a shout went up, and before she could make her escape, she had the pack on her heels, with shouts of "Inspector Martinelli!" and "How do you feel about the search being called off, Kate?" and "What will you do now?" being hurled at her from these strangers. She pulled her hood back up over her face, put her head down, and pushed her way through the microphones and pocket tape recorders to her ordi-nary-looking rental car. She had unlocked the door when a gloved hand came into her line of vision, covering the handle.

"Get your hand off this car," she said in a low voice, not looking up. The hand drew back quickly, and she begun to pull the door open against the weight of the people standing against it before her mind registered the question that she had been asked. She looked up into his expensive newscaster's face, and despite his superior height and her complete dishevelment, what he saw in her eyes made him step back onto his camerman's toes. "What was that?" she asked him.

"I said, Do you know where Jules Cameron is?"

Two years before, in another lifetime, Kate might have responded, might have given way to incredulity and fury, might even have attacked him. She had been through the wars since then, though, and by now not responding to the media was as automatic as breathing. She tore her gaze from his, shoved the filthy door back against their immaculate coats, and fell into the car. They continued to shout questions at her as she started the engine and put the car into gear; then they fell silent, looks of eager astonishment on their faces when she braked suddenly and rolled down the window. They surged forward, and she waited until they were beside her before she spoke.

Then clearly, for the benefit of their recording devices, she said, "For the record, no, I do not know where Jules Cameron is." She hesitated for an instant before adding, "I wish to God I did."

Rolling up the window, she drove off, reflecting that at least "Inspector Martinelli said she did not know where the girl is" sounded slightly better than "Inspector Martinelli refused to comment." Some of them might even relent and include her final phrase. Beyond that thought, her mind refused to look.

It was difficult driving while wearing slippery over-sized boots and bulky ski mittens, so before she reached the freeway, she pulled over to strip off various garments and lace on her lighter shoes. Had she not stopped, she would probably not have noticed the olive green car until it pulled up beside her in front of her motel, but in the mirror she saw it brake for an instant before accelerating past her, and when she saw the driver hide his face by lifting an arm as he went by, she knew that some enterprising reporter had decided to tail her. Too bad I didn't think of it earlier, she reflected grimly as she pulled off the gloves and bent down to the soggy laces. I could have led them off like the Pied Piper and given the other searchers a chance to get away. As it is, the search teams are in for a round of Kate Martinelli questions. Casting a mental apology over her shoulder, she struggled out of her boots and drove off in her stocking feet, too tired to bother with other shoes.

With a depressing sense of inevitability, she saw the green car in her mirror, pulling out of a dirt road behind her, keeping well back. It took her half an hour and several illegalities before the reporter's nerve broke and she lost him, but the effort cost her the last shreds of her energy. When she pulled up in front of the hotel, she was

172

trembling with fatigue and her head was throbbing along the line where the pipe had hit her skull. She retrieved her shoes, abandoning the wet boots and gloves, and dropped the car keys twice—once when she pulled them from the car-door lock, then again when she was digging in her jeans pocket for the key to her room—before she made it to the safety of her room. She let her shoes fall to the floor, fumbled with the bolt and the chain until they were fastened, and walked blindly across the sterile room to the bathroom. She went inside, then came back out to look across the room with dull incredulity at the still figure standing near the window.

"Lee?"

FIFTEEN

"HELLO, KATE," Lee said in a small voice. "You look . . . Oh God, Kate. You didn't find her?"

Kate didn't bother to answer, just stood, trying to absorb the sight of the woman standing beside the chipped veneer table, dressed in a flannel shirt, a puffy down vest, khaki trousers, and hiking boots. Her hair was down to her shoulders now, longer than it had been even in university days, and the arm cuffs of her aluminum arm braces had been covered with a solid band of Indian beadwork, a bright, complex pattern that drew Kate's eyes; they were easier to look at than Lee's face. Lee said something. Kate blinked, shrugged off her heavy parka, and tossed it in the direction of the bed, where it fell slowly to the floor.

"Sorry, I have to . . ." She knew she sounded idiotic, but she could not help it, and so she turned and went back into the bathroom. The toilet flushed, and when she came out again, Lee had not moved.

"I'm sorry," Kate repeated. "I don't seem to be working at top speed. What did you say?"

"Nothing that can't keep. You should have a hot bath and something to eat."

Kate made an effort to rouse herself.

"Sounds heavenly."

"I'll start the bath running." Lee moved then, using the arm braces to steady herself rather than throwing her entire weight on them. Lee was walking, actually walking, not hobbling anymore, moving easily around the end of the bed and past Kate, an arm's reach from her, then going into the bathroom. Kate heard the water start and sat down on the overly soft mattress. She thought about reaching for the phone and checking in with D'Amico, thought about lifting her foot up and peeling off the sodden, filthy socks, thought about Lee actually walking, and then she turned and lay down on the nylon bedspread. Kate was asleep before Lee came out of the bathroom to ask her about room service.

◆

Fourteen hours later, the telephone woke Kate. Lee already had it and was speaking into the receiver in a low voice.

"She's still asleep. Do you think I—"

"I'll take it," Kate said. She put out a hand and said into the phone, "Martinelli here."

"Kate, Al." She sat up sharply on the bed.

"Is there—"

"No news," he was already saying. "Not about Jules. I need to talk to you. I'm coming over."

"What is it? Something's wrong."

"Not on the phone. I'll be there in twenty minutes."

When she had hung up, Kate realized that she was wearing little but her knit cap and her corduroy shirt, which looked clean but stank of old sweat. She wondered how on earth Lee had managed to maneuver her wet jeans and socks off without waking her.

"You were out cold," Lee said, having read her face, or her mind. "The phone rang an hour ago, and you never twitched. Feel better?"

"I feel filthy. Al's coming over. I'd better have a shower first."

"Your clothes are unwearable. Better take something of mine. And don't tell me they won't fit, because they will. Just roll up the cuffs." Kate had her doubts, but it was true, laundry had been fairly low on her priorities the last few days, and her own clothes were so stale as to be offensive. And to her surprise, when she pulled on the jeans after her long and blessed shower, she found that they did indeed fit. The mirror told her the half of it, and a survey of Lee the remainder.

"You've put on weight," she said, sitting on the bed and pulling on a pair of Lee's socks. "It looks good."

"And you've lost some. Rosalyn told me you had a new image, sort of punk, she said. Actually, I think it's more a tough-guy look than punk, with that hat."

"Marlon Brando. Wait'll you see me in my tight T-shirt with the pack of cigarettes tucked in the sleeve. When did you talk to Rosalyn?"

"She wrote me a while back."

"I see. Did she tell you anything else about me?"

"Such as what?"

"Anything. Recently."

"Not recently. And really, it was only a passing mention, a month or so ago. I think she said you'd been there for Thanksgiving dinner."

"I was, yes. We had a good time."

"Did Maj cook?"

"Of course."

"I'm sorry I wasn't . . . Kate, it's . . . I'm so . . . Oh shit," said this woman who rarely swore. "Would you come over here? Please."

Except for the palm of her hand, and a couple of cheek-pecking hugs, Kate's body had not been in voluntary physical contact with another person for four months. It was awkward at first, no denying that. Too much had happened, and too many questions lay unanswered for it to be easy. However, there was no denying that touch, even with a woman Kate had cursed and resented and wanted to do violence to more than once over the past months, was a good and glorious thing. The fa-

176

miliarity of Lee's body slid past her defenses, and she was beginning to relax into the curves and angles when footsteps sounded in the hall outside, followed by a sharp rap at the door.

Flustered, she pulled back, then shot out an arm when Lee swayed insecurely. She steadied her, picked the arm braces off the floor and gave them to Lee, then went to let her partner in.

He came in, his eyes sliding past her to Lee. His tired face lit up.

"Lee! Woman, it's great to see you." He took three steps and enveloped her in a hug of his own, so that when Kate turned back from closing the door, all she could see of Lee was a pair of hands emerging from behind a plaid wool coat. She picked the braces up from the floor again, then waited until Al stepped back, his hand firmly on Lee's elbow until she had her arms in the beaded cuffs.

"You're looking great, Lee. The woods agree with you."

She acknowledged his remark with a nod, but her thoughts were all on him. She put her hand out and touched his arm. "Al, I was devastated when I heard. Is there anything I can do? Can I help Jani?"

"I don't know. Maybe. Can I let you know?"

"Of course. Kate said—"

Lee was interrupted by another knock at the door. Kate answered it and found a young woman in the uniform of the café next to the hotel. She was carrying two large brown bags.

"You ordered breakfast?"

"Did we order breakfast, Lee?"

"Yes."

"Come on in," she said. "I didn't know you delivered."

"We don't," said the young woman laconically, dropping the bags on the small table and pocketing the money Lee held out. An expensive breakfast, thought Kate, closing the door.

Lee had ordered for Al as well, eggs and bacon and

toast, only slightly leathery from the delay. Al took off his heavy coat and sat on the bed, Lee and Kate took the chairs, and they were silent until the food was nearly gone. Lee looked up first from her Styrofoam plate.

"I assume that if there had been any change, you'd have said something."

"No change. No sign whatsoever."

"There was a rumor yesterday at the search site," Kate said. "Someone may have seen a car?"

"D'Amico thought he'd found someone who saw a pickup with two people in it enter the freeway from the motel ramp just after midnight, the passenger small like Jules, but it's so vague as to be useless. Light-colored, full-sized pickup, it could have been from anywhere other than the motel. By the time the FBI finished questioning him, he wasn't even sure it was this exit."

"She vanished into thin air," Lee said quietly.

"Not under her own power she didn't."

"You're certain of that?"

"The dogs traced her to the back of the motel, period. She got into a car and was driven off."

"Got, or was put. Would the dogs have been able to track her if she'd been carried around the motel rather than walked there?"

"The handlers said yes, but that the animals wouldn't have seemed as confident as they did, if she'd been carried."

"And this killer, the Strangler. Could it be—I'm sorry, Al. You don't want to go over it all again."

Actually, Kate thought, he had seemed more comfortable now than when he had first appeared at the door.

"Lee, you couldn't possibly make it worse than it already is. Yes, it could be the serial killer who's working up here. Jules fits the physical description of his victims. He always takes them from near freeways, and there's no doubt he's moved south from where he first began."

"But?"

"The 'buts' are very thin. This guy normally kills immediately, takes his girls away, and lays them out ritually

178

in a place they're sure to be found within a few days. Always within a twenty-mile radius of where they disappeared. And then a few days later, some police station in the area will receive an envelope with five twenty-dollar bills in it. The first one, two years ago, had a typed note saying it was for burial expenses, but since then it's just been the money. And that, by the way, is a tight secret. You're not to speak of any of this to anyone. You, too, Kate. The FBI would string me up if they knew I'd told you two."

"Of course."

"Anyway, no note, no money, they haven't found her—" His forced attitude of detached professionalism slipped, and he choked on the word *body*. He cleared his throat and started again. "There are also indications that she left the motel, if not deliberately, then at least under her own power. Mostly the things that are missing—her shoes and coat she'd have taken even for a short trip out of doors, but probably not her hairbrush, and certainly not her toothbrush and her diary."

What is your word for the day, Jules? Kate wondered, and was hit by a wave of the grief and guilt that had dogged her every moment of the last ten days. To push it away, she shifted in her chair and asked, "You don't think she went off on her own, though?"

"No. She'd have left a note. I think someone took her, and I think he had a weapon, because there was no sign of a struggle and I know Jules would've raised bloody hell unless she had a damned good reason not to."

"How did he get inside her room, or get her to come out?" Lee wondered.

"I don't know."

"What is it, Al?" Kate asked. "You had a reason for coming over here."

His right hand went spontaneously to the pocket in his shirt, and Kate did not need the look of embarrassment on his face to know that it was time to brace herself. Hawkin had been a smoker when she first met him, and she had quickly come to be wary of what that gesture meant.

His hand fell away before reaching the empty pocket, and he raised his face and looked straight at her for the first time.

"I want you to go back to San Francisco."

Until that moment, Kate had managed to forget the question that had been asked at the door of her mud-spattered car the evening before. It had not been difficult to push it away, given the burden of extreme exhaustion, followed by the shock of Lee's appearance and then the heaviest sleep she'd had in weeks, but suddenly all she could see was the knowing look of accusation in the broadcaster's face and the shape of his leather glove spread out against the handle of the car. She waited, and although it was Lee who asked him why, he answered as if Kate had spoken.

"A whole lot of reasons. You need to see your doctor. There're at least three cases pending that one of us needs to work on. And—"

"Pardon me," Lee said. "Doctor? Kate? Have I missed something here?"

"She hasn't told you why she's not at work?" Al asked.

"No," she said slowly. "Somehow it hasn't come up yet."

"It's nothing, Lee," Kate said. "I got hit on the head, and until the headache goes away, I'm on medical leave."

Al Hawkin kept his mouth firmly shut at this vast understatement. Lee looked at him, but he gave nothing away. Finally, she struggled to her feet, picked her way over to where Kate sat, and reached out to pull off Kate's hat. Four weeks of hair did little to cover the scar, and she grunted in pain at the sight.

Kate picked the cap out of Lee's hand and pulled it back over her scalp, ignoring her. "Don't lie to me, Al. What is it?"

"I don't know how to say this."

"Jani wants me gone."

"That's part of it."

"And there's talk."

Hawkin exhaled. "Shit. You heard."

"I haven't heard anything, except one of the most offensive questions I've ever been asked by a newsman."

"Yes, that would be where it'd surface. That's undoubtedly where it started."

Lee said in a plaintive voice, "I'm really sorry, but I'm not following any of this conversation."

"Sweetheart, you'd have been better off staying put with your aunt Agatha. Maybe *I* should go and stay with your aunt Agatha. I was asked yesterday if I knew where Jules was."

"Why would you— Oh. Oh God, Kate, he couldn't have meant . . . Al?"

He stood up and went over to the window, his hand patting the front of his shirt again before he remembered and thrust both hands into his pants pockets instead. His voice was harsh, painfully so, when he began to push the words out. "I should have known it was coming. I should've gotten you out of here earlier. I mean, of course you're going to be a target. Even before, you would've been, but now, when half of San Francisco knows about the leathers and the bike, you're meat to their gravy. And Jules taking after you, that haircut she got, and the two of you riding around town on the motorcycle."

Lee positively radiated bewilderment, but neither Kate nor Al could spare her a thought.

"Al, does Jani think—"

"Jani's not thinking at the moment, but no, not really."

Which meant that she did indeed think something like that, or at least have her doubts.

"And D'Amico?"

"Florey doesn't listen to gossip. Besides, if he thought there was the least chance, he'd've had you down answering questions."

"And what—"

He whirled around, looking very large and extremely angry. "Martinelli, if you ask me whether I believe those filthy rumors, I swear I'll throw something at you."

Kate took what seemed like the first breath in minutes and felt her eyes tingle with relief.

"Thank you, Al."

"But when you get home, I'd leave that leather outfit in the closet for a while, and drive something with four wheels."

"Okay."

"You'll go?" He could not hide his astonishment.

"I don't have any choice. I'm not doing any good here, and if I stay, it'll only make things worse for everyone. It's already enough of a circus." Maybe I can do my Pied Piper act now, she thought bitterly, drag all the reporters back to San Francisco.

"I don't like it," he said unexpectedly.

"Al, she's your wife. And Jules . . . Jules is your daughter. But you've got to promise me, if there's anything I can do, you'll call."

"I'll call anyway. Look, I've got to go. I'm late for a meeting with the FBI; they've got a profile to go over."

"Another one?"

"Yeah. As if it does us one bit of good to know that there's a seventy percent chance he wet his bed as a kid and an eighty percent chance his parents were divorced."

"I'm glad they're keeping you in on it, Al."

"I had to call in a lot of favors," he admitted, and it dawned on Kate that one of the conditions they had made was her departure from the scene.

"Take care of yourself. And Jani," she said.

"You'll drive back?"

"I'll leave tonight."

"Watch the snow on the passes." He walked over to kiss Lee on the cheek, nodded to his partner, and went out. The door clicked, his steps faded.

"That was generous of you, Kate," Lee said.

Kate was on her feet. "Shut up!" she screamed. "For Christ's sake, just shut up!" She caught up a glass from the table, turned, and threw it with all her strength across the room, straight at the mirror above the cheap chest of drawers, then flung herself out the door.

Downstairs, panting, she told the startled desk clerk, "I'm leaving. Get my bill together. And you'll have to add something for a broken mirror."

◆

JANUARY

◆

SIXTEEN

IT WAS a long and mostly silent drive to San Francisco. They stayed the night in Ashland, waiting for the snow-plows to clear the road ahead of them, and it was an equally long and silent night. Kate seemed uninterested in how Lee had come to appear out of nowhere, seemed only half aware of her explanation of seeing a week-old newspaper on a trip into town for supplies. She could not rouse herself to give Lee anything but the most perfunc-tory account of her injury and the shooting of Weldon Reynolds, which simply seemed too far away to be of concern to anyone.

Eventually, Lee recognized the symptoms, and she forced herself to draw back. Kate was not still angry; she wasn't even sulking. She was merely hungover from the excesses of emotion, burnt-out and drained in every way, and fortunately Lee had the sense, and the experience, to see that Kate merely needed solitude, or as close to it as she would get with a passenger in the car. Lee wrapped herself in patience, biding her time, and allowed the miles to pass while she waited, with growing apprehension, for Kate to make the first overture.

The closer they drew to the city, the worse the traffic

grew, until halfway across the eastern segment of the Bay Bridge they came to a halt. Kate stirred, looked in the rearview mirror, and spoke for the first time in two hours. "What the hell is going on? Traffic should be dying down, not getting worse. What day is this, anyway?"

"I think it's Saturday."

Kate grumbled and threw occasional complaints at the grateful and relieved therapist at her side, who worked hard to preserve a detached air and paid no attention to the roadways outside until, once they were back on the ground and nearing the city center, a rapid movement came spilling in front of them. Kate slammed on the brakes, cursed, and laid on the horn simultaneously; at the same moment Lee began to laugh.

"What?" Kate demanded. "The whole goddamn city's gone nuts, and you're laughing?"

"Sweetheart, we're the ones who are nuts. Look at what they're wearing. This is New Year's Eve."

Kate leaned forward to examine the costumes, an equal number of men in diapers and in bedsheets, all of them carrying various noisemakers.

"Thank God," she said. "I thought the place had gone off the deep end for sure."

On Russian Hill, every house was lit up, including their own, which would have surprised Kate except that she had spotted Jon's car down the hill. She eased the Saab in between a convertible Mercedes and a Citroën DCV, coasted into the garage, and hit the button to shut the door behind them. Jon was already on the stairs. His skin looked brown even under the fluorescent lights of the garage, and he was wearing an apron and carrying a wooden spoon in one hand and a pot holder in the other.

He was at the passenger door before Kate had the key out of the ignition. "Lee! Oh my God, girl, look at you. You look like a woodsman; all you need is your ax. Where's your— Will you look at those. Have you taken up beadwork in your old age, my dear? Oh yes, give us a hug." Kate smiled at the sight of her two housemates pounding each other's backs (Jon holding the beaded arm braces now as well as the cooking utensils) before she went around to open the trunk and begin the process of unloading. When her head emerged, Jon was holding Lee at arm's length, still exclaiming. "I love the macha look; it reminds me of the seventies. Do you need a hand here? My God, she's walking. Look at her, Kate; it's a miracle of the blessed Jesus. We'll go dancing next week—can I have a date, dear? How superbly retro, dancing with a woman. God, you look great. You're glowing. Isn't she positively glowing, Kate? Hello, Kate, darlin', you look tired." Kate could see him hesitate, consider words of sympathy and expressions of horror, and then decide that this was not the time—for which she was grateful.

"Hello, Jon," she said, sidling past them with her arms full of bags and packs. "It's good to see you."

♦

The next day was Sunday, but Kate managed to track down the surgeon who had pieced her head together. He was at the hospital checking up on a trio of drunk-driving injuries from the evening before and agreed to see her.

When she saw him, their conversation consisted of "Does that hurt?" (No.) "What about that?" (Yes.) and "Any fevers or headaches?" (No, and Not for ten days.) With a warning to avoid hard things with her skull for a while, he scrawled a note allowing her back on limited duty. She took it, and broke out in a cold sweat.

She walked back to the car, unaware that she was getting rained on, and drove out of the parking garage, fully intending to go home. Somehow or other, she didn't get there. Instead, she drove out to the coast highway and parked, watching the waves pound furiously at the shore. The car shook with the gusts of wind, and the windshield became opaque with spray. After a while, she got out and walked into the maelstrom.

An hour later, face scoured raw and her entire body feeling cleansed, she unlocked the door and got back in. As she drove home, she tried not to think about Monday. Monday, when she would go back to work, to find that the storm of publicity and the lightning strikes of filthy rumors had moved south, directly into the Hall of Justice. How many obscene notes would be waiting for her? How many photographs confiscated from the collections of pederasts would find their way into her papers, appear on the walls of the toilet cubicles? How many disgusting objects could her colleagues come up with to torment a lesbian rumored to know more than she was telling about the disappearance of a child?

Kate did not know if she could summon the strength to cope with another campaign of whispers. She actually hoped, prayed, for a relapse, a headache powerful enough to justify her absence. However, Monday dawned with nothing worse inside her skull than the muzziness of a sleepless night. She put on her holster, feeling weary to her bones and cold with dread, and went to work.

♦

Kate's finger hovered over the DOOR CLOSE button on the elevator, but it did not actually make contact, and the door slid open at the fourth floor. She stepped out and walked down the hall to the Homicide Department. Inevitably, the first person she saw was Sammy Calvo, who could be offensive even when he was trying to be friendly. She braced herself, and he looked up from his desk and smiled at her.

"Casey! Hey, great, glad you're back. It's been really dull around here without you."

"Er, thanks. I guess."

The phone in front of him rang, cutting short any further, more devastating phrases. Kitagawa appeared next, his nose in a file until he was almost on top of her.

"Morning, Kate. How's the head?"

"Doing better, thanks."

"You still on leave?"

"I'm on a limited medical for the next three or four weeks."

"Right. When you get a chance, let's go over the cases you were working."

"Sure. I mean, fine." He put his nose back into the file and went out. However, his attitude meant nothing, Kate told herself. Kitagawa would have been polite to Jack the Ripper.

Tom Boyle caught her as she was stowing her gun and her lunch in a desk drawer.

"Hi, Kate, how you feeling?"

"Fine, Tommy boy. How was Christmas?" she ventured.

"Nuts, as usual. My brother-in-law broke his wrist playing kick the can in the street after dinner, and Jenny's grandmother cracked her dentures on a walnut shell in the fruitcake. How was yours?" He seemed to catch himself, and looked uncomfortable. "Oh, right. I don't suppose you had one, really."

"No, I didn't," she agreed.

"I think we'll go away next year, just Jenny and the kids and me. Disneyland or something. How's Al doing?"

"He's hanging in there."

"Yeah. Not much else he can do, is there? Well, I gotta go. See you."

Something was very odd here. Everyone was entirely too friendly. The messages on her desk, when she sorted through them, not only contained nothing filthy, but there were two generic greetings and a casual invitation to lunch from another detective, a woman Kate had worked with on a vice case some months before. Finally, when it began to seem that every person in the building—uniform, plainclothes, and support staff alike—was finding some reason to pass by her desk and say hello, she went to hunt down Kitagawa. She cornered him outside the interrogation rooms, ushered him inside one, and shut the door behind her.

"All right. What's up?"

"Ah, Kate. Is this a good time to—"

"I want to know why everyone is so goddamned cheerful around here. Everyone in the building knows that I'm fine, Lee's fine, Jon is just dandy, and Al's as

191

well as can be expected. Not one person has mentioned that Jules is still missing. Why the hell not?"

"They are probably aware that the subject causes you discomfort."

"Since when do my feelings—" She stopped. "Al. Al had something to do with this."

"He made a couple of phone calls, yes, to let us know that you might be back."

"What else did he tell you?"

Kitagawa squinted down at the form in his hand, although as far as Kate knew, he'd never had anything but perfect sight.

"You know," he said in pedantic tones, "the police, perhaps more so than other people, do not care for outsiders tormenting one of their own. Even when that member has not fit in terribly well before, if another group who is perceived as 'the enemy' begins pursuit, we have an extraordinary urge to close ranks around our threatened member."

Kate stared at him, openmouthed.

"An interesting insight into group dynamics, don't you think? Although you, with your background in sociology, would know all about it." He smiled, then reached past her to open the door, leaving her standing there.

When Kate went home that night, she told Lee about the conversation, and about a day surrounded by the gruff support of her colleagues.

"God," said Lee. "I couldn't think what was worrying you. I didn't even think of that. You must feel relieved."

"Relieved? I feel like I'd just heard the sirens start up in response to an 'officer down' call."

That night, for the first time since late August, Kate slept in the main bedroom.

For three and a half days after that, Kate succeeded in enduring the unremitting friendliness of the San Francisco Police Department. Then on Friday, in the late morning, there was a telephone call for her.

It was Al. He said, "We've had a letter."

SEVENTEEN

"YOU'RE NOT to know," Al said quickly. "Don't react to what I say. If the FBI or D'Amico find out I've been talking to you, they'll shut me out completely."

"I'm . . . glad you've had good weather." She smiled stiffly at Tom Boyle, standing next to her desk, and willed him to move away.

"There's someone near you. Okay, just listen. We had a letter, just a brief one, claiming to be from the Strangler. He said Jules wasn't one of his." Something of Kate's psychic message must have gotten through to Boyle, because he moved away.

"Surely you must be getting a hundred letters a day, saying all kinds of things," she protested in a low voice.

"He gave some details it would be difficult to know, unless he's got access to FBI records."

"My God," Kate whispered, trying with difficulty to keep her face straight. "Have you seen it? The letter?"

"A copy of it."

"And?"

"It's an identical typewriter to the original burial letter. And it has the right flavor. Indignant that he would be credited—his word—with a kill he didn't do. Plus that, it was mailed in the same way he sends the funeral money, to an apparently random name with the address of the police station, so it doesn't catch the attention of the post office until it reaches the local branch."

"Did it say anything else?"

"It said, I quote, 'I don't know why you're trying to credit me with the missing California girl. Asian girls don't have any curl in their hair.' The Strangler always takes a snip of hair from the back of the head, and there's never been a breath in any of the reports about it. So watch yourself with that knowledge, too."

"What's the reaction up there?"

"It's got everyone standing on their head. D'Amico thinks the Strangler's cracking, that this is the first step to turning himself in. There're three psychiatrists shouting at one another down the hall right now."

"What are you going to do?"

"What I've done all along: keep an open mind, and look at everything. All I can do."

"Any way I can help?"

"I can't think of a damn thing."

Neither could Kate. She asked after Jani, Al asked after Lee, neither listened to the other's reply, and both hung up feeling, if anything, more depressed then ever.

At one o'clock that afternoon, Kate thought of something she could do. She hunted down the file of the case that had begun, for her, with a search for a lost boy and ended with a piece of galvanized pipe, and after a bit of wading about, she found what she was looking for: the phone number of the foster home that had taken in Dio.

He was in school, of course, but she asked for, and eventually received, permission to meet the boy and have a conversation—alone.

She had to park illegally, but she was at the school when it let out. She almost missed him, he had changed so much in the last month, but his round-shouldered stance gave him away, that and the distance between him and the other students.

"Hello, Dio," she said, falling in at his side.

He stopped dead and looked at her warily. "Inspector Martinelli?"

"Call me Kate. What's the matter, didn't you recognize me on my feet and without a bandage on my head?"

"I guess not. You look . . . better."

"You look a little different, too."

She'd been referring to his obvious good health and the five pounds he'd put on, but he ran a hand through his neat haircut and said, with an attempt at humor that held a trace of bitterness, "My disguise. I'm passing for normal."

"Let me know if you manage. I never did. I'd like to talk with you for a little while. Wanda said it was okay."

"They like me home right after school," he said uncertainly.

"I told her I'd take you home later. Only, I'm parked in a red zone, so the first thing we have to do is move my car. Want to go get a hamburger?"

"Sure. Is this your car? Cool."

"Jules—" Kate stopped, occupying herself with the door locks for a moment. "Jules told me that *cool* was back in use."

They got into the car.

"Have you heard anything about her?" Dio asked, looking straight ahead.

"Nothing."

"Do you think that Strangler got her, like the papers say?"

"I don't know, Dio. I honestly don't know."

"She's the greatest person in the world," he said simply, then shut his mouth hard against further revelations.

Kate turned the key and put the car in gear without answering. Neither of them spoke to the other until they were seated, with their hamburgers on the table between them.

"How do you like Wanda and Reg?" she asked. Kate privately thought of the Steiners, whom she had met in any number of cases involving damaged children, as saints of God.

"They're okay. Kind of like boot camp or something, but she's a great cook. We eat at the same time every day," he said, as if describing the odd habits of exotic natives. "I even have a room to myself." Regular meals, privacy, and having a person to notice whether or not you were home from school was clearly foreign ground to Dio. Foreign, but, by the sound of it, not entirely unpleasant.

"Sounds like you come from a big, confused family," Kate commented. According to his file, he had consistently refused to speak about his past, where he came from, to give his full name, or even tell them if Dio was his real given name. It was no different now: He closed his mouth and his face, and Kate immediately backed away.

"Hey, man, I'm not trying to pump you. Dio, look at me." She waited until his sullen eyes came up. "I don't care where you come from, so long as you're better off now than you were before. I just want to know what you and Jules talked about."

He blinked. "I thought . . ."

"You thought what?"

"That you'd want to talk about Weldon."

"The squat isn't my case anymore, other than having to testify. No, I want to know about Jules. Do you mind telling me about her?"

"Why should I?"

"Dio, she's thirteen years old. She comes from a very sheltered background. She's missing, and I don't know why. It appears that there's a chance—a very, very small chance, but it's there—that the Strangler did not take her. Now, the FBI and everyone else up in Portland are working on the assumption that it was him. I can't do anything about that, but I can follow up on the other possibilities. What if she walked away on her own? Did some other son of a bitch kidnap her, or is she still out there somewhere, alone? You see, Dio, I thought I was getting to know Jules pretty well last fall, and then people started telling me things about her that made me realize there were whole parts of her I had no idea about. I'd like to know what you have to add to it."

"What kind of things?"

"For one, she ran away from another hotel last summer. Did she tell you about that?" She could see from his face that he didn't know what she was talking about. "Last summer when she and her mother were in Germany, they had an argument, and Jules walked out of the hotel. In a foreign country, where she didn't even speak the language. And she never told me about that. After I found out, I never asked her, because I figured that if she wanted to keep it to herself, that was her business. But not now. Now I need to know everything I can about her. Help me, Dio. It might make a difference."

Dio fiddled with the French fries in front of him, then put two in his mouth. Kate took it as a sign of conditional assent.

"First of all, did Jules ever talk to you about the Northwest? She told me one time that she'd lived in Seattle when she was very young. Do you know if she had any friends there?" Inevitably, she was going over well-trodden ground. The investigation, though concentrating on the Strangler, had not dismissed other possibilities quite as cavalierly as Kate had indicated. Nearly everyone who had come into contact with Jules Cameron, from her boy friend Josh to old neighbors and the families of Jani's colleagues at the university in Seattle, had been traced and interviewed. The address book Jules had left behind contained only one entry north of California: a school friend who had moved to Vancouver, British Columbia. She was away for the holiday and had written Jules to tell her that.

Dio thought for a minute, and looking at his face, deep in concentration, Kate realized that this was not a bad-looking young man. In another couple of years, in fact, if he could lose the wary sullenness, he would be handsome.

"I don't remember anything. She did tell me that she'd lived in Seattle, but all she could remember was when it snowed once. I think she moved when she was three or four."

Jules had been just barely three when Jani got a job at UCLA.

"Was she happy, do you think?"

"Jules? Sure. I mean, she didn't seem unhappy. Except—well, I don't know. Sometimes she acted kind of preoccupied. She used to get really pissed at her mom. I don't think her mother ever realized what an amazing person Jules was. Is."

"How did she feel about Al? Do you think she may have resented the marriage somehow?"

"She liked Al a lot. As far as I could tell, she was really looking forward to her mom and him getting married, when I saw her in December. Last summer, she used to talk a lot about families. She'd found out something about her own family, not very long before. She never told me just what it was, but she said it was 'ugly.' It made her feel ugly. And dirty, she said. Her mother's past made her feel dirty."

Kate could feel him opening out, but she was careful not to react. "Tell me what you know about her family."

He shrugged, but he wouldn't look at Kate, and she watched the muscle of his jaw jump.

"She must have said something to you . . . about her past."

He sat back and stretched his neck, as if easing his shoulders, and resumed play with the three limp fries in front of him. "Just that her mom divorced her dad. She didn't remember him—Jules, I mean. Just that he was somehow scary. He probably used to beat her mom."

The matter-of-factness of his last throwaway observation would have told Kate a great deal about his own family life, had she needed the confirmation.

"Did Jules tell you that?"

"No, it just sounded . . . you know, like something that would happen." He concentrated on slurping the last of his chocolate shake.

"You're probably right," she began to say, and was

startled when the boy across from her slapped the cup down and began to give out a stream of words.

"She really wanted a family, to be part of a real family, with a mother and a father and a dog. And a baby brother." His face screwed up in a wry humor that was painfully close to tears. "She wanted a baby brother to take care of. I told her she was stupid, that babies cried all the time and trapped you, but it was all just a fantasy, you know? She just used to talk about it, about making a family. She'd go on and on until I'd want to shout at her."

"She didn't want her own baby, though?" Kate asked cautiously.

"Ah shit, man," he burst out. "She was only twelve!"

"Have you never known a twelve-year-old with a baby?"

"Well, yeah. But that's different."

"Is it?"

"Of course. That kind of girl is—well, they're not really girls. Jules was different. She really was young. She was just a kid. Is . . . just a kid," he corrected himself. To Kate's amusement, the streetwise boy across the table from her began to blush. "She never knew anything about sex, not when I knew her last summer, anyway. I mean, she'd talk sometimes, you know, but it was just an idea to her, not a real thing. I'm sure she didn't know. And I never . . ."

"Did anything to disturb her innocence," Kate finished for him.

"No."

The brief flicker of amusement died under the bleak awareness that if Jules was by some miracle still alive, her innocence almost certainly was not. Kate refused to think about it, and she moved on to safer topics.

"When I was at her apartment once, just after you'd disappeared, the phone rang. She took it off and immediately hung up, without even answering, and she said something about strange telephone calls. Do you know anything about them?"

He squirmed in his seat, and all her instincts awoke. She'd hit something here; she could smell it radiating off him. He did not answer, just sat hunkered down, his blush gone, leaving him pale and very determined.

"Dio, she's missing," she said, nearly pleading. "I don't think she went under her own power, or if she did, she didn't mean to be away this long. She wouldn't have left us all hanging like this, Dio. Not Jules. She would have called, written, something."

"She . . . was getting . . . weird phone calls," he said jerkily. "A couple of times, maybe. It was a man."

"Were they obscene? Did she tell you what he said?"

"They weren't, no. That was the problem—if they'd just been some guy getting off on dirty talk, she'd have known how to deal with it, but this was just bizarre. He'd say things like, 'You're mine, Jules,' and then—no, wait, he called her Julie. 'You're mine, Julie' and 'I love you, Julie; I'll take care of you.'"

Kate felt the hair on the back of her neck prickle and rise. That kind of call was indeed seriously creepy. "Why didn't she tell anyone about the calls? Other than you?"

"I told her she ought to. They freaked her out, they really did, but she'd only had two or three, and he didn't actually threaten her or anything."

"God, she could be stupid," Kate began, but Dio, his brow furrowed in thought, was not finished.

"And I think there was something else."

She waited, and then coaxed, "What was that?"

"She seemed . . . this funny attitude . . . I don't know how to describe it." He was searching for words, though, so Kate waited, and after a minute his face cleared. He looked up at her eagerly, looking amazingly young and almost beautiful until he remembered who she was. He hesitated but then went on, although cautiously.

"I knew someone once—a friend's sister. His older sister, a year and a half older. They had a lot of problems in their family, but the two of them were really close. Then, when she was about fourteen, she started seeing this older guy. I mean a lot older, maybe thirty. He had a big car and he used to take her out, buy her clothes, and she began to get all secretive. She acted proud and excited and a little bit scared, like she had a big prize she was keeping to herself."

"What happened to her?"

"Dad—her dad found out and threw her out of the house. I don't know what happened next, because I left a few weeks later."

"And Jules reminded you of your . . . friend's sister?" Kate asked, drawing him gently back to the point he had been making.

"A little."

"You think she had a boyfriend, then?"

"Not a boyfriend. Like I said, she's just a kid. Not in her brain, but in a lot of other ways."

"But it was somebody she'd met?"

He began to look uncomfortable again, and suddenly Kate was certain that he knew more than he was telling.

"I don't think she ever met him, no."

"There's something else, isn't there, Dio?" She leaned forward, suppressing the urge to shake him. "Please, Dio. It could be what I need to find her."

"What if she doesn't want to be found?" he burst out angrily. "She's surrounded by goddamn college professors and cops. Who could blame her?"

"Did she tell you that, when you saw her in December?" Kate demanded, but it was too much for him. He stood up and threw his tall cup toward the garbage can, ignoring it when it missed. Kate scooped up the other wrappings, threw them and the cup in the bin, and hurried out the door after him. She caught him halfway down the block.

"Dio, you have to let me take you home."

"I don't have a home," he raged, throwing her hand off his shoulder, "and I don't have to let you take me anywhere!"

"I told Wanda I'd drive you back. If you come back on foot, she won't like it."

"Who gives a fuck?"

"She does, Dio. She's a good woman; don't push her around just because you're pissed off at me. It's not worth it."

He saw the sense of this, but no ex-con in cuffs went into a patrol car with less willingness than Dio climbing into the Saab, and he glowered out the side window the whole way back. She pulled up in front of the nondescript suburban house that had served as shelter for an endless trail of disturbed teenagers and turned off the engine.

"You're a good friend to Jules, Dio," she said quietly. His hand froze on the door handle. "I think she would be so happy to see how much you've done to pull your life together. I know it's tough, and if there's anything I can do to help you stick with it, I hope you'll call me. I don't agree with all the decisions you're making here, but I do understand that you only want to help Jules, and that you think this is the best way. I only ask you to think about something.

"Sometimes it's a sign of courage not to snitch on your friends. Other times, it's irresponsibility. Part of growing up is beginning to wonder which it is."

He didn't respond, but he didn't move, either.

"Jules saw the makings of a fine human being in you, Dio. I'm beginning to agree with her." She saw the color begin to creep up the side of his neck. "I gave you my card, didn't I? Phone me if you think of anything else," she said. "Anything at all."

EIGHTEEN

KATE DROVE the Saab away from Wanda and Reg Steiner's home, but around the corner she pulled over and turned off the ignition. After tapping her fingers on the steering wheel for a while and pursing her lips, she looked at her watch. A lousy time of day to get onto the freeway, but it couldn't be helped.

To her dismay, Rosa Hidalgo's apartment was silent, and there was no answer to the bell or Kate's knock. She walked back to the car, thought for another minute, then retraced her path toward the freeway, stopping at a gas station to buy a map and borrow a phone book.

Jules had said her summer computer class was at the university, which Kate took to mean the university her mother taught at. The departmental listings in the telephone book took up an entire column, but there was no answer, not in the Computer Sciences office, nor in the German department, nor in any of half a dozen others she tried at random. The secretaries had left for the weekend.

However, Kate reflected, the computer maniacs she had known would not be diverted by the hour hand of a clock—or, for that matter, by a ringing telephone. There wasn't much else to do, short of going home, so she bought herself a cup of bad coffee from the gas station cashier and drove to the university.

Darkness had fallen before Kate's flashed badge and firm reiteration of her name and rank got her into the computer labs.

"See?" said the elderly security guard who had been Kate's guide for the final stages of her quest. "Told you they'd be here."

The four people at the computer terminal did not stir until Kate had actually hung her badge down over the front of the monitor, and even then the only response was one of vague irritation. The hand of the man sitting next to the keyboard reached up and brushed her ID away.

"You'll have to wait a minute," he said.

Kate had to admit that she hadn't anything better to do, so she waited a minute, and then five more. After that, she got up and went into the next room, an office filled with copy machines old and new, a long table with a motley group of chairs, and various kitchen machines. She found a can of coffee in the refrigerator and filters in with the reams of Xerox paper. When the coffee was made, she carried the carafe into the lab, along with half a dozen Styrofoam cups, the top one filled with packets of sugar and creamer. The woman and the three men had not changed position, although it was now the woman's hands that flew across the keyboard.

"Coffee?" Kate asked loudly. One of the men, a young boy with red hair and freckles, tore his eyes from the monitor long enough to glance at his watch.

"Two minutes," he murmured, though not necessarily at Kate. She considered interrupting, by pulling out a few plugs perhaps, but decided to give them the two minutes. Actually, she thought as she poured herself a cup and sipped, it was almost refreshing to meet people who were not only unintimidated but also seemingly unaware of her status as an authority figure.

Two minutes and twenty seconds later, some invisible

sign on the screen caused the four attendants to slump back in their chairs. The woman gave the keyboard a few perfunctory taps, and across the room a laser printer hummed to attention.

"Coffee?" Kate asked again. This time, the four of them, chatting in incomprehensible shorthand, came over to where she sat at a worktable. She poured and pushed the cup with sugar and creamer toward them. The red-headed boy was the only one to add sugar, stirring it in with a ballpoint pen that he took from his pocket.

"What was all that?" Kate asked politely. "It didn't look like English."

"It wasn't. Bloke in Moscow," said the woman, her voice thickly Australian. "He can only talk when his partner goes on a break."

"Full of interesting stuff," commented the oldest man, who might have been thirty. "However, his English isn't up to it. Hence Sheila here," he said, nodding at the woman.

"Kate Martinelli," Kate offered, taking the name as an opportunity for introductions although the woman's name was Maggie, not Sheila. The others were Rob, the young redhead; Simon, the older man; and a young Chinese man with the unlikely name of Josiah. "My adoptive parents were missionaries," he said, offering a well-worn explanation in a voice with no accent.

"Do any of you know Jules Cameron?" Kate asked as soon as introductions had subsided. Four sets of eyes looked at her blankly. "She's a junior high school student who was in a class that was taught here last summer, something about programming. There was a boy in the class, her partner in some project. He sold a game to Atari when he was ten years—"

"Richard!" three voices chorused.

"We all know Richard," Maggie said. "We've all heard the story about Atari a thousand times."

"I haven't," said Josiah.

"You've only been here a week."

"I bet you know him anyway," said Simon. "He uses Albert Onestone as his *nom de clavier*."

"Oh, Albert. Sure, I know Albert. Is he as bigmouthed in life as he is on the net?"

"Worse."

"God."

"Do you know where I can find him?" Kate asked.

"He's always on the Internet. I don't think he sleeps. Or do you mean actually him, as in his body?" Maggie asked.

"His actual physical person, yes."

"I'm not sure where he lives."

"Could you ask him?" Kate asked.

"You mean when I see him?"

"If he's always on-line, what about now?"

◆

Richard, the computer genius whose pomposity had come across clearly even in choppy Internetspeak, had nonetheless agreed to meet Kate in the flesh. First, though, she needed to reach Rosa Hidalgo, to gain access to the Cameron (now Cameron-Hawkin) apartment. Richard, she trusted, would be able to open the computer inside the apartment, on the slim chance that Jules had left something—diary, letters, mutterings to herself—in its electronic recesses. It was this thin thread that she had followed down here, and she could only hope it led her a bit further before it snapped, or unraveled. She'd been an investigator long enough to be resigned to any number of fruitless days, but that did not mean she relished them.

Rosa was home. Her voice sounded strained, and she obviously held the memory of December's conversation with Kate in the front of her mind. Kate sat at the telephone in the corner of the computer lab and gradually wore Rosa down, grinding away with a steady application of Jules's name and an attitude of profound apology. She hung up feeling more than a bit nauseated, but with the permission at hand. Now all she needed to do was drag Richard away from his keyboard.

She was interrupted in her dialing of his number by the beeper somewhere on her person. She hung up, dug the tiny machine out of her pocket, and held it up. It displayed her own home number, with no message.

Old familiar panic feelings flooded over her as she punched the numbers, and when Lee herself answered, Kate went querulous with relief.

"What do you want, Lee?"

"Where are you? We expected you hours ago."

"Is that why you beeped me, because I missed dinner? I'm working." Damn it, Kate groused to herself. She can take off for months, yet I can't have a couple of hours without checking in. Well, she corrected herself after a glance at her watch, six hours. "Sorry, I guess it is late. I should've called. I've gotten out of the habit of having someone at home."

"It doesn't matter. Oh, look Kate, I'm sorry—I'm not thinking straight. I just got off the phone with Al Hawkin."

Kate held her breath.

"They've arrested the Strangler," Lee's voice in the receiver said.

"*What?*" The four people at the computer turned to look at her, but she did not see them.

"Just a little while ago. He wanted you to know before you heard it on the news."

"How good a make is it?"

"Sorry?"

"How sure are they that they've got the right man?"

"Al said it looks positive. He said to tell you a witness came forward who saw the letter being mailed. I assume that makes sense to you?"

"It does, yes. Where is he? Al, I mean."

"He said he was with D'Amico at the man's house, south of Tacoma, helping with the search, but that he'd call you tomorrow."

The help that Al would be giving, Kate knew, was to stand by and look at things taken out of the Strangler's house, to see if one of the trophies he had collected belonged to Jules. She shuddered and grasped the telephone as if it were a lifeline. Think, woman, she ordered. Don't go all soft now. She looked at her watch: just after eight o'clock. Lee was talking again, but Kate broke in, unheeding.

"Lee, I need you to make some phone calls. Do you have a pencil? Okay. Rosa Hidalgo: Tell her I won't be coming by tonight, but for God's sake, don't tell her why. Next, a kid named Richard." She gave Lee the number. "Same message as for Rosa; I'll call him in a few days. Next, call the dispatcher. Have her contact Kitagawa and tell him I'm going back on medical leave, that my head's killing me. . . . No, of course not; it's fine. And then the airport. Find me a flight; I'll be able to make it by ten o'clock. Wait a minute—did Al say more precisely where it was?"

"Just that it was south of Tacoma."

"Nothing about which airport?"

There was a silence on the line, then Lee said, "He did say something about it being too damn far from Portland, that he wished he'd flown into Seattle."

That answered the bigger question: Yes, Al knew that his partner would come.

"Right. Book me a flight into SeaTac, have a taxi at the house in, oh, an hour. That'll give me five minutes to pack. See you shortly."

"Drive carefully," Lee urged, but the phone was dead before she had finished.

♦

When Kate reached Russian Hill, she found her bag already packed and Jon bent over the duct-taped tear on her down parka with a needle and thread.

"Bless you, Jon," she said, and trotted upstairs.

"Do you want a sandwich, or coffee?" he called after her.

"No, I ate," she shouted back, ducking into the study to hunt down maps of Washington. As she pawed through the map drawer, she was dimly aware of the sounds of Lee making her laborious way up the stairs. When the click of her braces paused at the study door, Kate spoke over her shoulder.

"Have you seen those large-scale maps I brought back with me?"

"They're on the shelf."

Kate looked up and saw the bulging manila envelope. She kicked the drawer shut and stretched up for the packet, then shook it out on the desk and began sorting through it for the maps she might need.

"I'll call you tomorrow," she said. "Let you know where I'm staying. The car keys are on the table downstairs." She chose half a dozen sheets and put them back into the envelope, bent down the little metal wings to seal the flap, and turned to go.

"Kate, just hold on a minute."

"I can't, sweetheart. I'll miss the plane."

"Why do you have to go? Can't it wait until tomorrow?"

"It can't wait," Kate said gently. "I have to go."

"But why? They don't want you up there."

Kate winced, then said simply, "Al needs me."

I need you, Lee wanted to say, knowing that if she did, Kate would stay, and that Kate would resent it. And she couldn't help but be aware that she had relinquished the right to say that, after these last months, no matter how true it was. She forced herself to draw back.

"All right, love. Come back soon."

Kate stepped briskly into the hallway, then stepped back in. She kissed Lee, slowly.

"Good-bye, love," Kate said. "I'll call you."

Then she flew down the stairs to the waiting taxi.

NINETEEN

THE LIGHTS of Seattle did not rise up to greet the plane until nearly two o'clock the following morning. Waiting for the bag holding every warm garment Jon had been able to dig up took forty endless minutes, and renting a car nearly as long. She drove south on the empty freeways, through Tacoma and Olympia, and listened to the radio. Every news report trumpeted the arrest of Anton Lavalle, the homegrown American boy of French-Canadian stock, for the murders of at least three of the Strangler victims.

When she stopped at an all-night café to pour some coffee into her numb body, the name Lavalle was on the tongues of the waitress and the cook, the truckers and the highway patrolman, and when she spread out her map to consider the best route, the waitress was unsurprised at her destination.

"You want this turnoff right here, honey," she told Kate, tapping the map with an authoritative red fingernail. "Twenty miles up and then watch for the crowds." Kate laughed politely. "Want some more cream with that?"

"Yes, please, and could I have some toast or a muffin

or something?" She was dimly aware that a hamburger with Dio was the last meal she'd eaten.

"Got a nice bran muffin, fresh yesterday. Give you twenty-five cents off."

"That'll do fine. Thanks."

An hour later, Kate realized that the waitress had not been joking about the crowds: A line of parked cars and vans suddenly materialized at one side of the narrow two-lane road, with two figures carrying equipment trotting away from her headlights. She pulled over uncertainly, unwilling simply to park and walk into the night, but while she was trying to make up her mind, a car pulled up behind her. Its driver and a passenger got out with bulky bags slung over their shoulders and set off briskly down the road, which, she saw, was beginning to be visible in the first stages of dawn.

"Must be the place," she said aloud. She took her parka out of the bag and put on the boots she'd last worn to search the hills for Jules (both items cleaned and mended by Jon), then locked the bag in the trunk. In that time, two more cars had joined the line, three more intent men trotting down the road, their breath streaming out in the dim morning light. Kate tied her shoelaces and followed them.

There was chaos at the gate, where a dirt road branched off from the paved one. Kate held up her badge, put down her head, and shoved her way to the front. Even then, it took a long time to convince the short-tempered guards to let her through, a very long time after a local television man had recognized her and began to plague her with questions she could not possibly answer. The nearest guard let her in the gate, and when a convoy of emergency vehicles appeared, trying to push their way through the throng, he waved her on in disgust, then left to go and tear a few verbal chunks out of the nosy civilians.

"Hey, you!" he bellowed. "Yeah you, good-looking. You don't move your ass, I'm going to chain it to a tree." Kate slipped past him and set off up the hill.

The dirt road was nearly a mile long, climbing the side of a gentle hill. Once when Kate hit a patch of silence, free from the crackle of radios and amplified voices below and the growl of a generator from above, for a moment she found herself strolling along a country lane in the dappled sun of a crisp morning that seemed more spring than winter, complete with birdsong: nothing to say that she was nearing a pit of horror. Nothing at all, except for the faces on the men in the car she met around the corner.

She had known it was going to be bad, this lair of a killer, and the closer she drew, the greater the dread grew, until she felt the breakfast muffin like a fist beneath her heart.

Crime scenes invariably gave birth to the black humor of professional cleaner-uppers, and the worse the scene— a weeks-old body, a shotgun wound, an evisceration—the more mordant the jokes. Not many cops smile at the scene of unpleasant death, though they will occasionally bare their teeth, and often they laugh. But the grin is that of a death's-head, and the humor is blue, or, more often, black.

At a certain point, however, even the armor of humor fails, and the hard pleasure of triumph at the arrest of a stone killer has no chance against the reality of the man's acts. This was like approaching the epicenter of some horrendous natural disaster. The airy winter-bare woods and rutted dirt road were soon filled with grim-faced men and women who did not meet one another's eyes and whose shoulders were stiff with an aimless rage and despair. The short tempers that she had seen down at the main road were intensified up here into a barely controlled fury, and she let her face go blank and picked up her pace so as not to draw attention. It was going to be very bad.

But when she got there, she found no corpses being exhumed, no smell of death on the clean air. People were standing around or going about their jobs, but always, she soon saw, their glances returned to the ordinary rundown white trailer at the far end of the road—an old white box, its metal sides begrimed with mildew and rust, its roof hidden beneath lichen and leaves and layers of black plastic sheeting, ordinary except for the amount of attention being given it. The horror here was not in human remains; the horror reflected in the faces came from the knowledge of what sort of creature had inhabited the trailer.

The command post trailer was already in place, bristling with antennae and vibrating with foot traffic and the power generator, overwhelming its sick and decrepit white cousin. Two of the dozen or more vehicles packed into the clearing had their emergency lights on, pulsing the trees in syncopated bursts of color.

There was no sun here yet, if indeed there ever was on this side of the hill. It looked dank and the air smelled musty beneath the fumes of gas and diesel motors. Kate zipped her jacket to her chin, made sure her ID was clipped to the pocket, and approached the command post.

"Al Hawkin?" she asked a man in the uniform of the local sheriff's department. He shrugged and walked past her. "Al Hawkin?" she asked a plainclothesman. He tipped his head toward the trailer. "Al Hawkin?" she asked a woman who looked like a doctor, just inside the door.

"He's back there, with D'Amico. Can I help you with something?"

"I'm his partner. I need to talk with him."

"His partner? But I—" The woman stopped, studied Kate for a moment with a bit too much interest, blushed lightly when she realized what she was doing, and took a step back. "I'll just let him know. . . ." She turned and walked away into the noisy trailer, leaving Kate to reflect on the price of fame. Or was the word *infamy*?

Al appeared immediately on the woman's heels. He had his head down and kept it down, not greeting Kate, but merely gathered her up and propelled her down the steps ahead of him. He paused behind her, and she heard him say, "Harris, get someone to turn off those flashers, would you? It makes the place look like a goddamn movie set." Then he was beside her. "C'mon," he said, and set off through the trees. She had to trot to keep up with him, down a well-worn path between some shrubs.

The path ended at a sheer drop of about fifteen feet, which, judging by the cans and containers littering the ground between the bottom of the cliff and a busy creek some six or eight feet farther down, had served as the trailer's garbage dump. A bulky uniform was standing guard at the site. He looked up at their approach, flipped a gloved hand at Hawkin, and turned his back again.

Al moved to a fallen tree a few feet back from the cliff face. Kate went to sit beside him. It was quiet here, and all she could see was woods. No garbage, no cop, no serial killer's trailer, just growing things. Al took a nearly flat package of cigarettes from his shirt pocket, shook one out, and lit it. She did not comment.

"How's Jani?" she said instead.

"She's in the hospital."

"Al! What happened?"

"Couple days ago, before this latest. She's all right, just collapsed. They've got her on tranks and vitamins. She hasn't been eating, and I didn't notice it." Kate opened her mouth to protest at the tired self-loathing in his voice, then closed it again.

"Al," she started to say, but he spoke at the same instant.

"Videotapes," he said. The word burst out under pressure, from jaws that were held so tightly clenched, they must have ached. "Seven videotapes. One for each girl, more or less. A couple of them are mixed together."

"Oh shit, Al. Was there one—"

"No. No sign of Jules. None at all."

Kate could think of nothing to say.

"They're not finished yet, of course. But there're no traces so far, none of her clothes, no tape. And he's still saying he didn't do her."

She waited.

"However, there're two girls we know were his, and

they didn't have any videos, either. One of those he says he didn't do, but we know he did. There's even a necklace of hers here; he's just forgotten. Probably because he didn't have a tape for her, he forgot about her. D'Amico thinks . . . D'Amico thinks that he forgot the camera, or the battery was . . . the battery . . . Oh shit."

Al Hawkin threw his cigarette to the forest floor and slowly doubled over, as if he'd been hit in the stomach. He turned away from her, placed both of his fists hard against his forehead, and curled up fetally, his back to her. Kate was torn between the need to offer physical comfort and the man's intense need for privacy, and she held her hands out to his shoulders, hovering over his jacket for a long time, before she lowered them gently to touch him.

The tears he cried were few and small and bitter, and in barely a minute, he drew in a long breath and sat up straight. He threw his head back, blinking wide-eyed at the treetops and taking sharp breaths through his open mouth before he remembered his handkerchief and used it.

"I've got to get back," he said eventually, not looking at her.

She laid a hand on his arm. "Al, let me help. I'll finish looking at the tapes for you. I'd recognize her as well as you would."

"No," he said quickly.

"Al, I—"

"No! Martinelli, I sent you back to San Francisco. What the hell are you doing here, anyway?"

"I thought—" She caught herself, and instead of saying, I thought you wanted me to come, she said, "I thought I might be of some use."

"There's nothing for you to do here."

It was probably true; the place was swarming with cops already.

"I'll talk to D'Amico."

"I wouldn't," he warned. "He'll take your head off."

◆

Kate sat on the fallen tree and watched her partner pick his way along the pathway, and she continued to sit, with the smell of the killer's garbage mixing with the clean smell of woods and the diesel whiff from the growling generator, and she thought.

No, she would not again beg D'Amico for a meaningless task. However, she could not bear to go back to San Francisco, not yet. She had not even had time to think about the questions raised by the previous evening's interviews, and unfortunately Hawkin was in no condition to talk them over. All he could do was keep his shoulder on the load he had taken to himself. She had to admit that, other than stand by his side, there was nothing for her to do here, but she refused to go home and meekly return to work; she would at least carry through on the line of investigation she had started the day before, pointless though it undoubtedly was.

Assume, for the moment, that Jules was not lifted from the motel parking lot as a random girl by a recreational murderer. This left, as Kate saw it, three options. One, that Jules had chosen to leave, on her own and without so much as a note, for reasons unknown. Two, that there was a second killer, or a copycat, in the Pacific Northwest. Or three, that someone had been after Jules Cameron specifically.

The first one her mind recognized as a real possibility, despite her gut feeling that Jules would have left a note, however misleading its contents. The second, too, was possible, if statistically unlikely. But the third . . .

If someone had wanted Jules particularly, what would this mean? Why near Portland? And could it have had any connection with those strange telephone calls Jules had been receiving? "You're mine, Julie," the man had said. Was she now his? And why? Were there links to Dio? Or to Al? Or even to the Russian-speaking computer conversation, for God's sake?

Kate sat on her log a long time before she became

aware of the cold and her stiffness. She pulled herself off the tree and went back to the command post, which seemed quieter now that the strobes of the car flashers were off. She found Al outside with a cigarette, not so much smoking it as allowing it to burn itself down while he leaned against a car and stared off into the distance. The words rose up in her throat: Al, would Jules have the skills to survive on the streets? Al, how unbalanced is she? What didn't I see? She wanted badly to ask him, to take advantage of his experience and his ability to see things she often missed. She even tried to tell herself that offering him another option would be a kindness, but when she saw him, she knew that she could not. The familiar rituals of investigation, torturous as they were, were the only thing holding him together now. Remove those props and this man could break.

"I'm going now, Al," was all she said. "I have my pager; it seems to work up here. Do you know where you'll be tonight?"

"Here, maybe, or the hospital."

"Al, you're going to end up in the hospital yourself if you don't take care."

He looked at her blankly, noticed the long-ashed cigarette in his hand, and dropped it, grinding it under his heel.

"I'll call you later, okay?" she asked.

"Fine."

She grasped his arm and squeezed hard, then left him.

She was fortunate going downhill, catching a ride with a sheriff's deputy who took her smoothly through the gate and dropped her at her rental car, unrecognized by the press. She had the car turned and away in thirty seconds, feeling the immense relief of an escape from the gates of hell. For once, she did not mean the media circus, but the site behind them.

Long before she reached the freeway, she had decided that what she needed was a meal and a quiet hotel room. She'd been up in the hills for five hours, but it felt like days since her plane had landed at SeaTac. Her eyes were gritty, she craved a shower and badly needed a toilet, and her skin was twitchy with a combination of anxiety and adrenaline and simple lack of sleep.

Unfortunately, scores of law-enforcement personnel and media types had been there first, and the closest vacancy sign she came to was halfway to Olympia. She waited impatiently for the desk clerk to record her credit card number, then trotted across to her room. Half an hour later, bladder empty and hair still damp from the shower, she crossed over again and ordered from the "all day breakfast" page of the menu: eggs and bacon, a short stack of blueberry pancakes and hash browns, orange juice and coffee. The newspapers, waitresses, and other customers were all full of the arrest.

Back in her room, she eyed the telephone, decided she needed to sleep, and lay down with her shoes on, pulling the nylon bedspread over her, prepared to give herself over to the exhaustion loosed by the food.

Twenty minutes later, wide awake and tense as a drawn bowstring, she finally gave up, flung back the bedspread, and picked up the phone.

Lee answered.

"Hello, sweetheart," Kate said. "I thought I'd check in."

"Where are you?"

Kate told her, and gave her the motel's phone number.

"Have you seen Al?"

"Yeah."

"Is he holding up?"

"Barely. Jani's in the hospital." Her narrative punctuated by noises of distress from Lee, Kate told her what she had heard from Al. When she finished, she waited for Lee to speak. Eventually, Lee did.

"And?"

"What do you mean?"

"And so, if Al doesn't want you and D'Amico won't have you, why are you calling me from a hotel in Olympia instead of from the airport, telling me when your flight gets in?"

"I'll go nuts if I come home."

"Tell me more," Lee prompted. Kate had a vivid image of her settling back attentively into the therapist's listening position.

"I'm sure they're right—D'Amico and the FBI. This man Lavalle picked up Jules, and he killed her."

"But you're not sure, completely sure."

"No, I am, really. They're very good, Lee. They don't make stupid mistakes; they don't overlook things."

"Then what is the problem?"

"I don't know. I just know I can't stand the thought of walking away from it."

"Walking away from Jules," Lee said quietly.

"You could say that. Not without clear evidence of what happened to her. If she was on those tapes, or if they found her diary, her fingerprints, anything, I'd feel . . . well, not better about it, but resigned, I guess."

"The word you want is *closure*," said the therapist.

"That's right."

"You can't grieve until you know."

Kate did not answer.

"You may never have it. You know that, Kate."

As often as the idea had skirted the edges of Kate's mind, Lee's saying it hit her like a physical blow.

"I know. I do know."

"You'll have to face it sooner or later, Kate. Here or in Olympia. There may be no closure to this; you may need to make your own." Kate was silent. "Are you crying, my love?"

"I wish I could."

"I think you should come back home, Kate."

"I will, in a few days. I just need to satisfy myself that she didn't go to Seattle."

"Why would she have gone to Seattle?"

"She talked about it once. She and Jani lived there when Jules was very small. There's a chance she got it into her head to go back to her past, by herself." It sounded even thinner aloud than it had in thinking about it. Kate tried to elaborate. "You see, one of the things that's come out in all the conversations I've had about Jules is that she had a growing need for her own past. She found out this last summer that her father was like something out of a bad novel, violent and possessive. Jani left him when Jules was small, and he was killed in prison a while later. So she has a thing about her past, a need to find her roots. She talked about family a lot in the days before she disappeared."

"And you think she walked away from you to make her way—what, two hundred miles?—to a city you were going to anyway?"

"She had some money. And if she was going to Seattle, she wouldn't have waited to jump ship there, because it would have become the first place I'd have looked for her. Jules is a clever girl." Kate heard her own use of the present tense, and she felt obscurely cheered, as at an omen.

"How would you find her?"

"Shelters, halfway houses, squats. Bridges."

"It's a big place."

"And she's a distinctive girl. Oh, that reminds me: There're some pictures of her in the camera that I didn't get around to developing. Could you have Jon take the film into that one-hour place, and then choose one or two and have twenty copies of each made? Tell them they have to make a rush job of it. I'll give you a place to overnight them to when I get up there."

"Aren't there posters of her all over? I understood that's one thing they were doing."

"Sure, but I want a color photograph of her with short hair."

"All right." Lee's voice, patient and reserved, caught Kate up short.

"I have to do this, Lee. You do understand?"

"Not entirely, no."

"Lee—" How to say this? How to tell Lee that Jules had been the only thing to get Kate through this terrible autumn? "Lee, Jules and I became friends while you were away. Good friends. She reminded me of my kid sister Patty. You remember her?"

"I do. She was killed in an automobile accident when you were at Cal."

"I love Jules, Lee. She's family. I can't just walk off and leave it to the big boys."

"Even if there's no point in what you're doing?"

"Even if there's no point in what I'm doing."

Kate heard a sigh coming down the line, but no more objections. "Get those pictures together," she said. "I'll call you from Seattle. Oh, and I meant to tell you, my beeper extends this far up, if you need to reach me."

"Take care, sweetheart."

"You, too."

Now, Kate could sleep.

TWENTY

KATE WOKE up shortly before eight o'clock that evening, disoriented by waking to darkness, but rested. She wasn't hungry, there was nothing of interest on the television, and there was no reason for her to stay here. She threw her things back into her bag and checked out—to the mild consternation of the young desk clerk—got back on the freeway, and drove north.

At ten o'clock, she was checking into another hotel room, this one in downtown Seattle. She called Lee to give her the address, received Lee's assurance that Jon would drive down and drop the packet of photographs off that very night so she would have them tomorrow, and then pulled on her down parka, hat, gloves, and scarf and went out to prowl the streets.

This late at night, and without even a photograph in her hand, there would not be much point in cruising for the truly homeless, who would be under roofs or underground by now. However, she could get an idea of where young people would congregate and what part of town the squats were in, and return the next day armed with photograph and daylight.

She began with Pioneer Square and worked her way

up past the Pike Place Market and down along the water-front. She went into every coffeehouse and café, not bothering with the bars or the restaurants with linen on their tables. Jules might have an adult-sized brain, but she had neither the face nor the money for adult entertainment. If she was here, she would be with young people.

So Kate explored, entering a coffeehouse with a roaring espresso machine and a clientele that made her feel middle-aged, ordering a cup of decaf and nursing it, her eyes unfocused and her ears alert to conversation. Then, leaving the coffee half-drunk, she wandered along a few doors down to a vegetarian restaurant, where she ate some tasteless but undoubtedly nutritious soup and listened to a long and technical discussion about the growing of marijuana beneath artificial lights. She didn't finish the soup either, just left her money on the grimy plywood table and went on down the street to a bookstore that had a coffeehouse tacked on the side.

In and out, uphill and down. Eventually, the doors began to close, the people moving on to nightlife in more private venues. Kate walked under the raised freeway, saluted the lights of the city's space needle, and went back to her room, where she half-watched a violent movie on the television and tried not to think about the generous supply of alcohol in the minibar.

♦

On Sunday morning, Kate was out early. In her pocket was a paper with several addresses, copied from the telephone book's listing under "Housing and Emergency Services," and a map from the front desk with those addresses x-ed in. A call to the city's shelter hot line had given her the places most likely to be chosen by a teenager; those places were circled, and Kate went to them first.

It was a long, cold, and dreary morning among the outcasts, and when a listless snow began to fall a little before noon, Kate gave up and took a taxi back to her hotel. A hot, plentiful lunch helped thaw her out, and when the packet of photographs arrived at one o'clock, she decided that it was feeble of her to be chased home by some snow, which had more or less stopped anyway, and besides, she'd feel a real idiot when Jon asked her if his efforts to get her forty pictures of Jules Cameron had done any good. With a marker, she wrote, HAVE YOU SEEN THIS GIRL? along the top of each photograph, and along the bottom, CALL COLLECT, with her San Francisco telephone number. She drank the last of her now-cold coffee, slid the envelope into an inner pocket, and took herself back out onto the slick streets.

She posted ten of the one that looked like Jules now, and seven of the long-haired Jules, putting them on bulletin boards in busy coffeehouses and in the shelters. No one told her that they had seen Jules. She took a bus north through the city to the university district and spent a couple of hours there, asking questions, showing the pictures, posting a few. Two or three people thought the girl in the picture looked vaguely familiar, but it never went beyond vague.

The gray sky dimmed into dusk and the snow started up again. Kate took refuge in a restaurant and ordered a bowl of soup, sitting near the window and watching the flakes come hypnotically down, illuminated by the headlights of cars and the pools of light beneath the streetlamps. She was in the heart of the university district, and the people walking past looked like the students of any other university she'd ever seen, only more warmly dressed: backpacks and parkas, boots and woolen caps, an occasional foolhardy soul riding a bicycle and a number of others walking their bikes through the rapidly collecting layer of white on the ground. A young woman walked by with a dog, he trotting with a Frisbee in his mouth, she striding in knee-high boots under several thick skirts and wearing a colorful patchwork jacket and a loose rolled cap from Afghanistan. All she needed to complete the picture was a—

"Oh, shit," said Kate aloud, looking at the woman and seeing another. "Oh my God." A camera. All she needed was a camera. There had been a whole busload of Afghan gypsies, one of them with a camera, at the rest stop, with Jules, just as that fateful headache had been coming on. A camera . . . taking pictures.

Kate stood up violently and went for the door, shrugging her way into her damp parka. She stopped, turned back to drop some money on the table, and headed back toward the door, where she halted a second time, stood with her head down thinking for a moment, and then turned to search for the waitress. The entire restaurant had fallen silent and was watching her, with expressions ranging from amusement to apprehension. The waitress was one of the latter, and Kate's words to her did not soothe her much.

"Do you know the name of that bus company, the one that transports you but stops at places along the way?"

The waitress was looking positively alarmed by the end of the question, and it dawned on Kate that she'd been less than comprehensible.

"Sorry, I'm not making much sense." She tried a smile out on the woman. "There's a sort of hippie bus company, if you want to go to Los Angeles, for example, but they'll stop on the way to visit hot springs or the beach, things like that."

"You want to go to L.A.?" the woman asked hopefully.

A young man with matted blond dreadlocks and the face of a bearded angel cleared his throat. "You mean the Green Tortoise?"

"That's it. Do you know if they have an office around here?"

He shrugged. "Probably."

"How could I find them?"

He glanced sideways at his companion as if suspecting a trick question, then ventured, "The phone book?"

"Ah. Of course, the phone book. Thanks," she said.

"And thank you," she added to the waitress, then let herself out into the snow, heading to the phone booth she'd spotted across the street.

It was, of course, Sunday night, and there was no answer at the local number listed for the alternative bus company. Possessed of a raging impatience, Kate slipped and slithered her way around the district, showing off her pictures, to absolutely no avail. Eventually, she went back to the hotel, and a long time later she fell into a few hours of shallow sleep.

◆

The snow had warmed and turned sloppy during the night, sloppy and wet. Kate's shoes, once waterproof, were no longer, and her feet were frozen as she stood on the sidewalk, hugging herself and rubbing her hands, waiting for someone to come and open the Green Tortoise office. She'd been there for half an hour, and the office should have been open twenty minutes ago, at nine.

At half past nine, she spotted a longhaired couple making their slow and affectionate way down the street, and she was not much surprised when they stopped in front of the door. The man extricated an arm and dug into a pocket for a key ring, kissed his companion a long goodbye, and opened the door. Kate followed on his heels.

It was not much warmer inside than out. The man went around the room switching on lights, heaters, and a computer, and finally he took off his scarf and gloves, indicating that he was open for business.

"Can I help you?"

"I hope so. I'm trying to trace one of the passengers on a bus of yours that went through Portland just before Christmas."

He unbuttoned his coat, revealing a thick green fisherman-knit sweater beneath.

"Why?"

Reluctantly, Kate took out her ID and showed it to the man. He looked at it carefully and took off his hat.

226

His hair was not actually long, she noticed; in fact, it was surprisingly neat.

"This is not official business," she told him.

"That's cool," he said.

"I just need to find her."

"Like I said, why?"

"Frankly, I don't have the authority to go into that. I can only say that she may have seen something with a direct bearing on an ongoing investigation."

Without answering her, he picked up his coat, hat, gloves, and scarf and took them through a doorway. She heard a mild clatter of clothes hangers, and he came back, running both hands through his hair.

"You want some tea? Or there's instant coffee," he offered.

"Um, sure, thanks. Instant's fine."

He went back through the door. This time, she heard water running into a pot and the click of a switch turning on, and then he was back again.

"You know," he said, "if you're going to ask deceitful questions, you really ought to wear glasses or a fake mustache or something. Your face has been on the news."

"As I said, this is not an official inquiry."

"I'm a law student, and I can guess how close to illegality you're walking."

Kate stepped back and looked at him, and rapidly shoveled her original impressions of him out into the melting snow. She smiled wryly and held out her hand.

"Kate Martinelli."

"Peter Franklin," he said, and shook her hand. "What is it you're after?"

"A girl on your bus. She was taking pictures of the other passengers; there's a tiny chance she may have caught someone in the background."

"The Strangler himself? Lavalle?"

"He's denying any connection with Jules Cameron's disappearance," Kate said, which was the truth, although not in the way Franklin would hear it. "I want to pick up evidence while it's still fresh. If you're a law student, you're probably aware of how fast memories fade, how easy it is for evidence to become compromised."

The mild flattery got through. He nodded, started to speak, and was cut off by the whistle of the kettle in the next room, building to a shriek.

He chipped some coffee out of an encrusted jar, dropped a piece into a mug, and poured on the hot water. Milk was added to hers, honey to his straw-colored herbal tea, and Kate resumed.

"I could get a warrant if you think it's necessary," she said, feigning assurance.

"I don't know if it would help," Franklin said, blowing across the top of his steaming cup. "We don't really keep passenger lists."

"Oh Christ." Kate set the cup down so hard, the foul ersatz coffee slopped onto the counter. "Why didn't you just tell me that to begin with?"

"Whoa, lady. Would you rather I just said, Sorry I can't help you. Piss off?"

"Isn't that what you're saying?"

"No."

"Do you have a passenger list?"

"Not a passenger list. We keep records of the reservations made, but those are all along the line of 'Pick up Joe and Suzanne at the truck stop.' "

"No names or phone numbers?"

"It's not an airline."

"This doesn't sound very hopeful," she said aloud.

"Look, do you want to find your girl with the camera or not?"

"That's why I came here, but you just said—"

"Christ on a cross," he said to himself, turning away to a filing cabinet. "No wonder crimes never get solved."

Kate became belatedly aware that this was probably the most incompetent interview she had ever conducted. Frankin pulled a file from the drawer, pulled up the one in front to mark its place, and came over to her, laying it on the counter and opening it.

"Now, what was the date?"

"The twentieth. What is that?"

"The list of drivers."

"You think the driver might remember one girl?" Kate said dubiously.

"Our trips aren't like Greyhound. We have two drivers on all the time, and even on the straight-through trips there's a lot of interaction. We arrange a picnic, stop at a hot springs, that kind of thing—it can be more a brief impromptu tour than just a form of transportation, and the driver is a part of it. Portland, you say. Going which way?"

"Northbound."

He reached under the counter and came out with a piece of scratch paper, a recycled flyer of some sort torn neatly in quarters. He wrote a name and a seven-digit phone number on it, turned a few pages in the file, and wrote another name and number, this one with a 312 area code.

"That close to Christmas, we run four buses instead of two up and down, but there's only one that might've been there on the twentieth. That was Sally's bus. These are the drivers' numbers— No, wait a minute. Was that when B.J. had the brake problem?" He read on, then nodded. "Right, we had a delay and therefore a bit of an overlap. I'll give you their numbers, too." He wrote down a pair of names and numbers, one local and the other in the 714 area. Then he closed the file and went over to put it back in its drawer.

"One of these numbers is in L.A.," Kate noted. "Where is this other one?"

"Chicago. He just came out to drive the Christmas season. The local ones are between here and Tacoma." These were for Steven Salazar—Sally—and B.J.'s partner.

God, thought Kate in despair, if I can't do this over the phone, the airfares are going to kill me.

She pushed the thought from her mind and gave Franklin a look that was confident and grateful. She held out her hand.

"Thank you."

"I hope it helps," he said, his casual attire clashing strangely with the taut look on his face. "It's cases like these that make me question my opposition to the death penalty."

TWENTY-ONE

FOUR PHONE calls, four blanks drawn: All the drivers were out, presumably driving; two of them were expected back either tonight or tomorrow; another tomorrow night; the third, nobody knew where he was, hadn't seen him in a couple of weeks. Out again with the photographs, to soup kitchens and emergency shelters. She avoided the police, which would have involved uncomfortable explanations, telling herself that the police had already conducted their search for Jules Cameron.

Back to the hotel for phone calls to two drivers, one partner, and a lover. One driver had yet to surface and the other would be home at midnight Chicago time, but Kate was told that she'd damn well better not call then, because after a week on the road, the driver would have better things to do than talk on the phone. Al sounded as he had on Saturday, holding on by a mere thread; she told him nothing of what she was doing. Lee was patient and the conversation was short.

Tuesday morning, she caught the Chicago driver at home, but no, he had not pulled into that particular rest stop south of Portland a few days before Christmas.

Tuesday afternoon, three more people told Kate that

the girl in her photograph looked familiar, but one was so stoned, Kate didn't think his eyes actually came to a focus, and the other two were helpful and vague and suggestable.

Tuesday evening, she reached the driver Sally. He agreed with his codriver in Chicago that they had gone through the Portland area at roughly that time, but they had not shepherded their charges to the rest stop near the river.

This left the driver nobody could locate, and B.J. Montero, in the Anaheim area of the Los Angeles sprawl. B.J. was a woman, and her boyfriend worked a graveyard shift and had not been pleased at Kate's initial phone call. He did not seem any more pleased at subsequent calls, either, even though they didn't wake him in the middle of his night. This time when she called, on Tuesday evening, he just snapped into the phone, "She ain't here," and slammed the phone down before she could finish her sentence.

The next morning, timing her call to catch the man before he could drop into bed, she had the same response, only more obscene. Later, she called the Green Tortoise office again, but Peter Franklin could tell her only that B.J. had a couple of days off and had dropped the last of her passengers the day before. Kate supposed she was on her way home, taking her own sweet time—which, she reflected, was understandable if the boyfriend's ill temper was a general state.

Finally, at five o'clock Wednesday evening, the rude boyfriend, instead of hanging up, growled a curse and dropped the receiver onto a hard surface. A woman's voice came on the line. Kate introduced herself and explained that she was trying to find a passenger on the trip Montero had driven five days before Christmas, saying that she did understand that passenger lists were not kept, but that the local manager had suggested his drivers might have gotten to know some of their passengers.

"You just want whatever names I have?"

"It's more than I have now."

"Just a minute." The phone crashed back onto the table. Kate heard retreating footsteps, heard the man's voice say, "Wha' the fuck she want?" and, faintly, Montero answering, "Like you said, she's looking for someone who was on one of my trips." Bass grumbling and soprano giggling, punctuated by distant rustles and thumps, made Kate begin to wonder if they had forgotten her in the business of their reunion, but after a while the feet approached the phone again and the woman's voice came on.

"What was the date again?"

"December the twentieth."

"Right." There followed another silence, with faint paper noises. "Oh yeah, that trip. There was a leak in the brake fluid that took me forever to find, and that crew was really into singing. They must've sung 'White Christmas' a thousand times. Jesus, I thought I'd go nuts. I've got two names. Got a pencil? They're Beth Perry and . . . I think this says Henry James—could that be right? Yeah, I think so; I remember some joke about philosophy. You want their phone numbers?" Kate said yes, please, and wrote two strings of numbers down beside each name. "They're both students, so I took their parents' numbers, too. Students move around too much."

"Just out of curiosity, why did you take these names down? If you don't keep track of passengers?"

"I usually have one or two names a trip, like if someone has a car for sale, or does some kind of work I might need, or a friend needs. Or"—her voice dropped—"if it's a good-looking guy, you know?"

"And these two?"

"These two . . . let's see. Beth lives down here and does sewing, these sort of patchwork things. She was wearing this fantastic jacket, said she could make me one. And Henry fixes old cars. I thought he might be able to get a couple of parts my boyfriend needs for his '54 Chevy. Which reminds me, I forgot to tell him," she noted, but Kate did not hear the end of the remark. She had been struck by a vision of a thin young woman with two inches of black roots to her blond hair, furry boots, and a knee-length coat that was a riot of color in the drab parking lot, a garment incorporating a thousand narrow strips of fabric, silks and velvets and brocades, a coat that seemed to cast warmth on everyone in its vicinity. The girl in the coat had been there at the same time as Kate and Jules, one cold day three weeks before. Suddenly, with this tangible link between the driver and herself, the whole thing seemed possible, an actual investigation rather than aimless wandering.

It was a familiar feeling, and a welcome one, this almost physical jolt when an investigation began to come together around an unexpected piece of information, and after the brief distraction of her vision, Kate focused on what else the woman might have to say.

"Do you remember a photographer?" she asked. "A girl with a camera?"

"Everyone on these trips has a camera," Montero said unhelpfully.

However, Kate had thought a great deal about this particular girl and her camera, and she had a description ready. "She was about five two and looked like a sheep—not her face, but she was wearing a sheepskin jacket with the fur on the outside. She was young—maybe eighteen or so. Looked a bit Hispanic, maybe Puerto Rican. She had a truly ugly hat on, an orange knit thing that was all lumpy. Blue leggings, red high-top athletic shoes. The camera was a thirty-five millimeter with a long lens, kind of beat-up-looking, and she was running around telling people where to stand. I don't know what color hair she had, because of that hat, but I'd have thought she'd stand out in a crowd. Bossy in a ditzy kind of way."

After a pause, Montero said in a voice gone oddly flat, "Black."

"Sorry?"

"Her hair was black. Is black. And she's twenty-seven, not eighteen."

"You know her, then?" Kate felt a surge of hope out of all proportion to the actual information.

"My mother made that hat." Her voice had traveled from flat to disapproving.

"Your mother?" Realization began to dawn, along with an awareness that her description had not been as flattering as it might have been.

"What does 'ditzy' mean?"

"Um. Well, sort of unstructured," Kate said. "Freethinking. That was you, with the camera?"

"You really think that hat is ugly?"

"Oh no, not ugly, really. Just : . . handmade."

There was a snorting noise, and then the woman was laughing. Kate, much relieved, joined in.

"God, it is ugly, isn't it?" Montero admitted. "She's doing me a sweater to match, and I swear the arms are six feet long. You don't know any cold gorillas, do you?"

"I'll let you know if I meet one."

"Anyway, was it me you were looking for?"

"It sounds like it. What I'm after is a record of the people and cars in that rest stop when you were there. Did you have that film developed?"

"Sure."

"Do you have it there? Can you look for me and see what you caught?" Kate's voice was normal, conversational, but only years of experience kept it that way. Jules was almost certainly dead, murdered by Lavalle, but Kate could not suppress the crazy feeling that the child's life rode on this woman's answer.

"Sure. Do you want me to call you back, or do you want to hang on?"

"I'll hang on," Kate said firmly.

"It'll be a few minutes," Montero warned, then put the phone back onto the table.

It was more than a few minutes. Kate entertained herself by chewing a thumbnail, clicking her pen in and out, and listening to the conversation in the house in Anaheim. Montero and her boyfriend were arguing about dinner. Their voices faded and returned, drawers opened and closed, and finally Kate heard Montero shout that she was tired, too; she didn't feel like cooking; why didn't he go down and get some hamburgers; by the time he got back, she'd be finished on the phone.

The receiver was picked up just as a door slammed, and Montero was back on the line. "Found them. Now, let's see. I took seven or eight shots there, but they're mostly of people on the bus. What are you looking for? Is this some kind of insurance thing?"

"That sort of thing. What kind of background images did you get? Cars, people?"

"Okay. First picture: In the background, there're some people going into the toilets, a couple of cars sticking out behind the bus."

"License plates?"

"No, they're from the side."

"Go on."

"Um. Nothing on this one. Here's one of an old guy standing in the river fishing. Not a bad shot, either. Very evocative. Next is a picture of Beth whatsis in her coat— oh, there're some people and a car in this one. Mother and daughter, I guess, getting into a white convertible. Something foreign, I think."

"A Saab?"

"Hey, you're right. It is a Saab. How'd you know?"

It was an odd sensation, knowing that a stranger a thousand miles to the south was gazing at a picture of her and Jules.

"That's me," she said.

"I can't see you very well, but your daughter's gorgeous."

"She's not my daughter," Kate said before she could stop herself. Something in her voice gave her away.

"Who is— What are you after? Is this— Oh shit. Oh Jesus. Is this about that last girl who was killed by the Strangler? The policeman's daughter?"

"It is."

"And is this her, in the picture? That means . . ." The voice trailed off.

"That's her, yes. And she disappeared a few hours after you took that picture."

"And you think he was there? Stalking her? You want my pictures as evidence."

This was much the same thing as Peter Franklin had thought, and Kate again rejected the complicated truth in favor of keeping things simple. "That's what we're hoping. Are there any cars or people in the other pictures?"

A pause while Montero looked at the remaining pictures. "Well, yes, there's a bunch. Maybe a dozen cars and RVs, six or eight people walking around—people who weren't from my bus, that is. And a few more people inside cars, though of course you can't see them very well. What does Lavalle look like?"

Kate made her decision. "I'd like to ask you for the pictures and the negatives," she said.

"You can have them," Montero said emphatically and with revulsion. "Do you want me to mail them to you?"

"Would it be possible," Kate said slowly, "for you to meet me at the airport?"

TWENTY-TWO

ON THE ground, in the hotel room that had come to vi-
brate with frustration during the four days that Kate had
occupied it, the decision to fetch B.J. Montero's photographic efforts herself had seemed logical enough. A
combination of desperation and a vague sense of preserv-
ing some semblance of an evidence chain had made the
trip seem almost necessary.

Inside the plane, however, with the credit card receipts
for hotel, car, and airplane ticket weighing heavily in her
pocket, it was a different matter. She nearly got off before
the attendants shut the door; probably the only thing that
kept her in her seat was the knowledge of how difficult
and unlikely a refund would be.

How much had she spent on this fruitless quest? With
something approaching horror, she counted up the
charges put on her credit card in the last two months,
beginning with the waterproof shoes she had bought
Jules in Berkeley the day they headed out. Where were
those shoes now? she wondered. God, the card must be
nearly at the max now. How would she ever pay for it?
And what good had it done anyone? In the end, Jules

would still be gone, and she would be working to pay off an expensive wild goose.

The plane lumbered and rose, and three hours later dropped into Los Angeles. A remembered figure, wearing a much prettier hat, stood at the gate, manila envelope in her right hand and a large boyfriend at her left. She held out the envelope tentatively.

"Kate Martinelli?"

Kate took the envelope and held out her right hand, first to the woman, then to the man. "B.J. Montero? Good to meet you. I'm Kate Martinelli," she said to the boyfriend.

"This is Johnny," Montero said by way of introduction. He grunted and crushed Kate's hand a bit, in warning perhaps, or revenge for all the disturbance she had caused, or maybe just because he was a poor judge of his own strength.

"Good to meet you, Johnny." Kate extracted her hand. "Want to go for some coffee? I have half an hour before my return flight." The last flight to San Francisco, she thought, wondering why no one had written a song with that title. She then wondered if she wasn't getting a little light-headed. "A drink, maybe?"

"Sure," B.J. said, without so much as a glance at her companion. The top of her head was in line with the center of his biceps, but she handled him with all the ease of a mother.

Kate paid for two coffees and a beer for Johnny ("I'm driving," said B.J.) and, once at the table, opened the envelope. There were nine photographs, not eight. Middle-class gypsies in Afghan hats were caught in motion; the elderly fisherman stood in the frigid water, looking like a frost-rimed sculpture; Kate and Jules stood on opposite sides of the car, taking a last glance at the scene. Kate's door was open, as was the girl's mouth. Jules had been saying something about Montero's sheepskin coat, Kate thought, and remembered the blast of cold air against her nearly shaven scalp when she took off her hat before getting into the car, a jolt that seemed to have set off the headache.

The five remaining pictures were snapshots, hastily composed, though well focused. The focal points, however, were on the young people close to the lens, not on the cars parked in the slots or on the ordinary people walking to and from them. Kate glanced through them, not knowing what she thought she might see, but they were only pictures, memories of someone else's good times.

"You see anything?" B.J. asked. Kate tore her gaze from the picture and reached for her coffee. She shook her head.

"I didn't really expect to."

"You mean the man isn't there? Lavalle?" B.J. sounded both disappointed and relieved.

"I don't know what he looks like."

"You don't?"

Kate, seeing her astonishment, pulled herself together and gave a laugh. "I haven't been in on the interviews yet, and I wasn't there when he was arrested. A case like this, there're hundreds of people working on it. I'm only one." She glanced at her watch. "I better get moving. Let me give you a receipt, and if you'd just sign the backs of those photographs, so we know whose they are." A chain of evidence, as if anyone would ever look at them in a court of law. Would ever look at them, period.

Kate could feel herself beginning to run down. The brief push of zeal that had been set off by Peter Franklin at the bus company and the photographs taken by his driver was fading. If she hadn't already made an arrangement with the police photographic lab technician, she would have gone straight home from the airport, but instead, carried along by routine, she dutifully went to the lab, marked the photos for cropping and enlargement, and pointed out the faces and license plates she wanted brought out.

Then she went home.

It was nearly ten o'clock when she woke up the next morning, and the house was filled with the rich aroma of bread baking. She felt rested, but the sensation of being a piece of run-down machinery persisted. The last few days seemed unreal, like some stupid and pointless dream that had seemed profound at the time. Lee was home and Jon was baking. It was a sunny Thursday morning as she lay in bed while the rest of the world was hard at work. A bird was singing in the tree outside the window, and a dog barked somewhere.

And Jules was dead.

That brilliant, sweet, troubled, funny girl was gone, victim of the most revolting kind of killer. Kate had loved her, had been loved by her, and now she was gone.

She lay among the rumpled sheets, thinking bleak thoughts on a beautiful morning, and when the doorbell rang down below, she was caught up in a memory of another morning, in late August, when Jules had arrived on her doorstep and rung the bell, backpack over her shoulder, bandage on her knee, her hair still worn in long, childish braids, to ask Kate's help in looking for a friend. Kate had found him, and lost her, and suddenly, hit by an overwhelming upsurge of the grief that she had so long pushed away, she turned her face into the pillow and allowed the tears to come.

She didn't hear the sound of the bedroom door opening and then closing, but a minute later the mattress sank as Lee sat down on it, and she felt Lee's hand stroking her hair. Neither of them said anything for a long time, until Kate finally lifted her head, found a Kleenex, and turned onto her back.

The manila envelope Lee held was much thicker than it had been the night before. Kate took it from her without comment and slid the pictures out onto the bedcovers.

"A courier brought it from the lab," Lee said. "I thought it might be urgent."

Kate picked up one enlargement that she hadn't asked for but that had been done anyway: she and Jules on either side of the Saab, two heads of cropped hair, one on an ill-looking cop, the other on a girl with her life ahead of her. Except it wasn't life that awaited her a short distance up the road.

Urgent? These? No. The whole thing was pointless, a delaying tactic to avoid facing the truth, and she had finally admitted it.

Lee's fingers appeared at the top edge of the picture and tugged gently. Kate let it go and closed her eyes. Even with her arm across her face, she could feel Lee studying the two images, and she knew just when Lee began to cry. Kate held out her arms, and Lee curled up against her, and while the sun shone and the bread cooled and the dog was finally let inside, the two women mourned the brief life of Jules Cameron.

◆

And yet . . .

"You're like this terrier my parents used to have," Lee said. "He would not let go of a thing once he got his teeth into it." She was trying to be humorous, but her concern showed, and a bit of irritation, as well.

Kate licked the last of the sticky rolls from her fingers and turned her face to the sun. She had carried a table and chairs down to this, the newly rescued patch of garden, the only place in the winter that caught any sun. Jon had gone out, and the house felt silent and nearly content, as in the aftermath of a storm.

"I feel more like one of those high school biology experiments," she said ruefully. "You know, where you have some dead creature that you prod at and it jumps."

"Do you really have to do this?"

"It's a loose end, and it'll keep twitching until I tidy it up. After all, I did get all those people on the alert on Friday, then just took off."

"Rosa Hidalgo and some computer nut hardly count as 'all those people.'"

"It seemed like a lot more at the time. Anyway, it'll only be for the afternoon, and then tomorrow or the day after I was thinking about taking off for a couple of days."

"I think that would be a good idea," Lee said carefully.

"With you? Please? If you can get free," she added.

The joy dawning on Lee's face rivaled the morning sun, but all she said was, "Where?"

"Somewhere on the coast. Just drive?"

"South to Carmel or Big Sur?" Lee suggested.

"Fine."

"I'll need to buy a bathing suit. My only one has holes in unfortunate places."

"What fun."

"If you can guarantee me a private swimming hole, yes."

"Jon would love to take you shopping for a suit," Kate said firmly.

◆

Kate stared at the telephone for twenty minutes before she could work up her nerve to call Rosa Hidalgo. The question of legality—no, it was not even a question—the fact that what she planned was both illegal and unethical was actually of little concern when compared to the thought of Jani's anger if she heard that the woman she blamed for her daughter's disappearance had then been inside her apartment. Scenarios of shame and a permanent state of discomfort around Al almost drove her off—almost.

Very fortunately, Rosa was not home, and would not be home until late. Furthermore, her daughter, Angelica, had no hesitation about letting Kate into the apartment.

Albert Onestone, king of the Internet—Richard Schwartz to the rest of the world—took her a while longer, but she eventually got through to him, his real rather than virtual self on the telephone. Had she been conversing through the keyboard, she was certain he would have wriggled out of her grasp, but confronted by a live voice in his ear, he was out of his element and agreed to go with her to tease the secrets from Jules's computer.

Richard lived in a converted garage not far from the university, and when he came to the door, she almost laughed, so like the caricature of the computer nerd was he. Stooped, pale, bespectacled, and blinking at the sunlight, he was far from the overbearing persona that came across on the screen. She introduced herself, shook his damp hand, invited him to get in the car, waited while he logged off and shut down some machines, assured him that the jacket he had on would be heavy enough, helped him find a pen, and made sure he locked the door behind him.

"Richard," she said when they were in the parking area next to Jules's apartment, "for your own protection, I'm trying to keep anyone from knowing that you were here."

"Protection?" he said nervously. "I don't think—"

"Not that kind of protection—there's nothing dangerous here. It's just to keep you from getting involved. If anyone finds I've been here and broken into the computer, it's my responsibility. I don't want to bring you into it."

"Would you know how to get through the security blocks by yourself?" he asked dubiously.

"Probably not, but nobody could prove I hadn't stumbled through on my own. Don't worry, I'm great at bluffing. Now, you wait here. I'm going to go up and get the door open, then come back for you. I'll be five or ten minutes."

"Really?" He sat up, looking interested. "Do you use picks? I'd like to watch."

"Nothing so clever, just the key. Wait here."

Angelica was home, and she came to the door with a phone tucked under her chin.

"Hi!" she said; then she muttered into the phone, "Hold on just a sec." Turning back to Kate, she said,

"I've got the key. Do you want me to come up with you?"

"Oh, no, that's okay," Kate assured her. "Al told me where he kept his sweaters; it'll only take me a minute."

"Funny, Mom just sent them a bunch of things."

"Well, you know how men are," Kate said vaguely. Angelica laughed and went back to her phone conversation, leaving the door open. Kate trotted up the stairs and let herself in.

It did indeed take her only a minute to locate Al's unpacked boxes, piled to await his return from the aborted Mexican honeymoon. One in the bedroom held warm sweatshirts, so Kate pulled out three or four and some socks, bundled them under her arm, and went back downstairs with the key, carefully leaving the apartment door unlocked.

Angelica was still on the phone. She was sitting on the sofa with her feet on the coffee table, painting her toenails with bright red stars against a white background. Kate held up the key between two fingers. "Where does it go?" she asked.

"Oh, stick it on the hook next to the kitchen phone," the girl answered, waving at the door. Kate found the hook and returned the key to what she hoped was the same place that Angelica's mother had left it. When she came back through, the girl looked up from her task.

"Just a sec," she said again into the receiver, and to Kate: "Did you find what he wanted?"

"I did, thanks. And look, Angelica, maybe you shouldn't mention this to your mother. Actually, she sent the wrong stuff, not what Al had asked her for. She'd be embarrassed if she knew."

Angelica giggled conspiratorily, and Kate shut the Hidalgo door behind her when she left.

Richard was reading the driver's manual from the glove compartment.

"Come on," Kate said, throwing the clothes across the backseat.

"Wait a minute. I don't know if I— What are those?"

"Old sweatshirts. Let's go."

"Just how illegal is this?"

"Not at all. He's my partner," which had nothing to do with it, but it seemed to reassure him. He allowed her to take the manual from his hand and pull him out of the car.

"I really don't—" he whined.

"Shhh!"

"I really don't understand," he said in a whisper. "You never explained why you need to get into Jules's computer."

"I told you she disappeared. She was kidnapped."

"Yes, I know."

Feeling she had given the feeble explanation so often that it was nearly threadbare, she sighed. "If Jules disappeared voluntarily, she may have left behind an indication of why—a friend's address, for example, or a phone number. She kept a written diary, but she took it with her. She may also have kept a diary in her computer."

"It's an invasion of privacy," he said desperately. "There are laws against it. I'm sure there are."

They were on the stairs now, the back ones, which did not run right past the Hidalgo door. "I thought hackers believed in freedom of information," she commented.

"Corporate or governmental information, sure, but not private stuff."

"Never mind, Richard, I won't make you read it. Just unlock the door and I'll rob the place."

They got into the apartment without being seen. Richard booted up, then tapped and scowled at the keyboard for a while before giving a brief grunt of satisfaction as Jules's files fell open before them.

"Before I open these," he said to her, "I need to know if you want to hide your tracks."

"What do you mean?"

"Well, as it is, when I go into one of these, the computer will record that it was opened on this date and time. If you don't want that to happen, I have to change the date on the computer so it thinks it's last month, or last year. It's not perfect, and someone looking for it would probably see it, but it's a way of escaping a quick glance. I can be more elaborate if you like, and nobody would ever know, but that takes more time."

"No, we don't need to be paranoid about this. Go ahead and do the simpler cover."

The files Richard opened were as tidy as Kate would have expected, clearly delineated between work and private material. She had him open each one to be sure, but many of them were simply for school—science and English assignments, book reports and homework of various kinds.

There were three oddball files, and Kate, knowing that Jules used a compatible, if more advanced, version of the word processing program that Lee had on their computer, had him copy them onto a disc. He then closed down the files, restored the proper date to the computer's brain, and shut it down.

"Should we wipe off our prints?" he suggested eagerly.

"No," she said, to his disappointment. When they left, it was quite dark, and again nobody noticed their presence.

TWENTY-THREE

THERE WAS a lot of material on the disc, and Lee's archaic printer was smelling overheated before Kate finished. But that was nothing compared to what the stuff did to her brain as she read far into the night, lying on the couch in the guest room.

She fell asleep at some time before dawn, waking three hours later with a drift of papers covering her and the floor around the sofa, like a caricature of a park-bench sleeper with a blanket of newspapers. She groaned, eased her rigid neck, and cobbled the papers together in rough order before walking stiffly down the stairs to the coffee-pot.

"Sleeping beauty," commented Jon. He was constructing a shopping list, which always seemed to involve turning out the entire contents of every cupboard. Fortunately, there was a bit of cold coffee in the pot. Kate splashed it into a mug and put it in the microwave to heat.

"Do you think we could bear to have lentils again?" he asked her. He was tapping his teeth with the eraser end of the pencil, a gesture Kate suddenly recognized as pure Lee, adopted by her caretaker.

"I like lentils," she said finally.

"Maybe I should substitute flagelot. Such a saucy name, don't you think?"

"They sound delicious," she said absently, turning to remove the still-cold coffee from the whirring machine. Dio—she'd meant to call Dio before he went to school.

She took the cup into the living room, making a face when she sipped it, and paused to get her notebook from her briefcase. She flipped through it to find the phone number she wanted, sat down, dialed, sipped, and grimaced again, then sat forward when the phone was answered.

"Wanda Steiner? This is Kate Martinelli."

"Hello, my dear. How is your poor head?"

"Much better, thanks. How is Dio doing?"

"He's coming along nicely. I do like him. He's one of the nicest boys we've had in a long time. Not a mean bone in his body, despite everything he's been through."

"Has he given you any other ideas about his past? Where he came from, what his name is?"

"As you know, Inspector"—Kate grinned to herself: When being official, both Steiners invariably called her Inspector Martinelli; otherwise, to the wife, she was Kate, dear—"I try to give my boys as much privacy as I can, and they know I won't violate their confidence. However, having said that, there's really nothing to tell. I think he may have come from a medium-sized city in some western state, and I believe his mother died within the past five years."

"That's more than he told us."

"Oh, he hasn't said anything directly. I judged it by his habits, and the fact that he has very pretty manners when he chooses. He spent a childhood around a woman who loved him and taught him well, but he's had a fair amount of rough treatment since then. There are scars on his back, you know."

"Are there," Kate said grimly.

"From a belt or a switch, I'd say, which drew blood, and more than once." The words were cool and factual—

she had, after all, seen worse beneath her roof—but the voice was not.

"And he hasn't let a name slip?"

"Never. In fact, he's taken the birth name of his friend, your partner's daughter."

"Jules?"

"When he first came to us out of the hospital, we told him he needed two names for the records, at school and so forth, so he asked her permission to borrow it temporarily."

"Good . . . heavens."

"I thought it was rather sweet."

"I wonder what her mother thinks."

"I doubt that she knows," Wanda said complacently. "So, were you just asking after the boy, or was there something in particular I could help you with?"

"There is, yes. I'd like to talk to him again after school, if you don't mind. I'll drive him home afterward."

"He was a little upset last time, dear," she said in oblique accusation.

"I know; I'm sorry. And I can't promise he won't be upset this time, as well."

"Tell me about it."

"Dio knows something about Jules that may have some bearing on her disappearance."

There was a long silence while Wanda Steiner thought it over. "You're not going to arrest him?"

"Absolutely not."

"Or threaten him with arrest."

"I won't threaten him with anything. I like the kid, too."

"That doesn't mean you won't do your job, Inspector Martinelli. Very well, you may talk with him after school, under two conditions. One, that you tell him clearly, at the beginning, he does not have to talk with you, and two, that you keep firmly in mind, Inspector, that if you cause him to run away from here or lose the progress he has made in the last month, I will be very upset."

It was funny, Kate thought, how this gray-haired lady

with the grandmotherly act could produce a threat of sharpened steel with her voice.

"Yes, ma'am," she said meekly.

♦

However, when she called Dio's school to leave a message, she was disconcerted to find they had no student by the name of Dio Cameron.

"I was just told he was with you. In fact, his guardian gave me your number."

"Just a moment, please. I'll let you talk to one of the vice-principals about it."

Before Kate could stop her, the call clicked and hummed, and a woman answered.

"Cathryn Pierce."

"My name is Kate Martinelli. I'm trying to leave a message for one of your students, and I was just told that he isn't registered there."

"But you think he should be?"

"I was told so—by his current guardian, Wanda Steiner."

"This is one of Wanda's boys?"

"He's using the name Dio Cameron, although—"

"Dio Kimbal."

"Kimbal?"

"That's how he registered, although I was told that wasn't his actual name. Why, is there something wrong?"

"No, no. Sorry, I must've misunderstood Wanda. But there couldn't be two kids named Dio who live with the Steiners."

"Not likely," the vice-principal agreed.

"Anyway, I'd appreciate it if you'd get a message to him, to say that Kate Martinelli would like to speak with him after school. Tell him he doesn't have to but that she'd appreciate it."

There was a pause while Pierce wrote the message down; then she said, "Okay, I'll have it delivered."

"Thank you very much. How's he doing, by the way?"

"Surprisingly well. Are you a friend?"

"I found him, when he was sick."

"You're the police officer who saved his life and was nearly killed?"

"Both exaggerations. But I'm glad he's doing okay."

"He seems to have a lot of catching up to do, but by his tests, I'd say he's a bright boy. Not that being bright is everything."

"It probably helped him survive."

"There is that, yes. Well, thank you, Ms. Martinelli. Let me know if there's anything else I can help you with."

Kate thanked her in return, and cut the connection with her finger. Kimbal? After a moment she allowed the button to come up, and dialed the Steiner number again.

"Wanda? Kate here. Tell me, why is Dio using the name Kimbal?"

"I'm sorry, I assumed you knew. Kimbal is apparently the girl's birth name. I ought to have made it clear, but I thought you knew her so well."

"Who told you her last name was Kimbal?"

"I suppose Dio must have. That is to say, I know her name is Cameron now, but I assumed her mother changed it after the divorce. Is this not the case?" she asked, sounding more resigned than concerned. "Has Dio been lying to me?"

"No. I mean, you seem to know more about Jules than I do."

"I never met her, or her mother, but it sounds like she was a lovely girl."

Kate felt her throat constrict at the flavor of eulogy in Wanda Steiner's words, but she forced herself to say, "Yes, she was. Thanks, Wanda. I won't bother you any more."

"It's not a bother, dear. Tell me, do you want me to say anything to Dio about the name? I will if it's important, but at this stage with my boys I generally find it best to keep the number of confrontations to a minimum."

Kate agreed that it was a question that could be put off for an easier time, thanked her again, and hung up.

After a minute of staring unseeing at the carpet, she blinked and then went in search of Lee, whom she found in the consulting rooms, where she saw her clients. There was no client this morning, just Lee, tidying the crowded shelves of figurines used in the therapeutic process.

"Can I consult?" Kate asked.

"The couch is free."

"Not for me, Frau Doktor. A consultation about a mutual friend." Lee put down her cleaning cloth and lowered herself into a chair. Kate sat in the chair across from her, picking up a glass unicorn to fiddle with. "As you know, I'm trying to reconstruct why and how Jules disappeared."

"There's been nothing to connect her with the Strangler, then?"

"Al would've called. No, I think something else happened to her."

"But I thought— Are you saying you think she's alive?"

"No." Kate took a breath, then forced herself to say it. "I think Jules is dead. But I'm not convinced the Strangler did it. There are too many oddities: Jules was getting weird phone calls from a man; on the drive north, she seemed at times preoccupied, touchy; and unless she was snatched from the parking lot at the motel, which is unlikely, she opened her door to her abductor. Voluntarily. No, I'm uncomfortable with a number of things, and I think there's a chance that someone either watched her or communicated with her over the Internet, or both, then either followed us on the freeway—which wouldn't have been difficult to do, and I certainly wasn't watching over my shoulder—or else arranged to meet her along the way, as soon as she was away from the fairly tight watch Jani kept over her." She rubbed her forehead with her free hand. "I don't know, Lee. I'm just trying to find an explanation that makes sense."

"What did you want to consult about?"

"I broke into Jules's computer."

"How on earth did you do that?"

"I had some help. A lot of what I found was what you'd expect, school assignments and such, but there were three files that bother me. One of them seems to be a kind of novel she's writing, all about a little girl—her words—named Julie. I should mention that according to Dio, one of the things her strange phone caller said was, 'You're mine, Julie.' The story is an endless round of these idyllic episodes, picnics and horseback rides and travel and camping and cooking dinner at home, with her in the middle of a family: Mommy, Daddy, and Julie. Pages and pages of detail, actually very monotonous. If it hadn't been in her personal files and had her kind of vocabulary, I wouldn't have thought she could write such drivel.

"The second file was a lot more like Jules. It was notes and references and statistics, all about relationships."

"Relationships?"

"Marriage, mostly. Pieces of articles about marriage and divorce, statistics about the effects of divorce on children, things that sounded like advice-to-the-lovelorn columns—how to keep your man, things like that—next to a part of some university study with a hundred footnotes, all of them copied. Oh, and personal research she'd done, as well. I recognized several conversations I'd had with her over the last few months, transcribed. She had an amazing memory."

"And the third file?"

"That was the strangest of all. She named the file 'J.K.,' just the initials. Now, I just got off the phone to the vice-principal of Dio's high school, and she told me that Dio is using the last name Kimbal. Wanda Steiner, who's fostering Dio, thought that was Jules's original last name."

"J.K."

"Yes."

"What's in the file?"

"A name. That's the whole file, just a name: Marsh Kimbal."

Lee thought for a moment, looking progressively more unhappy. "You've got to talk to Al, ask if he knows who Marsh Kimbal is."

"And how do I explain how I got the name? Broke into his apartment, violated Jani's privacy?"

"You did get the name from Dio's school."

"The last name, yes, but the name Marsh would take some explaining. I know I'll have to tell him eventually. But first I need to talk to Dio: There are things he's not telling me. And I'll run a search on the name Marsh Kimbal, see if anything turns up, though it's probably a pseudonym."

"You still haven't asked me a question," Lee said mildly.

"I have several. First, would you say those first two files indicate a normal reaction on the part of a single-parent child?"

"A highly intelligent thirteen-year-old who doesn't have a family aside from her mother; who, as you told me the other day, just learned her father was a violent criminal; who, furthermore, is going through a rough time with her mother and is facing the upheaval of having a new father wished on her, even a father she's fond of—all this considered, I'd say yes, it's an unusual interest in family dynamics, but an understandable one."

"Okay. Now, you know Jules; you know how smart she is. Could someone who found out about this fixation—"

"Not a fixation, I'd say that was too strong a word."

"Okay, this strong interest—could he sucker her into running away by playing on a sense of family?"

Lee saw immediately where she was heading. "There've been a number of cases like that lately, haven't there? Kids making friends through the Internet and running away to join them."

"Exactly."

"And you're asking me if Jules might have done that?"

"I can't believe it. I'd have thought she was way too bright to fall for a con."

"A con she wants to believe in? A fantasy to fit her own, a way out of the problems she's had building up in school and at home, a way to follow the romanticized notions of homelessness she may have built up around Dio? Kate, you know as well as I do that a teenager always believes he or she is both isolated and invulnerable—'You don't understand' and 'It can't happen to me' form the bedrock of her age group."

"So you'd say she could have done it?"

"Gone with someone who presented himself as a father figure? Sure. Were there any Internet conversations in storage?"

"None. Richard—the computer kid—said there were signs she'd dumped files. But she'd done it so cleanly, he couldn't retrieve them."

"So what do you do next?"

Kate put the delicate horned figure back on its shelf. "What I've been doing all along. What I always do. Ask ten thousand pointless questions and follow any answer that doesn't feel right."

"But we're still planning on going out of town?"

"Tonight. After I've seen Dio."

◆

"Wanda told me not to harass you," she told the boy over their hamburgers. He looked startled, then smiled uncertainly.

"Did she think you were going to?"

"She knows I'm going to." Calmly, she ate a bite of her food and took a pull at the straw in her milk shake. "But she wanted you to know that you don't have to talk to me if you don't want to."

"And do I? Have to talk to you?" He was thrown off balance by her odd attitude.

"No."

"So, why should I stay here?"

She shrugged. "Be a shame to waste your burger." She took another bite, and after a minute, he followed her example.

"So," he asked after a while, "when does the harassment begin?"

"It's been going on since I left the message for you at school. I plan to make you so sick of little notes and big hamburgers that you tell me what I want to know."

His jaws stopped, then started moving again, more slowly.

"What do you want to know?"

"The same thing I wanted to know last time. Whatever you're not telling me about Jules."

"What am I not telling you?"

"If I knew that, I wouldn't have to harass you."

"What makes you think there's something I'm not telling you?"

"I don't think; I know."

"How do you know?"

"You tell me every time you open your mouth."

"Maybe I'll just keep my mouth shut, then."

"See? You just did it again."

Resentment and outrage mingled in Dio's face as he searched for the proper reaction.

"Dio, you're going to tell me sooner or later, because you want to. You can tell me now, or you can tell me after I've beaten you into submission with hamburgers and milk shakes. Oh, and ice cream. You like ice cream?"

"Yeah." He was beginning to look alarmed.

"There's a killer ice cream parlor in the other direction from the school. I can bring in the big guns; they have a brownie sundae that makes you think you've died and gone to heaven. That ought to bring you to your knees. And if it doesn't, I'll have to torture you with the occasional ball game."

Suddenly, it dawned on him: This adult, this policewoman, was making a joke. She could see him rejecting the idea, trying it on again, and slowly working around to considering the possibility. Eyeing her curiously, he ventured a response: "If you really wanted to hurt me, there's a movie I was thinking of seeing."

She threw the remnant of her hamburger onto the paper-lined basket; he jumped; she reached for the napkins and began to wipe her hands in disgust. "Wouldn't you know," she said bitterly. "Here I try to threaten some-one, it turns out he's a goddamn masochist."

His mouth went into an O, and then he saw the skin around her eyes crinkly slightly, and he suddenly began to laugh.

Kate was inordinately proud of that laugh, but she gave no indication. Instead, she finished dramatically wiping her hands and fought hard to keep a look of dis-gust pasted on while the boy dissolved in snorts and choking laughter. She doubted he'd laughed like that in a hell of a long time.

It wiped away his fear of her. However, when the brief episode was over, he became suddenly shy, and she de-cided that Wanda Steiner was right: It was best to take things in stages—too soon to ask about the name Kimbal. She led him off to the car and drove him home, chatting about nothing.

But when they were in front of the Steiner home, she caught him before he could open the door.

"Jules was my friend, Dio," she said quietly. "I intend to find out what happened to her, and I can't afford to ignore what you know. Think about it."

He walked away, subdued. She drove away, buoyant with the knowledge of a step taken, and with the thought of some days alone with Lee.

◆

"Has Jon been home since this morning?"

"Just to drop off the swimsuit he bought me. You like it?"

Kate turned from her examination of the closet to look at the piece of nylon Lee was holding up.

"Good heavens, it looks like you could actually swim in the thing. I'd have expected something that looked like spiderwebs, or with plastic fruit hanging off it, or made out of snakeskin. How on earth did you get him to buy just an ordinary suit?"

"I told him I'd make him go back until he got me one that I would wear, that I'd pay for only one suit, and that if he succeeded, he could have three days off."

"Clever you. Does it fit?"

"More or less."

"Will wonders never cease? But anyway, he does know we're going away?"

"I told him I doubted we'd leave before tomorrow morning—I didn't think you'd actually get away, to tell you the truth."

"Ye of little faith. Do you want the sweatshirt or the sweater?"

"Both. I did tell him we'd leave a note if a miracle happened and we actually got away before he gets back. Which reminds me, did you make any arrangements with work, or are you just calling it medical leave?"

"I called in two days of vacation. Have you seen those rubber sandals I bought last year?"

"Jon put them in the box on the left. Sweetheart," said Lee in a different voice, "what do you want to do with these?"

Kate turned from the closet and saw Lee holding the envelope and loose pictures.

"Ah, hell," she said. "I don't know. Send them to Al, I guess. No, not the one of Jules. And leave the negatives out, as well; he won't need those. Just stick them in the drawer, and here, give me the envelope." She sealed the flap and, downstairs, paused in the act of carrying out the suitcases to address the envelope to Al in care of D'Amico's department. She then added a P.S. to Lee's note, asking Jon to mail it, and then she carried the suitcases out to the car.

She left her gun in its drawer and the cellular phone on its charger. After much agonizing and changing her mind three times, she left her pager too, on the table next to the phone. Like it or not, this would be a holiday. She felt that she owed Lee the symbolic commitment of leaving the beeper behind.

◆

Three hours later, Jon came in, his arms filled with grocery bags. The puzzled look on his face cleared when he found the note propped against the saltcellar, and he looked pleased, then mildly irritated as he glanced at the food he had just bought, and then he began to look even happier as he realized he did not, after all, have to cook it. A phone call and a quick distribution of groceries into the refrigerator and freezer, followed by a trip downstairs for a change of clothes and a small overnight bag, and he was also out the door. However, a minute later his key sounded in the lock. He went back to the kitchen, picked up the manila envelope, and went out again.

◆

At the shipping place, Jon hesitated briefly over the methods of delivery before deciding that the other jobs he'd done for Kate lately had been matters of life and—no, maybe that wasn't the best phrase—had been urgent as hell, so he might as well treat this the same way. If Kate was too busy to mail it herself and couldn't be bothered to give instructions, well, she'd just have to pay for it. Besides, the expense made him feel he'd had revenge for having had to put that lovely fresh bit of salmon into the freezer instead of directly onto the grill. He sent the envelope the fastest way they offered, and the most expensive.

He then climbed back into his car and headed across the Golden Gate Bridge to Marin and the mountaintop house of friends.

◆

In the other direction, near Monterey, Kate and Lee found a hotel with a room on the ground level and a glimpse of the ocean. One of the first things Kate did was to leave a message for Jon on the machine to tell him where they were: the freedom from responsibility represented by leaving her beeper and gun behind extended only so far. That done, however, she forced herself to relax. During the night the rhythm of the waves pervaded their bodies, and during the day they walked and did tourist things at the aquarium, and they talked.

For the first time since August, they began tentatively to explore this new stage in their relationship, with both of them now convinced that Lee was, literally, back on her feet and able to shoulder a real part of the burden. Cautious of hurting each other, careful not to wield grievances, trying hard for a clean beginning, they talked.

One of the things they talked about was a topic that had lain between them for five months, ever since the argument about Aunt Agatha's letter. Yes, Lee still wanted a child. No, she hadn't forgotten it; she hadn't said it in a fit of madness; it had not been a passing fantasy. She also was not about to go ahead with it unless Kate agreed. If she had a child, that child would have two parents, not a mom and an "other."

She had, she told Kate, gone so far as to research the problems. On the medical side, there were actually a few doctors out there who regarded pregnancy in a woman who had poor use of her legs as something other than a prescription for an abortion. On the legal side, she felt she could now present a case, if called for, that she was competent to perform the tasks of motherhood. She might not be able to run after a two-year-old, but she could hobble fast. The dual legal threat concerning the status of the child of a lesbian and a handicapped woman would remain, but she was as prepared as she could be.

Kate did not agree with any of this. She did, however, listen.

◆

All the members of that family—householder, partner, servant, and the ghost of an as-yet-unformed child—spent a quiet two days in their various places of rest, blissfully unaware of the storm that was moving in on two fronts.

◆

At 1:15 on Sunday afternoon, the telephone in the empty house on Russian Hill began to ring.

◆

By the time Jon Samson arrived home later that afternoon, relaxed and slightly rosy from the wintery sun beating down on his friends' sheltered swimming pool, the tape on the answering machine was filled, almost entirely with the same message, delivered in Al Hawkin's increasingly frantic voice. When Jon got out of his car, he was pounced upon by a burly but not unattractive uniformed police officer who had been doing drive-bys all afternoon, waiting for a sign of life at the house.

◆

While Jon was rescuing the salmon from the freezer and preparing to grill it with some tiny red-skinned potatoes for his new friend, Kate and Lee, also sunburned and satisfactorily tired, were approaching the city.

"Do you want to go somewhere for dinner, or just pick something up?" Lee asked. "If we just go home, Jon will feel obliged to cook."

(Jon, meanwhile, was trying hard to cook, although the telephone calls were becoming very frustrating, not only because he hadn't the faintest idea where the pictures in the envelope he'd sent had come from but also because they kept interrupting his attempts at conversation with the burly cop. The beeper's intermittent noise also drove him bats, because it was locked into the small table with Kate's gun. He finally had the uniformed officer carry the table into Lee's consulting rooms and shut the door on it, and went back to his charcoal.)

"I don't feel like a restaurant," Kate said. "Shall we just stop for a burger? In fact—would you like to meet Dio?"

"I'd love to, but you can't just drop in on him on a Sunday night."

"Oh yes I can," she said, a shade grimly.

Wanda Steiner opened the door. "Kate! Hello, dear. Do come in."

"Hello, Wanda. Sorry to drop in on you like this. I was wondering if Dio was in. I don't know if you've had dinner, but I thought he might like to come out and have a hamburger with us."

"I'm sure he'd love to—you know how boys his age can eat, and he did seem to enjoy your last meeting—but he's still out at the park with Reg, kicking around a soccer ball."

"Oh well, that's okay. Another time."

"No, dear, why don't you just pop down and see if they aren't nearly finished? Reg won't admit when he's had enough, but he did pull a shoulder muscle the other day playing basketball. That's why they're playing soccer, to give his arm a rest. No, I'm sure he'd be happy for an excuse to quit, and I think Dio wanted to talk with you, anyway."

"Did he?" Kate said, feeling her pulse quicken.

"I think so. Anyway, you go see. It's only at the park—that's two blocks up the way you were going and one over to the right. Just have him back by nine. School tomorrow, you know."

TWENTY-FOUR

AT THE park, a graying man with the stocky build of a lifelong athlete was running up and down the otherwise-deserted playing field with three boys. What they held over him by young muscle, numbers, and speed was countered by experience and wile, although to Kate's eye, he appeared to be flagging a bit. She got out of the car and walked slowly toward them across the soggy winter grass, enjoying the thud and scuffle and snatches of breathless exclamations across the cold dusk air.

"Watch out, Jay."

"He's got—"

"No you don't!" shouted the older voice, a laugh lodged in the back of it.

"It's mine!"

"Pass it, Dio. Pass it!"

"I—oh shit!" came Dio's voice as he caught his foot on a stray toe and went sprawling.

"Language," chided Reg's voice.

"I meant shoot," Dio called, but the action was moving rapidly away from him as Reg ran with the ball in a zigzag pattern down the field, deflecting the teenagers with his broad shoulders, stopping abruptly twice to change direction and run around them, and finally booting the black-and-white ball ahead of him through some invisible goal. He threw up both hands in triumph, but as the boys stood around him protesting his sly maneuvers, he bent over and stood with his hands on his knees, sides heaving.

Dio looked up at Kate's approach.

"Did you see that?" he demanded. "He fouled me. It was deliberate."

"I wouldn't put it past him," she agreed amiably. "Hi, Reg. Still sitting out an easy retirement, I see."

"That's me." He gasped, and stuck out a hand filthy with sweat, mud, grass, and God knew what else. She shook it.

"See, she agreed! That was a foul."

"So maybe next time you won't insist on three against one," Reg said.

"Cheating old man," Dio protested, without sounding actually angry.

Reg Steiner ignored him. "What can I do for you, Ms. Martinelli?"

"Wanda told me I could steal Dio for a little. If he wants to join us for dinner," she added, making it a question.

"Sure," Dio said. "Is that okay, Reg?"

"Fine. I'll drop Jason and Paulo home. Better get your sweats from the car."

Sweatpants on and sweatshirt in hand, Dio climbed into the back of the Saab, filling it instantly with the vigorous smell of fresh air, crushed grass, and male sweat.

"Dio, this is my friend Lee Cooper. Lee, this is Dio, known as Dio Kimbal, for reasons known only to himself."

Dio absently wiped his right hand on the leg of his sweatpants before putting it over the seat for Lee to shake, but he was looking only at Kate.

"More third degree, eh?" he asked.

"I have my truncheon ready."

"Where are we going?"

"Someplace quiet, where your screams won't be heard."

They ended up at a place where indeed screams would barely be heard, but not because of the quiet. There could be little attempt at interrogation over the blare of the jukebox, or even conversation, although Lee's mouth moved a great deal as the music played up and down through the songs of her own adolescence. They had burgers and shakes and apple pie, and it was half past seven when they went back out onto the street, all three of them beaming and replete.

In the car, Kate paused with her hand on the key. "Wanda said you wanted to talk to me."

"Maybe you'd like to drop me somewhere first," Lee immediately offered.

"No, that's okay," Dio said. "I didn't really want to talk."

Kate wondered if she'd imagined the very slight stress on the final word. "What did you have in mind?"

"I thought . . ." He took a deep breath. "I thought I'd show you something."

"Good," Kate said approvingly. "Showing me things is good. While you're thinking, though, you might also think about where the name Kimbal came from."

"It's Jules's name."

"Her name is Cameron," Kate pointed out.

"Her real father's name was Kimbal."

Kate whirled around so fast, she nearly strangled herself on the seat belt. "She told you that?"

"Yeah."

"Marsh Kimbal?"

"I don't know. She never told me his first name."

"What is Cameron, then?"

"I don't know that, either, but it's not his name. It isn't her mother's name, either. At least that's what Jules said."

"How did she find this out? Did she come across her birth certificate?"

"It isn't on her birth certificate, not the one her

266

mother has. There isn't a father listed on that one. Jules hunted it down in the records of some hospital somewhere, over the computer."

"How long have you known this?"

He wouldn't meet her eyes. "Since last summer," he said in a small voice.

"Shit, Dio." She turned and smacked her hand hard against the steering wheel. "How could you keep this kind of information to yourself? I've been trying—"

"Kate," Lee said quietly. "He's given it to you now. Work with it."

Kate grasped the wheel firmly with both hands and took several slow breaths. "Okay. I'm sorry, Dio. Thank you for telling me. I'm glad the hamburger torture worked. Now I'm going to have to find a phone." She pulled the keys out of the ignition and began to peer at the surrounding buildings, but she was interrupted by Dio's hand tentatively touching her shoulder.

"Could the phone wait?" he asked. "I promised Reg I'd be back by nine, and I'd really like to give you the other thing tonight."

"What is it?"

"An envelope Jules gave me last month, with something lumpy in it. I didn't open it."

"Where is it?"

"At the squat. It was the only place I could think of to hide something."

She looked at the clock. To the squat and back across town would indeed leave little time for hunting down first a telephone and then Al Hawkin.

"Why didn't you ever have a car phone put in?" she complained to Lee, starting the engine and pulling out with a squeal onto Van Ness Avenue.

♦

The three of them sat in the silent car and looked at the dark, dreary bulk of the warehouse.

"We don't have a key for the padlock," Kate said, "and they've nailed the metal sheet down."

"I got in another way last month," Dio told her. "It'll only take me a minute."

"I'll go with you."

"You don't have to."

"Yes, I do." She left the keys in the ignition and turned to Lee. "If anyone comes, anyone at all, lean on the horn. I'll be here in twenty seconds."

"Be careful," was all Lee said.

"I wonder if my tetanus shots are up-to-date," Kate muttered, reaching under the seat for the flashlight.

The boy's alternate entrance was around the back of the building. He dragged a crate from its resting place against the wall to a position under the metal fire escape and boosted himself up onto it. To Kate's relief the box proved itself sturdier than it looked by not collapsing as Dio jumped up to catch the lowest rung. He pulled himself up, Kate following with a good deal more effort. Halfway up the stairway, he swung his leg over the handrail and onto a narrow decorative ledge on the building. Kate kept the light shining on his feet as he picked his way along to a small window half a dozen feet away, which easily pushed open. He turned and grinned at Kate, his teeth gleaming in the indirect glow of the flashlight.

"I was afraid they'd fastened it shut." He placed both hands on the sill and pulled himself up and over. After a muffled thump, he reappeared and stretched his hand out for the light, then guided Kate's steps until she, too, had dropped into the strategically placed mattress. She coughed violently at the dust raised, and moved away.

"Let's hurry this up. I'd rather not have to explain what we're doing to the local patrol."

They went down the hall, passing the room where Kate's head had been bashed in, and down the stairs past the communal living quarters to the ground floor. It was still filthy, and there were still heaps of decaying carpet filling one of the rooms and sagging Sheetrock on the walls.

"Can I borrow the light?" Dio asked. Kate handed it

to him, watching as he picked his way across the floor to one bit of ruined wall, where he shone the light up into the dust-colored studs and then worked his hand up into the recesses. When he drew out the envelope, Kate released a breath she had not known she was holding: She did not like spiders.

He came back and handed her the dirty white envelope. She took it by one corner and looked at it curiously. The back had been opened and then taped shut. "It was like that when Jules gave it to me," he said. "Look at how it's addressed."

She turned it over. On the front was typed:

JULIE KIMBAL
(JULES CAMERON)

"Can we open it?" he asked eagerly.

In answer, she patted her clothing, found a lack of anything that would do as an evidence bag, and shook her head. "Not yet. Jesus, I hope this case never comes to trial; the defense will have a field day. No, Dio, we can't look at it yet. Give me the light."

Still holding the lumpy envelope by the same corner, she retraced her steps upstairs to the small window and peered down in dismay. One-handed and backward, it was an ugly proposal.

"Isn't there another way out?" she asked.

"The top of the fire escape is at the roof, but there's a padlock on the door. This window's so small, nobody bothered."

"The hell with it. Let's see if we can break the padlock."

It was a small lock and a thin chain, held on by a couple of feeble staples. Kate raised a leg and kicked it, and the whole thing went flying out onto the roof. She had Dio prop the door shut against the wind when they left.

"Why didn't you guys ever take that off?"

"Weldon said it wasn't right to break things in the squat." Kate turned to stare at him, but he was serious.

She followed him, shaking her head at the logic of a man who would shoot a cop but not break a lock.

At the car, he asked again, "Are we going to open it?"

"I'm going to take you home."

"Please. I really want to see what's in it."

Oh hell, Kate thought, he deserves it. And I'm not about to take it into the lab without opening it, anyway.

She cut the envelope open on Wanda Steiner's kitchen table. Wanda had placed a paper towel down to protect the scrubbed wood from the dirty paper, and she'd given Kate a lethally sharp kitchen knife with a long, narrow blade. Kate slit the paper, leaving the tape intact, lifted the slit open with the tip of the knife, and slid out the thing inside.

It was a small, lumpy wad of tissue paper wrapped around something. With the tip of the knife and the end of a fingernail she began to undo it. The object whispered slightly inside the paper, the metallic whisper of a chain shifting, and with a shudder of premonition she knew what would be inside the envelope.

She was right: dog tags.

A set of dog tags, scratched and dull from long wear. The name stamped onto them was KIMBAL, MARSHAL J.

Kate stood up. Her body felt numb with cold, but she was vaguely aware of relief that her brain was still functioning.

"I've got to talk to Al," she said, looking at Lee.

"Do you have his number?"

"It's at home. I left everything at home."

"Jon's probably back, if you don't want to wait."

"He'll find it for me." Kate went to the phone on the kitchen wall, and only when she had begun to punch in her home number did she realize that it was a strange phone, and then she noticed that she had an audience. Awkwardly, she held out the receiver to the Steiners. "Do you mind if I . . ."

"Of course not."

She turned to complete the dial sequence and remembered something. "None of you touch that paper or the dog tags," she ordered. After a minute, she frowned. "He's got the answering machine on."

"He may be screening calls. Leave a message."

Kate nodded, and when the recorded message had played to the end, she started to say in the stilted tones of someone speaking into a recording device, "Jon, it's Kate here. Lee and I will be home in—"

The others in the room heard the phone give forth a whoop, and then a loud and vastly relieved voice was shouting into Kate's ear.

"Kate, darling! My God, it's been like Grand Central Station around here. Where on earth are you?"

"Why? What's wrong?"

"Something about some pictures you sent to Al Hawkin. You've stirred up a veritable ant's nest there, dear. I thought he—"

"Pictures? What pict—B.J. Montero's photographs. Jon, what about them?" she said urgently.

"I don't know; he wouldn't tell lowly old me. Just said that there's a man in them who shouldn't be, or something."

"Was it Lavalle?"

"Well, you know," said Jon, "I really don't think so. Anyway, you'd better call the poor man before he ruptures a blood vessel or something. He was sounding a wee bit stressed."

Al wasn't the only one, Kate thought. She hadn't heard Jon this arch in months.

"Right. Did he give you a number?"

"Only a few dozen times. Do you have a pen?"

"Just a minute. Lee? Hand me that pencil? Okay," she said to him. He gave her a Portland number. She repeated it, hung up, punched in the lengthy sequence that would bill it to her credit card, and when it rang she asked for Al Hawkin. He was there in a matter of seconds.

"Kate? Thank God. Where the hell did you get those pictures?"

"It's a long story, but they were taken at a rest stop south of Portland where Jules and I went—in the afternoon, a few hours before she disappeared. Some people were there, taking pictures of one another, and I tracked them down. I sent them to you on the off chance Lavalle's car was there."

"Not Lavalle, no. Jesus. When I got them, I didn't know what the hell they were. Nobody else recognized them, so I stuck them in the team room—I'm back in Portland—and Jani saw them when she came to bring me some lunch." Jani's on her feet again, Kate noted in passing. "She just looked through them. In fact, she'd put them down and walked away, when it hit her. I thought she was going to pass out again."

"She saw Marsh Kimbal," Kate said.

But for the background noise, she would have thought he had hung up. Eventually, he spoke, his voice high and breathless.

"How the fuck did you know that?"

"I've been busy, Al. I just found out. He's been sending Jules messages. He sent her a present, too—his old army dog tags. I assume he was in the army?"

"Yes. Jani . . . Jani told me he was dead. I still don't know if she honestly thought he was, or if she told herself he was so many times that she began to believe it herself, or— Anyway, that doesn't matter. What matters is, if Jules's father snatched her, there's a good chance she's still alive."

"Al, tell me, please tell me there's something visible on his car's license plates," she prayed.

"The car's registered to a Mark Kendall. He lives in the middle of nowhere in southern Oregon, two, three hours from Medford."

"It's him?"

"Sounds like. We've stayed away until we knew what the hell we were dealing with, but the FBI's already set up a team in Lakeview.

"I'll leave tonight, be there before morning. Where should I go?"

"They've taken over a building at—where the hell's

that address? Here it is." He read it off to her. "It's a bank that just went bust; the FBI is borrowing it."

"Where will you be?" she asked him.

"I'll be there," he said, and hung up.

She lifted the receiver from her ear and placed it gently on the base that was mounted on the wall, staring at it for a long moment before she turned to the others. Struggling to contain the riot of emotions set off by the rebirth of hope, she looked first at Lee, then at Dio.

"Jules may be alive," she said.

TWENTY-FIVE

"His name is Marshal James Kimbal, known as Marsh," the FBI man had begun, but that had been a long, weary time ago, and Kate now felt as if she'd been sitting for a week in this chair around the long table in the anonymously corporate boardroom in this building in southern Oregon. She'd arrived here at some ungodly hour on Monday morning, having driven through the night, and had sat here, it seemed, ever since. It was now Wednesday, and as far as she could see, they were setting off on a second full day of the same circular discussion that had occupied part of Monday and all day Tuesday.

Even the photograph of Jules that was pinned to the wall, blurry from enlargement and the dust in the air between the girl and the telephoto lens, failed to charm anymore. When she'd first seen it on Monday afternoon, she couldn't take her eyes off it for the sheer joy of seeing evidence of Jules alive. Now her attention, what was left of it, was all for the man who walked in front of Jules, the man with the gun in his hand, the man who had tracked Jani and found Jules and taken her out from under Kate's unconscious nose.

Since those introductory words on Monday afternoon,

the compilers of evidence—those not occupied with Anton Lavalle two hundred miles to the north—had been in high gear. Photographs, a couple of nearly inaudible long-range recordings, and a detailed history of an obsessed father had been wheeled in, and analysts and recommendations had begun. And they had continued, until Kate was beginning to regret that the investigation was as high-key as it had turned out. Normally, a father kidnapping a daughter would not merit two FBI agents, a sheriff and his deputy (who knew the land like the backs of their sun-beaten hands), and two highly qualified psychiatrists, experts in the field of kidnapping (one speaking for the mind of the villain, the other, the only woman in the room aside from Kate, sharing her expert opinion on the mental state of the child victim). The experts were there as spillover from the Lavalle case, having been sent down because they were more or less in the neighborhood; the others were there because of Al, and because it had begun as a highly visible case in the media. One of the agents was unhappy about being in the sticks rather than in Portland, and both of the experts were tired and just a bit bored. Al was present because he was, after all, experienced in the field, and Kate had a seat at the table because he wanted her to. Various other people had been in and out of the boardroom during the last two days, from Jani (for an uncomfortable time, causing a collective sigh of relief when she left) to D'Amico (who shuttled back and forth a few times from one end of Oregon to the other before it was decided that he was best used on his home ground in Portland) and a handful of technicians and other law-enforcement personnel, who came and went as they were needed.

Two things had justified the cautious and high-tech approach they were taking: Kimbal had a well-documented tendency toward violence, and the girl's stepfather was a cop. There was no way they could use the standard approach, which would have been to take a couple of sheriff's deputies and bring the girl back. The core eight people had spent the last two days discussing evidence and options, and by now they were thoroughly fed up with one another.

"Look," Al was saying tiredly, "even you guys aren't allowed just to take the guy out without even giving him a warning."

"We're not suggesting that," began the FBI man at the head of the table.

"Sounds to me like you are. You just said you couldn't go in at night because of his dogs and because he and Jules are always in the cabin together, but during the day you can't get in fast enough to separate them without alerting him. Short of cold-blooded murder with a sniper scope, what're you going to do, disguise yourselves as rocks?"

Several angry voices spoke up at once, and Kate half-listened to the argument, her eyes drawn to the enlarged photos of the small cabin where Jules had been taken by her father.

It was literally out in the middle of nowhere, in an expanse of knee-high scrub and rock, five miles from the nearest neighbor. For a paranoid ex-con with survivalist leanings out to save his only daughter from the wicked world, it was perfect: He could see the enemy coming, miles away.

Other photos tacked up on the carpeted walls showed fuzzy images of Marsh Kimbal, lanky and black-haired. In several of them, Jules followed behind, but the pictures, taken over a considerable distance with lenses like telescopes, were too hazy to give a hint of the girl's expression. To Kate, though, the girl's body language told of her confusion and doubt.

The argument was coming around again, and it was time for Kate to say her bit. She stirred, waited for an opening, and spoke up.

"I still think you're wrong. I know kidnap victims always fall in love with their captors, but I don't believe Jules would fall for his crap, not in the long run. I mean, look, the man's a fascist."

"He's a survivalist," corrected the male psychiatrist,

and Kate went on hurriedly before he could present a lecture on political niceties.

"Same thing," she said. "He's a sexist and a swine, and Jules would never go for it. You won't have any trouble separating her from him."

"She's only a child," he insisted.

"She's got more brains than any three adults, present company not excluded."

"She may be bright," commented the woman expert, "but that doesn't mean she is not gullible."

"Okay," Kate conceded. "Granted, intelligent people can be really stupid. But not Jules, not in this case. I know that if I go in there all by myself, let her see me, just ease in and out again, she'll read it as a warning, so that when you come in with force, she won't panic. She'll be ready to come to us. On the other hand, if you just descend on her with guns blazing, then she probably would hang on to Kimbal, because she wouldn't know what the hell was going on. An adult wouldn't, either."

At this point in the argument's cycle, the head man normally either redirected the flow or called for a break, but this time, before he could do more than place his hands on the table preparatory to shifting his chair back, the woman expert sat forward and placed her gold pen onto the glossy wood with an authoritative click.

"Inspector Martinelli may be right," she stated. The room went still in surprise. "If she did succeed in going in, making contact with the child, possibly even conveying a message, and coming away, then we would be in much the stronger position: Jules would be forewarned, and we would have had a direct look into Kimbal's defenses. If she failed, one of three things would have happened: She would be driven off, taken hostage herself, or shot outright. In the first case, we would not be much worse off than we are now, nor in the second, which would also give us the thin advantage of having a trained adult present to oppose Kimbal. As to the third possibility, I don't know that there is much to say, other than noting that Inspector Martinelli is clearly aware of the risks involved, has had a good deal of field experience with decoy situations, and does not appear to me suicidal."

Well, thought Kate, feeling her mouth go dry, it's always good to have a clear mind to tell us how matters lie. She glanced at Hawkin, but he was not looking at her.

"I still think I should be the one to go," he was saying.

Both psychiatrists began immediately to shake their heads. Even the man agreed that, with this particular hostage taker, any casual intruder would have to appear blatantly harmless. Were they in a city, an aged drunk might do, but not miles from the closest bar. The analysts knew enough about Marsh Kimbal to feel certain that he would take an adult male intruder as a threat. He might believe that a woman was harmless, though, and that she was stupid enough to get lost among the dirt roads of eastern Oregon.

For once, Kate agreed with the experts.

And for once, to everyone's astonishment, the disparate law-enforcement personnel assembled in the room seemed on the verge of agreement, as well. So tired of waiting that they were willing to go along with any proposal actually involving forward motion, they found themselves, with varying degrees of reluctance, agreeing to Kate's proposal.

The rest of the morning was spent laying out plans and fallbacks, and then Kate was excused so that she could put on her fancy-dress costume.

◆

Kate sat, clenching and loosing her hands on the wheel of the little Japanese car, staring through the streaked windshield and over the carefully dirtied hood at the bare road that stretched out into the distance.

Beside her, Al Hawkin rubbed his hand over his mouth, grimacing at the scratchy sound, and broke the silence.

"You don't have to, you know."

"Al, the sooner you get out of the car, the sooner I can get on with this."

"I could go."

"Al," she said warningly.

"All right." He made no move toward the door handle. "Are you scared?"

"Of course I'm scared. I'm always scared when I dress up as a decoy. It's gotten so I start to sweat whenever I pick up a tube of lipstick."

He smiled dutifully at the feeble joke. "Christ, I hate sending you out there without a backup."

"You're not sending me out anywhere," she said, bristling slightly. He turned to look at her for the first time since they'd left town an hour before.

"I wonder if Jules will actually recognize you."

"My new look," she said. "I thought the lace on the collar was a really nice touch." With her tired blond curls, light pink lipstick, trim brown penny loafers, and tan polyester trousers—she'd drawn the line at the flowered skirt that had been offered—she looked like a conservative young woman, the sort who could easily get lost out here in the middle of nowhere.

"In my youth, they used to call that a Peter Pan collar."

"Did they? Funny. Jules told me once she hated Peter Pan—the idea of lost boys made her furious. This was when we were looking for Dio," she explained.

"Yes? Well, I'm sorry Lee can't see you."

"Jon would love it even more. Get out of here, Al. I need to go."

"Watch your back, Martinelli," he said, and surprised them both by reaching out an arm to embrace her shoulders briefly. In a moment, he was standing on the roadside, watching her drive away, before he turned and got into the back of the governmental car that followed her for a while before turning off to join the rest of the watchers on the low hillock three miles south of the cabin where Jules Cameron was being kept by the man who would be her father.

◆

Kate decided that sweaty hands and heart palpitations were not unsuited to the role she was supposed to be playing, so she might as well not try to hide them. She pulled up in a tentative manner in the dirt space in front of the cabin and sat for a moment, studying the two sleek Doberman pinschers who stood inside their high-wire cage that adjoined the house. They were studying her in turn through the wide spaces of the wire, their heads down, their jaws shut in concentration, their eyes hungry, as she opened her door and cautiously got out of the car. Nothing moved, including the dogs, although she knew that Kimbal and Jules had been inside as recently as when she'd dropped Al, or the FBI men following her would have let her know. Besides, his pickup truck was still there, parked under the bare tree that in the summer would shade a part of the dog run.

She walked around the back of the car, keeping it between her and the dogs, and walked up the two worn wooden steps to knock at the screen door. She stepped back down onto the packed earth, turned her back on the door, and waited.

Tense as she was, she didn't hear the inner door open until the man spoke.

"Yeah?"

Kate spun around, laughing nervously at the shadowy figure behind the screen. His right hand was on the door, his left hand resting on the jamb at shoulder level. She squinted up at him.

"You startled me," she said, with just the slightest drawl in her voice, and tittered again.

"What do you want?" he said.

"Well, I'm lost, I think. At least none of the roads much resemble the directions I was given, and haven't for some time now. I wonder if you might tell me where I am."

She felt his eyes on her, and wondered where Jules was. "Where d'you want to be?" he asked.

"A place called Two-Bar Road? Here, let me get my map. I'll show you." She went to the car, aware of his suspicious gaze burning her, a gaze echoed by the two animals off to her right. She opened the passenger door, took out a crumpled and completely unfolded Oregon road map, and carried it back to the house.

He had not moved. He did not move when she stood on the lower step and fumbled with the awkward sheet, balling it up rather than folding it to the place.

"See, I was here, and—here's the place. It's just a driveway, but they call it Two-Bar Road. It's there where the circle is—see? D'you mind if I open the door so you can see it? That's better. So, can you tell me where I am now?"

No sign of Jules, not even in the slice of tidy room she could see when he allowed the door to open just enough to bring his right shoulder out and point to a place on the map with his index finger while his left hand stayed glued to the inside doorjamb—with a gun, she speculated, nestled up against the wood trim and held tightly in place? Kate fancied she could smell gun oil.

"You're right here," he said, his finger in the blank space forty miles from the imaginary Two-Bar Road.

"Am I really? Oh no. And it'll be dark by the time I get there. How on earth did I get way over here? Oh well. Let me just make sure I have it right. I don't suppose you have a pen? No, don't bother," she drawled, although he had made no move toward stepping inside his house. "I'm sure I have one in the car." She went back to the passenger side of the car, rummaged about in the fake leather handbag, and came back with a cheap ballpoint pen. One of the dogs was smelling the air for her scent, its muzzle protruding from the cage up to its eyebrows. "Those are certainly powerful-looking dogs you've got there," she said to their owner. No response, and Kate was torn between the building fury that nothing whatsoever was happening and the need to maintain her line of helpless chatter.

"Let me just mark this down here. Now where was

it?" Where the fuck is Jules, you bastard? she thought. "Okay, I've got it. So I go back to here and then turn left; that should get me there." God, this *is* her father; she's got his hands, and they have the same eyebrows. "I don't suppose I could use your telephone, just to call and let them know I'm coming?" She knew that he had no telephone, but it was, after all, the sort of thing a lost woman would ask.

"I don't have a phone."

"You don't? Well, I guess it's quite a ways from nowhere. Yours was the first place I saw for miles." Surely she's heard me, Kate thought in desperation. She has to be here, and the cabin is too small for her to be out of earshot. I'm going to have to leave; he's not going to let me in. She wavered, then decided to try just one last nudge. "Just one more thing, then, and I'll let you get on with your evening. I wonder if I could be really intrusive and ask if I could use your bathroom? If I have to go another hour on these roads, I'll just burst." At least I know you have indoor plumbing, you bastard. I don't have to worry about being pointed to an outhouse.

He studied her, looked over her shoulder at the beat-up car, and then took his right hand off the door and stepped to his left. Taking a deep breath, and mightily tempted to elbow him in the gut as she went past, regulations be damned, she went up the two steps and walked past him into the house, into a room with a threadbare braided rug on the worn linoleum floor, mismatched sofa and chairs in front of an oil-drum woodstove, and the arsenal of a survivalist on racks on the walls. She had just time to notice an open book, a spiral notepad, and a pen on the Formica kitchen table when her body froze at the sound of a shotgun shell being jacked into place.

"Turn around," he said. She did so, slowly.

"What are you doing?" she demanded in outrage and fear, neither of which were feigned, not with the barrels of a shotgun two feet from her chest.

"A woman like you would rather pee her pants than come into a lonesome house with a strange man. Who sent you?" Shit, it wasn't just Jani who gave Jules her brains, thought Kate wildly.

"Marsh?" a tentative voice said from behind Kate.

Kate jerked, and then with her hands well out from her sides, she swiveled her head to look at the inner door.

Jules was wearing grubby, overly large jeans and a plaid shirt that had to belong to Kimbal. On her feet were the boots they had bought in Berkeley, one of them with string in place of the original laces. Her haircut had grown out and had a hacked-off appearance. A wide bruise darkened her left cheekbone, and her eyes looked at Kate without recognition.

"Go back to your room, Julie."

"But Marsh, I just wondered—"

"Julie," he said in a voice like a quiet whip crack, "I said go."

The child looked out from under her lank bangs at her father, and at Kate, then stepped back into the room and shut the door quietly. Kate turned her head back to the man with the shotgun.

"Is that what you wanted to see?" he demanded. "That's my daughter. She's mine, and if that bitch of a mother of hers sent you to fetch her back, that's just hard luck for you. Out."

For a moment, Kate felt weak with relief: He was going to let her drive away, thinking her an informal envoy, and no great damage would have been done. However, halfway to the car he said, "Stop right there. Hold out your left hand."

She knew the sound of the rattling metal even before the handcuffs hit her wrist. The sharp jab of the shotgun barrel against her spine kept her from moving, but she broke out in a sweat, oozing fear, and it was all she could do to keep a whimper from finding its way up her throat.

"Other one," he ordered, and when she did not move, he barked, "I'll shoot you down right here if I have to."

He won't, she tried to tell herself. There's no reason for him to do more than drive me off his land in some humiliating manner. Besides, I do have backup; a dozen men are watching through their scopes from that small hill off in the distance. Just keep him calm, and delay. If Jules has the sense to go out the back window, they'll see her and move up quickly. Just take it slowly. . . .

She bent forward so he could have her right hand, and felt the metal cuff slip around it. Kimbal took the gun out of her spine. "I used these on Julie when she tried to run away, back in the beginning. I knew they'd come in handy again."

"What are you going to do with me?"

"Me? I'm not going to do a thing. However, those dogs of mine, they know it's about time they were let out, and they're not going to be too happy about you trespassing."

Kate heard another jingle, and she looked back, to see him thumbing through a key ring. He selected what looked like the key to a padlock and began to move toward the cage and the quivering dogs.

"Marsh," came the voice again.

"Julie, go back in the house," he said without looking up.

"Marsh!"

"Julie," he began in a growl, and then stopped. "Baby, we won't need that. This lady's leaving on her own." Kate turned and saw Jules in the doorway. She had a revolver in her hand that looked as if it belonged in a Western, but it was clean and looked well cared for, as had all the rifles on the wall. She had it in her right hand, pointing at the ground.

"You can't hurt her, Marsh."

"Julie, this is Daddy's business. Take the gun and put it away before you hurt yourself." He sounded as if he were talking to a six-year-old, but then Jules was acting strangely young, as well.

But determined. "Let her go, Marsh. Don't let the dogs out."

Both adults stood still, squinting into the late sun at the thin young girl in ill-fitting clothes, hanging on to a gun that probably weighed more than her arm did. Kate stared not at the gun, but at the tear that was trickling down the young face.

"Julie, you're going to be in big trouble, girl. It'll be the belt for sure if you don't get yourself inside right now." His anger at her disobedience was under thin control.

"Marsh," she said around her tears, "I can't let you hurt her. Let her go. I'll stay here with you. Just let her go. Please!"

That was when Marsh Kimbal made his mistake. Had he simply walked up to Jules to take the gun from her hands, she would certainly have let him, but he lost his temper. He pivoted around with the shotgun coming up, centering it on Kate.

"Daddy!"

It was more a scream for help than a warning, but Marsh Kimbal's entire body jerked in reaction. He whirled, and Kate turned, and they saw Jules standing on the ground now, thirty feet away, the big revolver held in her trembling hands in the position Kate had taught her on the shooting range, pointing straight at her father. Tears welled up and no doubt obscured her vision, but she was biting her lip in concentration, and Kate knew that if Jules fired a shot, there was a good chance that she would hit him. Kimbal knew it, too.

"There's a bullet in the chamber, Daddy. I know how to shoot. Let her leave."

He wavered. If she had been anyone but his daughter, he might have turned the shotgun on her, but this was the daughter he had sought for over ten years, and he could not bring himself to kill her. At the same time, had she been anyone but his daughter, he would have known that if he simply approached her, talking calmly, he could have had the gun for the taking.

But this was his own child defying him, and the step he took toward her was not conciliatory, but furious. She saw it, and she closed her eyes and pulled the trigger.

The shot almost hit him. Had she kept her eyes open, it would have, but it went wide—not by much, but enough. It tore his left shirt sleeve in passing, then went zinging and bouncing against the wire of the dog cage before raising a long plume of dust out into the floor of the scrub desert. One of the dogs went yelping for shelter; the other snarled and leaped at the wire.

But Kate did not see the results of the shot; she only saw that for one brief instant, Kimbal had forgotten her. Hoping fervently that Jules would not continue to pull the trigger in her panic, she threw herself against him.

The shotgun went off, deafening Kate and taking out half the windows in her rental car but drawing no blood, and Kate continued to shove against him with her head and shoulder, butting him off balance and backward, knowing full well that, cuffed as she was, there was a point at which he would regain control, and then either he would kill her or Jules would shoot him, and Kate didn't know which possibility caused the greater panic. So she shoved hard against his stumbling body until she felt the jar as he fetched up against something solid. She leaned into him hopelessly, knowing it would be over in a matter of seconds, and then, inexplicably, he screamed. Startled, she drew back slightly; he screamed again, and looking up at him, she saw that he had flung out his left arm to catch himself as he hit the wire cage. Half the hand had gone through the wire and the excited dog, growling murderously, had seized it between its teeth.

She moved half a step back, braced herself, and with all her strength swept her left foot against his legs. The momentum unbalanced her and she went down on one knee, but he, too, fell, screaming again as the dog's teeth tore free. While Kate struggled to her feet, he cradled his left wrist in agony, started to rise, and then fell limp and silent as Kate's conservative leather shoe connected with the side of his skull.

Pain shooting up her arms and down the leg she had landed on, bent over double, her arms behind her back,

Kate looked around for Jules. She found her standing as before, unhurt, lowering the heavy gun to the ground.

"Hey, J," she panted, and felt a grin begin to grow on her face.

"I knew you'd find me, Kate. I knew it."

TWENTY-SIX

"Jules, sweetheart, where are the keys to these hand-cuffs?" she demanded.

"I don't know."

Kate racked her brain, trying to visualize the key ring that Kimbal had taken out and probably dropped back into a pocket when he was interrupted by Jules. She couldn't remember seeing a handcuff key, and there had only been half a dozen keys on the thing, but then she'd only seen it for a moment. She looked at the man speculatively.

Jules spoke up. "He doesn't keep them on his key ring. They're somewhere in his room."

No time, then; he was stirring already. The wound in his hand, though dramatically pumping dark red blood all over him, would not be enough to keep him unconscious, and Kate was loath just to keep kicking his head until her backup arrived. She wavered; he stirred again; and she knew that she could not be standing there helpless when he came to. Jules could tie him—but one look at the girl's face and Kate knew she couldn't ask her to go near the injured man. That left two options: awkward flight, with the dogs behind them as soon as Kimbal woke, or Kate's freedom.

"I have to get these cuffs off. You're going to have to shoot them."

Jules tore her eyes from the man who was her father. "There was only one bullet in the gun."

Kate paused for a look of admiration. "God, girl, you sure made it count. Okay, there'll be another shell in the shotgun; that'll have to do." She gently nudged the shotgun across the uneven ground until it lay at Jules's feet. "Now, you haven't shot one of these before, so I'll talk you through it." Words, Kate thought; words would keep Jules moving as nothing else would, her only tool to keep the shock in the girl's face from immobilizing her completely. "Our word for the day is ballistics, okay? First of all, sit down, on the ground with your legs apart. That's right—we don't want you to shoot your nose off here. Now, pick up the shotgun and point it at the sky, kind of jam its butt into the ground to keep it stable, because it has quite a kick. Fine. Now, I'm going to try and get the chain of the handcuffs over the barrel, and you're going to pull the trigger."

Kate bent down close to Jules, facing the opposite direction, trying to look over her shoulder and see her hands, trying at the same time to put as much of herself as possible in front of Jules to protect the girl from stray shot.

"Maybe I should go look for the keys."

"There's no time, Jules. He's waking up."

"I don't think he'll—"

"Jules! We have to do this now or he's going to bleed to death!" Kate didn't think it likely, but she needed Jules to keep going. "Hold the butt steady and ease the trigger back slowly."

"I don't think—" Jules started to say, but over her voice and the noise of the frenzied dogs Kate thought she heard a groan, and cold panic shot through her.

"Jules, pull the trigger!"

Jules pulled, and for the second time, the gun exploded

a foot from Kate's head, sending her sprawling on the weedy ground, her shoulders feeling as if they had been ripped from their sockets. She got to her feet and stumbled over to Kimbal, fighting to unbuckle her belt with her sprained and trembling arms. With the remnants of the handcuffs riding her wrists like a pair of punk bracelets, she wrapped the length of fake white patent leather around the man's arm, putting on pressure and watching the pulse of blood slow. She hoped it was because of the tourniquet rather than the approach of death—not that he would be any true loss to the world, but the girl did not deserve to see it.

"Someone's coming," said Jules.

"About time," she muttered. Indeed they were coming, car after governmental car. It had seemed longer, but within four minutes of the shot, the tide of men began to spill out of the cars and wash over them, taking over the care of the wounded man and transforming the remote shack into a bustling center of forensic activity.

Sometime later, after Kimbal had been taken away but before the animal-control officer had arrived with the dog tranquilizers, someone thought to slap some bandages on Kate's scraped knees and the parts of her hands that had been singed by the shotgun blast. She sat on the edge of her car's backseat, brushed clear of glass crumbles, and looked elsewhere while the medic swabbed and taped. He finished, she thanked him, and when she looked up, Jules was in the door of the shack, wrapped in a blanket and cradled in the shelter of Al Hawkin's arm. She was pale with shock and red-eyed, and she looked at Kate with an unreadable expression on her face. Kate got to her feet.

"I'm okay, Jules. Marsh Kimbal's going to be okay. You're safe."

Jules did not answer, but in a minute she turned to Al and allowed him to fold his arms around her. He held her, looking over her head at Kate with a face nearly as devastated with relief as his stepdaughter's.

"Kate, I . . ." he began, and choked up. She stumped

over to where they stood and draped her own arms painfully around the two of them. They stood that way, oblivious of the activity and noises, until the aches in Kate's arms began to turn into shooting pain, and she reluctantly stood back. Al blew his nose, Kate reached into her pocket for a Kleenex and blew her own nose, and finally Jules looked up and said in a small voice, "Can I borrow that?"

Kate began to laugh, and in an instant the three of them were dissolving again, this time in tears of laughter.

"Kate—" he started again, when he could speak, but she interrupted him.

"Take her home, Al. Jani's waiting."

He hesitated, then nodded, and with his arm still around Jules's shoulders, he began to guide her toward the cars. When they had taken a few steps, Jules stopped and eased her head out to look at Kate.

"I knew you'd come," she said. "I knew it."

ABOUT THE AUTHOR

LAURIE R. KING lives with her family in the hills above Monterey Bay in northern California. Her background includes such diverse interests as Old Testament theology and construction work, and she has been writing crime fiction since 1987. She is the winner of the Edgar, the Nero, and the John Creasey awards.

Visit her website at www.laurierking.com.

If you liked WITH CHILD, the third in Laurie R. King's, Kate Martinelli Edgar-Award-winning mystery series, you won't want to miss the other titles in this series:

THE ART OF DETECTION
A GRAVE TALENT
TO PLAY THE FOOL
NIGHT WORK

And turn the page for a preview of one of the exciting latest mysteries in Laurie R. King's beloved Mary Russell mystery series, A LETTER OF MARY. Look for A LETTER OF MARY at your favorite bookstore!

A
LETTER
OF
MARY
by
Laurie R. King

PART ONE

Tuesday, 14 August 1923—
Friday, 24 August 1923

*A pen is certainly an excellent instrument
to fix a man's attention
and to inflame his ambition.*

—JOHN ADAMS

ONE
alpha

THE ENVELOPE slapped down onto the desk ten inches from my much-abused eyes, instantly obscuring the black lines of Hebrew letters that had begun to quiver an hour before. With the shock of the sudden change, my vision stuttered, attempted a valiant rally, then slid into complete rebellion and would not focus at all.

I leant back in my chair with an ill-stifled groan, peeled my wire-rimmed spectacles from my ears and dropped them onto the stack of notes, and sat for a long minute with the heels of both hands pressed into my eye sockets. The person who had so unceremoniously delivered this grubby interruption moved off across the room, where I heard him sort a series of envelopes *chuk-chuk-chuk* into the wastepaper basket, then stepped into the front hallway to drop a heavy envelope onto the table there (Mrs Hudson's monthly letter from her daughter in Australia, I noted, two days early) before coming back to take up a position beside my desk, one shoulder dug into the bookshelf, eyes gazing, no doubt, out the window at the Downs rolling down to the Channel. I replaced the heels of my hands with the backs of my fingers, cool against the hectic flesh, and addressed my husband.

"Do you know, Holmes, I had a great-uncle in Chicago whose promising medical career was cut short when he began to go blind over his books. It must be extremely frustrating to have one's future betrayed by a tiny web of optical muscles. Though he did go on to make a fortune selling eggs and trousers to the gold miners," I added. "Whom is it from?"

"Shall I read it to you, Russell, so as to save your optic muscles for the *metheg* and your beloved furtive *patach*?" His solicitous words were spoilt by the sardonic, almost querulous edge to his voice. "Alas, I have become a mere secretary to my wife's ambitions. Kindly do not snort, Russell. It is an unbecoming sound. Let me see." I felt his arm come across my desk, and I heard the letter whisper as it was plucked up. "The envelope is from the Hôtel Imperial in Paris, a name which contains distinct overtones of sagging mattresses and ominous nocturnal rustling noises in the wardrobe. It is addressed simply to Mary Russell, no title whatsoever. The hand is worthy of some attention. A woman's writing, surely, though almost masculine in the way the fingers grasp the pen. The writer is obviously highly educated, a 'professional woman,' to use the somewhat misleading modern phrase; I venture to say that this particular lady does not depend on her womanliness for a livelihood. Her *t*'s reveal her to be an impatient person, and there is passion in the sweeps of her uprights, yet her *s*'s and *a*'s speak of precision and the lower edge of each line is as exact as it is authoritative. She also either has great faith in the French and English postal systems or else is so self-assured as to consider the insurance of placing her name or room number on the envelope unnecessary. I lean toward the latter theory."

As this analysis progressed, I recovered my glasses, the better to study my companion where he stood in the bright window, bent over the envelope like a jeweller with some rare uncut stone, and I was hit by one of those odd moments of analytical apartness, when one looks with a stranger's eyes on something infinitely familiar. Physically, Sherlock Holmes had changed little since we had first met on these same Sussex Downs a bit more than eight years before. His hair was slightly thinner, certainly greyer, and his grey eyes had become even more deeply hooded, so that the resemblance to some far-seeing, sharp-beaked raptor was more marked than ever. No, his body had only exaggerated itself; the greatest changes were internal. The fierce passions that had driven him in his early years, years before I was even born, had subsided, and the agonies of frustration he had felt when without a challenge, frustration that had led him to needles filled with cocaine and morphia, were now in abeyance. Or so I had thought.

I watched him as his long fingers caressed the much-travelled envelope and his eyes drew significance from every smudge, every characteristic of paper and ink and stamp, and it occurred to me suddenly that Sherlock Holmes was bored.

The thought was not a happy one. No person, certainly no woman, likes to think that her marriage has lessened the happiness of her partner. I thrust the troublesome idea from me, reached up to rub a twinge from my right shoulder, and spoke with a shade more irritation than was called for.

"My dear Holmes, this verges on *deductio ad absurdum*. Were you to open the envelope and identify the writer, it just might simplify matters."

"All in good time, Russell. I further note a partial set of grimy fingerprints along the back of the envelope, with a matching thumbprint on the front. However, I believe we can discount them, as they have the familiar look of the hands of our very own postal-delivery boy, whose bicycle chain is in constant need of repair."

"Holmes, my furtive *patachs* await me. The letter?"

"Patience is a necessary attribute of the detective's makeup, Russell. And, I should have thought, the scholar's. However, as you say." He turned away, and the sharp zip of a knife through cheap paper was followed by a dull thud as the knife was reintroduced into the frayed wood of the mantelpiece. There was a thin rustle. His voice sounded amused as he began to read. " 'Dear Miss Russell,' it begins, dated four days ago.

Dear Miss Russell,

I trust you will not be offended by my form of address. I am aware that you have married, but I cannot bring myself to assign a woman her husband's name unless I have been told that such is her desire. If you are offended, please forgive my unintentional faux pas.

You will perhaps remember me, Dorothy Ruskin, from your visit to Palestine several years ago. I have remained in that land since then, assisting at three preliminary digs until such time as I can arrange funding for my own excavations. I have been called back home for an interview by my potential sponsors, as well as to see my mother, who seems to be on her deathbed. There is a matter of some interest which I wish to lay before you while I am in England, and I would appreciate it if you would allow me to come and disturb your peace for a few hours. It would have to be on the twenty-second or twenty-third, as I return to Palestine directly my business is completed. Please confirm the day and time by telegram at the address below.

I believe the matter to be of some interest and potentially considerable importance to your chosen field of study, or I would not be bothering you and your husband.

I remain,

Most affectionately yours,
Dorothy Ruskin

"The address below is that of the Hôtel Imperial," Holmes added.

I took the letter from Holmes and quickly skimmed the singular hand that strode across the flimsy hotel paper. "A decent pen, though," I noted absently. "Shall we see her?"

"We? My dear Russell, I am the husband of an emancipated woman who, although she may not yet vote in an election, is at least allowed to see her own friends without male chaperonage."

"Don't be an ass, Holmes. She obviously wants to see both of us, or she would not have written that last sentence. We'll have her for tea, then. Wednesday or Thursday?"

"Wednesday is Mrs Hudson's half day. Miss Ruskin might have a better tea if she came Thursday."

"Thank you, Holmes," I said with asperity. I admit that cooking is not my strong point, but I object to having my nose rubbed in the fact. "I'll write to let her know either day is fine but that Thursday is slightly better. I wonder what she wants."

"Funding for an all-woman archaeological dig, I shouldn't wonder. That would be popular with the British authorities and the Zionists, would it not? And think of the attraction it would have for the pilgrims and the tourists. It's a wonder the Americans haven't thought of it."

"Holmes, enough! Begone! I have work to do."

"Come for a walk."

"Not just now. Perhaps this evening I could take an hour off."

"By this evening, you will be bogged down to the axles in the prophet Isaiah's mud and too irritable to make a decent walking companion. You've been rubbing your bad shoulder for the last forty minutes although it is a warm afternoon, which means you need to get out and breathe some fresh air. Come."

He held out one long hand to me. I looked down at the cramped lines marching across the page, capped my pen, and allowed him to pull me to my feet.

♦

We walked along the cliffs rather than descending the precipitous beach path, and listened to the gulls cry and the waves surge on the shingle below. The good salt air filled my lungs, cleared my head, and took the ache from my collarbone, and eventually my thoughts turned, not to the intricacies of Hebrew grammar but to the implications of the letter that lay on my desk.

"What do you know of the archaeology of Palestine, Holmes?"

"Other than what we discovered when we were there four and a half years ago—which trip, as I recall, was dominated by an extraordinary number of damp and hazardous underground chambers—almost nothing. I suspect that I shall know a great deal more before too much longer."

"You think there is something to Miss Ruskin's letter, then?"

"My dear Russell, I have not been a consulting detective for more than forty years for nothing. I can spot a case sniffing around my door even before it knows itself to be one. Despite what I said about allowing you to see her alone, your Miss Ruskin—yes, I know she is not yours, but she thinks she is—your Miss Ruskin wishes to present a puzzle to the partnership of Holmes and Russell, not merely to Mary Russell, a brilliant young star on the horizon of academic theology. Unless you think my standard degree of megalomania is becoming compounded by senility," he added politely.

"Megalomania, perhaps; senility, never." I stood and watched a small fishing boat lying off shore, and I wondered what to do. The work was going slowly, and I could ill afford to take even half a day away from it. On the other hand, it would be a joy to spend some time with that peculiar old lady, whom I indeed remembered very well. Also, Holmes seemed interested. It would at least provide a distraction until I could decide what needed doing for him. "All right, we'll have her here a day sooner, then, on the Wednesday. I'll suggest the noon train. I'm certain Mrs Hudson can be persuaded to leave something for our tea, so we need not risk our visitor's health. I also think I'll go to Town tomorrow and drop by the British Museum for a while. Will you come?"

"Only if we can stay for the evening. They're playing Tchaikovsky's D at Covent Garden."

"And dinner at Simpson's?" I said lightly, ruthlessly ignoring the internal wail at the waste of time.

"But of course."

"Will you go to the BM with me?"

"Briefly, perhaps. I had a note from the owner of a rather bijou little gallery up the street, inviting me to view the canvas of that Spaniard, Picasso, that I retrieved for them last month. I should be interested to see it in its natural habitat, as it were, to determine if it makes any more sense there than it did in that warehouse on the docks where I found it. Although, frankly, I have my doubts."

"That's fine, then," I said politely. Suddenly, Holmes was not at my side but blocking my way, his hands on my shoulders and his face inches from mine.

"Admit it, Russell. You've been bored."

His words so echoed my own analysis of his mental state that I could only gape at him.

"You've been tucked into your books for a solid year now, ever since we came back from France. You might be able to convince yourself that you're nothing but a scholar, Russell, but you can't fool me. You're as hungry as I am for something to do."

Damn the man, he was right. He was wrong, too, of course—men have a powerful drive to simplify matters, and it would be convenient for him to dismiss the side of my life that did not involve him—but as soon as he said it, I could feel the hunger he was talking about, waking in me. I had in the past discovered the immense appeal of a life on the edge of things—walking a precipice, pitting oneself against a dangerous enemy, throwing one's mind against an impenetrable puzzle.

The waking was brief, as I ruthlessly knocked the phantasy back into its hole. If Dorothy Ruskin had a puzzle, it was not likely to be anything but mild and elderly. I sighed, and then, realising that Holmes was still staring into my face, I had to laugh.

"Holmes, we're a pair of hopeless romantics," I said, and we turned and walked back to the cottage.

TWO
beta

SHORTLY BEFORE midday on the appointed Wednesday, I drove my faithful Morris to the station to meet Miss Ruskin's train. It was four and a half years since we had met near Jericho, and though I would have known her anywhere, she had changed. Her chopped-off hair was completely white. She wore a pair of glasses, the lenses of which were so black as to seem opaque, and she favoured her right leg as she stepped down from the train. She did not see me at first, but stood peering about her, a large khaki canvas bag clutched in one hand. I crossed the platform towards her and corrected myself—some things had changed not at all. Her face was still burnt to brown leather by the desert sun, her posture still that of a soldier on parade, her clothing the same idiosyncratic variation on the early suffragist uniform of loose pantaloons, tailored shirt, jacket, and high boots that I had seen her wear in Palestine. The boots and clothing looked new, and somehow ineffably French, despite their lack of anything resembling fashion.

"Good day, Miss Ruskin," I called out. "Welcome to Sussex."

Her head spun around and the deep voice, accustomed

to wide spaces and the command of native diggers, boomed out across the rustic station.

"Miss Russell, is that you? Delighted to see you. Very good of you to have me at such short notice." She grasped my hand in her heavily calloused one. The top of her squashed hat barely reached my chin, but she dominated the entire area. I led her to the car, helped her climb in, started the engine, and enquired about her leg.

"Oh, yes, most annoying. Fell into a trench when the props collapsed. Bad break, spent a month in Jerusalem flat on my back. Stupid luck. Right in the middle of the season, too. Wasted half the year's dig. Use better wood now for the props." She laughed, short coughs of humour that made me grin in response.

"I saw some of your finds in the British Museum recently," I told her. "That Hittite slab was magnificent, and of course the mosaic floor. How on earth did they make those amazing blues?"

She was pleased, and she launched off on a highly technical explanation of the art and craft of mosaics that went far above my head and lasted until I pulled into the circular drive in front of the cottage. Holmes heard the car and came to meet us. Our guest climbed awkwardly out and marched over to greet him, hand extended and talking all the while as we moved inside and through the house.

"Mr Holmes, good to see you, as yourself this time, and in your own home. Though I do admit that you wear the djellaba better than most white men, and the skin dye was very good. You are looking remarkably well. How old are you? Rude question, I know, one of the advantages of getting old—people are forced to overlook rudeness. You are? Only a few years younger than I am, looks more like twenty. Maybe I should have married. A bit late now, don't you think? Miss Russell—all right if I call you that? Or do you prefer Mrs Holmes? Miss Russell, then—d'you know, you've married one of the three sensible men I've ever met. Brains are wasted on most men—do nothing with their minds but play games and make money. Never see what's in front of their noses, too busy making sweeping

304

generalisations. What's that? The other two? Oh, yes, one was a winemaker in Provence, tiny vineyard, a red wine to make you weep. The other's dead now, an Arab sheikh with seven wives. Couldn't write his name, but his children all went to university. Girls, too. I made him. Ha! Ha!" The barking laugh bounced off the walls in the room and set the ears to ringing. We took our lunch outside, under the great copper beech.

During the meal, our guest regaled us with stories of archaeology in Palestine, which was just getting under way now in the postwar years. The British Mandate in Palestine was giving its approval to the beginnings of archaeology as a science and a discipline.

"Shocking, it was, before the war. No sense of the way to do things. Had people out there rummaging about, destroying more than they found, native diggers coming in with these magnificent finds, no way of dating them or knowing where they came from. All that could be done with 'em was to stick 'em in a museum, prop up a card saying SOURCE: UNKNOWN; DATE; UNKNOWN. Utter waste."

"Didn't Petrie say something about museums being morgues, or tombs?" I asked.

"Charnel houses," she corrected me. "He calls them 'ghastly charnel houses of murdered evidence.' Isn't that a fine phrase? Wish I'd written it." She repeated it, relishing the shape of the words in her mouth. "And during the war, my God! I spent those years doing nothing but stopping soldiers from using walls and statues for target practice! Incredible stupidity. Found one encampment using a Bronze Age well as their privy and rubbish tip. Course, the idiots didn't realise their own water supply was connected to it. Should've told 'em, I know, but who am I to interfere in divine justice? Ha! Ha!"

"Surely, though, most of the digs are more carefully run now," I suggested. "Even before the war, Reisner's stratigraphic techniques were becoming more widely used. And doesn't the Department of Antiquities keep an eye on things?" My rapid tutorial at the hands of one of the British Museum's more helpful experts at least enabled me to ask intelligent questions.

"Oh, yes indeed, improving rapidly, things are. Of course, there's no room for amateurs like myself now, though I'll be allowed to make drawings and notes when I get back. There's talk of opening the City of David, really exciting. But still, we get Bedouins wandering in with sacks of amazing things, pottery and bronze statuettes, last month a heart-stopping ivory carving, magnificent thing, part of a processional scene, completely worthless from a historical point of view, of course. He wouldn't tell us where in the desert it came from, so it can't be put in its proper archaeological setting. A pity. Oh, yes, that's more or less why I'm here. Where's my bag?"

I brought it from the sitting room, where she had casually dumped it on a table. She opened it and dug through various books, articles of clothing, and papers, finally coming out with a squarish object wrapped securely in an Arab man's black-and-white head covering.

"Here we are," she said with satisfaction as she displayed a small intricately carved and inlaid wooden box. She laid it in front of me, then bent to replace various objects into the bag.

"I'd like you to look at this and tell me what you think. Already gave it to two so-called experts, both men of course, who each took one look and said it was a fake, couln't possibly be a first-century papyrus. I'm not so sure. Really I'm not. May be worthless, but thought of you when I wondered whom to give it to. Show it to whomever you like. Do what you can with it. Let me know what you think. Yes, yes, take a look. Any more tea in that pot, Mr Holmes?"

The box fit into one hand and opened smoothly. Inside was nestled, secure in a tissue bed, a small roll of papyrus, deeply discoloured at the top and bottom edges. I touched it delicately with my finger. The tissue rustled slightly.

"Oh, it's quite sturdy. I've had it unrolled, and the two 'experts' didn't coddle it any. One said it was a clever modern forgery, which is absurd, considering how I got it.

The other said it was probably from a madwoman during the Crusades. Experts!" She threw up her hands eloquently, eliciting a sympathetic laugh from Holmes. "At any rate, the experts deny it, so we amateurs can do as we please with it. It's all yours. I started on it, but my eyes are no good now for fine work." She took off her dark glasses, and we saw the clouds that edged onto the brilliant blue of her eyes. "The doctors in Paris say it's because of the sun, that if I wear these troublesome things and stay inside all the time, it'll be five years before they have to operate. Told them there was no point in having the years if I couldn't work, but, being men, they didn't understand. Ah well, five years will get me going, if I can get the money to start my dig, and after that I'll retire happy. Which has nothing to do with you, of course, but that's why I'm giving you the manuscript."

I took the delicate roll from its box and gently spread it out on the table. Holmes pinned the right end down with two fingers and I looked at the beginning, which, as the language was Greek, began at the upper left. The spiky script was neat, though the whole eighteen inches were badly stained and the edges deeply worn, in places obscuring the text. I bent over the first words, then paused. Odd; I could not be reading them correctly. I went back to the opening words, got the same results, and finally looked up at Miss Ruskin, perplexed. Her eyes were sparkling with mischief and amusement as she looked over the top of her cup at me.

"You see why the experts denied it, then?"

"That is obvious, but—"

"But why do I doubt them?"

"You couldn't seriously think—"

"Oh, but I do. It is not impossible. I agree it's unlikely, but if you leave aside all preconceived notions of what leadership could have been in the first century, it's not at all impossible. I've been poking my nose into manuscripts like this for half a century, and though it's somewhat out of my period, I'm sorry, this does not smell like a recent forgery or a crusader's wife's dream."

It finally got through to me that she was indeed serious. I stared at her, aghast and spluttering.

"Would you two kindly let me in on this?" interrupted Holmes with admirable patience. I turned to him.

"Just look at how it starts, Holmes."

"You translate it, please. I have worked hard to forget what Greek I once knew."

I looked at the treacherous words, mistrusting my eyes, but they remained the same. Stained and worn, they were, but legible.

"It appears to be a letter," I said slowly, "from a woman named Mariam, or Mary. She refers to herself as an apostle of Joshua, or Jesus, the 'Anointed One,' and it is addressed to her sister, in the town of Magdala."